The Agora Trilogy: Book I

The Midnight Charter

David Whitley

SQUARE
FISH

ROARING BROOK PRESS
NEW YORK

For Mum and Dad

SQUARE
FISH

An Imprint of Macmillan

Square Fish and the Square Fish logo are trademarks of Macmillan and
are used by Roaring Brook Press under license from Macmillan.

Cataloging-in-Publication Data is on file at the Library of Congress
ISBN: 978-0-312-62904-5

Originally published in the United States by Roaring Brook Press
Square Fish logo designed by Filomena Tuosto
First Square Fish Edition: 2010
10 9 8 7 6 5 4 3 2 1
www.squarefishbooks.com

Contents

This mournful Truth is ev'ry where confest,
Slow rises Worth, by Poverty deprest:
But here more slow, where all are Slaves to Gold,
Where Looks are Merchandise, and Smiles are sold,
Where won by Bribes, by Flatteries implor'd,
The Groom retails the Favours of his Lord.

—SAMUEL JOHNSON

It is hereby agreed that

         until the time when the Antagonist

              preserve the structure

      the Protagonist must, with full support

will lead to dissolution

as stated below

and every citizen of Agora has the duty to

        until the Last shall fall, and then

the truth will be secure

CHAPTER ONE

The Staircase

BEING DEAD was colder than Mark had expected.

When his mother had told them all tales of the afterlife, she had drawn him close into her woolen skirts and painted a picture of another city, one where it was always summer. A world where the river glowed clean and bright, a land where all debts were forgotten. Mark had trusted every word, until he awoke in a stone cell, shivering and wrapped in a shroud.

His mother had been the first to go. At least she would have found out before him how wrong she had been. She had turned as gray as the stone. He had held her hand right up until the end. Then the Reaper had come. It had looked like a man in a black coat until he had glimpsed its face — smooth and white, without mouth or nose, but with two huge black eyes. Mark had shrunk into a corner as it passed by. The other children had said that to touch it was to turn to dust.

It came three times. The first time for his mother, then for his brother and sister. On each occasion he heard his father mumbling something and the low answering tones of the Reaper, just out of earshot. Only once had his father's words become loud enough to make out. He was shouting something about the water, that there was no other water to drink. The Reaper had left with a slower step that time, as if it knew it would be back.

After that came the tiredness, the lightness. Mark had watched the backs of his own hands turn gray. He knew it would be soon. Then there were only feelings. The sense of a burning mouth, and of noise. Of being half pushed, half lifted past whirling shapes and sounds. Of a final, blissful coolness filling him.

When he awoke, he was cold. It was obvious he was dead. Everything felt different. The gray was gone from his skin, the noise from the air. In life, the stench of the river had mingled with the tang of fish, clinging to his hair and clothes. The afterlife smelled of dust, with a whiff of vinegar. For a while he shut his eyes, drawing the sheets around him to ward off the draft that crept around his feet, but it was no good. He peered around the room. It was not large. The walls and floor were of gray stone. He could make out a fireplace where a few embers still glowed. And beside it, a door.

Mark waited, though for what he was not sure. An angel? Had he been good enough for that? He'd always helped his father gut the fish. And he'd cared for his brother and sister as the plague claimed them. Was that enough? Stiffly, he slid his feet over the edge of the bed and got up. He shuffled toward the door. It was old, the wood warping around the hinges. It did not look like an angel's door. With a shaking hand, he pushed it open.

An ancient stone staircase spiraled up before him.

In the back of his mind, something stirred. Something his mother had said about the legend of the man who was not good enough to get into heaven, who had climbed there himself. In the distance, up the stairs, he thought he saw a glimmer of light.

He raised a bare foot and placed it on the first step.

The staircase was uneven, the stone crumbled away in some places. When he looked down, he could see that it carried on, past the room he had come from, and disappeared into murky depths. After that, he tried not to look down again.

He passed doors. Thick doors of dark wood. No light came from behind them. What if they were where the damned went? Those who left their work unfinished, their debts unpaid. Mark had seen them dragged screaming out of their homes by the receivers, the men in blue. They were never seen again.

He went on, twisting higher and higher. The staircase seemed to grow steeper. His legs were weaker than in life, and he leaned against one wall. His fingers felt something carved into the stone. It was too dark to see what was there, so he traced it with his fingertips. Six shapes in a circle. Pointed shapes. Stars. Should he know what that meant? He tried to remember more of his mother's stories, but thinking about her was painful.

Then, below him, he heard the squeak of hinges.

He began to move faster. He scrambled up, pushing himself with hands and feet, his heart pounding. Behind him he heard another step, slow and firm. Nothing good would be coming from those musty depths, and he was so close to the light.

And then he saw it.

Above him one of the old doors stood open. Light streamed through from beyond — pink, orange, and gold. Mark pressed forward, clambering higher still. As he moved, he glanced back. The Reaper was on the stairs behind him, his black shape blending into the deeper shadows. He willed himself upward. *Just a little further, just a few more steps. No Reaper could ascend into heaven.* He reached the door, gasping, pulling himself around the frame, throwing himself into the room.

His eyes hurt from the brightness; he had to screw them up. Beyond the door was a landscape of pure white. And ahead of him, bathed in streaming light, stood a figure, a girl, staring into the heart of the burning radiance. She turned; Mark dropped to his knees, fixing his gaze on the floor. Mother had said that to look upon a dweller in heaven was to feel your soul burn away. His eyes were already on fire.

From behind, he heard the approaching step of the Reaper. He flattened himself on the ground. The angel would save him.

"Sir . . . who is this?"

The voice wasn't that of an angel. It was wary, guarded, and unmistakably young. It reminded Mark of his sister.

"His name is Mark." Another voice, male, older, and soft.

Mark felt his breath catch. The Reaper was behind him now; he heard the rustle of its coat as it bent over him.

"He belongs to me now."

"Is he ill?"

"Not any longer. Isolation from further infection was the only way to achieve a full recovery. Certainly seems more lively now, although I don't see the reason for all this panic."

Confused, Mark opened his eyes a crack, turning his head slightly. The angel stood before the Reaper — he tall, in black robes, and with a ghastly, pale face; she in white, apart from the darkness of her face, hair, and hands. He tried to raise himself, but the angel turned her head his way. He looked at her imploringly.

"If you will permit me, sir," the angel said, her deep brown, almost black, eyes curiously meeting Mark's gaze. Then she reached up and deftly removed the Reaper's face.

For a moment, Mark felt dizzy, his head spun.

4

And then he came back to life.

The tower room grew darker as the setting sun, which had been streaming through the narrow window, sank beneath the ledge. The room, Mark now saw, was full of furniture covered in white dust sheets. The angel's robes no longer burned with light. In fact, they were not much better than his own clothes — only a rough, cotton working dress and a cream-colored apron. As she bent over him, a few strands of thick, black hair fell forward over her face, slipping loose from the white ribbon she had used to tie it back. And in her hands the dark-skinned girl now held a white, strangely shaped mask, together with a pair of thick, dark pieces of glass which Mark would soon learn were called goggles.

As for the Reaper, his true face was human. A young man, his short, straggly brown hair beginning to recede, a thin mustache perched upon his lip.

Mark sat up.

"Am I alive?" he said, his voice rattling painfully in his dry throat.

The girl nodded. "Thanks to Dr. Theophilus," she said.

She stared at Mark, her dark eyes taking him in. Then she turned to the man.

"Sir, the Count's note said that he wanted to see you at the fifth hour. I have taken him his meal."

The doctor nervously ran a finger over his mustache.

"Don't suppose you could tell what kind of mood he was in, Lily?"

The girl, Lily, frowned. "I would be . . . tactful, sir."

She glanced down at Mark, who was still sitting between them, and said, "Are you hungry?"

It took Mark a few seconds to realize that she was talking to him. Then, at once, he found that he was ravenous. He nodded furiously. Lily smiled.

"Can he have food now?" she asked the doctor, who pursed his lips.

"I believe so," he answered cautiously. "Yes . . . some food first, and then show him around. Grandfather and I have important business to discuss."

Lily responded with a brisk nod of the head and turned back to Mark. She held out a hand.

"First part of the tour: The kitchen is this way."

Mark put his own hand in hers. It seemed paler than normal against her dark fingers, but maybe it was because the usual grime had been washed away. Shakily he rose to his feet. He was taller than she was. She let go and gestured down the stairwell. From up here, it looked less supernatural.

"Five doors down," she said. "Go in and wait for me. If you touch the pots you'll be sorry. I just need a moment with the doctor."

Mark nodded again, trying to think of what to say even as he stepped back onto the stairs and began to descend. He was still trying to figure it out when he reached the fifth door and turned the handle. Then all thoughts of words were driven from his mind by the overpowering smell flooding through the open doorway. The smell of food simmering in pots over a smoky fire. All at once, it was like being back by the river, before the gray plague had come, where in the evening the different scents of a hundred broths and stews would lead him through the alleys and home to huddle around the bowl with his brother and sister and pick clean the remains of his father's last catch of the day. He was about to rush in, to pull the lid off the nearest one, when he heard a sound above him. Lily and the doctor were talking. He hovered by the door, curiosity fighting with hunger. Then, silently, he moved back up the stairs, straining his ears.

". . . not to let the old man know," the doctor was saying. "Not just yet. He doesn't think we can keep another servant. I've tried to explain that I cannot manage without assistance but . . . you know him."

"Very well, sir. I take it Mark will be helping you."

"As soon as he is well enough, Lily. He's my first full recovery," the doctor said with a touch of pride in his voice. "I'd better be careful."

Mark smiled. He didn't know what was happening, but whoever these people were, they were going to keep him.

"And . . . ," Lily's voice drifted down, "does he know yet that his father sold him?"

There was a pause.

"I thought you might break that particular piece of news, Lily," the doctor sighed, "as one who knows what it's like to adjust . . ."

"As you wish, sir."

Numbly, imperceptibly, Mark's appetite died.

 The Signet Ring

"**W**ELL, LILY?"

"Sir?"

"How is the boy doing?"

"Much the same."

It was their ritual for the first few days. Lily sat on the stone staircase just outside Mark's room, stitching tablecloths or reading by the light of a candle. Every hour or so, Dr. Theophilus would ascend from his cellar rooms, make his gentle enquiry, his eyes full of hope, and, receiving the same reply, would nod with concern and turn away. Mostly he would return to his studies. Lily never went down there. She knew he kept human corpses in the cellar — the bodies of plague victims — for dissection. It was necessary, of course; if he was to cure this plague he had to understand it, but Lily shivered to think of working all day surrounded by their fixed, ghostly stares.

This time, the doctor sat down beside her on the step. He stroked his thin mustache thoughtfully, a sure sign that something was worrying him. Not that this was unusual.

"How long do you think he will be in there?" he asked.

Lily considered for a moment, wondering whether she should tell him about the sobs she heard when Mark thought everyone was asleep, about the red-rimmed eyes that peered through the crack of the door as she slipped in his food.

She looked up into the doctor's own eyes, seeing the heavy shadows underlining them from sleepless nights of work.

"Not long, sir."

Of course, the doctor was being soft. By law, Mark should have been working the second he arrived. She had, as soon as she knew where the dusters were kept in this ancient tower. But she didn't bear a grudge; that wasn't going to help.

The doctor sighed.

"I wish I didn't have to conceal him like this. Perhaps if he were free to wander the tower on his own he would adjust better, but . . ."

The doctor trailed off. He always did when he thought of his grandfather. Old he may have been, but Count Stelli had lost none of his presence or his power. Lily put down her book, trying to think of a practical solution.

"Perhaps, sir, if you stressed how important he is to your research, as the first patient to recover from the plague — "

"Mention plague to the old man and he'll throw the boy into the street, and me with him," Theophilus interrupted with a shake of his head. "Perhaps it would be different if the plague ever touched the elite, but they think my research is worthless or, worse, dangerous. They see no profit in trying to cure a disease that lurks in the Piscean slums, and if Grandfather knew I had brought a carrier into his home, even a healthy one . . ." The doctor turned his gaze on Lily, eyes too sad and weary for his age. "Why can no one see how much suffering it causes, Lily?"

Lily looked up at the doctor. There was an answer to that question, and they both knew it. Lily knew that the blindest people were those who would not see. That was why she always kept her eyes open.

Their moment of reflection was interrupted as, in the distance, a bell jangled, accompanied by a low rumble like distant thunder.

The doctor frowned. "Looks like the old man has woken up," he said with resignation.

Lily got up. "He'll be wanting his breakfast."

And like any other day, she left the doctor to drift back down to his work, his thin, tall shadow disappearing into the depths, as she climbed up the spiral staircase to the kitchen.

The Count had barely left his rooms for years, according to the doctor. As always, after waking she had read the note left for her the previous night on the bronze door at the top of the tower and obeyed the clipped instructions to the letter. Summoned by the bell, she loaded a tray with the Count's breakfast of bacon and carried it carefully up to the bronze door. Seeing that, as most mornings, it was closed, Lily slid open the wooden hatch beside the door and placed the breakfast tray on the platform within. Then she closed the hatch with a click and rang the bell, listening for the rumble as the food was winched up the shaft to the Observatory. Only once had she tried to enter uninvited, and sometimes she thought that her ears still rang with the roar that had told her she was not welcome.

She had never dared to do that again. She knew what happened if a servant angered their master. She had seen it at the bookbinder's, how the other girl had cried and clung to the legs of her master in vain. It was a rare master who would take someone in who had been thrown away or publicly shamed. "Damaged goods" they were called—the disgraced. Unable to work or trade or live. On the streets, with plague and thieves, she would be lucky to last a week. Lily's master, the Count, held her fate in his hands, and he was known for his temper. She never asked about the person who had worn her working dresses before her and tried not to notice that, although Lily was not large for her age, they were just the right size. One apron had been halfway through being patched, the needle and thread hanging loose, as if just put down for a moment.

When she returned to Mark's room, the door was ajar. Cautiously, she opened it further.

He was sitting on the simple bed, facing away. His hair had been shaved during his treatment, to check for signs of infection the doctor said, but it was starting to grow back now, a dirty blond color. He was already looking less thin than he had when he first arrived; he would be sturdily built when fully returned to health. As if he felt her gaze upon him, Mark turned, his face blotchy and pale, his mouth set in determination. He stared up at her defiantly.

Lily looked at him, tilting her head to one side. His gray eyes were dull still, but there was something new there, something she recognized. Curiosity.

"Want to see the tower now?" she asked.

He nodded.

After that, the next couple of days were easier. The tower had so many rooms to show, often all Lily had to do was to throw open the door. Mark's eyes grew wide at the simplest thing. When she showed him the old, musty dining room he gaped for minutes before gingerly stepping in. One eyebrow raised, Lily followed him.

"It's only a table, Mark," she said, tapping it with her knuckles. "It doesn't come to life."

"But . . . it's real wood . . ." Mark said, stroking it with his fingers. "Why would anyone make a table out of something this valuable? If my dad had this much wood, he'd have the best fishing boat on the Ora. He'd take me out with him and catch enough to feed all of us ten times over—"

"If you think that's impressive, you should see the silverware!" Lily interrupted hastily and stooped to open the sideboard.

It felt stupid to be parading the Count's possessions like this, but she had to distract him. Anything was better than thinking about his family. Especially since the doctor had told her that by the time he took Mark away, his father was the only one left.

Lily lifted a vast silver platter onto the table and pushed it toward Mark.

"Care for a canapé, sir?" she said playfully, gesturing to the empty platter.

Mark stared at her, and Lily felt her cheeks flush with embarrassment. She was making a fool of herself.

"Sorry, sometimes I mess around with this stuff," she offered in explanation. "Passes the time when I'm on my own, after I finish my duties. Otherwise I think too much." Lily drew up a dining chair and sat down. "That isn't always a good idea."

"I . . . suppose so," Mark said, looking at his reflection in the polished silver. "A place like this . . . it must make you think. It's like a legend," he carried on, gesturing around him in the silent dining room. "An enchanted tower, full of old, forgotten rooms . . . huge staircases . . . magical windows into other worlds . . ."

"If they were magical, they'd manage to dust themselves," Lily muttered.

Mark's mouth twitched and inwardly Lily grinned. The beginnings of a laugh.

"It's just a tower," she continued quietly. "The Count needs it for his business."

"The Count?" Mark asked.

"Count Stelli. My master."

"I thought the doctor . . ."

"Dr. Theophilus is *your* master," Lily said, and instantly regretted it.

Mark cast down his eyes; she could see him lose his color again. She knew how he must be feeling. She had been the same when the orphanage had sold her to the bookbinders when she was half Mark's age. Suddenly no choice but to work because they had the right to stop feeding you. No one listened to a tool that talked. You lived on borrowed time, waiting for the day when you were declared useless and thrown away.

Mark sat down on one of the chairs, his lips pushed together, bloodless. Lily reached out to him across the table, letting her hand rest near his.

"He's the Count's grandson, but the Count lets him run his practice from the cellars of the tower. The doctor's a good man," Lily said, as gently as she could manage, and stopped. What else could she say? *I'm sure he gave a good price for you even though you were ill? It probably saved your life to be taken away?* All true, of course, but would it help? Lily did not waste her words, especially when they could cause more harm. At least she had only been sold by the matron of her orphanage. She had never had a family to lose. Mark's life had been signed over by his own father.

"Lily . . ."

Lily steadied herself for a question she didn't want to answer.

"Is . . . is his name really Theophilus?"

Lily laughed, the knots in her stomach loosening.

"It's an old family name, apparently. It means 'loved by God.' "

"Mom used to tell me stories about gods," Mark said quietly.

Lily cursed herself. Just for a moment she'd managed to make him think about something else. Fleetingly, they had been almost cheerful.

"Anyway . . . ," Lily continued, trying to sound as if she hadn't noticed his change of mood, "how long is it until your title day?"

13

"My what?"

"Your title day."

Mark still looked blank.

"Twelve years since your birth," she prompted, "one grand cycle of the stars."

Mark frowned. "Two weeks," he said. "I was born on the last day of the month of Scorpio. Is that important? Mom said that your twelfth birthday was special, but wouldn't tell me why."

Lily smiled.

"Then he only owns you until then. That's the day you own yourself." Lily shook her head in bemusement. "You don't mean that no one has ever told you about—"

"I'm free?" Mark interrupted, his eyes shining. "I can go home?"

Lily's smile faltered. Looking at his sudden excitement, she couldn't bring herself to explain, to point out that she hadn't said that. Not quite.

"That's the day you can make a choice," she said.

In his eagerness, Mark didn't notice the difference.

As the next two weeks passed, Lily saw less and less of Mark in the daylight hours. The doctor was instructing him in his duties, mostly cleaning a wicked-looking set of scalpels and brewing up foul-smelling drugs, and Lily had to get on with her tasks. As usual, she dusted the ancient, empty rooms, as usual she tried to get Dr. Theophilus to eat something at least once a day, and as usual she took the Count's meals up and lingered by the Observatory door, willing it to open.

The Observatory. Lily had only been allowed up there once, to polish the huge brass telescope. Then it had been daytime, but the Count had drawn the thick velvet drapes across the tall windows that filled every wall. The only sky she had been able to see had been the painted ceiling, frozen into an eternal night. Lily could hear a rumbling snore from his bed on the far side of the room as she scrubbed away. She had seen the shafts of sunlight slipping through holes in the ancient fabric, sparkling off the metal before her. She had felt the hairs on the back of her neck stand up, willing her to turn around, to fling aside the curtains and look down on the city. It was mad; the Count spent his days in a room full of windows, yet only ever looked up into the night sky.

It was Lily's secret passion — to find windows. The tower was gloomy and most of the shutters were locked tight to keep in the warmth. But every time she had a moment, she slipped away to the old bedroom, the room where she had first met Mark. There was a window there, though it was barely more than a slit in the wall, just enough to let a little breeze in. Peering out, there was almost nothing to be seen in the dense shadow of the tower other than a tangle of roofs and brick-work. But at sunset, when the sun angled itself just right, the light shone through, warming her face. At that instant, she could see the city, transformed from a threatening shadow to a glowing whirl of color and spectacle. Then she could see other people hurrying past, see the distant sparkle of the River Ora and the far-off towers of the Directory of Receipts. There, in that moment, all Agora was laid out before her.

This wondrous sight was the only thing that thrilled her out of the daily routine. Apart from those rare occasions when the doctor had the time to talk to her, she had learned to keep herself quiet, to wrap herself up in practical detail, to choose her words, and even her outward emotions, with the greatest care. No one at the orphanage wondered about the city beyond the boundary wall. To them, the orphanage had been their home, but for Lily "home" encompassed so much more. It was strange to think of Mark surrounded by a family but still so ignorant of the city, so sheltered. While she, who had never known any adult she could talk to without fear of punishment, had scrambled for any piece of knowledge she could find. He still had no idea how important his title day would be, while she had spent as long as she could remember waiting for hers — for her chance to get out into the city and live.

Wearily, she contemplated the pile of dirty plates before her. Of course, that had been before her title day had arrived and she had learned that owning herself was not the same as being free.

On Mark's title day, Lily slept late. She had been mending clothes all night and for once the Count's irritable ringing did not rouse her. As she awoke, however, she could understand why, even in her windowless room, she could hear the lashing of the rain outside. Last night would not have been a night for stargazing, so he was probably still asleep.

The doctor had taken Mark out with him on his rounds for the first time, and Lily knew better than to disturb the Count if he had not summoned her. So she settled herself down in the kitchen, lit one of the thick wax candles, and, squinting at her needle, began to stitch. The Count had a new formal cloak — perhaps he was expecting visitors — and his symbol, six golden stars in a circle, had to be sewn on. It would not do for the greatest astrologer in Agora to receive guests in an old robe. Lily frowned. All this for looking into the sky and predicting the future.

Around lunchtime, the sound of knocking echoed through the tower. Lily rushed to the front door, the rain from outside spitting through the keyhole, but by the time she eased it open, only wind and water were visible. On the ground, wrapped in brown paper, a small box sat forlornly. Lily bent to pick it up, scanning the narrow streets for the deliverer. But, as her hand closed around it, she saw the name "Mark" inked on its surface, already running in the onslaught of water, and she caught her breath. She knew what this was. This was an official delivery from the Directory of Receipts itself.

Wringing out her hair, Lily returned to the kitchen and put the box next to the fire to dry out. Then, going back to her work, she waited.

The candle had burned low before they returned, but Lily did not get up. She listened to the sound of their footsteps. She heard the doctor mutter something about being busy all evening, then his steps faded away, down the stairs into his workrooms, the deepest cellars.

Lily looked up as Mark came in and sat heavily on the wooden chair before the fire. Dr. Theophilus had given him a long black coat like his own, and he held it around him. His face, always wan, seemed paler than ever. He stared for a while into the fire and shivered. He did not speak.

"It will get better," Lily murmured. She didn't need to ask if it had been bad; that was etched into every fresh line on his face. Mark made a noise. It was too weak to be a scornful snort, but it carried the same idea.

"So many of them, Lily . . . so many people . . ." he said at last, his voice barely rising above the crackling fire. "Pressing against you, pushing past. Seas of people, and they all . . . all end up . . ." Mark closed his eyes. "So many of them. Stacked in rows . . . I thought, if I looked hard enough, I'd find my sister . . . my mom . . ."

Lily cast down her eyes. So he had taken Mark to a plague hospital. That was where his work was, at the moment. Had the doctor even thought? Had he considered how fresh the memories were for his new assistant? From what Mark had told her, it had been less than two months since his family had first caught the same disease. When the doctor became wrapped up in his work, he never noticed the effect on the healthy.

"And the worst part . . ." Mark stood up suddenly, his eyes darting around. "They all had it. I could see it on the workers. They all had spots of gray on their hands. Dr. Theophilus told them that if they touch others they will pass it on, but they didn't care! Like fish swimming for the hook . . . going out into the city, pushing through the crowds . . ."

Mark sat down again, suddenly exhausted. "If they knew what it was like, they'd never go out. Like you, Lily. Like us."

Quietly, Lily put her stitching to one side. She felt as though she should do something—comfort him, hug him, tell him everything was going to be all right. She had read about it. But Lily had never known that kind of affection, so she didn't have the words. Instead, she rose and reached up to the shelf where she kept the bowls. She filled one from the pot of stew she'd prepared and pushed it into his hands.

"Have some food," she said firmly. "You'll feel better."

Lily watched him eat without speaking. For a long while, even after he had finished, they sat in silence. The only sound was the crackle of the fire, and every now and then an alarming rumble from beneath them as the doctor worked on his latest medicine. Eventually, still not quite sure of what she was doing, Lily drew her stool near to Mark and tentatively placed a hand on his arm.

"Tell me about it," she said.

"It . . ." Mark began falteringly. "The medicine that cured me, it doesn't work for everyone. It poisons some. He gave it to one man and he started screaming . . ." Mark gripped the arm of the chair, his knuckles white. "After that, there were other things to do. Boils to lance, bandages . . . He cut off a man's leg as well." Mark relaxed a little. "I didn't mind that so much, the man couldn't feel it, and we went into a little room. Not many people there. I got to clean the knife."

Lily raised an eyebrow, involuntarily drawing back her hand.

"You *enjoyed* that?" she said.

"More than the disease. You can't catch someone else's leg." Mark gave a tiny smile and stretched out his own legs, looking around the room. His eyes came to rest on the damp parcel sitting on the table. He picked it up thoughtfully. "Is this yours?" he asked.

"It's for you," Lily replied, puzzled.

Mark squinted closer. "How can you tell?"

"It has your name on it. See."

Mark looked up sharply.

"You can read?" he said with a wary air. "Only receivers read where I come from."

"I taught myself when I worked at the bookbinder's, before I came here," Lily said gently.

Mark gave her a look of bewilderment. Lily shook her head and reached down to one side of her chair. She lifted up a leather-bound volume.

"Have you ever seen a book before?"

"Only the ones the receivers had . . ." Mark shifted in his chair, uncomfortable. "My father said that they used them to keep track of debtors."

"This one isn't for business," Lily said, holding it out to him.

Tentatively, Mark touched the cover.

"So . . . what *is* it for?" he asked.

Lily looked down at the tome in her hands. How could she answer a question like that? This book had been her escape for over three years, ever since it was nearly sent to the furnaces for being badly bound. It had been the first one she had learned to read, the first book that had been more than another job to her. She knew every tale by heart.

She smiled wistfully. "It tells you stories," she said.

"Really?" Mark reached out, but Lily pulled it back.

"Open your parcel first."

Mark turned back to the box, his hands nervously reaching out. Slowly, he slit open the damp paper with a fingernail. The wooden box inside was soaked through.

"So that's how you write my name?" he said, tracing the outline of "Mark" carved into its lid.

"Yes," Lily said quietly, remembering how she had felt, only a couple of months earlier, when a similar box had arrived for her.

Mark lifted the lid and gasped.

"Is it . . . gold?" he said, breathing reverently.

Lily laughed. "Some kind of brass, I think. You can get them in gold, but you need to be a little richer than we are." She got up and looked over his shoulder. "Happy title day, Mark. You own your-self now."

Mark reached into the box and plucked out its contents. Sitting there in his hand it was less impressive: a flat, round disk mounted on a cheap brass ring. But carved on that disk, solemnly floating, was something Mark later said he had seen only once, when his dad had brought it proudly home from a rare catch, saying that it was a good omen. It was stylized, but there was no mistaking the five points of a starfish. Mark sat and stared. A signet ring.

"Haven't you ever seen one before?" Lily said softly.

"Of course I have, but . . ." Mark paused, tracing the outline of the seal. "I used to ask when I'd get one. My brother and sister were both younger, so I think I knew that I'd be first. My dad told me to wait until I was grown up, said it would be a surprise. Mom always looked sad when she thought about it. She never said anything about title days . . . All her stories were about witches, and ghosts, and cities made of gold . . . nothing to do with the real world, but they always felt more real than anything I'd ever known. After a few stories, I always forgot what I'd been asking her about . . . I think that was the point."

Mark held it up to the firelight, then gingerly slipped it onto his ring finger. Lily couldn't see his expression, but his voice was a whisper.

"Dad kept his hidden in the blankets where he slept. Only brought it out when he was going to sell the catch. He was afraid the neighbors would steal it. 'Steal your ring, steal your soul,' he used to say." Mark held out his hand. "Lily, how . . . how do you use it?"

Lily considered for a moment. Mark needed to make his first trade and receive his title gift — even the most lowly beggar received something on their title day. But what would the doctor give him? He owned nothing but tools for which Mark would need years of training before he could use them. And then, almost without realizing it, her eyes drifted down to the book in her hands. She held it tighter. It was important to her, one of the few things that she had ever been able to call her own.

But what was the point of a story you could not share?

She picked up the candle.

"I'll show you. Wait here."

After a few minutes of rummaging in a cupboard, Lily returned with paper and a long, thin pen. It had once been a goose feather, but all remnants of fluff had been stripped from it and now it was a very simple means of moving ink from a copper pot to the paper. Carefully, she wrote, reading aloud as she did so:

> I, Lily, give to Mark, one book.
> In return, Mark gives nothing, for it is a title gift.

Then she reached for the candle and, tilting it, let hot wax run down onto the contract.

"Press it in, like this."

Fishing in her apron pocket, Lily pulled out her own signet ring and pushed it down into the wax. As she pulled it back, both saw the shape of a flower, a lily, growing out of an open book.

"Now you."

His hand shaking, Mark pushed his seal down beside hers. The starfish seemed to grin up at him.

"What now?" he said.

"Nothing. You own the book." Lily felt a twinge of sadness but covered it with a sly smile. "Do you want to know how to read it? That's extra."

"Not fair," Mark grumbled. "I can't even use the present."

"You can look at the woodcut pictures," Lily replied, handing him the book. "Anyway, be grateful. My title gift was a cart ride."

"Where to?"

Lily paused. Images of her few belongings being thrown into the mud rose up in her mind as she heard the doors of the book-binder's grinding shut. Inwardly, she shuddered.

"Away," she said simply. "The bookbinders didn't want to keep me once I had my signet ring. They didn't own me anymore, and they needed smaller fingers for the stitching. I was lucky. They let me stay on for a week, before I was—" Lily gave a mirthless chuckle—"asked to leave. It feels like a lifetime ago."

Mark picked at the cover of the book awkwardly.

"I suppose you get used to it," he said hopefully, "after a couple of years . . ."

Lily gave a tight smile.

"I probably will, but it still feels new to me." She folded her arms. "My title day was only two months ago, on Agora Day."

Mark looked up sharply, his surprise visible.

"Really?" he said. "I mean . . . not that you look much older than me . . . It's just . . . the way you act and talk . . . you remind me of my mother sometimes."

Lily flinched.

"Gee, thanks," she said, a little more sharply than she had meant.

Mark shrank back into his chair. "She used to be the one who explained things," he said quietly. "She was the one who told me stories, who kept all this stuff away from me. She . . . she made me feel safe."

Lily breathed out slowly, her annoyance fading away. Now she thought about it, it was strange to think how little time she had spent at the tower. It already felt as though she had been through its dull routines a thousand times. She pulled her chair closer to Mark's.

"I started work years ago, Mark. The orphanage sold me to the bookbinders when I had seen only six summers. I wasn't even the youngest worker there." Lily bit her lip; she had never talked to anyone about this before. "I didn't have a mother or a father, just an orphanage matron who was so distant I never even knew her name." Lily shrugged. "I suppose that kind of life makes you grow up fast." She leaned forward. "I can tell you everything I've picked up, Mark—try to help as best I can. But I can't be your mother, and I wouldn't want to be. She sounds special."

Mark looked away. "She was," he said.

For a while they sat with their thoughts, Mark gazing at the signet ring and Lily at Mark. She couldn't tell what he was thinking.

"So," Mark said at last, "the doctor doesn't own me anymore?"

"He won't in a week. They give you time to find someone new."

"And then you sell yourself?"

"You sell your service. It's all we have." Lily rolled up the contract. "There are no more gifts, Mark. Not ever."

There was a pause.

"Lily . . ." he said. "What do we do?" When he looked up at her, he suddenly seemed so lost.

Lily took his hands into her own. "We survive, Mark. That's the only thing we can do. We try to live, try to find somewhere we can call home." She saw her own dark eyes reflected in his gray ones. "We do what we can for ourselves." She squeezed his hands. "And for each other."

For a long moment they both turned away to look into the fire, but if there was a glimpse of the future in the flames, Lily could not see it. Then Mark took the cover of his new book and flipped it open.

"Clean the kitchen for you in exchange for a reading lesson?" he said.

Lily smiled.

"I'd say that's worth a couple of hours."

CHAPTER THREE

The Deal

I T WAS A FEW MONTHS later that Mark discovered, to his astonishment, that he was happy. Or at least closer to happiness than he had expected to be.

It wasn't as if he had much to be happy about. At night, when he lay curled up against the tower's many drafts, dark thoughts would come back to him. The face of his father would swim into view, stamping down a brass seal into wax, selling his dying son to a doctor for a few weeks of treatment. Then the same doctor would rouse him, announcing that they were setting off again to walk the streets.

He was a different man out there. In the tower the doctor relaxed a little. He often apologized to Mark for the worst parts of their work — the dissection of corpses, the foul-smelling mixtures — but down in the basement, between the dry stones, it felt safe and secret. Mark could pretend to himself that it was nothing more than an intriguing game.

But when they were on the streets, it became all too real. The doctor donned the mask of the Reaper, the smooth white face and goggles of black. He made Mark wear a mask too; it would protect them from other diseases in the slums, he said, and it acted as a badge of office. Outside, Dr. Theophilus walked swiftly and spoke as little as possible. Mark could see the tension in his hands as he handed over the instruments and bottles. He often concentrated on the doctor's hands — it meant he didn't have to look at the gasping, desperate faces around them.

Mark couldn't help it. He knew the doctor was right when he told him that it was impossible for him to catch the gray plague again. He didn't understand, of course, something to do with "the vile humors" having been purged, but there could be no reason for his master to lie to him. However, when he was out there, on the streets . . .

It was the smell. He was used to the smell of rot, of moldering fish and foul river mud — the stench of the River Ora as it lapped against the banks of the Piscean slums — which had been with him his whole life. But by the river he could see the sky. Now, crushed into the alleyways in the depths of the Pisces District, far from the waterfront he had called home, it was as though the odors were being pushed into his nose and mouth, as though his head was swelling up in the rush of diseased air and clattering footsteps. He was shoved and jostled by a thousand rushing shadows. No one greeted each other as they rushed by.

Sometimes he thought of going back, of seeing whether his father was still alive, but something always stopped him. He told Lily that it was the thought of the city, huge and imposing, stretching out between the tower and his old home, and she said she believed him. He was grateful for that, particularly as both of them knew it was not the only reason. If he went back he would find one of two things: a dead father or the man who had sold him. The trouble was, he didn't know which would be worse.

He had learned to enjoy the atmosphere of the tower — dry, dusty, and safe. The building had changed in his mind over the four months he had known it: Once it had been terrifying, but now it seemed to stand out like a beacon, calling him home. No disease would survive long in a place so empty. When the time had come to sign his apprenticeship to the doctor, a week after his title day, he barely waited for the wax to drip onto the paper. The doctor's signet had six stars on it, like his grandfather's. But in addition there were two snakes twisted around a stick: the symbol of a healer.

Having his own signet was also strangely comforting. Sometimes, lying in bed, he would keep his scrap of candle lit for a few minutes before he dropped off to sleep so that he could stare at the little brass ring. The starfish seeming to flex and move in the flickering light. It was like discovering a new part of himself, as if he had fallen asleep with just one name, like everyone else, and woken up with a hundred. He was no longer just Mark; he was Mr. Mark of the starfish signet, apprentice to Dr. Theophilus. He felt, for the first time, as if he really knew who he was.

However, his life wasn't perfect. He still had to hide whenever the Count's bell rang. Never mind that the old man had not left his Observatory for years; new servants were not permitted, especially those who might be contaminated.

When Mark had asked Lily how she came to be accepted as his servant, she had smiled wearily before replying.

"I wrote to him, as soon as I knew the bookbinders wanted to get rid of me. Said I wanted to work for the great Count Stelli, that I'd read every one of his books." She had then given a rare chuckle. "Almost true actually. Not a lot that's worth reading when you're working in the astrology section. He replied the next day, sending me the contract, his seal already on it. I handed it to the receiver on the way to the tower." She had looked down for a moment before continuing. "I've never seen him in the light, barely spoken to him. He communicates in notes. First one said he wanted to put my literacy to the test."

Lily. Mark had had to think again about her. She certainly wasn't an angel; angels didn't clean the privies. But it was still as if she had stepped out of one of those stories his mother used to tell him. He'd known a few of the other kids on the waterfront — they used to throw mud at each other — but she was nothing like them. She seemed older, more serious, yet she could still be fun; in the evenings, when their work was done, she was always ready to talk, or they would explore the old dust-sheet-covered rooms. If he managed to make her laugh, it was always a bonus. He had found that, with the assistance of a couple of dust sheets and a few improvised moans, he could pretend that the tower was haunted. This never failed to raise a giggle, although he was not quite sure whether she was laughing at the game or at how ridiculous he must look.

But if he bumped into her during the day, when she was not expecting him, that was different. Just for a second, before she greeted him, she would stop what she was doing — cooking and cleaning mostly — and stare, as if she was coming back from thoughts far deeper than he had ever had. It was at times like these when he noticed her eyes. Dark eyes, just like her skin. He knew that she kept no secrets, she spoke frankly and simply, and Dr. Theophilus thought her invaluable, but sometimes Mark found her unnerving. Once, his mom had told him of an ancient spirit who could draw your soul out with its gaze. It would have had eyes just like Lily's.

His mom's stories had been nothing like those in Lily's book. As the weeks passed, Lily continued Mark's reading lessons, drawing their stools closer to the kitchen fire to stave off the winter's cold. Under her guidance the letters, words, and sentences began to make sense, but Mark found that there were no heroes or demons in what he read. In fact, for several days he labored to understand a passage that eventually turned out to be about nothing more than making a shepherd's pie.

"I thought you said this was a storybook," he grumbled, squinting up at her.

Lily sighed. "It is. That pie's important because the son had to steal the meat to make it, because otherwise his mother would have starved. That's why the receivers come for them."

Mark shivered. "I prefer the old stories. They don't have receivers, only demons. You can trust demons."

He didn't want to admit it, but the fact that there were no receivers here in the tower also made it feel safe. The receivers hadn't come often to the slums, but when they had it was always to take someone away, someone who had failed to settle their debts or cheated or, worst of all, stolen. All the children would cry and dive for cover as the midnight-blue uniforms came into view, then watch in fascinated horror as another family were dragged apart by gloved hands, while an inspector looked on and wrote his report. Of course, adults dealt with the receivers all the time. Every contract was handed in to them for safekeeping; as the representatives of the Directory of Receipts, they would even write contracts for those who could not do so themselves. Once sealed, the contracts were taken away, and in due course a receiver brought you an official receipt. One of them would knock on the tower door weekly to collect and deliver, but Mark always hid. He was perfectly legal, he had no debts, but . . . It was whispered that the receivers sold the debtors back to those they had wronged, in pieces if necessary, and the shrill whistles of their patrols made him tremble.

Worse still, the most wretched of the debtors were said to be taken before the Director of Receipts, the ruler of Agora himself. Even the storytellers fell silent when they mentioned the Director. No one other than the highest in the city had ever seen him, or even knew precisely who he was, although several great families claimed him as one of their own. All anyone knew for certain was that those who entered the Directory vanished from the world. It was said that the Director held a great ledger with the name of every Agoran written in it. It was said that he could see each person's life written in their name, and that if he erased the name, struck it out with a stroke of his pen, it would be as if that person had never existed — their life forgotten, their passing brushed away.

Mark mentioned all this to Lily, who raised an eyebrow and said dryly, "A lot of things scare you, don't they?"

After that, Mark's fear was replaced with irritation for most of the rest of the day. He was only being sensible.

In the meantime, he continued learning about the world's dullest family in his book. Lily told him that his reading was improving far faster than she would ever have expected, but it still felt achingly slow to him.

During one lesson, when the afternoons had begun to brighten with the approach of spring, Mark complained loudly, "Nothing happens! They don't do anything except moan about their lives, then every so often someone dies or gets arrested for their debts. Aren't there any other books? I'm cleaning the dining room for you for this."

"Not unless you fancy reading about infections of the bowels in the doctor's books or want to try stealing from the Count," Lily retorted, keeping her eyes fixed on the page. "Anyway, it's about real people — people with fears and hopes. Are you saying you never worry about the future?"

"The only things that frighten me are things I've seen happen,"

Mark shot back and was pleased to see Lily's face soften. It was a victory of sorts.

She pulled back her hair, bent over his shoulder, and pointed to the next line. "What does it say?" she said patiently.

Mark frowned. "This is really going to help me?" he asked.

Lily nodded firmly, but kept her eyes fixed on the page.

"It's a huge city out there, Mark. How can we learn about it if we don't let others do some of our seeing for us?" She turned her head then, her gaze meeting his. "Don't you want to think about other people? Do you want to stay in this tower and know nothing about the world outside?"

Mark dropped his eyes. It was silly, but he didn't want to look at her. He felt that she would extract his answer, which was that he had tried the world outside and didn't much like it.

"If I were them," Mark grumbled, closing the book, "I'd find a way to make the world work for me. I wouldn't sit and wait for the next disaster. I wouldn't be trampled on," he added fiercely.

Lily gave him a look that he couldn't read.

"What?" he snapped.

"Nothing," Lily said thoughtfully. "Except . . . so much of it wasn't their fault. Don't you feel sorry for them?"

"It's only a story," Mark grunted.

Lily's gaze was still on him.

"That's not an answer," she said.

"It's not how a real family would behave anyway. There definitely aren't enough arguments . . ."

"Yes, well," Lily said softly, "I wouldn't know."

Instantly, Mark felt a sharp stab of guilt.

"I'm sorry, I didn't mean . . ." he began, but Lily shook her head.

"It doesn't matter," she said, taking the book from him. "Don't stop."

"Stop what?"

"Telling me what a real family would do," she said hesitantly. "I'd like to know."

Mark was thrown. He had never really thought about it before.

"Um, the brothers and sisters would probably fight sometimes, but not really mean it . . . The mother would try to make peace and make everyone feel safe . . . She would love them all . . . and the father would . . ." Mark faltered. "He would protect his family . . . and keep them close to him—every one of them. That's what a good father would do."

"He would," Lily said, with quiet fierceness. "That's what he should have done."

They stared at each other, unsure of what to say next. Mark wanted to thank her but he knew, just by looking in her eyes, that she understood.

Then, as if nothing had happened, Lily opened the book again, a half smile on her face.

"Come on, enough distractions, back to your reading lessons," she said in a breezy tone. "Unless you want me to convince the doctor to sell your contract to a sewage worker . . ."

Mark relaxed, all of the tension in the room fading away.

"I'd like to see you try," he replied, peering down at the page.

This, then, was his happiness—living in an ancient building with a strange girl, a master who talked of things he could not understand, and a fierce voice from above. It felt timeless, as if it would continue forever.

But it didn't. And it was his fault.

It was also the day he discovered the other important use of reading. A little more attention and he would have noticed his name on the receipt delivered to their door by the receiver, the receipt for his title gift contract with Lily, finally processed by the Directory. A little more knowledge and he would have hidden it away, not left it in the pile of papers for the doctor to take up to his grandfather at their weekly conversation.

The voice of the Count shook the tower; Mark felt the vibrations all the way down in his room. He shrank back, hiding from the sound of running feet. He heard the doctor call his name frantically, but he couldn't move. He sat on his bed, his knees drawn up under his chin, shaking. He had been discovered, and they were going to throw him out. Out there.

His door burst open, and he buried his head in his knees, clinging to the meager sheets. He wouldn't be taken. He felt a hand grab his shoulder and shake it.

"Mark!"

It was Lily's voice. He looked up, clinging to her sleeve.

"Don't let them take me out there," he said, his stomach lurching. "I'll live in the deepest cellar, I'll work all night, just don't let them take me . . ."

"It's not just you, Mark."

He stopped. Lily's face was strangely intense.

"It's Dr. Theophilus," she continued breathlessly. "The Count found out about you and they argued. The doctor explained that you weren't infectious anymore, but the Count said that it was about trust, about hiding people in his own home . . ." Lily slowed down, gathering herself. "The Count owns the tower, and he's throwing him out, so as his servant you go where he goes . . ."

Mark collapsed backward onto the bed, groaning.

"Don't let them send me out there, Lily. I'll die . . . I can't . . ."

"Then swap with me."

Lily's voice cut through his thoughts, clear and firm. He sat up. She was holding out a contract, her seal already on it.

"You don't want to leave," she said, "but I do. This is the only chance I'll get. I don't want to leave you behind, but it's either you or me who walks out into the streets."

Mark stared at the contract. It was so simple; even he could read it all. Trembling, he reached into his pocket and pulled out his signet ring, its brightness barely dulled. He hesitated.

"Can we do this? Is it allowed?"

"It's legal, just about," Lily replied. "We're nearly the same age and haven't officially been working here long enough to have different skills. As far as the law's concerned, we're worth the same."

Mark thought about this, his brain racing.

"The Count won't keep me if he thinks I'm diseased."

Lily shook her head.

"The doctor says he managed to convince him that you're no longer dangerous. He told me this wasn't just about you, that it's been coming for a long time."

"I'll be alone with the Count."

"True," Lily said. "He's a hard master and you'll work all day. But he's rich, he'll keep you fed, and you'll never have to leave the tower."

Mark slipped on the ring and moved it toward the blob of still-soft wax. He looked up.

"And you?" he said quietly.

"I don't know," she replied, and Mark noticed that, despite her determination, the contract quivered as she held it. "I'll write to you somehow. I'll visit if I can. I'll let you know. And you write back to me, all right?"

For a moment, they stared at each other. Then he nodded.

"I'll miss you," he said softly.

Lily pushed the contract forward.

"I know," she said, "but that's Agora. You take your chances when they come if you want to survive." She paused as Mark pressed his seal into the wax. She nodded and grabbed his hand. "Keep surviving, Mark."

And then she was gone.

Some hours later, Mark was still sitting numbly on the bed. The flurry of activity, the shouts and bangs, had all long since faded away. Somewhere in the back of his mind he wondered vaguely what time it was.

In the distance he heard the ringing of a bell. The Count was calling for his supper.

Silently, Mark trudged up the grand staircase that got narrower and darker as it wound its way up the center of the tower. Finally, at the top of the stairs, he stood before a door that he had never seen. Lily had described it well. It was a door of burnished bronze. A door to the stars.

"Sir?" he said at last. His voice squeaked as he spoke, but he managed to keep the trembling out of it.

There was a pause, followed by the slow tread of heavy footsteps descending a flight of stairs. Mark held his breath, but the door did not open. Instead, he heard a low rumble from within the closed chamber.

"Who is that?" The voice was not loud, but it carried infinite menace, like distant thunder.

"Uh . . ." Mark felt his throat go dry. "Mark, sir. Your new servant." Silence from behind the door. "Lily . . . she went with Dr. Theophilus. I stayed. I think . . . you know about me."

There was a long pause.

"You are fortunate, boy, that I have no time to hire a new servant at present. I am told that you are now free of disease," the voice of the Count rumbled. "Nevertheless, if you infect me, I shall see that you are thrown from the top of my tower before I die. Is that clear?"

"Yes, sir."

"I want no food tonight; I am working. Bring breakfast early tomorrow morning, boy. I am expecting visitors. Now be gone."

Mark's legs obeyed the final instruction before his brain registered it. The Count's commands carried a lifetime of authority.

He wandered down to the kitchen. The fire had gone out and Lily's sewing had been left on a chair. Mark sat down heavily. This was it, then, just the two of them in this vast old place.

He still hadn't decided how he felt about it all when he fell asleep.

CHAPTER FOUR

The Glassmaker

THE RAIN LASHED against her face, but Lily didn't care. She breathed in deeply. She was outside. The walls were no longer there.

She looked up at Dr. Theophilus, but he was once again swathed in coat, mask, and goggles. She had not had long to read his expression when she told him about her and Mark's arrangement, but she had seen that he wasn't angry. Sad might have described it better.

Then again, the doctor often looked sad. Lily did not see him very often, but she had noticed how his step grew slower every day, how his brown hair was already showing signs of gray, even though, according to an old diary of his that she had found in one of the disused bedrooms, he had seen little more than two grand cycles. It gave the date of his title day fifteen years ago. He had sounded so proud.

Lily could have wished for a better day on which to see the city.

When the cart had taken her to the tower she had tried to imagine what the outside world looked like. Lying stuffed among the bales of cloth like old linen, she had listened to the rain spatter on the tarpaulin covering her. Now she looked and felt that same oily, foul rain on her face as she stared up at dingy gray walls and a leaden sky. Still, the streets around the tower itself were broad and clean, a sign on the wall proudly proclaiming this as part of the prosperous Gemini District, the seat of learning.

Shielding her eyes against the rain, Lily looked around her. Everywhere the people who pushed past were packed in so tightly that she could barely see the buildings around them. As they went on, the crowds grew louder and the shops grander. The cobblestones below her feet were replaced with smooth, even flagstones. Ahead a huge ornamental arch, carved with two identical figures gazing at each other, loomed above the sea of heads.

And then the streets opened out.

Even in the driving winter rain, even when shoved and jostled from all sides by the hordes of cloaked people, the Central Plaza took Lily's breath away. The River Ora, channeled by engineers many years before, flowed around the circular hub, while twelve arched marble bridges, one for each district, crossed over its greenish waters to the twelve vast arches which led to the rest of the city. And in the distance, visible always despite the gloom, the towers of the Directory of Receipts loomed out of the clouds. Lily had never been this close before, but she didn't need anyone to tell her what the building was — it stamped its authority upon the plaza as if its mastery of the city was infused into every stone.

She so wanted to linger by the hundreds of stalls set up on the plaza, covering it in a carpet of wares. She wished she could have shown Mark this. Shown him that the outside world was not always terrible.

But there was no chance of that now. Perhaps not ever.

She was jolted out of her reverie as she saw Dr. Theophilus carrying on, crossing the bridge ahead of them to the Plaza and plunging through the crowd. She had to run to catch up with him. They continued together toward another of the arches on the far side, this one bearing the carving of a strange creature. Half-man, half-horse, it stretched back a bow and arrow, as if to send its shaft plunging into the heart of the Directory or maybe even soaring over the distant city walls.

As they crossed another bridge and then passed beneath the arch, Lily read the inscription on the archway: *Sagittarius District*.

Beyond the arch, the streets began to constrict, but the mass of bodies seemed only to increase, the roar of people hawking their wares even louder than before. But Dr. Theophilus's silent tread lay away from that, down the alleyways where huddled forms pushed past them, not wanting to linger.

The stones grew grimier, the streets rougher, and sometimes Lily's shoes swam up to the ankles in mud. Looking at one figure, Lily noticed that all she had to sell were pieces of brick and stone that she had scoured from the crumbling buildings around her. Soon, as they progressed deeper into the district, the makeshift stalls vanished altogether. Now those they passed had something quite different to sell, and it couldn't be displayed.

Looking at them, Lily heard again the words of the matron of the orphanage: *There are no beggars in Agora, children. Everyone makes their way by bartering something, for there is always someone who will trade.*

Lily drew the collar of Mark's coat around her face. It was too big for her, but it had been part of the contract, and now she used it to hide her face. Some of the shadows in doorways turned their heads as she walked past, holding out their hands, which were spotted with patches of gray. Lily shrank back. She suddenly had the urge to hold the doctor's hand. It was ridiculous; she was a servant, but just then she felt so alone.

She reached out, and to her surprise, he grasped her hand. He gave it a squeeze. Not much, but she concentrated her eyes on it, saw her dark hand clasped in his black gloves. He stopped then and looked down at her. His face was hidden behind the mask, but there was something in the way he passed her a thick cloth to use as a headscarf that suggested concern. Her feet ached now, and she was dizzy with new sights. The buildings seemed to stretch up into the sky, looming over her.

"Sir," she said at last, "I don't think I can go on . . ."

"Almost there, Lily," Dr. Theophilus replied, breaking his silence. "Just a few more streets."

As Lily dragged her weary feet over the cobblestones of the Sagittarius District, she realized with a start that she had no idea where they were going.

There were shops here, regular buildings, but they pushed together like a mob, squeezed nearly on top of each other. And still they walked on, until, in one swift movement, the doctor dived down a side street and produced a set of keys.

"Here we are," he said.

The building looked very ordinary from the outside. Its stone was dark red, and it had no colored banners hanging from its windows to advertise its presence. It rested in the shadow of a shop whose walls were covered in pieces of sparkling glass. A small, thin woman appeared at the shop's doorway, peering at the doctor as he tried to fit one key after another into the lock.

"Theo?" the woman said at last, as the doctor dropped the keys with a muffled exclamation. He turned and pulled the mask from his face.

"Yes, Miss Devine," he said, with a brisk politeness. "I wonder, this lock . . ."

"I had it changed," she said, sidling over to the door. "The locksmith was getting a little too interested . . . I was charged with caretaking by your parents, Theo."

"Oh." Dr. Theophilus frowned, his eyes flicking to one side. "If we could have the key, Miss Devine, I intend to practice here. I believe the property still belongs to me."

"To an extent, Theo, to an extent." She raised a hand, stained with some kind of bluish smear, and ran a finger over the door. "Since your parents did not settle all of their debts before they left, much of the property now belongs to me."

"They died, Miss Devine."

"True. Still, I am not ungenerous. A regular contract with a doctor, for free, will go some way toward the new rent." The woman smiled.

Lily shivered. There was nothing malicious in the smile. And that was what was so unnerving; it was as if she couldn't see the pain crossing the doctor's face.

"I shall need some new glassware as well," he said at last, gesturing toward Miss Devine's shop. "Let us decide on the rate. Lily, come with us."

Mutely, Lily followed the adults into Miss Devine's shop. The entire front wall was covered in tiny multicolored shards of glass that glinted in the dying light, their red pattern proclaiming her trade as a glassmaker. As Lily pushed her way through the heavy curtain that served for a door, the light dimmed dramatically. Inside the room, the shelves were full of glass vials. Inside each one was something that shimmered in the half-light of an old lantern. The doctor and Miss Devine slipped behind the long, low counter, and went on into a back room that was lit by the flickering glow of a glassblower's furnace. Left on her own, Lily began to sweep her eyes across the shelves. Each miniature bottle had something written on it, but in the gloom she couldn't quite make out the words. She squinted closer, focusing on one deep maroon liquid. There was something scratched into the glass — a name: *Ambition*.

"That's a good one."

Lily jumped. A figure had emerged from the shadows. For a moment, she thought it was Miss Devine, but then she saw that this woman was younger and even thinner. Red curls, tangled and knotted, obscured much of her pale face, so all Lily could see were two large blue eyes peering at her with a strange brightness. Lily noticed that she held one of the vials between her fingers — a pale yellow liquid that seemed to shake even though her hands held it steady.

"Is it some kind of perfume?" Lily asked, trying to be polite to cover her unease. She had seen something like this in the old dressing room of the tower, a relic from the Count's mother.

The woman laughed. "Nothing but the smell of success there, young miss. That's pure ambition, bottled for sale. Expensive too. One of Miss Devine's finest. They say she milks it out of servants in the old houses, keeping them docile for their masters. Makes everyone happy."

Lily looked back at the bottle. This must be a joke, surely, but the woman spoke as if it were the most natural thing in the world.

"Gloria!" The sharp voice of Miss Devine, who had reappeared from the next room, cut across their thoughts. The woman looked up, smiling. Miss Devine gave a businesslike nod.

"Your usual, I take it?"

"Yes, Miss Devine," Gloria said hurriedly, holding up the vial of yellow liquid for inspection. "I wouldn't dream of going anywhere else."

"Good girl."

Lily watched as Miss Devine tore off a strip of paper from a long roll on the counter. She wrote with practiced speed, dripping the wax and sealing it almost before Gloria had detached a small leather bag from her belt and placed it on the counter. Lily watched as Gloria fumbled with her signet ring, before plunging it into the wax, leaving her symbol, a pedestal within a wreath of leaves, next to Miss Devine's stamp — a vial of liquid. The glassmaker took hold of the bag, opened it, and gave a deep sniff.

"I see the spice merchant on Aurora Road has been using your services again, Gloria. Fine wares, very useful."

"Is it enough?" Gloria asked, twisting her long sleeves between her fingers.

Lily noticed that she had begun to rub her wrists together nervously.

Miss Devine smiled. "For today, Gloria. Since you are such a good customer."

Gloria nodded gleefully and tucked the tiny bottle into her pocket. Smiling, she turned to Lily.

"The best emotion in the city, miss," she said, as if imparting a great secret. "The very best." And with that she left the shop.

Miss Devine deftly rolled up Gloria's contract and slipped it, along with the drawstring bag, under the counter.

"Your master may be some time, girl. He is selecting alchemical equipment from my storeroom." The glassmaker stepped around the counter, resting one hand on Lily's shoulder. It felt hard and dry. "How long have you worked for this physician?"

"Not long, madam," Lily said, easing herself away from Miss Devine's touch, while keeping her eyes respectfully lowered. There was no point in being bold with someone she didn't know, especially when she seemed to have power over her master.

"Are you prepared for your duties?" Miss Devine took a strand of Lily's dark hair and twisted it around her finger. "You've seen work, girl, I can see it in your hands. But have you seen death?"

Lily felt her stomach begin to churn. She had tried to keep that thought out of her head.

"Only once, madam," she said. "When I took the doctor his lunch . . . down in his workroom . . ." The awful blank stare began to rise before her and she shuddered.

"A doctor's assistant must see much death, girl. Wounds and sickness, and then there are the flies . . ." Miss Devine smiled. "Forgive me, but you must be prepared. You look pale at the thought of it."

"I . . ." Lily swallowed. She could feel her insides squirming.

It was stupid; she had always told herself that a dead person couldn't harm her, but . . .

"It's blood. It makes me feel sick . . . It . . ." Lily faltered. She didn't know the word for what she felt.

"Don't worry. Lily, is it?" Miss Devine said, walking back behind the counter. "Disgust is natural, one of the prime emotions. Of course — " she leaned forward, resting her arms on the counter, a motherly smile on her face — "it is also quite a valuable commodity."

Lily looked up, startled, as Miss Devine continued.

"Useful to people to have a little extra disgust sometimes. It works wonders as a slimming aid for society women, while a touch of repulsion helps people to take a more balanced view of their business. I do quite a brisk trade in disgust. And a child's disgust is the freshest, of course, before we become hardened to the world."

Lily looked up. All around her the shelves stretched up to the ceiling. On them, the tiny bottles clustered together, hundreds of them, perhaps thousands. And each one, every one, contained part of someone, some piece of their mind, boiled down and ready for sale. She shuddered.

"Miss Devine . . ." Lily stopped. It seemed unnatural; her feet itched to run away, to wait for the doctor outside. But then again, what use was disgust? Fear kept her safe, anger gave her drive, but disgust? She could have done without that when they served food at the orphanage.

"In payment for some of that glassware that your master is choosing, shall we say?"

Miss Devine pulled forward another length of paper and cut it off with a blade of glass. Lily watched as the contract formed before her. Three pieces of alchemical equipment in exchange for her disgust. She felt dazed, still not quite able to take it in. Her heart was beating in her mouth. But then, out of her churning thoughts, a practical voice asserted itself. She would be able to help the doctor without flinching; he could continue his research. It would solve so many problems.

She pressed her ring down into the warm wax.

Miss Devine rolled up the paper and drew aside a curtain in a corner of the room. Beyond it, a dark chamber filled with a large and tangled shadow greeted Lily's eyes. As Miss Devine brought in the lantern, the light gleamed off a web of glass tubing curling around in a labyrinth of globes and beakers. In the far corner, a mass of pipes fed into a large, squat device covered in cogs and pistons. In the center of the apparatus, beneath the largest of the glass spheres, there was a leather chair.

"Sit down, Lily. It will only take a moment."

Lily moved forward, her footfalls resonating through the apparatus. As she sat in the chair, a feeling of unease stole over her. Miss Devine lowered a mask of smoked glass from the middle of the machine. Lily opened her mouth to speak, but her words were stifled as the glassmaker covered her face with the mask. She could feel tubes spiraling out from it as it pressed down over her eyes, nose, and mouth.

"Don't move, my dear," Miss Devine called out, as she scuttled across to the machine in the corner.

Lily lifted her hand to move the mask, deciding to speak, to say that perhaps this wasn't a good idea.

There was a deep hum. The machine was on.

For a moment, Lily felt nothing. Then she became aware of a rushing behind her ears, as though wind was howling through the pipes above her. The noise grew louder and louder. Her head was filling with air, and the wind was reaching down, deeper and deeper . . .

Then, rising inside her, Lily felt happiness, sadness, fear, elation, horror, indifference; each flashed through her more intensely than ever before, bubbling up from within, passing into her head and then, with a rush, out through her eyes and mouth. Dimly, she saw a rainbow of fizzing, glowing gases escaping up into the tubes above her, spinning faster and faster around the web of glass beyond.

Lily was numb. She sat dully, watching the colors whirl. Somewhere above, she saw a thick, black gas separate from the others, saw it sink down, condensing, dripping into a flask beside her—her disgust. She felt emptied out, hollow. Then there was another noise. Lily turned her eyes. The doctor had pushed his way into the room. He was shouting something, but she was too tired to listen, too sluggish to move her head. He pulled one of the controls.

With a rush, the machine shuddered into reverse. For one awful moment, the colored gases hovered above her. Then they all fell at once, streaming into her. Lily gasped, clutching at the mask, trying to tear it off her face as every emotion she had ever felt forced its way into her head. Laughing and crying, screaming and smiling, she leapt up from the chair. Behind her, she heard the wrench of glass and then a crash. The mask flew from her face, shattering on the ground.

She looked up as the doctor loomed toward her, his face full of rage. She had never seen him angry before. Even as she looked,

Lily felt another surge of emotion, but just one this time — fear. Overwhelming, petrifying fear of that face. She turned and ran.

She ran through the shop. She ran out into the streets. She kept running, faster and faster, running until her legs ached and her lungs screamed for rest. But it was not until the fear faded, until her overwhelming panic settled again into the back of her mind, that she stopped and sank to her knees, gasping from exhaustion.

She lay down in the filth and mud, and closed her eyes.

CHAPTER FIVE

The Manservant

MARK WAS AWAKENED by a tremendous knocking at the front door.

Rubbing his eyes, he stumbled down the stairs, wondering if Lily had had to do this every time a visitor came. Then again, in all his time at the tower, he could not remember a single visitor.

Gritting his teeth, Mark tugged at the rusting bolts that held the door shut. A voice from the other side spoke impatiently.

"Open up! The Count asked us here at the fourth hour after midnight precisely. I am not in the habit of rising at such a time."

Grunting out apologies, Mark dragged the heavy door back. The next moment, he was pushed aside by a young man in a thick brown coat who swept into the hallway. He glared at Mark, plucking a three-cornered hat from his head and shaking out a mane of red hair.

"Is it a common practice for you to leave your master's guests out in the cold, boy?" he demanded, thrusting the hat into Mark's hands.

Mark scowled at the hat, but muttered something about being new to the job.

The visitor gave a mirthless laugh. "Carry on in this fashion and you are likely to be new to a great number of jobs in quick succession." Elegantly, he peeled off the coat and dumped that too in Mark's arms.

"Pay no attention to the boy, Laud. We waste our time shouting at the staff."

Two more coats — one of gaudy green silk, the other of cheaper, black cotton — fell into his arms as two more men entered, bringing with them a blast of chill night air. The speaker was a large, genial-looking older man who leaned on a walking stick, his brightly patterned vest straining under his bulk; the other, a man of middle years in impeccably neat, formal black, stayed silent. The older man gave a cough.

"I think it is better if we see ourselves up." He turned to Mark. "Boy, has your master ordered breakfast at this unnatural hour?"

Mark nodded, even as his heart sank. He had never cooked anything in his life. The men seemed satisfied.

"Bring it soon," the redheaded visitor ordered, before turning to the older man. "Come, sir, we must not keep the Count waiting."

Mark hurried back up the stairs to the kitchen, behind the guests, wishing that the Count had warned him how early the visitors would arrive. This was not what he would have called morning. Not sure what to do with the hat and coats, he laid them on the kitchen table, as neatly as he could, and began to open cupboards frantically, seeking anything that might be edible. They were well stocked, but the meat was still raw, the eggs uncooked. As he stood in the cold kitchen, Mark realized that he didn't even know how to get the fire going. He was jolted out of his thoughts by the jangling of the Count's bell and fell to scrambling for whatever he could find, hoping that somewhere, despite her rush, Lily would have left instructions as to what the Count liked.

A few minutes later, he surveyed his findings. Hungry as he was, he could not say he was tempted by the lump of cold ham he had found in one of the more obscure cupboards, even when he had piled some homemade bread around it. He hoped that the dark liquid in the thick bottle would make up for it. It looked a little like his father's old rum, but smelled fruitier.

Grimly, he loaded up a tray with this fare and began the long climb to the top of the tower. As he stumbled up the last steps, however, he stopped in his tracks. The door ahead of him was ajar. Lily had told him everything she knew about the Observatory and one thing was certain — the Count *never* left the door open. Mark shivered. All Lily had had to do was ring the bell and push his meal through the hatch. Mark had wanted to do the same, perhaps then the fury of the Count might be held off. No chance of that now.

Gingerly, balancing the tray on a hand and shoulder, Mark knocked on the door. It reverberated, but there was no response. He pushed it open.

Beyond, a circular antechamber presented itself, lit dimly by two old oil lamps. In the center, a spiral staircase made of wrought iron and decorated with sharply pointed stars curved upward, through an open trapdoor, into the ceiling. From above, Mark could make out the rumble of the Count's voice, just out of hearing, and the answering sharper tones of someone younger, probably the red-headed man. Mark's heart sank. It had been hard enough to come through the door; now it seemed he was going to have to walk into the middle of their conversation. He hesitated, not knowing what best to do.

"Are you going to wait there all day?"

Mark jumped and the tray fell to the floor with a clatter. In desperation, he lunged for the bottle, which was, miraculously, unbroken but had rolled away from him. Mark fell to his knees, but then watched in dismay as it came to rest under a shiny black shoe.

"I appreciate your eagerness, boy, but I prefer my liquor in a glass. So much more efficient."

Mark looked up. A curious smile and a raised eyebrow appeared out of the gloom, followed by a proffered hand. He took it. The skin was rough, but as the man helped him up, Mark noticed that his nails shone in the lamplight as though they had been polished. Between two fingers, something gold glimmered.

Mark stood up, clutching the bottle. Now he looked more closely, he recognized the man as the third visitor, the one who hadn't spoken. No wonder Mark had missed him; in his black vest and breeches he was almost invisible in the darkness. Even his hair, unremarkable brown in ordinary light, seemed to melt into shadow in this gloom, making his startlingly green eyes seem all the brighter as they caught the glow.

"Thank you, sir . . . I . . ." Mark gestured hopelessly at the ham that lay on the floor.

The man laughed. "No need to 'sir' me, boy. I am a mere servant, such as yourself. And don't trouble yourself about the meal. The Count, I am reliably informed, goes without eating for days on occasions. As for his guests —" the man flicked the gold object between his fingers idly —"the elder gentleman, my own master, the Honorable Mr. Prendergast, has recently become a vegetarian teetotaler on the advice of his doctor, so you have saved him from the social embarrassment of having to refuse your offerings."

"What about the redheaded man . . . Laud?" Mark asked.

The man smirked.

"I think, perhaps, that Mr. Laudate should speak more civilly to servants if he wants efficient service, don't you?"

The man's smile broadened into a grin. His teeth too were surprisingly bright in the murky room. Mark couldn't resist smiling back as he bent down to pick up the ham.

"What's your name, boy?" the man said, suddenly leaning forward.

Mark told him while he pulled the remains of the meal together, and the man gave a sigh of satisfaction.

"That's a good name. Strong, simple. You can build on a name like that. Tell me then, Mark, do you know what this is?"

Mark looked up. The man held out his hand, then flicked the tiny golden object from finger to finger. It was some kind of metal disk.

"No, sir," Mark said.

The man tutted. "What did I say about 'sir'? Snutworth is my name." Seeing Mark's look of incredulity, he added, "My parents were blessed with many things, Mark, but judgment in choosing my name was not one of them. I wouldn't mind, but it is such a mouthful, and impossible to shorten without making it worse."

Snutworth chuckled and Mark found, to his surprise, that he was joining in.

"Anyway," Snutworth continued, raising one finger conspiratorially, "I'll tell you what this is, Mark." He leaned very close, holding the disk between his thumb and forefinger. "It's a mark!" He drew back triumphantly, letting the disk drop into Mark's hand.

Mark looked at it. It seemed like the seal of a signet ring, covered with an unknown script that didn't resemble any of the words in Lily's book. In the center of one side, there was a portrait of someone looking away.

"What is it?" Mark asked.

Snutworth plucked it delicately from his grasp.

"A piece of history, Mark. A token used to represent something real. An illusion. They called it a coin once. Men would kill for them. Often did."

Mark looked at him, incredulously.

"It isn't *that* pretty," he said, squinting at the coin.

Snutworth closed his hand around it.

"But it is something to hold on to, Mark," he said softly. "You would be amazed how important that is."

"Snutworth!" The voice of Mr. Prendergast, the old visitor, called from the room above. "Has that servant arrived yet?"

"He wishes you to know that the cupboard is bare, sir," Snutworth called up with a wink.

Mark smiled his gratitude.

"Irrelevant, Snutworth. We want the boy for something else. Send him up."

"Of course, sir," Snutworth said.

Mark stepped backward, but Snutworth laid a reassuring hand on his arm.

"My master has approximately four hundred and thirty-two different tones of voice and that one was definitely not anger. I'd hazard a guess at curiosity, with just a hint of smugness." Snutworth pushed Mark to the base of the stairs. "That is most definitely one of his better moods. It looks like you are going up in the world."

Mark put one hand on the banister, feeling the cold iron beneath his hand. He turned back to Snutworth, who nodded encouragingly. Mark took a deep breath.

As he climbed the stairs, up toward the square of lamplight in the ceiling, where the trapdoor to the Observatory above lay open, his newfound confidence drained away. If he did even one thing wrong . . .

He had seen those no one would take, the damaged goods. They huddled together on the streets, watching for scraps to grab. They never bothered to ask anyone for aid, for they had nothing to give in return.

The lamplight grew brighter. Mark gripped the banister harder and climbed up.

In an instant, the gloom of the chamber below vanished in a burnished glow. Mark's eyes opened wider than ever as he caught his first glimpse of the telescope. Vast and complex, a monolith of shining brass, it dominated the center of the room, pushing its way out through the walls of glass. And beyond that, through the windows, the stars seemed to rush toward him, so many in the crisp night sky, all so clear through a thousand interlocking windows.

"The boy shows interest. That is promising."

The voice of Mr. Prendergast, warm and encouraging. The stars shone brighter.

"He would, I suppose, be an adequate replacement for the girl," said Mr. Laudate, the harshness of his earlier voice overlaid with an intrigued lilt. It was impossible for Mark to tear his eyes from that glorious sight.

"Mark, come here."

The Count's words worked their way into his consciousness. Suddenly all thoughts of stars and skies were banished from his mind. Now he was, once again, a shabby servant boy standing in the midst of three powerful men. He bowed his head. His feet, he noticed, were still bare and grimy. He shuffled forward.

"You wanted me, sir?" he ventured.

"Look here, Mark."

He raised his eyes.

The Count's clothes glinted with gold stitching. Like a warlock of legend, he wore a deep blue coat that glimmered with stars, but for him the stars were more potent than any spell. They were the symbol of Count Stelli. The old man held his gaze, the deep lines on his face made darker by the flickering candlelight. Mark couldn't begin to imagine how old the Count was, but despite the white hair and the dry skin he was sitting upright, utterly still, as though not even a bolt from the heavens would move him from that spot.

Beside the Count was a desk covered in papers and curious brass instruments. As he watched, the Count held out one of these papers.

"Read, boy," he said, in a voice of distant thunder.

Mark frowned, almost blurring the letters with his concentration.

"Pri . . . Principles of Astrology," he said, trying not to sound as if many of the words meant nothing to him, spelling them in his head first and dragging out their syllables as long as he dared. "The First House of Libra," he continued, growing in confidence, "can be found within the con . . . stellation . . ."

"Enough!" The Count thrust his hand toward him.

Mark flinched instinctively, but then saw that he held a quill pen, a few pieces of feather still attached to the far end.

"Copy this," the Count said, gesturing to a diagram.

Mark hesitated. It showed a strange, angular box drawn around a roughly circular set of dots. He reached forward to dip the pen in the ornate inkwell, just as he had seen Lily do, and put it to a sheet of parchment. The ink pooled out, blotting through, but, all too aware that the visitors had come forward to look over his shoulder, he persevered. The diagram was beginning to take shape when Mr. Laudate gave an impatient hiss, so loud it made Mark jump, tearing the parchment.

"With all due respect, Count Stelli," he said, glaring at Mark, "this was not part of our arrangement. I was prepared to agree to the girl, without once meeting her, purely because her letter to you suggested that she had some intelligence. But it will take months to train this boy to the appropriate standard."

"Months that we have in abundance, Laud," the Count said, a hint of the usual thunder in his tone. "So strange that the young, who have so much time, are always so keen to rush." He rose from his chair stiffly, one hand on an ornate cane. "Or would you rather do it yourself?"

Mark thought he caught a brief look of fear in Mr. Laudate's eyes and he wondered just what this "training" was for. Then a rap from the cane on the stone floor brought his attention back to the Count. The old man's eyes peered out from his face, surveying him up and down.

"I think it is time to draw up your contract properly, Mark," the Count said. "Your arrangement with my former servant simply to exchange places is not sufficient for a future apprentice."

"Does the boy have the talent?" Mr. Laudate asked, his voice trembling.

Mark thought he must be angry and turned to leave, but Mr. Prendergast stepped forward and patted Mark on the head. He smelled of perfumed oils.

"The boy can read, that is a good start. And the Count does not grow any younger. He has no family to carry on this noble business."

Mr. Laudate looked up sharply.

"I thought . . ."

"None," the Count agreed, with a look at the young man that dared contradiction.

Mr. Laudate returned the stare for a moment, then turned away. Pretending he hadn't noticed, Mark went back to his work, filling in the last of the dots.

"Sir?" he said, holding up the paper.

The Count took it, studied it intensely, and then held it up. Through the window behind him, Mark saw the night sky in all its blackness. Then he saw them. The five stars in a rough circle, scattered across the darkness — the stars he had been drawing, capturing something so vast on a scrap of parchment. The thought made him smile.

"It will do for now," the Count muttered. "We can continue when my guests have gone. Leave us now and sleep until the sun rises."

Mark stepped backward, away from the stern look of the Count and the jowly smile of Mr. Prendergast. He felt his step lighten as he reached the stairs. Snutworth, who had clearly been listening at their base, clasped his hand and shook it in congratulation, but Mark barely registered him.

He walked down to his room, his head filled with stars and visions, his thoughts a mass of twinkling lights. Somehow, the stars alone knew why, the Count had taken him as his apprentice. Already the letter he would write to Lily about it was forming in his head, though maybe he would keep secret the part about the role being meant for her. There was no need to spoil the wonderful news — that his days as a kitchen servant were over before they had barely begun. He was apprenticed to the greatest astrologer in all Agora and one day, if he fulfilled his duties and performed whatever project the Count and his guests were preparing him for, then maybe . . . just maybe . . .

It was later, just as he was falling asleep, that another image rose into his mind. It was only then that he remembered Mr. Laudate as he descended the steps. If he hadn't been so thrilled, so full of the future, he might have wondered why the redheaded man had looked at him strangely, with something almost like pity.

CHAPTER SIX

The Violinist

LILY OPENED HER EYES, and the night sky stretched above her. For a few peaceful seconds she lay still, staring at the stars spread out in all their splendor. Then, as usual, reality intruded on her thoughts. Her coat was covered in mud and her feet were still sore from running across cobblestones. She thought that perhaps she had slept for a little while because her hair lay across her face. And she was cold, so cold. Her breath misted in the air before her.

Shakily, she rose to her feet. She felt an instant stab of sadness, which caught her unaware, and tears filled her eyes. She closed them and took a couple of deep shuddering breaths.

"It's just a side effect . . . something to do with the machine," she whispered to herself, fighting the urge to howl with grief. Deliberately, painfully, she began forcing the emotion to fade, just as she had every other time she'd felt like this.

"There isn't time," she hissed, clenching her fists. There was never time. That was what made it so hard. But she hadn't cried since her first night at the bookbinder's, and she was not about to start now.

Gradually, as always, her feelings subsided. Lily gave one last brush to her coat, blinked hard, and looked around.

She had not chosen a bad part of the city to collapse in. She was far from the Sagittarius District, with its winding alleyways. Here, the ancient houses stood tall against the chill night sky. She had no idea how far she had run or what time it was. In fact, for once the stillness was what struck her. There was not a sound to disturb the night air. Lily breathed deeply. For a moment, a glint of happiness flared in her brain. But when it faded, it left behind something that felt more genuine, more natural. Hunger.

She cast her eyes around and spotted a piece of bread lying in the gutter. She reached down without a thought to pick it up and was about to put in her mouth when she stopped, feeling something shift in her hands. She held the bread up to her eyes. There were tiny worms living in it. She felt a cold chill even as she found herself still considering eating it. Maybe by the time Miss Devine's machine went into reverse her capacity for disgust had already gone. She shuddered at the idea and hurriedly threw the bread down, trying to think of something else.

She soon wished she had not. As she walked, her footsteps seemed to echo, disturbing the shadows. Things shifted and scuttled in the darkness. In every corner she thought she saw thieves lurking, thieves who would turn all the more dangerous when they found she had nothing to steal. She couldn't call for the receivers — she had broken a contract by running away. If they found her now, it was prison, at least. Her only hope was that the doctor would not report her missing before she got back to him. She began to run, but the shadows seemed to whisper to her: *Damaged goods . . . debtor . . . debtor . . .*

Then, at the edge of her hearing, something stirred. It was so faint that Lily barely knew if she was imagining it. It hung on the night air like a scent carried by the breeze. Music.

Intrigued, Lily followed it.

She had heard music before, of course. At the orphanage she had sung dull songs in praise of Agora along with everyone else, and once at the bookbinder's one of the men had brought in a guitar and some raucous voices had been raised, until she was sent off to another room because it "wasn't suitable." But this was different. It wasn't a voice, there were no words, and yet it sang, ebbing and flowing on the wind.

Eventually, Lily arrived at a run-down house on an old square. In the moonlight, she could just make out that there had once been designs on the flaking plaster that covered the façade of what had been a grand and beautiful house. Now bare beams were exposed and an ancient wooden door hung ajar. But it was from within that the haunting sound still came.

Lily hesitated. She was cold, dirty, and far away from her master. Her brain, working feverishly, told her to turn around, find out where she was, get back to the doctor, and seek his forgiveness before he gave her up for lost.

Her hand had other ideas. It pushed at the door.

Inside, the house seemed too bare. Spaces on the walls bore the ghostly outlines of paintings that had once hung there, and an old chair that should have been part of a set stood alone in a corner.

Lily moved forward, willing her feet not to dislodge anything, not even to press down on the floorboards, which might cry out at any moment.

Another room — a sitting room this time, to judge by the sofa with three dusty cushions — and there, at the far end, another door, wide open. Silently, Lily crept closer. The tune, which swelled and rose, was coming from within.

Lily peered through.

Beyond, in the moonlight, she saw a little courtyard, its walls covered in withered ivy dusted with frost. At the center, a muddy trickle of a fountain gurgled into a mossy basin. And sitting on the edge of that basin, wrapped in black shawls, a woman, her hands caressing some kind of instrument that she held up to her chin. Her hair seemed silvery, although much of that could have been the moon, and she stared into the distance, her dark eyes set on something only she could see.

Lily stood mesmerized as the music filled the courtyard, a simple tune, its only accompaniment the rustling of leaves. Dimly, she remembered an illustration she had once seen in a book. This was called a violin.

Lily felt something bubble up inside her. This was nothing like what had happened before, when the emotions had been forcibly dragged out of her. This feeling of melancholy grew from within, stealing up on her as she listened. All other sensations were blotted out.

She felt a hand on her wrist.

She nearly cried out, but something in her stopped it — perhaps because it would have interrupted the music. Instead, she stiffened, turning as slowly and silently as she could.

Her eyes met another pair, at about her height. She took in a pale, curious face, blue eyes, and short, red hair. She opened her mouth, but the figure raised a white finger to her lips, shaking her head. Lily understood. As quietly as they could, both of them stepped backward across the room, out of the sitting room and into the hall. The figure, Lily could now see, was a girl her own age in a shabby white nightgown. She closed the door and the music was now muffled, though it could still just be heard. She then turned to face Lily and, to Lily's amazement, her face broke into a smile.

"What do you think of Signora Sozinho's playing?" she whispered.

"Amazing," Lily replied truthfully.

This seemed to please the girl.

"You're privileged, you know that?" Her voice was hushed but breathless. "She never gives concerts anymore. Around here they only know her as the violin maker . . . She hates anyone to hear her. Lucky for you I left the door open or . . ." The girl stopped, her head on one side. "You're not a thief, are you?"

"No."

"Good. I have a bell to ring and a whistle to blow if you are, but there's not much to steal here anyway. We don't even have any of the Signora's violins at the moment; she's just sold the last . . ." The girl seemed to have another idea. "But maybe . . . are you one of her fans, from the old days?" She looked her up and down. "You don't look old enough to remember, but I've been wrong before. She might sign something if you come in the morning . . . I . . ." The girl stopped, shaking her head wistfully. "Sorry . . . I don't get the chance to talk very often. There're no other servants here. You a runaway?"

It took a moment before Lily realized that a question had been asked. She began to nod, then changed her mind.

"If I can find my way back to the Sagittarius District, then I won't be much longer," she said.

The other girl frowned.

"I should turn you in, you know," she whispered cautiously. "You did break in. And you got a concert for free. There's some in the high houses of the Leo District who would trade everything they owned to hear the Signora play." The girl studied her again. "Would you fight me if I tried to run for help?"

Nervously, Lily considered. The girl did not look unfriendly, but she was the one with the power. After a moment's thought, Lily nodded.

"I'd have to," she said. "It would be my only chance."

The girl considered this for a while and then nodded.

"The Signora would never forgive me for that. She hates to be interrupted." Then the girl gave Lily a broad grin and said brightly, "So I'll just have to show you the way back. We'll go via the Central Plaza."

Lily waited while the girl got dressed in a dark heavy dress that looked rather too old and large for her. She could hardly believe it. *It must be a trap of some kind*, she thought. *The girl must be planning to take me to the receivers*. More than once she considered bolting there and then, trying to find her own way back. But then the girl opened the door and smiled, and Lily saw it, that same look that Dr. Theophilus had at his best moments, one of warmth and trust. Marveling at her luck, not quite believing that anyone, let alone another servant, would help her for nothing, Lily quietly slipped out of the front door. The girl followed her, closed the door, and laughed.

"Good thing you chose the one night this week it isn't raining," she said as they began to walk. "I don't share the Signora's love of all types of weather. I truly believe she doesn't feel the cold. If it had been wet I'd have remembered to lock up the house, and you'd be drowning in the streets. It becomes like the river down here in the depths of the Virgo District. I'm from Taurus myself. We're so much drier over there, but it's bad news in the summer. My name's Ben, by the way, short for Benedicta. What's yours?"

"Hmm . . ." Lily found herself distracted. Something about that music had lingered in her mind. "Er . . . Lily, short for . . . well . . ." That was odd. For just a moment, she felt sure she had been going to say something. But as far as she knew Lily was the full length of her name. "Short for nothing. Just Lily." Seeing that Benedicta was about to launch into another speech, she got in first. "That music . . ."

"Wonderful, isn't it?" Benedicta enthused, stepping lightly

through the uneven streets. "You wouldn't think that she's never played it before an audience. Why keep something like that to yourself?"

Lily frowned.

"I thought you said she had fans . . ."

"Of course," Benedicta said, "she was a singer once. The best in the city. She and Signor Sozinho were heard all over Agora. Before we were born, everyone would have known about them." Benedicta sighed. "If it was anything like the violin . . . They said she could make even the debtors smile."

"What happened?" Lily asked softly.

Benedicta winced, as if unsure whether to answer that question. For a few minutes they walked in silence until, with sadness, Benedicta went on.

"An admirer happened. One who got too friendly with the Signora . . . until Signor Sozinho found out. The divorce . . . it took everything. The Signora so wanted to keep the old house that she had been brought up in and he let her. But he took everything else. The money, the paintings . . . and her voice." Benedicta touched her throat. "He took that too . . . She'll never sing for anyone else again."

The morning before, Lily would have been shocked by that. Now, thinking back on her day, she could easily believe it. It was far easier to accept that than to believe that this redheaded stranger, who spoke to her as if they had known each other for years, was real and not some guardian angel.

"She earns a living by making violins," Benedicta continued. "Not enough to support that old house. She should have an army of servants working in it, but she can only afford me. I have a knack for languages, even sign language." She paused.

They had reached the ornate arch that marked the edge of the district, this one bearing the symbol of a young woman draping herself over clouds. Ahead lay the bridge to the Central Plaza, which was eerily quiet at this time of night.

"But even I don't know what she means when she plays that violin. That language doesn't use words." Benedicta bowed her head. "I used to love to hear her play, when I first came, but after I learned her story . . . I still listen, but it hurts. I can't imagine what it's like for her . . ."

For a moment, Benedicta closed her eyes, her easy cheerfulness gone. Then, shaking off her gloom, she brightened and turned back to Lily with a smile. "Sorry. My brother says that I talk too much. You can make your own way from here, can't you? The Signora doesn't like me to go out after dark." Then she grinned. "But she doesn't mind visitors during the day, though, if you like."

"Yes," Lily said, smiling, "I know the way." She hesitated, wanting to hug this strange creature, partly out of gratitude, partly to check that she was real. "Thank you," she said instead. "Thank you, Benedicta."

"No trouble. Good night, Lily," Benedicta said, looking up to the east. "It'll be good morning soon."

Lily nodded, but before she could say anything else Ben had smiled, turned, and vanished back into the ancient streets.

Lily found her way back to Miss Devine's shop in a trance. Deep in thought, she barely noticed the figures huddled in doorways or heard their racking coughs until she saw the glittering walls of the glassmaker's once again. Outside the shop, the doctor had waited, tall and imposing in his black coat in the darkness. Lily looked up at him.

"Sir . . . I . . ."

"It doesn't matter. I've offered Miss Devine a cut of any profits we make in exchange for damaging her machine, in addition to the rent. I also got this."

He put his hand in hers and gave it a comforting squeeze. When he took his hand away again, a vial of black liquid lay in her palm. On the side, etched in rough strokes, the word *Disgust* looked back at her.

"You can conquer it without selling yourself, Lily," the doctor said softly. "If you take it back into you before a day has passed it will be as if you never sold it, otherwise it will be gone forever." He turned his face away. "I am sorry for my anger. You didn't know."

Lily opened her mouth to speak, to tell him it was all right, but stopped when she realized he hadn't finished. He looked out into the dark night and continued.

"In the end, after my father died, my mother tried everything to keep up our rent. Everything except going back to her father, the Count. She started selling off her emotions, just little ones she could do without. Then one day she sent me off to Grandfather's, with no word of explanation, along with enough jewelry to put me through medical training at the University. I wondered for a long time what she could have sold that was precious enough to pay for all that."

The doctor turned away and fitted a new key into the little door in the wall.

"Her love for me was particularly fine, apparently."

He opened the door and went through. Lily followed, the little bottle of her own emotion pulsing faintly in her hand.

Inside, it was so dark that Lily could barely see anything at all. But there was a new smell, an odd one, like dust and fruits. Silently, the doctor reached up to light an old brass lamp.

As the amber glow rose, carved wooden pews became visible. Two statues looked down with benevolent gaze at the far end of the room, and high on the walls, almost invisible with the night sky behind them, strange windows covered in black lines appeared.

"This was called a temple in its day," the doctor whispered. "At one time, they were fashionable. My father was the priest here. My mother came for an hour each week, just to sit and think about something other than what she owned. Then it was twice a week, then every day. Eventually, she did something my grandfather called "foolish." He bowed his head. "She married a man who valued things you couldn't touch, and hold, and have. It was her ruin, but she didn't regret it for a day." He sighed. "Poor woman."

As Lily looked, her eyes opening wider and wider, the sun began to rise and the dawn light streamed down through the windows of colored glass.

"It was always meant to be a place of healing." Dr. Theophilus looked up, his wistful brown eyes sparkling in the multicolored light. "Now it can be. Welcome to our new practice, Lily."

"Our practice," Lily repeated, under her breath. Yes, she liked the sound of *our*. No one had ever said that to her before.

And the sunlight felt so warm.

INTERLUDE ONE

THIS ROOM groans under the weight of history.

Its ceiling is tall, but lost in shadows. Somewhere up in the rafters there are lamps, but their light barely illuminates the vast gilt-edged portraits that line the wall, frowning down on the polished floor as if it had gleamed brighter in their day. But this room has never been light, not since the Directory of Receipts was built.

It is quiet. Even the sharp tap of a pair of high-heeled shoes, crossing its marble floor with steady step, vanishes up into the ceiling, to fade away to nothing.

The shoes reach a desk of mahogany. There is a falter in the step. Nothing that anyone would notice—no one except the figure behind the desk, whose quill stops moving.

"Something troubling you, Miss Rita?"

A dry voice, a patient voice, but a voice that causes the woman before his desk to breathe in sharply. He notices that too.

"No, Director. Except . . ."

A pause, the echoes of the woman's last words linger. Her foot taps nervously. The Director, his face hidden behind the light of a thick candle, puts down his quill.

"Your project. How does it progress?"

"Nearly a year has passed since the girl's title day, sir. But . . ."

"Go on."

The shoes take a step backward. The temperature in the room seems to drop.

"Are you sure that these two need our attention, Director?"

"Patience, Miss Rita," the Director says, his quill once again scratching on the parchment. "All debts will come in, given time."

The shoes shuffle and Miss Rita raises her head.

"But are they who we think they are?"

The room holds its breath.

"It is impossible to be certain. They are young, but soon they will show their natures. Then all we need to do is watch."

"Of course, sir."

The Director's secretary turns and walks away. And the Director of Receipts, surrounded by the cavernous space of his ornate, empty office, turns back to the papers on his desk.

CHAPTER SEVEN

The Dumbwaiter

Virgo 18
Dear Lily

*Sorry it's been so long since I last wrote. It's been so busy
here at the tower and the Count keeps me working all night
long. I've been copying out his patterns, transcribing (bet
you don't know what that word means!) old texts — I don't
have time to sleep or to eat or . . .*

The ink ran out. Hurriedly, Mark jabbed his quill into the inkpot
with a clink, flicking droplets over the page. He sighed, looking at
his fingers, which were nowadays permanently stained blue-black
from his constant work. Months of learning, and the ink still
found its way to everywhere except where he wanted it. He began a
new line.

*I think my writing's gotten better. Of course, I spend
most of my time drawing diagrams, but the Count's always
teaching me new words.*

Not always. Not anymore. Those first spring months had been
fabulous — for all of his thundering, the Count had taught him well.
Now Mark could recognize a planetary conjunction in an instant,
and at night he dreamed of the zodiac, which turned into fabulous
beasts and figures before his eyes. The Count had even organized
for their meals to be brought in from a local restaurant so that
Mark never needed to brave the kitchen again, much to his relief.

But as the weather grew warmer and summer progressed, the
Count retreated into his personal winter, demanding that Mark
remember more and more, stuffing him with arcane facts until his
hands ached from copying and his eyes streamed in the dim light.

*Prognostication. That's a good one. It means telling the
future. That's what I'm going to do at last! I've been
counting off the days to Agora Day . . .*

Mark paused, laying down the quill. He'd been thinking about
what would happen on Agora Day ever since he had started his
apprenticeship, of course, but writing it down made it sound so
immediate — so real.

*I've been practicing, writing down the signs I saw. Last
night there was a shooting star in Libra. That means
something important and sudden next month, maybe even
the first day.*

The first day of the month of Libra and of a new year. Agora Day.
The day of the Grand Festival. The most important day of the year.

The day he was set to make his first public prophecy and be formally accepted into the Astrologers' Guild.

> *I hope it means success. It was in conjunction with*
> *Jupiter. I think that's a good sign. The Count said he'd guide*
> *me, but all astrologers make a prediction on Agora Day. It's*
> *part of the celebration. Everyone expects it. So much for you*
> *saying that I'd never do anything with all this stuff! Which*
> *one of us will be up on the podium for everyone to see?*

Mark stopped to think, hoping that Lily would take that last line as he intended—as a joke. It had been so much better when she had been able to visit, even if it was only once or twice a month. It could get lonely in the tower, particularly as the Count never allowed him to leave. But Mark had only dared to invite Lily to visit when he had been given a day off and he was sure his master would not see her. The Count even frowned on Mark writing to her, knowing that she was still the doctor's apprentice.

Not that Mark would have had the time to see her now. As Agora Day approached, the Count worked him harder than ever.

He held the pen up to the candle flame, the only light in this windowless room. He'd tried so hard, but everything seemed to have so many different interpretations, so many possible futures. He had wanted to tell the Count that he wasn't ready, but his master's glare froze the words on his lips. The Count made no secret of the fact that Mark had only one chance to be accepted by the rest of the guild, or it was back to the kitchens for the rest of his life.

"The time is near, Mark," the Count had told him one morning, after a long night of stargazing. "Soon you will be ready. On Agora Day you will make your predictions and my rivals will be silenced."

"Your rivals, sir?" Mark had ventured.

73

The Count had looked at him then, his sunken eyes gleaming in the morning light.

"There are some who doubt the worth of astrology, Mark, some who see it as little more than trickery, and not the highest science of the gifted mind. They seek to undermine us, to destroy a family name as old as Agora itself. But you will prove them wrong, Mark." The Count had come toward him, grasped him by the shoulders, and spoken in a whisper: "You will prove the true nature of the stars."

And Mark had felt very proud at that moment. Whatever the Count needed him to prove, he would do his best. This great man had put his faith in him. He was worth something in the Count's eyes. Mark would not disappoint him.

He dipped his quill in the inkwell again.

> *The Count has visitors again today, the same ones I told you about before. Mr. Prendergast, the lawyer, is all right, I suppose, but he always talks to me as if I was a little kid, and he smells of rotting flowers. Snutworth told me he agreed to be paid in this awful perfume once, and no one would trade it for anything, so he wears it all the time now, out of spite. Snutworth's got hundreds of stories like that. If it wasn't for him I'd never have anything but work to think about. You've got to meet him, Lily. He's like you — he notices things.*

Mark cast his eyes up to the ceiling, suddenly feeling lonely here in the anteroom beneath the Observatory, waiting until the Count needed him. He wished he had Snutworth to talk to now, but Mr. Prendergast had sent him off to fetch news of the festival preparations. Only two weeks to go.

> *And then there's Mr. Laudate. Mr. Prendergast calls him Laud for short. I don't think he likes me at all. Won't even*

look at me when he visits. Then again, Snutworth says he
doesn't much like anyone. Comes of spending his whole life
praising people for a living. Mr. Laudate seems pretty
important to them, but I don't think he's much older than
us, maybe a few years.

Mark stopped again. He was nearly at the end of the sheet. His quill hovered above the page. Should he ask about Dr. Theophilus? Lily might like it, but the one time he had asked about him the Count had found the letter and thrown it into the fire before he could send it. The doctor's rooms had been locked up, and his picture had been taken down. Mark was fairly sure that he was wearing some of Dr. Theophilus's old clothes, since they were better than anything else he'd ever had but were made for someone taller and thinner than him. However, he didn't dare ask. The Count grew mellower with familiarity, but the old temper could still rise in a second.

I hope everything's fine with you. And thank . . .

From above, he could hear fragments of the conversation drifting down through the floor. He wasn't sure, but it sounded as though the Count had raised his voice, while a younger voice, Mr. Laudate's, grew louder to meet it. This was not the time to try the Count's patience.

Thank your master for the medicine he sent. It helped
me to sleep, and it keeps my father out of my dreams.

A pity it had not helped him to forget. After a few nights of heavy, dull sleep, the nightmares only came back stronger than ever, the ring on his father's finger gleaming like a star as he signed his son's life away to a stranger. He never saw his father's face any-more; even in dreams he couldn't bear to look at it.

The sound of the trapdoor opening brought Mark out of his reverie. He looked up hastily at a clatter of footsteps on the wrought-iron stairs, as Mr. Laudate hurried into the room. His face was flushed, his eyes sparking with something that looked like fury. From above him, the voice of the Count rumbled.

"You're a fool, Laud! Why did you take on the business if you don't have the stomach for it?"

The voice seemed more mocking than angry, but Mr. Laudate spun around to shout back up to the Observatory.

"A question I ask myself every day, Stelli. Perhaps out of a youth-ful desire to believe that you had some good intentions behind it all. I shall be careful not to make that mistake again. Mark! Where is my coat?"

Startled to realize he was being addressed, Mark jumped up to retrieve Mr. Laudate's hat and coat from pegs nearby at the side of the room. He held them out, but Mr. Laudate did not take them. He just stared at Mark, the same strange, intense look that he had given him the first time they had met. Just as he seemed about to speak, another voice floated down from the top of the steps.

"I must say, Laud, I fear you are turning down an excellent opportunity."

Mr. Prendergast descended the steps, leaning heavily on his cane, its silver handle glinting in the candlelight. Instantly, Mr. Laudate's expression hardened. He turned and gave a stiff bow.

"Nevertheless, Mr. Prendergast, I feel that the time for my involvement has ended. I have already publicized your event and ensured that everyone is prepared. That is the sum of my personal expertise."

"That's true." Mr. Prendergast eased himself forward, placing a flabby hand on Mr. Laudate's shoulder. "But it hardly seems fair that you should not reap the rewards of your effort."

Deliberately, the younger man shrugged off the older one's hand, his gaze never wavering from Mr. Prendergast's eyes.

"My mind is made up. I wish to have nothing more to do with this. I have other business to attend to."

For a second, Mr. Prendergast's smile faltered, then it returned, twice as broad as ever.

"And I wish you the greatest of success."

"You are too kind, sir," Mr. Laudate said icily, taking his coat from Mark's arms and wrapping it around his shoulders. As he did so, he peered down at Mark's desk.

"If you intend to write letters, boy, then try to get a basic grasp of spelling and grammar," he said, his tone as sarcastic as ever.

Mark opened his mouth to protest, but Mr. Laudate silenced him with a fierce look. Almost casually, he reached over and picked up the quill and a piece of fresh paper. "Let me show you."

"Ever the perfectionist, Laud," said Mr. Prendergast from the bottom of the iron staircase. "A virtue that is difficult to maintain. Old men such as myself have learned the value of compromise."

"Perfection is a noble goal, sir. Even if not achieved," Mr. Laudate replied.

Irritated, Mark glanced down to see what the young man was writing.

Get out of here.

He looked up, surprised, but Mr. Laudate avoided his gaze, instead addressing himself to Mr. Prendergast, even as he continued to write.

"I have always prided myself on knowing when I am no longer required."

You are in danger. They are deceiving you.

"Indeed." Mr. Prendergast polished the handle of his cane with a handkerchief. "And, I believe, we can count on your discretion. So important in a man whose livelihood depends on the goodwill of the powerful."

You'll be damaged goods forever if you follow them.
Break your contract if you have to. Stelli has enemies,
a powerful society. They might take you in. They have the
power to cancel debts. Even if they don't, it's better than
staying here.

Mark stared, dumbfounded, as Mr. Laudate continued, not a waver in his voice betraying what he was writing.

"I trust I understand thoroughly what is important, Mr. Prendergast."

I never thought they would take it this far.

"Sensible man." Mr. Prendergast began to come toward them. "Is the boy really so incompetent? I believed his writing had come on immensely."

Mark didn't dare to look up, suddenly terrified that he would see what had been written. Clearly Mr. Laudate recognized the danger too. Faster, he scribbled his final words:

I'm sorry.

Then, as if nothing had happened, he straightened up, sweeping his hat onto his head. As he did so, he knocked over the inkwell with a flick of his wrist. Mark snatched up his letter to Lily, but in a second Laudate's note was soaked, its message blotted out. Straightening up, he made an impatient sniff.

"The boy only succeeds in making a mess, Prendergast. Would you walk with me to the front door? I have a few final matters of business to discuss."

For a moment, Mr. Prendergast's eyes flicked between Mr. Laudate and Mark, something hard glinting in them. Then he nodded and opened the bronze door to the stairs. Mr. Laudate followed him, but as he turned to close the door, his eyes met Mark's once again with another look of sudden intensity. Mark gave a quick nod, to show that he understood, and then the door was closed and they were gone.

Mark sat down heavily, staring at the piece of ink-soaked paper that lay on his writing desk. It was ridiculous. Why would his master try to trick him? Why bother, when he was bound to follow his every command? And what was this deception anyway? The Count taught him out of books that every astrologer had to study. Was every apprentice being deceived? Mark looked upward, trying to hear his master moving in the room above.

But why would Mr. Laudate lie?

The door hinges creaked. Mark brought his gaze back down, ready to defend himself against Mr. Prendergast's enquiries. Instead, the welcome sight of Snutworth appeared before him, a sheaf of papers clamped to his chest and one eyebrow raised quizzically.

"Has there been another argument?" he asked carefully. "Something seems to have ruffled my master. And was that Mr. Laudate I saw being shown the door?"

Mark nodded distractedly.

"I don't know," he said. "Mr. Laudate thought . . . I mean . . . he knows . . ."

Mark's mouth dried as he looked at Snutworth standing in the doorway. He wished he could ask Lily what to do; she was always so sensible. But she was far away and there was no one else. He needed someone to trust, and Snutworth had never shown much loyalty to his master.

"I think . . . something is going on," he whispered in a rush. "Something involving me, and the Count, and your master, and a plot . . . I don't know what . . . Mr. Laudate wouldn't say."

Snutworth pursed his lips, frowning, his eyes flicking around the room. For one horrible moment, Mark thought he was going to go and tell his master his suspicions. Then he took a step back and fixed his eyes on something just outside the room, something Mark could not see.

"There may be a way of finding out."

Snutworth raised one long finger to his lips and motioned for Mark to sit quietly. Mark did so, stuffing his letter to Lily into the pocket of his breeches. He was about to ask what Snutworth was planning, but when he heard the heavy tread of Mr. Prendergast on the stairs he busied himself with clearing away his quill and ink. He kept his head down as the lawyer entered, wheezing from the climb, and muttered for Snutworth to return to the Observatory. Snutworth followed his master up the wrought-iron staircase.

Mark could hear his heart pounding in his ears. From the room beneath he couldn't pick out words — no matter how hard he tried, he could only hear the tone of voice — but the Count sounded angry. A moment later, Snutworth descended the stairs, shutting the trapdoor behind him, blocking out the voices above. He no longer held the paperwork, but he was smiling in triumph. Mark jumped up.

"What did you shut it for?" he hissed. "We've got no chance of finding out what they're talking about now!"

In reply, Snutworth glided silently over to the open bronze door and beckoned. Curious, Mark followed him out. Snutworth shut the door behind them.

"Tell me, Mark," he said softly, "do you know what that is?"

He pointed to the closed wooden hatch set into the wall beside the bronze door.

"Of course," Mark whispered, confused. "That's where I put the Count's food if he doesn't want to be disturbed at mealtimes. Lily used to use it all the time. There's a platform in there that winches up food to the Observatory . . ."

"I believe the technical term is a 'dumbwaiter,'" Snutworth said thoughtfully. "A useful device for an old man who doesn't want to carry trays of food upstairs. Of course, they have their disadvantages. They can cause terrible drafts." Snutworth placed his hands on the hatchway. "You see, there needs to be an open shaft in the wall between the room below and the one above. And if someone were to accidentally open the hatch in the upper room while his master was distracted with papers . . ."

Deftly, Snutworth slid open the dumbwaiter with a barely audible click. Understanding dawning, Mark eagerly pushed his head through the hole, leaning on the tray at the base, craning up to see the light spilling through from the Observatory hatch. Initially he could hear only muffled noises, but then, as his ears adjusted, the words became clear.

". . . I don't think Laud will spread the word, Stelli," Mr. Prendergast was saying. "He knows that Ruthven's allies will not employ him now that he is known to have worked for us, and he has a business to maintain. Without the support of our friends, he and his family would be starving in a matter of weeks."

"A family? At his age?" the Count rumbled.

"Sisters, Stelli, not children," Mr. Prendergast replied, with a smirk in his voice. "You really should take my advice and learn about your employees; it can be most beneficial. Laud may be reckless enough to break a contract of silence on his own account, but he knows full well that he would drag his sisters onto the streets with him. A man like that is dependable, to a point."

"You should never have convinced me to hire him," the Count snarled. "There must be many others who would take their payment without a murmur."

"Laud is the best, Stelli. He will have made sure that everyone who matters knows about Mark's debut performance. Particularly those who would like to see our 'learned friend' Lord Ruthven taken down a peg or two. It is already the talk of the elite circles that Ruthven has privately declared that this boy of yours will make the most accurate predictions of the entire festival."

Mark felt a strange glow of pride for a moment, until the Count gave a harsh laugh.

"Yes, let Ruthven try to wriggle out of that one. Let him rue the day he issued that challenge to me in the newspapers." Mark heard a rustling noise, as though the Count were waving a piece of paper. "Listen to this! 'We ask ourselves why members of the Astrologers' Guild are held in such high regard, when any sensible Agoran can see that their starry pronouncements concern only versions of the future that benefit them, and them alone. They claim to know the truth, but wrap their prophecies in such a fog of mystery that they could mean anything. I believe that anyone, if schooled in the right words, would have just as much chance of unveiling the truth. A common child may prove to be as profound a seer as the venerable Count Stelli himself!' "

Another sound, this time of a newspaper fluttering to the ground.

"So be it," Stelli growled. "Let him stand by his words. Let him have his common child. A child trained by the very best." He pounded his fist on the arm of his chair. "Let him watch this child stumbling his way through the mysteries of the ancients and hear the scornful laughter as each prophecy proves empty and worthless beside our own." His voice sank lower, became more conspiratorial. "You are certain that everyone believes the boy to have been chosen by Ruthven?"

"I told you," Mr. Prendergast replied with calm assurance, "Laud is the best. He knows how to set the whisperers going. I cannot speak for the common man, but for everyone who matters . . . it is a certainty. The more extravagant the plot, the more certain the elite are that there must be some truth in it. As far as they are concerned, Ruthven has staked his argument — more than that, his reputation — on Mark, 'the common child,' outdoing your most venerable astrologers in his visions of the future. Worse, he has attempted to skew the results by sending the most talented child he could find to train with you, without your knowledge, perhaps even offering him guidance behind your back. Even if Ruthven were stupid enough to deny it, it would only make the rumors stronger. All you have to do, Stelli, is to ensure Mark's predictions are suitably preposterous, and Lord Ruthven will be disgraced, humiliated. And if a man who judges others for his living is found lacking in judgment . . . well, the city is not forgiving. His opponents have been waiting for a reason to bring him down for years. And our dear Mark will give them all the pretext they require."

At this point Mr. Prendergast laughed — a high, unpleasant sound that pierced Mark's ears, driving home the terrible realization of just how much he had been deceived.

"And with it, of course, Ruthven's Libran Society will lose considerable influence while they try to find a new leader," Mr. Prendergast continued. "Unpopular he may be, but my spies tell me that it is only he that holds them together. Although I do wish you would explain to me why it is so important to damage the Librans. I know you have never been happy with their power, but surely you must have the Director's ear? You and he were friends once, were you not?"

"A lifetime ago, Prendergast," Stelli grunted. "Perhaps, after the festival, I will tell you about the dreadful crimes of the Libran Society. But for now, suffice to say we must not fail." A note of grim mirth entered his voice. "Although I can't deny it—the chance to see Ruthven fall after his attempt to ridicule me adds extra sweetness to the affair. You are certain that the boy will not prove problematic?"

Mr. Prendergast snorted.

"I don't think we will have much trouble with the boy revealing anything. After the festival he will be the worst kind of damaged goods—a laughing stock for the whole city. No employer will be willing to give him a second glance. He would not be worth the investment, or the risk that he would fail again. It will be irritating for you to have to train a new apprentice, of course, but . . ."

"I shall be training *no* new apprentices."

There was a surprised pause.

"But, surely . . . after your great success?" Prendergast ventured.

The Count sniffed.

"I am an old man, Prendergast; I have watched more than eighty summers roll past. In all that time, I have had only two ambitions: to become the greatest astrologer in all Agora . . ."

"Which you have undoubtedly achieved—you are respected and loved by all of your brother astrologers—" Prendergast began, but the Count interrupted him with a grunt.

"Do not flatter me. They fear me, no doubt, but there is little love. My 'brothers' who would abandon me in an instant were I to lose face. I am no more immune to that than Ruthven." The Count sighed heavily. "My other ambition has been to see Ruthven fall, to punish him and his Libran cohorts for their dark and secret crimes. On Agora Day, I shall either achieve that or I shall fall. I have no time left to start anything new."

Mark heard a creak, as though Prendergast had leaned forward in his chair.

"Come now, Stelli," he said soothingly. "Let's hear no talk of falling. We hold all of the cards. Thanks to our brilliance, Ruthven does not even have any influence over the boy he is supposedly supporting . . ."

"Please, let us speak no more of *him*." The Count said wearily. "It has taken a great deal of patience to make the boy sound even slightly competent. There must be the appearance that I trained Mark to the best of my ability, but that even I cannot work miracles on a boy without a scrap of natural talent." There was a sound of shuffling papers. "But that is the sacrifice I have made for this venture, and I shall not have to endure his presence for much longer. I shall continue to tell him that he makes progress, however much it sticks in my throat." He coughed, suddenly businesslike. "Now, these preparations for the astrologers' platform in the Central Plaza . . ."

Mark could not listen anymore. Shaking, he pulled his head back. He barely noticed Snutworth sliding closed the hatch of the dumbwaiter. He felt numb, as if the whole world was very far away. It was Snutworth who broke the silence.

"Something of a setback, Mark."

"Can . . . can they do this?" Mark said at last, finding his voice.

Snutworth shrugged. "It isn't illegal. My master is a competent lawyer, so he will have seen to that."

Mark tried to speak, but couldn't. Instead, he opened the bronze door, silently walked over to his writing desk and began stuffing his few pens and hand-copied papers into his shirt.

"What are you doing?" Snutworth asked, a thoughtful look on his face.

"Getting out, just like Mr. Laudate said," Mark replied, refusing to turn around. "If you keep quiet about me, I can be halfway across the city before they realize I'm gone. These papers are mine. Maybe I can trade them for food until I can find a new job and make enough to trade back to the Count for breaking my contract . . ."

"And your clothes?" Snutworth said. "They are merely loaned to you by the Count. Take one step out of that door and you're a thief and a debtor. No one will take you in. There will be nowhere to go."

"What choice do I have?" Mark turned fiercely, fighting to keep his voice quiet enough not to be heard by those above. "You think I'll have any chance of finding another job after the festival? You think anyone will want me when it's known that I'm worthless?" Mark felt sick as he forced the words out: "That I'm damaged goods?"

He stopped then, his head swimming. He was shivering as if he could already feel the cold of spending his next winter on the streets, the last he would feel. Maybe, if he was lucky, disease would find him before he starved.

Snutworth seized his arms, shaking him once.

"Stop this!" His voice was low and urgent. "You've been given a chance, Mark. Don't squander it."

"What do you care?" Mark hissed back, pulling free of Snutworth's grasp. "This will be good for your master. You'll be going up in the world."

"True," Snutworth replied. "And the fact that you recognize it tells me something about you, Mark. You have such great—" Snutworth seemed lost for the right word momentarily and then, with a smile, he found it—"potential. You have a quick mind, Mark, and a willingness to adapt to changing circumstances. You can turn this to your advantage."

Mark sat heavily on the edge of his desk.

"It doesn't take an astrologer to see where I'm going, Snutworth. There's no way out. No amount of good fortune can save me."

Snutworth leaned in close, his eyes glinting in the flickering candlelight.

"True," he said, "fate has turned against you." He paused, a glimmer of a smile on his thin face. "But fortune can be given a little . . . push. Will you trust me, Mark?"

Mark looked up at the manservant then, his pale face inscrutable, but his hand extended in friendship. He breathed out, a long sigh. It wasn't as if he had much choice.

"What's the plan?" he said.

CHAPTER EIGHT

The Past

LILY LOOKED ONCE again at the tattered piece of paper in her hand. This was definitely the right place. A squat, solid building of gray stone on a dull, functional street. Even the crowds in the Aries District seemed less energized than in the rest of the city. This was certainly not somewhere to try and hawk your wares. Everyone here knew their place — usually, it seemed, working for the vast paper factory that loomed over the district. But this building was different, and not just because it was a little larger and a little cleaner than those around it. This was where she had spent the first six years of her life.

Receiving Mark's latest letter had made up her mind. It had been brief, and the ending seemed sudden, as if it had been finished in a hurry, but one line had stood out for her: *It keeps my father out of my dreams.* This had made her think. As she spent her days measuring out the remedies or cleaning the doctor's scalpels, the thought had grown in her head, nagging at her, demanding attention: *At least Mark had a father to dream about.* She hated herself for thinking like this. It wasn't as if Mark much wanted to remember the man who had sold him in exchange for medicine to save himself, but even if he felt nothing other than hurt, that was something.

In the end, she decided she had to find the orphanage. This wouldn't be hard because her records were held at the Directory. It would only take one letter to find out which of the city's orphanages had been her first home. Even so, it needed all her resolve to send it. It had sat on a table in the former temple for days, unmailed, until Benedicta, paying one of her visits, had picked it up.

"Do you want me to mail this for you?" she had asked.

Lily had taken it back, confused, telling her in a mumble what it was about. Benedicta had gone quiet for a moment, before saying gently, "You should mail it, Lily. Who knows? Your family might be looking for you . . . I don't know what I'd do without my brother and sister."

"It's . . . difficult, Ben," Lily had replied. They had been friends for months now, yet Lily still found it hard to talk about her past. "They could be anyone. Right now, I can imagine what I want . . . invent a new family every day . . . But if I really found out . . ."

"They might not want you?" Ben had suggested.

"Yes . . . How did you . . ."

"The Signora wrote a letter," Ben had said, sadly. "She wrote to her husband, to ask his forgiveness." Ben had taken Lily's hand. "She wrote it ten years ago. I have to dust around it. It's been waiting on a table in the hall all of that time. I think she still believes that she'll send it one day."

Lily had mailed the letter within the hour. And had a response by the next evening.

Lily fingered the little glass vial she wore on a chain around her neck, the word *Disgust* still visible on its surface, although it was long since empty. It reminded her that the fear she was feeling was perfectly natural. Her memories of this place were not good, and even though she had been so young when she last saw it, no more than six summers, the oppressive atmosphere of the place flooded over her as if it had been yesterday. But she would not be sent away, not this time. If any sign of her past, of her unknown parents, could be found in Agora, it would be found here and she had to know.

She reached up, lifted the door knocker, and brought it down three times. The sound echoed within. After a while, she heard shuffling footsteps and iron bolts being drawn back. The door eased open to reveal a thin-faced boy who could have seen barely seven summers peering from behind. He stared at her expectantly. Lily took a deep breath.

"Miss Lily, to see Matron Angelina," she said.

The boy nodded, unspeaking, and pulled the door open a little further. Steeling herself, Lily stepped through, and the boy closed the door, shutting out the daylight.

She recognized the smell first, that musty odor of damp. Then the corridors began to feel familiar. She remembered them as larger than they seemed now.

In the distance she could hear the chanting. She remembered that too: the matron's idea of lessons — filling their heads endlessly with "The Glory of Agora" without once showing it to them.

The boy led her past an open doorway lit by guttering torches. Through it, Lily could see a dormitory. It was even sparser than she remembered, little more than shelves, with a few mats and blankets. On one of the shelves, a girl lay coughing. She couldn't have been more than five. Lily looked away. She had always thought that it was only the ill who disappeared in the night. Until it had happened to her and she had woken up sold, in a building she had never seen before. One of the most important nights of her life, the night she had finally left the misery of the orphanage, and she had slept right through it, without a glimpse of the city she had longed to see.

Lost in her thoughts, Lily took a moment to notice that the boy had stopped. He knocked on a large wooden door and, before Lily could thank him, he had scurried away down the corridor.

"Come in, do!" a voice called from behind the door.

Lily paused. The voice sounded far lighter and younger than she remembered. It had been years, but the matron was burned into her memory as a formidable lady, her hair pulled back tightly and her expression severe.

"Well? It's rude to keep your hostess waiting," the voice complained.

Hurriedly, Lily pushed open the door and entered another world.

For a few seconds, she squinted at the sudden light, which streamed from the windows and reflected off a hundred glittering ornaments. Then, as her eyes adjusted, she saw her hostess. The face and shape marked her out as three or four years older than Lily, but the dress was too young for her, all bows and satin, and her hair was a mass of blonde girlish ringlets. For one strange instant, Lily thought that she had picked her clothes to match the room, where it seemed there was barely an inch of space not covered in frills or knickknacks. In one hand, the hostess held an ornate, silver teapot.

"Tea?" she asked, pouring out a cup for herself. "Not the best, I'm afraid. Mommy will insist on that being used only on important occasions. Sit down, do. You must be Lily."

"Yes . . ." Lily said warily, looking around for a chair.

The hostess was sitting at a round table in the middle of which was a handsome cake stand full of cakes. Each place was already set with a cup and plate, and each seat was occupied by a large doll with glassy eyes. Unsure what to do, Lily picked up the doll on the seat nearest to her, meaning to put it to one side. Out of curiosity, she turned the doll's face toward her and immediately froze. The resemblance was slight, the doll was not particularly lifelike, but the thick, midnight black hair and soulful expression were unmistakable—in her hands, she held a replica of herself neatly dressed in a white linen smock.

The hostess giggled in glee. "It's a hobby of mine. Mommy lets me play with some of the healthy babies, and after she takes them away I add to my collection." She beamed as she poured Lily a cup of tea. "I made her myself, and called her Lily, of course, after you. Say hello."

Gingerly, Lily put the doll down beside her, turning its gaze to the wall. Something about the glass eyes unnerved her. Distractedly, she picked up the teacup and took a sip, grimacing as the liquid burned her tongue.

The hostess tittered. "Milk?" she said, with a look of amusement.

Lily smiled thinly.

"No, thank you, Miss . . ."

"Cherubina," she said, putting down her own tea. "Mommy . . . that is, Matron Angelina, is busy today, preparing for the Grand Festival next week. She runs several other orphanages all over the city, and they want a choir this year. She said I'd be able to answer any of your questions."

"She did?" Lily murmured, trying to keep the skepticism out of her voice.

She noticed a vast and complex dollhouse on the other side of the room, its small occupants spread throughout its richly furnished rooms in elegant poses. In the attic, she even noticed a toy maid—rosy, plump, and as flawless as her toy masters. She was dressed in a silk replica of a working dress, unpatched and pristine, pressing sheets of satin with a miniature iron of solid silver. She made quite a contrast to the ragged boy who had met her at the door and the hollow-faced girls she had known when she had been here.

"Oh, yes, I've been looking through the files," Cherubina said with a grandiose air, and then added, with a giggle, "I think I put it in one of the jewelry boxes. Just a moment . . ."

She rose with a rustle of skirts and began to pull drawers out of a wooden bureau. Lily watched her, oddly fascinated. Try as she might, she could not remember Cherubina. She hadn't even known that the matron had a daughter. Then again, looking around her at the crowds of baby dolls, she doubted whether Cherubina's interest would last beyond the point when the children could talk back.

"So," Cherubina continued as she rummaged, "Mommy said you wanted to know about your past."

"Yes," Lily said, watching as the pile of necklaces, bracelets, and earrings began to mount on the table. "I want to know if I had any family."

"If you did, you don't anymore." Cherubina's voice was muffled. "They would have sold you, or they could have died, I suppose."

"Even so," Lily said, biting the inside of her lip, "I want to know."

Cherubina's face rose out of a drawer, turned sideways in puzzlement.

"How odd," she said, with a petulant frown. "Then again, you were an odd baby. I remember you, even though I was only tiny. You never cried, just sat there in your little white smock, watching us."

Cherubina gave a grin of triumph as she extracted a folded piece of paper from the bottom drawer.

"That's why I called you Lily."

Lily managed to keep her expression steady.

"You named me . . . But surely you were too young?"

"I was really, but Mommy could never deny me anything." Cherubina beamed. "I was so set on calling you Lily . . . I can't remember why, I had only seen four summers at the time. Maybe because it was my favorite flower when I was little, and you looked like one, dressed all in white! Of course, I prefer hyacinths now, they're all the rage . . ." Cherubina paused, casting a critical eye over Lily's patched working dress. "A pity you couldn't keep it up. You hardly look like one now . . . but of course that's not your fault."

She patted Lily's hand with a simper and slipped the paper into it.

"There you are. Your report. Lucky for you Mommy is so organized."

Lily stared down at the piece of paper between her fingers. Then slowly, carefully, she unfolded it and began to read.

> *Name: Lily*
>
> *Assumed date of birth: Libra 1, year 129*
>
> *Origin: Unknown. Left as a baby, approximately one year old on our porch on Agora Day, beginning the 130th year of the Golden Age. Due to lack of other information, and for the sake of convenience, we have recorded her first birthday on this date.*
>
> *Abilities: Few. As of current age — six years — she has developed some skill with sewing.*
>
> *Possible troubles: Has a stubborn nature, which should be corrected.*
>
> *Additional information: Left without details about parentage, but with a pouch of unusual gemstones. Baby blankets also of good quality, but marred by having the child's name — Lilith — embroidered on them. After this*

name was picked off, the blankets were more easily traded for initial care.

There was nothing more. Lily read it over twice, trying to see if there was anything else to learn, any hidden messages, or speculation on where the gemstones or the blankets might have come from. Cherubina draped herself over the back of Lily's chair, her blond curls dangling onto the paper.

"Slow reader, aren't you?" she said with a chuckle. "Oh, I remember those gemstones! We kept a couple until quite recently. You should have seen them. Beautiful, smoky crystals, until you held them up to the light. Then they seemed to shine from within, like they had a tiny fire inside . . . I think Mommy should have let you keep one, but she said that we had to trade them all."

Lily got up from the chair, unable to gather her thoughts. She went over to lean on the dollhouse.

"Lilith," she muttered to herself, rolling the unfamiliar name, *her* name, around her mouth and tongue.

Cherubina, who was now scooping jewelry back into the drawers, looked up.

"Oh yes, that was Mommy's idea. Said that Lilith was too grand a name for an orphan girl, and it did sound awfully stuffy, like some dreadful old governess." She laughed. "I knew that there had to be another reason that I settled on Lily. Funny, I'd forgotten that. Lily . . . Lilith . . . it's not that important really."

"Not important?" Lily said, her voice deathly calm. She picked up one of the dolls from the house, looking into its dull glass eyes. "Isn't it important for me to know my own name?"

"What's in a name?" Cherubina replied, seating herself back at the table and pouring another cup of tea. "Do you like that? It's terribly profound . . . it's from a play I was reading last week."

"*What's in a name?*" Lily repeated, feeling the crunch as her

95

hand tightened around the old paper. "I'll tell you what. My name is all I have. It's all I've ever had."

Lily felt her heart beating faster as her voice grew louder.

"It's the one thing I could call my own when I was stuffed into storage with a hundred other girls, huddled together for warmth. It was the way I remembered who I was as your mother taught us to submit, to be no different from any other drudge." She threw the doll to the floor. "It was all that kept me from despair when I woke up and found myself sold in my sleep, tossed into the back room of a bookbinder's, stitching leather by candlelight for the right to eat. It was the name I signed on the bottom of the letter to the Count. The letter that saved me from being left in the streets when my fingers grew too large for the tiny stitches."

Lily came forward now, her face flushing. She felt like grabbing Cherubina by the shoulders, to shake the stupid girl until her blue eyes rattled and her golden ringlets fell from her head. Instead, she stood there, quivering with fury.

"It's the only thing anyone has a right to in this city. Not family, not compassion, just a single word to call your own. And you and your mother took half of it away from me and didn't even notice."

Cherubina stared at her for a moment. Then she gave a sniff.

"I think I liked you better when you were a baby." Icily, she turned her back on Lily and began to sip her tea. "You can see yourself out."

Lily stalked down the corridors, seething within. She barely noticed the boy open the front door once again; she didn't feel the crowds jostle her as she forced her way through to return to the Central Plaza. Even the decorations that were being put up for next week's festival, adorning the already elaborate stalls, did not get a second glance. It was only when she arrived home, opening the side door with a clatter, that her hands unclenched and the piece of paper fluttered to the ground. She slammed the door behind her and leaned back against it, breathing in the calming air of the former temple.

"Lily? Is that you?"

Dr. Theophilus's voice drifted up from the cellar. Lily grimaced. Was it her? Before she had seen that note she'd thought she knew who she was — just another street orphan, probably with parents already turned to dust that blew through the endless streets. But now, with a head filled with strange gemstones and her new grand, mysterious name, she felt like she knew less about herself than she had that morning.

"Hello?"

The voice sounded more concerned, and Lily raised her own in reply.

"Yes, Theo, it's me."

It still felt odd calling him Theo. Using the shorter version of another's name was always a sign of friendship, and he had insisted upon it. She was his apprentice now and, while she still felt a shudder during operations, he relied on her to mix his medicines. He always insisted that they were a partnership, not a master and servant. Thinking about that made her jaw relax a little.

"That's a relief," the doctor replied, his long, thin form emerging from the cellar door. "Miss Devine is getting a little prickly over the rent again. I tell her it's all a matter of time but . . ." He stopped, his face filling with concern. "Are you all right, Lily? You look awful."

Lily gave a wan smile.

"I'm fine, Theo. I just . . . didn't have a good time at the orphanage."

He sighed.

"I tried to warn you. There's nothing to be gained by stirring up the past."

Lily nodded distractedly, moving over to the former altar, which had been converted to a workbench. She picked up her pestle and mortar.

"I need to get on with grinding these ingredients," she said, her mind still lingering in Cherubina's room, hovering over those dolls that had better clothes than the children just a few rooms away.

Dr. Theophilus stroked his mustache, frowning.

"Only one patient today, Lily, and he's still sleeping. I have some time if—"

"I'm fine."

Lily pulled the mortar toward her, adding minerals and herbs from the boxes beside her, and then she began to grind. The pestle pounded, each strike becoming louder than the last. She found her breathing rising again and cursed silently. Why was she so angry? Had she really been expecting anything else? And yet . . .

"I just thought that maybe," she began, grinding the pestle against the side of the mortar, "if you ran an orphanage, you might occasionally, once in a while, notice the children. Maybe be a little bit interested in who they were or where they came from." Lily heard her voice turn bitterly sarcastic. "Not *care*, of course. It's too much to expect that a place dedicated to looking after abandoned babies would care about anything other than how much profit they could make from their living goods." She threw in some more roots angrily. "But I thought they might at least pay some attention . . ."

"Speaking of paying attention," Dr. Theophilus said gently, pointing.

Lily looked down. Most of the contents of the mortar were spread across the altar, having been sprayed out by her rough pounding.

Embarrassed, she scooped the powdered medicine toward the edge, catching it in the bowl.

"Lily, we can't change the world. We do our best, healing the sick . . . Three more recovered from the gray plague last week, and there are fewer and fewer cases every day. We're beginning to make a breakthrough."

"It's not enough, Theo," Lily interrupted, feeling her anger mount again. "Why don't we treat debtors? Why are those who need your cures most left to die in the streets? They spread the disease, Theo. It would make sense — "

He shook his head. "I've told you, Lily, we can't afford to treat those who can't trade for it. We're barely getting by as it is, we ask for so little in return."

"There *should* be a way," Lily insisted.

The doctor twisted his hands together, closing his eyes in exhaustion.

"Suppose I treat one debtor for free. What hope is there for him? He's still on the streets. He'll be infected with something else within a week. And what about the others? What about the thousands of debtors we didn't save? What about the hundreds who will suffer when we're forced onto the streets ourselves?" He spread his hands helplessly. "We can't live on dreams, Lily."

Lily turned her back on him, fury catching in her throat. To her shame, she felt her eyes begin to heat up and prickle with tears.

"What about Mark?" she said, turning suddenly to face the doctor. "Why did you help him, trading for a boy who was as good as a corpse when his father sold him? Or are you going to pretend that he was nothing but an experiment?"

Dr. Theophilus stepped back, as if stung, and Lily instantly regretted it. She hated being angry with the doctor. He had been so kind to her over these past six months, but she couldn't seem to stop herself.

"Why did you have to hide the urge to do something kind?" She leaned forward on the old altar, her words coming in a stream, "Why did Benedicta never tell her mistress that she showed me the way home for nothing? Why did *I* make Mark clean for me for reading lessons, when I so wanted to teach him? Why, Theo? Why? Shouldn't we be able to do such things out in the open? Are we ashamed of doing something that has no profit?"

Lily dropped her head and bit her lip, her hair falling forward to cover her face. Her throat began to constrict, and she had to stop talking to avoid sobbing. She felt as though years of frustration were trying to escape from her, but the doctor did not deserve to bear the brunt of her fury.

To her surprise, she felt the touch of his hands on her own, flat on the altar, and looked up into his eyes, which were full of concern. Lily swallowed hard.

"If there was just one person who could show everyone there is another way, Theo," she said more steadily. "If someone stood up in the middle of the city, with everyone watching, and did something that brought them nothing in return, and happiness to others . . . it might start something that couldn't be stopped. It might make people see and think . . . and change . . . and stop letting Agora be the sort of city where six-year-olds can be taken away in the middle of the night, all alone . . ."

Lily trailed off. Dr. Theophilus was looking at her oddly. For a moment, she thought she could see hope in his eyes. But when he spoke, his voice was sad.

"I believe, once, I used to think like you. When I was younger." He paused, pursing his lips. "I forget sometimes how young you are. But believe me, Lily, this is all we can do. If we make things better in a little way, and for as long as possible . . ."

His shoulders slumped and he suddenly seemed far older than his twenty-eight years.

"That's as good a life as you can lead. I've had to learn that, Lily." He sighed. "But don't believe me, not yet. This city ages you far too quickly." He straightened up, keeping hold of her hands. "I'd better check on the patient. He's paying in grain, so we'll be eating this week."

He gave her a weak smile, but Lily did not return it. Quietly, deliberately, she pulled her hands away. She watched him walk over to the door, his step slower than ever, and listened as he descended the stairs. Then she closed her eyes, feeling a shudder pass through her.

She breathed deeply, trying to control her urge to hurl the mortar at the wall. But it was expensive; they couldn't afford to trade for a new one. Besides, she had to finish her work. Benedicta was coming over later to find out how the orphanage visit had gone, and Lily had to look as if nothing was wrong.

Her friend was having a hard time this week. Signora Sozinho's wedding anniversary was approaching—the day of the festival— and thinking of her mistress was the only thing that seemed to banish Benedicta's usual cheerfulness. She was so very fond of the Signora, and Lily couldn't help but share her affection and her sadness. The Signora had once been loved by the whole city, but now she drifted through life like a ghost and there was nothing that either Ben or Lily could do about it.

What if Theo was right?

Savagely, Lily seized the mortar and pestle and began to pound away again, grinding more herbs into dust.

Pound . . .

She saw herself in her mind's eye, age seventy, still standing at this table mixing medicine. Helping with the same diseases.

Pound . . .

She looked just like Theo—caring, concerned, and defeated.

Pound . . .

She would not be defeated. Theo was wrong.

Pound . . .

He had to be wrong.

Pound . . .

There had to be a way to show the city that she was right. To open everyone's eyes.

Pound . . .

And perhaps . . .

Pound . . .

Lily stopped, an idea beginning to form in her head.

Perhaps there was.

CHAPTER NINE

The Future

"**B**EST OF FORTUNE,** Mark. Do us proud."

That had been the hardest moment so far, having to hear Mr. Prendergast's remark, complete with a good-natured slap on the back. At least the Count had been his usual self, giving him looks as if he were worth less than the dust that was kicked up as they rattled along in the carriage to the Central Plaza. It was strangely honest—the Count had never pretended to like him. But Mr. Prendergast, reeking of perfumed oil, continued to smile his jowly smile, and Mark was forced to return it. If they suspected a thing, they would cancel his appearance and, having spent months preparing him for it, the Count was not likely to be forgiving.

Mark squirmed in his seat, trying to see through the crowds that surrounded the astrologers' platform. Old men pressed in around him on every side, eager to talk to the Count, who sat stony-faced beside him. Mark had never seen the Count in daylight before. He seemed frailer, physically. His descent from the Observatory had been achingly slow, and the few steps he walked from the carriage to his throne at the heart of the astrologers had wavered, but only Mark had noticed this. In public, the Count wore his years like armor. He walked upright, refusing all offers of support, and, as his fierce gaze fell on those around him, they parted to let him through. Mark felt almost in awe of him. It was hard not to be swept up by the majesty of the occasion.

Seeing that the Count was deep in conversation, and Mr. Prendergast had disappeared into the crowds, Mark got up and pushed his way to the edge of the platform. He leaned on the ornamental rail, so highly polished he could see his reflection in it. For a moment, as an unfamiliar face stared back at him — clothed in ceremonial royal-blue coat and hat, his starfish signet gleaming back in gold from every button — the whole thing struck him as funny. How many of the Count's possessions had been traded for these fine clothes? The sleeves were so soft, they had to be trimmed with satin; even his stockings were of silk. And all for one day, all to prove a point and ruin another man's reputation.

Mark gazed out at the spectacle around him. He had never been allowed to go to the Grand Festival, not even as a little child. His father had been too busy to take him, and his mother had thought it was full of thieves and con men. Probably it was, but looking out now at the colorful banners, the weaving processions, the noisy, bustling liveliness of it all, he couldn't help feeling an urge to run out there among the vendors and lose himself in the celebrations.

Then he remembered the scroll of predictions, clasped firmly in one of his gloved hands, and his heart sank again.

Mark had heard the other astrologers as they made their predictions for the year ahead. He'd listened intently to the generalized warnings, the nebulous suggestions, the promises of good fortune that could apply to almost anyone. That was what astrologers were supposed to do, that was the lesson that Snutworth had taught him as they were preparing the day before — keep it vague and the audience will fill in the gaps.

No chance of that, Mark thought, thanks to the Count. His master had practically dictated the prophecies himself. He'd pretended to be giving guidance, of course, pretended only to be pointing out which of the stars seemed most significant. And despite everything he knew, Mark had been forced to smile and look grateful.

There were only three. As the youngest astrologer, he was required to make only three prophecies. But these were the most risky of all — predictions written and circulated days ago, predictions about the festival itself. Even now, the important festival-goers would be reading their copies and waiting.

Silently, he mouthed the familiar verses to himself again:

The Glory of Agora this day will shine
And prophecies three shall encompass the sign.

The hour will be marked with double the joy
And bells ever ringing their sweetness employ.

The stars will be falling for that which would rise
The whole then will crumble, the small win the prize.

And lastly the lonely will silence amaze
And hymning her happiness rise up in praise.

And with these three signs removed to the past
The Glory of Agora ever will last.

He had tried every trick he could think of to make it easier. He tried to ignore the influence of the more difficult planets, took the most conservative interpretations he could find, even made it rhyme in order to pad it out. The only thing he had discovered from that was that he was no better at poetry than he was at astrology. He couldn't seem to get the feel for the mystery.

In his mind, Mark had seen it play out. The awful silence as he read them aloud, his voice quivering. The deathly hush as they waited for something, anything, to happen. Then the laughter began, the whole crowd erupting into hoots and giggles, as he jumped down from the platform and pushed his way through the crowd, losing himself in a sea of bodies, publicly shamed forever.

As he mused, he caught sight of a black-suited figure slipping quietly through the revelers toward the clock tower in the middle of the Central Plaza, his face concealed from the platform by the angle of his tricornered hat. No one else would have paid attention, but to Mark it was a sign of hope. Snutworth was on his way. Everything depended on him. What he was doing was dangerous, of course, but part of Mark longed to be with him, anything to get away from the platform and the curious eyes of the astrologers. Not for the first time, he wished that he had told Lily about what he was going to do. She was probably out there somewhere in the throng, waiting for the celebrations to truly begin. But the Count still read his letters and secrecy was vital. In any case, Mark considered with a shudder that the last thing he wanted was to drag Lily down with him, and not just because she was his friend. If he failed today, she and the doctor might be the only people in the whole of Agora who would take him in.

As he turned back to look at the other astrologers, he saw the cluster around the Count part. The Count had risen, slowly, and bowed to a new figure who was approaching him. This man, elaborately dressed in powdered wig and gown of purple velvet, and bearing a golden chain of office, seemed to command as much respect as the Count, and lesser astrologers stepped away hastily. The two powerful men stood face-to-face, talking politely, but even Mark could feel the crackle of tension between them. Then, to his concern, the Count raised a withered finger and beckoned Mark toward them. Keeping his eyes lowered, he shuffled closer.

"Where are your manners, boy?" the Count snapped. "Greet the Lord Chief Justice as is his due."

Mark scraped a bow, then felt a gloved hand grasp his chin and his face was turned upward for inspection. The Lord Chief Justice was old in Mark's eyes, but of a younger generation than the Count, and his grasp was firm and strong. His gaze appraised Mark swiftly.

"So, Stelli, this is the boy I have heard so much about." The Lord Chief Justice's voice was deep and restrained, as if he could say anything he wished, but chose not to. "He is certainly young to be making his first predictions, even for an apprentice. I trust you have taught him well."

"The very best tuition, Ruthven," the Count replied, and Mark felt his throat go dry. So this was Lord Ruthven, the "rival" the Count and Mr. Prendergast had spoken of. The Lord Chief Justice himself! They said he was only one step down from the Director and was his public face because the Director never left his office.

"I don't doubt it, Stelli," Lord Ruthven said, in a tone that suggested the opposite. "Nevertheless, as the whole of the city's elite talks of our wager, and of my apparent support for the lad, a demonstration would be appreciated."

"Naturally, My Lord," the Count replied, his disdain palpable. "Mark, what is the significance of the house of Virgo?"

Remembering the lessons drumming this into his head, Mark gabbled, "Work, sir. At the present time, as the sun is leaving the house, it signifies a fall in profits for some, but tempered by a larger celebration as Mars is in retrograde and Jupiter is in conjunction with—"

"Enough, enough!" Lord Ruthven gave a smile and withdrew his hand. "The boy has clearly had his head stuffed with all of your precious science. You must forgive me for my concern over so trivial a matter, Stelli."

"Not at all, Ruthven," the Count rumbled, with polite malice. "It is entirely understandable, especially considering that much of the city believes our wager to be rather more than trivial. Some might even say that our reputations rest on the boy's predictions." He paused, then added pointedly, "I am pleased that he lives up to your expectations of my noble art."

"I believe you overestimate the boy's importance." Ruthven's voice grew colder and quiet, so only the Count and Mark could hear. "Look at this crowd, Stelli. The rabble do not know of any wager. All they will see is the Count's prodigy. I wonder whose reputation they will link to his success or failure?"

The Count smiled icily. Mark had the impression that the two old foes had forgotten that he was there, or perhaps they both thought him so ignorant that he would not understand what they were talking about.

"Come now, Ruthven," the Count said. "We are not men who care about the common herd. Everyone who matters, who holds power, knows that the battle lines have been drawn."

"Nothing but rumors," Lord Ruthven replied, his composure beginning to crack. "No one will ever believe that I had anything to do with—"

"You are the politician, My Lord," the Count rejoined, fixing Lord Ruthven with a steely glare. "Would you claim that rumors have no power?"

Lord Ruthven did not respond, but Mark felt certain that if such a thing were possible on this warm autumn day, frost would have formed in the air around him.

"Now, surely you are required elsewhere, Ruthven?" the Count continued, loud enough for others to hear, putting his hand on

Mark's shoulder in a parody of fatherly concern. Mark could feel the old man's fingers digging in like claws. "Mark needs to prepare for his recitation."

"On the contrary, Stelli, I consider it my duty to stay and observe." Lord Ruthven made an expansive gesture, all traces of his coldness vanishing too rapidly to be genuine. "Today is a day when all differences should be set aside in the wonder of the occasion. We are celebrating nearly twelve grand cycles since our city entered its golden age. One hundred and forty-one years of prosperity. Surely that is worth more than petty arguments?" Lord Ruthven beamed, placing his hand on Mark's other shoulder.

Mark grunted, suddenly wishing more than anything that he had grown taller over the past months. Between them, the two men seemed determined to force him into the ground.

"In any case," Lord Ruthven continued nonchalantly, "as you say, I have taken a personal interest in the boy, so I feel it is only fair that I witness his first predictions."

Mark's spirits sank further still. No matter how much he wanted to believe that Lord Ruthven would protect him if he failed, he could not. Indeed he knew that if he was disgraced today, the Lord Chief Justice would be the first to condemn him. Lord Ruthven didn't need his name linked to that of a failure. Even he could become damaged goods if the whole city saw him as a fool.

Looking out over the sea of stalls, Mark watched as the people buzzed and swirled before them, while the vendors called their wares. Ribbons and banners hung from every awning. In the distance, the twelve bridges and the arches gleamed from their recent polishing. The sun shone down remorselessly, as if determined to be indifferent to his fate. By rights, there should have been a sinister shadow at the very least, giving an inkling that something was about to go horribly wrong. But the weather ignored his inner storm.

Mark glanced up to the clock tower at the center of the plaza.

He was due to read his predictions at midday, and now it was nearly . . .

The first chime rang out.

He felt his world contract. He barely noticed the two men release his shoulders, propelling him forward to the podium on the ornate balcony from which the astrologers addressed the crowd.

The second chime and Mark was aware that the crowds had begun to grow quiet. How many people knew about this?

The third and he stepped to the podium, holding up his scroll.

The fourth.

Out of the corner of his eye, Mark saw Count Stelli and Lord Ruthven sit down to one side, watching.

Fifth . . . sixth . . .

Now the whole crowd seemed to be looking up to the astrologers' platform.

Seventh . . . eighth . . .

Mark felt sweat trickling down the back of his neck. He unrolled the scroll.

Ninth . . .

He scanned the crowd, trying to pick out the tiny black-clad figure. Snutworth had to be out there. He couldn't let him down now.

Tenth . . . eleventh . . .

Mark cleared his throat.

Twelfth . . .

This was it. The moment.

The crowd held its breath.

Thirteenth . . . fourteenth . . . fifteenth . . .

Whispers began to ripple through the crowd. Mark was hidden behind his scroll, so no one saw his face split in a huge grin of relief. He'd done it!

Even as he cast his eyes down the predictions, he remembered slipping the copy to Snutworth at their last meeting. Remembered the servant studying them and then wincing.

"Not the easiest to achieve, Mark," he had muttered. "Still . . . just make sure you draw out the reading as long as possible and I'll deal with the rest."

And now he had. Even as Mark watched a distant, shadowy figure slip out of the base of the clock tower, he recalled his first prophecy:

The hour will be marked with double the joy
And bells ever ringing their sweetness employ.

Every single note of the second twelve peals was the sweetest sound Mark had ever heard. Finally, on the twenty-fourth chime, they stopped.

He forced himself not to turn, even though he so desperately wanted to see the expression on the Count's face, to watch him realize that his "talentless" pupil's first prediction had come true. Who cared that Snutworth had been fiddling with the works of the clock? Even the Count would have to agree that it fitted perfectly. But instead Mark swallowed hard. The most difficult part was still to come.

He lifted his scroll and, in a voice that shook only slightly, he began to read:

"The Glory of Agora this day will shine
And prophecies three shall encompass the sign."

He grimaced. In the midst of everything, he wished he hadn't used the word *encompass*. He wasn't quite sure what it meant, and if even part of this prophecy was wrong the whole scheme would collapse.

"The hour will be marked with double the joy

And bells ever ringing their sweetness employ."

A pleasing buzz greeted those lines. Mark looked around the crowd. Was Snutworth in position yet? Had he found the right place? Mark took a long pause and tried to look mystical.

"The stars will be falling for that which would rise . . ."

The buzz grew louder.

"Come on . . . come on . . ." Mark muttered under his breath.

Nothing. The crowd seemed to be losing interest.

"The whole then will crumble, the small win the prize."

A shriek went up.

Mark craned his neck with everyone else. At one of the central stalls a man was holding something up. Mark couldn't quite see. Was that the baker's stall? It had to be if the next prophecy was going to work, but for some time the prophecies were forgotten in the new excitement.

"Dreadful business . . . dreadful . . ."

Mark spun around. Panting and wheezing, the round shape of Mr. Prendergast was ascending the steps up to the platform, one hand firmly gripping the rail.

"Trouble, Prendergast?" Lord Ruthven asked, pointedly not getting up to help the lawyer.

"Indeed, My Lord, most appalling," he wheezed. "I understand from my contacts among the receivers that the baking competition, a little piece of harmless low-life amusement, has been ruined. A rat was found burrowed into the center of the winning loaf. It could signal the end of that poor baker's career, such a public humiliation, and to think he had such ambitions . . ."

"A baker indeed," Lord Ruthven mused. "Isn't bread, when baking, said to 'rise'?"

"I had no idea that Your Lordship was so interested in cooking," Count Stelli growled, giving Mark a vicious look.

Mark could see the veins standing up on the back of the Count's hands as he gripped the arms of his chair, his eyes twitching back and forth at the astrologers who swarmed around him, as if challenging them to comment. Lord Ruthven seemed unruffled, however.

"I was just considering how very apt the boy's words are at this moment, 'The stars will be falling for that which would rise,' and of course the rat, that is, the smallest creature, could be said to have triumphed."

"Thank you, My Lord," Mr. Prendergast interrupted with an air of irritation. "I think we are all capable of drawing our own conclusions. It is a shame that my servant, Snutworth, is not here. He is a man who delights in word games. However, I doubt that he will be joining us for a while. That was a bad business indeed."

It took a moment for Mark to realize what Prendergast had said. When he did, however, all caution deserted him.

"Bad business? What bad business?" Mark said, a little too loudly.

Mr. Prendergast turned his attention to him. For once, his eyes held no friendliness, not even falsely. But his mouth continued to smile.

"Quite sad really. It seems that his envy finally got the better of him. I found, this morning, that my priceless silver-topped cane had disappeared. I live alone and keep very few servants. There was only one person who had the opportunity."

Barely were the poisoned words out of Mr. Prendergast's mouth before Mark remembered something he had glimpsed that morning amidst the panic of preparation: The lawyer had forgotten his cane and sent Snutworth to fetch it for him. For a brief instant, he wanted to shout that out, to reveal how he was twisting the truth in the hope that someone would believe him instead of the old fraud. But the words froze in his throat. There was something more urgent to know now. He heard the Count ask the question.

"Have the receivers caught him?"

"Fortunately, yes," Mr. Prendergast said, his eyes never shifting from Mark. "They found the cane on him, of course. Strangely, they found him over at the animal pagoda. He seemed to be prying loose the lock on a cage of rare solitaire doves." Mr. Prendergast shook his head. "He probably intended to create a diversion." The lawyer turned back to Mark, his words slow and significant. "It is remarkable what the criminal will do to cover his tracks."

Mark felt his hands shake. *Solitaire* doves. He didn't know much about other languages, but only the day before Snutworth had told him what this word meant: alone.

And lastly the lonely will silence amaze
And hymning her happiness rise up in praise.

It wasn't going to happen. It wasn't enough to get two out of three.

"Come now, Mark," Mr. Prendergast said softly. "You must finish your pronouncements. I'm sure we cannot wait to see your triumph."

Mark looked around. Mr. Prendergast seemed to be taking pleasure in his words. The Count was impassive once again, but in his eyes Mark could see glowering hatred. An expression of curiosity crossed Lord Ruthven's face, but he was hardly stepping forward to help. And all around them the astrologers muttered to each other, passing notes back and forth, glaring in his direction. As their eyes flitted toward the Count, looking anxiously for his approval, Mark felt something else stir inside him. His mind heard again their "prophecies," each one a vague promise of rising fortunes or auspicious signs, so empty that they could mean anything. Why should they succeed, when all they did was shadow the Count and feed off the respect he was accorded? The respect given to a man who used his apprentice as bait in a political game.

Determined now, Mark turned back to the crowd. Maybe he would fall this day, but at least he had found his own voice. He wasn't going to be anyone's puppet anymore.

"And lastly the lonely will silence amaze
And hymning her happiness rise up in praise.
And with these three signs removed to the past
The Glory of Agora ever will last."

Mark finished and held his breath. The crowd remained silent.

Nothing. There was no chorus of cooing doves, miraculously released despite Snutworth's capture. Not a sound broke the air. Mark looked out over the endless shifting of the crowds, a mass of people all looking to be told something they could believe. He felt his legs tense, ready to jump into their midst, to scurry and push his way through and vanish, running from the Count and his politics, for even he could foresee that there was no future for him there.

He put down his scroll.

And he heard the first note.

It was a pure, clean sound, rising out of the crowd. A single note, crisp, bright, and high.

Mark was the first to see her. A woman, her black hair streaked with silver, ascending the musicians' platform on the far side of the plaza. From here, he could not make out her face, nor that of the man whose voice mingled with hers, sounds of darkness and light resonating and trilling together.

But he could make out the word. The one word they were singing over and over again, rising in runs and twirls of notes, filling the plaza.

"Glory. . . . Glory . . . Glory be to our city fair . . ."

He heard a rustle and Lord Ruthven was beside him, leaning on the rail. He looked out to where the crowds were gathering around the platform.

"It has been so long since I heard Signora Sozinho sing. I had thought her voice was lost." Lord Ruthven spoke with a trace of nostalgia. "Sozinho, of course, is an ancient name. I believe it means 'alone.' " He turned to face Mark and smiled, satisfied. "Truly a miracle, young man."

And Mark listened. Listened as the murmurs and shouts from the plaza seemed to echo with the music, watched as the people turned from the singers back to him, cheering, and felt the old astrologers jostle around him, suddenly suspiciously keen to show their support and shake the hand of their newest, brightest star.

It was much later before anyone noticed that the Count and Mr. Prendergast had vanished into the crowd.

CHAPTER TEN

The Song

H ALF AN HOUR earlier and on the far side of the Central Plaza, Lily put five round white pills onto a counter. "Is that enough?" she asked.

The vendor peered at them for a moment and then gave a nod.

"Since it's you, Miss Lily. Always good-quality painkillers."

Lily absently stamped her seal on the contract. She had been overcharged, of course. Theo had warned her that at the festival everything was traded for twice what it was worth, and under normal circumstances she would never have bought the rather sickly and unpleasant-looking pieces of candied fruit, but she needed something to distract her. The eleventh hour was already past and still no sign of either of them.

For the fiftieth time she went over the wording of her letters, trying to remember if she had given offense or told too much. If one of them did not turn up, then her grand idea would come to nothing. She wished she could have gone over the plan with Theo, but he was too busy making ends meet. He now had twelve patients under observation in the cellar alone. Besides, she couldn't bear to see his sad smile as he helped her, sure that what she was doing was foolish but trying his best anyway.

Even Benedicta had not been convinced when Lily had first explained her idea. But being Benedicta, she had not hesitated for a moment once Lily had asked for her help, even though if something went wrong it would be a disaster for her. Lily didn't want to admit it, but at that moment Benedicta's faith in her was all that was keeping her from abandoning her plan. The longer she stood there, the more hopeless it seemed.

Nervously, Lily popped one of the candies into her mouth and winced. It tasted not unlike the medicines she had been mixing out of riverweed earlier that morning, stuffed with something sticky and vaguely alive. She shuffled away from the stall, pushing through the mass of revelers, choking on the smells and noise of the markets. Grimly, she made her way past a pile of discarded flowers and fallen bunting that was already being trampled underfoot and glanced up at the clock tower.

Half past eleven.

She frowned. The musicians' platform was still empty. He was supposed to be here by now. His butler had said that he had been commissioned to compose and sing a new work for the midday celebrations. It was said that the Director himself would be listening from the tallest tower of the Directory.

She walked back and forth, scanning the people around her. Every now and then she thought she saw faces that looked familiar, but they continually faded away, returning to the mass of humanity around her. She had never been to the festival before. Although she had been given leave to go with the rest of the workers at the bookbinder's the previous year, the arrival of her signet ring that very morning had changed everything. For one blissful hour, she had been so happy, so thrilled to finally own herself, to face Agora Day as an independent person. Then the chief bookbinder had called her into his office and told her that she was to be thrown out of the only home she had known since the orphanage. It seemed that everyone had been celebrating on her title day except for her.

She knew that Mark would be here, of course, but she was sure that he would be even more nervous than she was. She would have to make sure to catch his appearance at the astrologers' platform, although he hadn't sounded as thrilled as he usually did the last time he had written. She had not had time to tell him of her plan, and in any case he would probably have laughed at her. As she stood in the middle of the crowd, every passerby totally absorbed in the festivities, her own resolve began to falter. Of course she believed that what she planned to do was worth doing in its own right — just as she had said, an act of kindness that brought her nothing in return. But at the same time the thought gnawed at her that she did want something out of it, desperately. She wanted it to be seen, to show everyone around that there was another way to live. And she wanted to prove to herself that it could be done.

Someone in the crowd jostled her. She turned, annoyed, only to see a black-suited stranger slip past. He made an apologetic gesture but kept on toward his target, which seemed to be the clock tower. Curious, Lily turned to look after him and froze.

There, just next to him, was the man she had been waiting for. All thoughts of the stranger went out of her head as this new figure approached. His coat long and flowing, his black hair touched with gray, there was no mistaking him — his face graced most of the woodcut pictures pinned up on the musicians' platform.

"Signor Sozinho!" Lily called out, pushing her way through the throng, dropping the bag of candies to the ground. "A moment, please, Signor . . ."

Airily, Signor Sozinho glanced over in her direction, a look of irritation playing over his features.

"A child," he said, looking down at Lily. "And a scruffy one at that. I hope that Miss Lilith keeps more servants than you, girl. The great Signor Sozinho does not grant an interview to just anyone. As I recall from her letter, your mistress said that she would meet me personally."

His voice was rich and musical, but there was something strange in its overtones. As though every word was followed by a ghostly echo. Lily stuck out her hand, trying to act a great deal older than she felt. It was time to own up.

"Thank you for giving me a few minutes of your time, Signor." She paused, noticing that her hand was still stained from the morning's work. Embarrassed, and feeling younger and more hopeless with every second, she wiped it on her apron. "I am Miss Lilith."

The man looked down at her, one eyebrow raised.

"You must get someone else to write your letters. They are surprisingly well written," he said, withdrawing his hand with a flinch, as though she had dirtied it. "Still, a good joke, so I shall not be angry. Perhaps if you are very good, I shall give you an autograph, but only after the performance. Now, I have more pressing matters to—"

"Signor, please . . ." Lily jumped into his way again. "It will only take a moment, if you will just come with me."

"Girl, I do not have time," Signor Sozinho snapped. And there it was again, louder this time, an echo to his words, higher than his own voice, almost feminine. Angrily, he pulled a bundle of manuscript sheets out of his pocket, waving them in Lily's face. "This work has been commissioned by Lord Ruthven himself, to be performed at midday. I must prepare and study my notes."

"You don't know it by heart?" Lily said thoughtfully, a desperate plan forming in her mind.

The great singer sniffed.

"When one composes every day, one can scarcely be expected to recall each note with perfect accuracy, if that is any concern of . . . What are you . . . Let go of that! Stop! Stop, thief!"

But Lily was already plunging through the crowd, the manuscript clutched to her chest.

"Not my best plan ever . . ." Lily gasped to herself as she hurtled onward.

Already she could hear the sounds of the receivers gathering at Signor Sozinho's outraged shouts as he followed her. But there were so many people and Lily could slip between them, while Signor Sozinho had to push them out of his way. Ahead, she could see the elegant curve of the Virgo District bridge, and beyond that the Virgo archway, decked with its statue of a maiden among the clouds. If she could just get that far, hide from the receivers until the others arrived, then maybe she wouldn't end this day in prison.

She reached the bridge, panting as she hurried up its steps, and risked a glance back. Receivers in their midnight-blue uniforms were beginning to cut through the crowd, but Signor Sozinho was nearer, his face red from exertion. She dashed on, down the steps on the other side of the bridge. The shadow of the archway loomed up before her. She stopped, glancing around.

A hand closed on her shoulder.

Lily froze, turning as slowly as she could. Signor Sozinho's expression was grim.

"I shall not ask for my music, girl," he said, his tone menacing. "I want the receivers to see that you are holding it when they arrive. I do not know what you mean by this, but it matters little. You will be given the maximum penalty for stealing my work."

Lily bowed her head, cursing herself and her stupidity. So much for her grand ideas. Then she stopped. Something had caught Signor Sozinho's attention behind her.

A flicker of hope stirred inside her, but she didn't dare turn around. Not yet.

"It has been a long time," Signor Sozinho said, his voice flat, no longer talking to Lily but to someone behind her. "A lifetime."

Lily smiled, shook herself free of his hand, now slack, and turned.

Standing in the shadows of the great archway, her eyes cast down, her hands clasped before her, was Signora Sozinho. Beside her, half hidden behind her mistress, stood Benedicta. Lily walked over with an encouraging smile and Benedicta nodded back, her attention fixed on Signor Sozinho.

Slowly, cautiously, the great singer walked closer to his former wife. In the shelter of the archway the Signora had found a refuge on the edge of the noise and rush. Even the pursuing receivers, Lily was pleased to notice, seemed to have lost them without the Signor's shouting to guide them. Nothing, not even a breath of wind, disturbed the air between the couple. Eventually, the Signor raised a haughty eyebrow.

"Strange to see you accompanied by girls. I thought young men were more to your taste."

Lily winced. The Signora stepped forward, her hands gesturing before her expressively, her mouth moving soundlessly. Meekly, Benedicta translated.

"She says, 'There was only ever one young man for me.'"

Signor Sozinho sneered, "Your lawyer made that clear at the time." He glanced around. "What happened to him?"

Signora Sozinho made more signs. Benedicta paused, a wistful smile on her face, before translating.

"He grew old. We still sang together, but the music was gone." The Signora raised her eyes to meet those of her former husband and continued to sign. "I tried to find that music again. In the end, I tried to find it with someone else. But it never came back . . ."

Benedicta frowned. "I think she says *carissimo*. It's an old language." She lowered her voice. "I think it means 'dearest.' "

"I did nothing wrong," Signor Sozinho muttered. "The court found in my favor, a wronged husband. I never betrayed our life together."

"Not in your acts," Benedicta said, her eyes fixed on the Signora's fluttering hands, "but in your eyes, and in your heart. You took everything from me. My life, my voice . . . I gave my name away for you and took yours."

"Enough!" Signor Sozinho shouted. The echo was clear this time: It was a woman's voice, rising within his own like a half-heard duet. "I will not listen to your lies anymore. You broke everything we had, and you will not have it back. You will not sing for anyone else, even if I have to listen to your voice for the rest of my life . . ." He broke off, turning away, and Signora Sozinho turned too, her face ashen.

Lily exchanged an anxious look with Benedicta. This wasn't supposed to have happened. From what her friend had told her about the pair, she had thought that just seeing each other again would be enough. Instead, she seemed to have made things worse. Behind them, some of the people in the passing crowd had stopped and were watching, whispering to each other, seeing the opposite of what Lily had wanted to show them. With no clear plan in her head, Lily stepped forward and asked the only question that she could think of.

"Why did you keep her voice within you all this time?"

"It is no business of yours, girl," the Signor snapped, but Lily pressed on, her mind whirring.

"Didn't you have the choice to have it bottled? That's normal, isn't it?"

"You are correct, girl." The Signor turned baleful eyes on his former wife. "But that was not my desire. Call it a reminder never to trust again."

Softly, hardly sure where the words were coming from, Lily spoke again.

"I don't believe that."

The Signor turned on her, his voice scornful and bitter.

"*You?* Who are you? What do you know of the pain I have suffered thanks to her?" he said, frenziedly jabbing his hand toward the Signora. "What do you know of the agony, the broken life? You, who have barely begun to live, how can you know what it is like to have twenty years turn into a lie? To feel the soul ripped from your music?"

There was a long pause. Even the noises of the Central Plaza's festivities seemed muted. Then, slowly, the Signora raised her head and made six simple gestures. Benedicta looked and spoke.

"I didn't think you cared so much."

Signor Sozinho sighed.

"Once, *carissima*, once. Once I thought you gave me all you had."

"I have now," the Signora signed, a sad smile appearing on her lined face.

The Signor shook his head. "Nothing but a substitute."

They stared, frozen, looking at each other. Lily took a deep breath. Now was her chance, this moment of stillness. Hundreds of possible words poured into her mind, arguing, cajoling, willing them to understand. But, when at last she spoke, she found an odd feeling descend upon her. Just for that instant, none of her big ideas mattered. The words were not calculated, nor were they any longer about proving a point or starting a crusade. They came direct from her, Lily, standing between two people who belonged together, and she meant every one of them.

"It's not too late. No," she said, before Signor Sozinho could speak, "please, Signor, listen, just for a moment. Then you can lock me up, anything. But first, tell me this." Lily walked over to Signora Sozinho, but she kept her eyes fixed, unblinking, on that lady's former husband. "You are the most successful singer in all of Agora. The Director himself commissions new works from you. You have armies of servants, everyone sings your praises. They tell me that women line up to be introduced to you. So tell me, Signor Sozinho, why haven't you remarried?"

The Signor drew himself up to his full height, but his face seemed suddenly to bear the full weight of his years. As he spoke, his wife's voice spoke along with him, resonating in his throat.

"My name is in an old tongue. It means 'alone.' It seems that is how I am destined to be. All those around me have been proven false."

There was a rustle of skirts. Signora Sozinho clasped his hand, mouthing something. He looked back at her, his face showing confusion. Benedicta stared at her lips and smiled.

"She says, 'I'm sorry. I was wrong, *carissimo*. I thought you didn't know me. But it seems our thoughts were the same.' "

"Maybe," the Signor said, drawing away, "but it is too late now. There are wounds we cannot heal."

"Why not?" Lily said, burning with fierce passion. "Look around you, both of you! Don't you see a thousand people who have servants, ten thousand who have fame, a million with riches? Everyone in this city grabs what they have and holds it. But you . . . you had something you cannot trade for anything, something worth more than pride. Don't throw it away," she said, with one final, exhausted sigh. "It doesn't make sense."

The two looked at each other, did nothing but stare. Lily caught Benedicta's eye. The other girl smiled nervously, unable to tear her eyes away from the scene before them.

And then the clock chimed twenty-four.

It was as if the world had paused. Somewhere nearby, people

were shouting, saying something about a prophecy being fulfilled. Lily barely noticed. She simply saw Signor and Signora Sozinho moving closer, still holding each other's hands.

On the twelfth strike, they'd kissed. A strange mist seemed to play around them. When the bells had faded, after the final peal had rung out, they pulled back, the last wisps of smoke leaving his mouth and flowing into hers.

"*Carissimo* . . ." Signora Sozinho said.

Lily felt relief flooding her from within. Outside, she was just about aware of Benedicta squeezing her hand in delight. With her other hand, she proffered the manuscript that she was still grasping.

"I think this is yours, Signor. I'm sorry I had to take it, but . . ."

"Look at this, *carissima*," Signor Sozinho said, taking it from Lily and handing it to Signora Sozinho. "It is the same tune that we wrote all those years ago."

Signora Sozinho looked over it, her eyes moist, her face breaking into a sad smile. "We wrote it as a duet . . ." she said, her voice a little unsteady still.

"Can you remember it?" Signor Sozinho asked gently.

His wife's smile grew wider.

"Every note," she said.

"Go," he urged her. "Begin, at the musicians' platform. I shall join you in a moment."

The Signora paused, her hand stroking her former husband's cheek, and then she danced away across the bridge and through the crowds. Signor Sozinho watched her go, his own years slipping away.

He turned to Lily. "I shall draw up a contract later, of course. But for this service you shall have some of our instruments, I think, and of course the charges of theft will be dropped . . ."

Lily held up her hand.

"I want nothing, Signor."

He paused, a look of suspicion on his face.

"Nothing? Did someone hire you to do this?"

"No, sir. There is nothing to repay." Lily struggled to find the words. "It is right . . . correct . . . that you should be together. That's enough for me."

Signor Sozinho looked at her blankly.

"Nothing?" he repeated, staring in bewilderment.

Lily shrugged.

"I'd prefer it if you didn't set the receivers on me for taking the manuscript." She stuck her hands in her apron. "And some thanks would be nice."

The Signor looked at her as if she were some strange, alien being. Then, in the distance, he heard the first strains of the Signora's voice. And he smiled.

"Thank you, Miss Lilith. Thank you."

And he was gone, beginning his part of the duet as he left.

Filled with excitement, Lily followed him, climbing the bridge until she was standing at its peak and could see over the whole of Central Plaza. Then, she stopped to watch, a smile twitching on her face as Signor Sozinho slipped through the mass of people around the platforms in the Central Plaza. Her plan was proving a success. Already she could hear the whispers in the crowd passing by, mutterings of surprise and intrigue. It wouldn't be long before people started asking questions, before the story was told. It wasn't much yet, no one came up to her to ask what it was all about, but right now that hardly mattered. It had worked . . . it had really worked . . . and if once, why not again?

In any case, the crowd seemed to be distracted by something happening on the other side of the Plaza. There was quite a gathering around the astrologers' platform. From her vantage point on the bridge, Lily peered into the distance. Wasn't that Mark standing there? She jumped as she was jolted out of her reverie. Mark's prophecies! She must have missed them! Guiltily, she began to push her way forward.

"Come on, Lily," Benedicta said, tugging at her sleeve, her face flushed with delight. "Let's go and listen to the Signora sing. I knew this would work . . . that is, I know I said you were crazy when you first told me . . . but still, I knew it!"

Lily smiled, raising her hands to calm down her excitable friend.

"You go, Benedicta. And have a good time. I want to try to see Mark. Then I'd better go home because I've got some things to think about . . ."

"You're not going to leave!" Benedicta crashed across her thoughts and seized her hand. "You've just made my mistress happier than she's been for years and not even asked for a reward. I demand you enjoy yourself for the rest of the day! First, we'll go and congratulate your friend, if we can get anywhere near him, and then there's some candied fruits on sale I know you'll love." Benedicta grinned. "Don't forget, the festival only comes once a year."

Lily looked into Benedicta's face, so bright and cheerful, and gave in. After all, she did have something to celebrate.

"All right," she said, taking Benedicta's arm, "but you're trading for the candies. I can't stand them."

"Only if you agree to try one of the games."

"Games? What kind of games?"

"All sorts! Honestly, don't you ever have any fun?"

"I help cut off people's limbs for a living, Ben . . ."

And, talking about everything and nothing, the two girls plunged into the crowds to enjoy the rest of celebrations.

But, even then, it did not stop Lily from thinking.

Nothing ever could.

CHAPTER ELEVEN

The Star

MARK COULDN'T SLEEP that night. He paced through all of the rooms of the tower, too full of energy to stop for a moment.

His ears were still ringing from the cheers and from the excited babble of old astrologers talking to him about planetary conjunctions just loud enough so that everyone around could hear. After a while, Mark was sure that his answers made no sense, which was fine, as it was clear that no one was listening. They were all too busy, taking questions from the throngs and relaying his confused answers. At some point he was presented with a scroll of some kind. It said something about admitting him to the Astrologers' Guild, but he barely had time to read it.

All day, as the unfamiliar faces had pressed in around him, he had been searching for familiar ones, dreading their appearance. At his celebratory dinner, held in a vast marquee, he was expecting the room to grow silent, the cheers to stop, and for the shadow of the Count to fall over the room. But it never did. Nor did he once smell Prendergast's perfumed oils. Even when, in a carriage hired by Lord Ruthven, Mark had returned with trepidation to the tower, he found just echoing emptiness. The only clue that the Count had been there at all was that the front door was hanging open. As far as Mark could see nothing had been touched.

But he couldn't be sure. He had searched the tower from the depths of the cellar, still reeking from the doctor's experiments, to the heights of the Observatory, yet all was still and dark. The ever-present dust lay undisturbed.

The tower was strange without the Count. He had infused every crack in the stonework; his voice hummed through every hall. Without him, it was just a shell.

It was around midnight when Mark started to consider what would happen if Count Stelli didn't come back. Up until then, he had prepared his speech, promising that he would give the Count full credit for his success, as long as he kept him on as apprentice, on a more equal basis. He felt that, after his miraculous achievement, he had the right to ask for more. Fate must have been smiling on him after all, to have restored Signora Sozinho's voice like that. Either that or his talent for astrology was far greater than anyone had suspected, himself included.

He remembered how the crowd had flowed up onto the astrologers' platform and hoisted him onto their shoulders, parading him as a genius. And all he could think of as he was carried away was the first note of the Signora's song, the moment when one of his prophecies really had come true. For that second, he had believed it; he was sure he could feel the power of the stars flowing through him. And then, with a jolt, he remembered how he had managed his first two "miracles." He wondered if the Count had ever felt like this — the only one who could not enjoy the show, because he alone could see the puppets' strings.

But if the Count didn't come back, what would he do? Where would he go? Could he stay here without him? Even if he did, how long could he trade his predictions? How long would his fame support him?

He couldn't find any answers. Not even though he struggled with these questions all night. Not even as he stood in the Observatory, looking down on the dark city below. A city picked out in tiny specks of torchlight as though all the stars had fallen to earth.

This was when he really needed Lily. He had spotted her in the crowd that afternoon, but in the crush of admirers she had not managed to get near. He had spent the whole day wishing he could find anyone he knew. Anyone at all. So many celebrations all around him and no one to share them with.

Mark paused, the black, clouded night sky surrounding him.

For a moment, he thought he smelled fish. He remembered being tiny, listening to his mother's stories, his father coming home with the day's catch.

His mother would have been proud. But she was dead now. And his father . . . even if he was not dead, he was to Mark.

"Look at me now, Dad," he said aloud, his voice echoing back from the walls of the Observatory. "I wasn't worth keeping? But here I am. Standing at the top of the world. They called me a prodigy yesterday. A miracle." He swallowed, his eyes moist. "They thought I was worth more than something to pay a bill."

There was no reply.

Mark sat in the Count's chair as the dawn came up, breaking through the clouds, dyeing the roofs of Agora red and purple. In the distance, the towers of the Directory loomed back, the only thing as high as he was. And far beyond, the gray shadows of the city walls, the edge of the world, emerged out of the morning mist. Legend said that there was nothing outside the city — nothing but mountains, barren and lifeless, stretching on forever. Mark imagined himself flying, rising higher and higher, up above the topmost towers, to gaze down at Agora, a glimmering spark of life and energy in the midst of empty darkness. For once, the city seemed totally still.

Then a loud knocking at the front door broke the silence.

Mark galloped down the stairs, sure that this was the Count back again, demanding to know why no one had been sent to look for him. Already, Mark's weary brain was trying to frame excuses. He pulled back the bolts and opened the door.

It was not the Count.

"Snutworth!" The word came out as a sigh of relief.

The servant also looked as if he hadn't slept. He bore an ugly bruise on his cheek and was walking with a limp, supported by a familiar silver-handled cane. But as he hobbled into the tower, there was an expression of triumph on his face.

"Sensational! Truly, an utter success!" he said as he sank into a chair in the entrance hall.

"Are you all right?" Mark asked.

Snutworth waved his hand dismissively.

"Our friends in the receivers were a little enthusiastic when they arrested me, that's all," he said, wincing as he stretched out his injured leg. "Fortunately, once my accuser's crimes came to light, my own paled into insignificance."

"Your accuser?"

"My former master," Snutworth said, leaning back. "The inspector informed me that several other lawyers have discovered a number of shady dealings in his name, including the fixing of legal cases and the running up of debts on confidence." Seeing Mark's look of confusion, Snutworth smiled. "To put it bluntly, the most exclusive businesses were prepared to lend to Mr. Prendergast, the great lawyer and possible future Lord Chief Justice, well known to be the confidant of our greatest and most respected astrologer. They were less keen to lend to the associate of a discredited old man who had just been embarrassingly shown up by a boy still a month or two shy of his thirteenth birthday." He shrugged. "Damaged goods, you see. It matters little to the elite that he was playing dirty, everyone does that, but no one wants to deal with a politician who cannot even control his own schemes or gets caught by the very rumors he started. It appears that his reputation for cunning was all that my former master had to keep his 'friends' loyal. They called in their debts, and the receivers . . . collected. They caught him in the small hours. He tried to sneak back into his house, and the receivers were waiting for him."

"So they let you off?" Mark asked.

Snutworth shook his head.

"Not quite. But fortunately the law has an interesting feature. Prendergast has no living relatives, so on his imprisonment he becomes the property of the Directory. His possessions were sent to cover his debts, and what remained, little of any value, was divided among his servants." Snutworth gave a strange smile. "In the eyes of the law, we were his only children." He sighed. "Unfortunately, the fine for damaging that birdcage and attempted theft of those rare doves swallowed everything I inherited, apart from this cane." Snutworth tapped it on the ground thoughtfully. "I should be grateful that they didn't connect me with the sudden appearance of a rat in the baker's prize loaf, or notice me fiddling with the workings of the clock tower. Otherwise I might have lost the very clothes I wear."

"Snutworth, I . . ." Mark felt a burning guilt settle in his stomach. "I didn't mean for you to lose everything . . . If it hadn't been for me—"

"Nonsense!" Snutworth interrupted airily. "Prendergast would never have achieved his ambition. Lord Ruthven has seen off better attempts on his title than this. And, in any case, to reveal to future associates that I assisted, in some small way, in the rise of one of our city's brightest stars will be payment enough."

"Brightest stars . . ." Mark repeated.

Snutworth smiled.

"But of course. I spent the night in prison, yet even in there I heard the news. It was a plan of genius, Mr. Mark, to have such a backup as Signora Sozinho; a moment of foresight greater than any I could conceive . . ."

"Um, well . . . not all that great . . ." Mark mumbled. "But are people impressed?"

"Mr. Mark, there is not a person in Agora who would not see it as an honor to have their fortune read by you today. You have given them the most accurate Agora Day predictions they have ever heard. They are calling you a marvel, a prodigy, a matchless seer!" Snutworth drew back with a smile. "They have also noted that you have the favor of Lord Ruthven, which for as long as it lasts may be the most astounding triumph of all."

Mark's head was spinning as he tried to take everything in.

"But the Count — "

"The Count has disappeared," Snutworth interrupted, "and if he's wise he'll stay that way. All people value their reputation, but for an astrologer . . . it is everything, all that separates him from a madman." Snutworth frowned. "The Count staked his entire reputation on besting Lord Ruthven. It seems that his and Prendergast's agents had been defaming you in the upper circles of society for weeks, to distance themselves from your failure, so any possible benefit he could have gained from your being his apprentice has been squandered." Snutworth thoughtfully polished the head of his cane with his sleeve. "Do not waste any sympathy on the Count, Mr. Mark. He played a dangerous political game and lost. I wouldn't be at all surprised if he was found to have been involved in Prendergast's crimes."

"But he never left the tower!" Mark said, amazed to find himself defending the old tyrant.

Snutworth shook his head. "That would have been no barrier. Besides, I never said that he *was* part of the crimes, but that may not prevent him being found guilty." He shrugged. "Making an enemy of the Lord Chief Justice can have that effect, especially if you are no longer quite the figure of respect you once were."

"Snutworth . . . don't be so . . ."

Mark struggled with his feelings. Of course the Count had been prepared to sacrifice *him* without a second thought. But he was over eighty; he wouldn't last a day on the streets.

"Cynical?" Snutworth suggested. He leaned forward earnestly. "Mr. Mark, we must accept realities. Try to play another game and you'll be trampled underfoot, which, considering the vast possibilities open to you now, would be such a waste."

Mark met Snutworth's gaze, not quite sure what he meant. Then, slowly, some things that the servant had said began to click into place.

"Snutworth . . . did Count Stelli have any other family . . . apart from Dr. Theophilus?"

"All dead, Mr. Mark. And the doctor was disowned months ago, all ties officially severed." Snutworth smiled. "And you know full well that he didn't keep any other servants. The receivers will hunt for the Count, but if he has disappeared he too will be declared a nonperson. In the eyes of the law, dead." Snutworth looked up and around at the entrance hall. "Its upkeep may be a little expensive, but I'm sure your readings will more than cover that."

"It's . . . mine?" Mark said, his mouth gaping. "But surely Dr. Theophilus—"

"The law would require him to trade for it—he's a little old for title gifts. A disowned grandson has no more right to inherit than a passing debtor," Snutworth said simply. "Besides, I believe he has a practice already."

"It's still his family home. He should have something out of it, at least the medical equipment . . ." Mark said, but less forcefully. He was beginning to warm to the idea of staying here as the owner of the tower.

"You've earned this, Mr. Mark." Snutworth looked him in the eye. "Do you want to be at the mercy of others for the rest of your life? Would you give away everything that is yours?"

Mark frowned and opened his mouth. Then he closed it again. He did not need to answer that.

"And now, if you will excuse me." Snutworth rose, leaning stiffly on the cane. "I won't take up any more of your time."

"Wait!" Mark said, hurriedly rising also. "Stay a bit longer. If it hadn't been for your plan—"

"You are very kind, Mr. Mark, but I cannot afford to delay," Snutworth said as he adjusted his hat. "I am unemployed and have little to trade for my lodgings. I must find a new master without delay." He put his hand on the door. "Although I fear that the desire for professional assistance is not as popular as it once was."

"Snutworth," Mark said, taking hold of the man's sleeve, "look . . . I've got no idea how much I've inherited. I couldn't offer as much as Mr. Prendergast, at least at first. But, if you're interested . . ." Mark took a deep breath. "You understand this city. I still don't. Not like you do. Would you consider . . ." Mark paused, wishing that Snutworth would interrupt, as he had every other time. But he kept looking back, waiting, and eventually Mark had to finish the sentence himself: ". . . working for me?"

There was a long pause. Mark was sure that Snutworth was insulted, that he would stalk away and leave him alone. Instead, eventually, Snutworth's face broke into a smile and he bowed low.

"It would be an honor, sir."

It was the first contract that Mark had ever written himself. He blotted it three times, but in the end it was finished. He stamped his starfish into the wax, and it was joined a moment later by an outstretched hand, the symbol of a servant. It felt strange to Mark as Snutworth had to be nearing forty summers, yet as they shook hands up in the Observatory, Mark felt a strange thrill of partnership. Even though Snutworth was a head taller, he could look him in the eye as an equal. Mark was the master, but Snutworth could be his guide, his protector.

Snutworth would never have sold him.

"Now, sir, to business," Snutworth said briskly, as he folded the contract. "We had better wait until the Count is officially declared a nonperson before we show that to the receivers. In the meantime, however, I think we should set up a few more public prophecies, make use of recent publicity. A little more vague than last time, perhaps. We don't want to have to 'help' them again. Then, of course, there's the matter of expanding your interests. Best not to put all of your wealth in one area, too unstable. I would recommend trading some of your new possessions for influence in other commodities." Snutworth smiled. "Fish, perhaps. Then, of course, there's — "

"Just . . . just wait a moment," Mark said, collapsing back into the Count's — no, into *his* chair. "It's a lot to take in. Yesterday I was just an apprentice."

"I can see it now," Snutworth said, stretching out his hands. "Every newspaper will carry it: 'Apprentice's meteoric rise.'" He laughed. "Or something like that. Perhaps you can hire Mr. Laudate to do your publicity. He certainly seemed inclined to help you."

"Uh . . ." Mark clutched his head, the pounding in his temples reminding him that he hadn't slept for at least twenty-four hours.

He felt Snutworth put something into his hand and, looking up, saw a tiny bottle filled with sea-green liquid. There was something scratched on the side: *Calm*.

"What's this?" Mark asked, squinting at it.

"Something useful," Snutworth said, kneeling beside him. "Pure emotion, distilled and prepared for use. Always keep a little on me. An old friend of mine is in the business. It's rather helpful for moments of stress."

Mark looked at the bottle, which was no bigger than his smallest finger. It seemed so simple, so convenient. Perhaps too simple.

"No thanks," he said, pushing it away. "I think I just need to sleep."

"As you wish, sir," Snutworth said, returning the bottle to his pockets. "Maybe another time. If you wish to retire, I shall draw up some suggestions for your first acquisitions."

"Don't you ever sleep, Snutworth?"

"Not when my master's business is calling." Snutworth straightened up, his eyes bright. "Not when the future has so much potential."

Mark looked at his new assistant framed in the light streaming through from the dawning sun. For the first time, he saw the Observatory in daylight — the velvet curtains tied back, the brass telescope gleaming. And through the windows he saw a crowd, already gathered at the base of the tower, waiting for admittance.

"I'll tell them to come back this afternoon, sir," Snutworth said.

But Mark was barely listening as he nodded. In his mind, he was already dreaming. Dreaming of the new life that now stretched out before him. A year ago, he had been worth less than the clothes he stood up in. Now he had wealth, respect, even some influence and power.

He could do anything.

And he would.

CHAPTER TWELVE

The Idea

IT WAS A WEEK before the receivers came.

Lily had been waiting for them every day, wondering whether they would give her any warning or just barge in with a warrant for her arrest. She could not tell, since she did not know if what she was doing was illegal. So when she heard that authoritative rap on the door, the first thing she felt was relief.

She caught Benedicta's eye across the room, where the red-headed girl was gathering up the blankets that they had laid across the old pews. She gave a look of encouragement, anxiously smoothing down the stained apron that she had thrown on over her dress, another of Signora Sozinho's castoffs, which was both a little too large and too grand for her work, despite its age. Lily readied herself and tried to calm her mind. She had to look businesslike, to act as old as she could. The rap came again, louder and more insistent. Lily drew herself up to her full height and made her way over to the door.

No sooner was it open than an official-looking document, sealed with the stamp of the Directory, a furled scroll, was thrust into her face. As she stepped back to read the warrant, she examined the man who was presenting it, a craggy-faced receiver wearing the shining silver brocade of an inspector. His expression was encouraging: disapproving but not immediately hostile. Certainly not as hostile as that of the younger sergeant behind him, who was peering through the doorway with clear disgust, his nose wrinkling as though he thought them diseased.

"On the authority of the Directory of Receipts," the inspector intoned, sounding as if he had repeated these words a thousand times before, "we are to investigate these premises on suspicion of illegal actions. You have no right to refuse and — "

"Certainly, sirs," Lily interrupted. "Will you come in?"

Lily felt a ripple of amusement as the inspector was stopped in his tracks. Evidently he was not used to cooperation. Recovering himself, he nodded briskly and entered, followed by his sergeant.

"Can we get you anything?" Lily said sweetly.

"Or perhaps take your coats and hats?" Benedicta added, coming forward with a smile, plucking at the sergeant's midnight-blue sleeve.

The sergeant recoiled in alarm. "Is this some kind of trick?" he said, his eyes narrowing. "Attempting to steal from a receiver is punishable by — "

"No, thank you," the inspector interrupted firmly, flashing a look of annoyance at his fellow receiver. "Sergeant Pauldron, remember that these young ladies are not currently accused of anything. And I'm sure there is no risk of them overpowering you."

Lily wasn't sure, but she thought she detected a flicker of a smile in the corner of the inspector's mouth. Internally, she also felt a twinge of pleasure at being referred to as a "lady." She had been a legal adult since she turned twelve, but so far few people, other than Theo, had treated her as anything more than an attention-seeking child. The good feeling was soon gone, however, as the inspector's eyes swept over the interior of the temple.

Lily followed where he looked. They hadn't added much. There were still the tables which Theo had set up for examinations, and a few more oil lamps had been added, as trying to operate under the light that shone through high stained-glass windows was impossible. Meanwhile, Lily noticed that the sergeant was busy inspecting the font at the other side of the room. He gave a sniff and jerked back in surprise. Despite herself, Lily had to smother a laugh at his expression of surprise.

"Medical alcohol, Sergeant," she explained. "Very important for cleaning wounds. I can show you the receipt for it if you want to check."

The sergeant scowled and began to run his hands along the pews. Lily exchanged a look with Benedicta, who had returned to folding blankets, and then turned her attention back to the inspector. He was quite different from his sergeant. He searched only with his eyes, but Lily was sure that he noticed far more things. Indeed, it was he who came upon the most recent addition.

"I don't know how many patients you have, Miss Lilith," he said, looking into one corner, "but it must be many. That's a large cooking pot you have there."

"That's for a very special kind of patient," Lily said quietly, meeting his gaze, preparing herself for the argument she had rehearsed long into the night. "It is designed to cure those whose only disease is hunger."

"Something of a backward step, isn't it?" the inspector remarked. "A bright girl, apprentice to a doctor, cooking food for debtors? My wife certainly wouldn't stand for it. She's a receiver too."

"If you have a skill, you use it," Lily said simply. "Show me someone willing and able and I'll be happy to pass the job on to them."

The inspector nodded, seeming satisfied with her answer.

"Pauldron!" he called out.

The sergeant put down an old incense burner, which he had been examining with great suspicion, and marched forward.

"Sir?"

"Take notes on this conversation."

Pauldron reached into the pocket of his coat and withdrew some sheets of paper and a stick of charcoal. He poised the charcoal, ready to write. The inspector cleared his throat.

"Investigation into . . ." He paused, frowning. "What do you call this place again?"

"An almshouse," Lily said clearly. "A-L-M-S," she added, looking at the sergeant's paper, "not weapons."

"Investigation into the Temple Street Almshouse, Inspector Greaves and Sergeant Pauldron of the receivers presiding." The inspector pursed his lips. "Miss Lilith, this building seems to have seen some strange businesses. It looks like a temple to me, a fad from a couple of cycles ago, as I recall. I believe they were selling something called 'enlightenment and spirituality' . . ." The inspector rolled the words around his mouth as if they had a peculiar taste and then shrugged. "It never quite caught on. I see from the reports that we closed it down in the end."

"Complaints of being robbed, sir," Pauldron added with a sniff. "Some of the customers felt no different, even after multiple purchases."

"Indeed," Greaves concurred. "Records indicate that this building was left abandoned until the middle of last year, when it was taken over as a medical practice by a certain Dr. Theophilus."

He frowned. "Records also state that he owns part of it and that he is renting the rest of the property from Miss Devine." The inspector looked around the room thoughtfully. "In other words, he is legally responsible for whatever happens under this roof. I hope he's not avoiding questioning."

"No, sir, the doctor is visiting a patient," Lily lied.

That is what he had told her, but she knew him better than that. He had barely been in the practice since he had heard that his grandfather had disappeared. It had been nearly three weeks since Agora Day, but still every day he went out and every night he came back looking paler than ever. If he kept up these searches in the slums it would only be a matter of time before he caught one of the new diseases. Diseases that made the gray plague look like a mild cough.

"Anyway," the inspector continued, ignoring Lily's look of concern, "you are his apprentice?"

"Yes, sir."

"That is unusual in itself. Your records do not indicate any form of medical training. Do you come from a background in healing?"

Lily paused briefly before replying, her head filling again with what she had discovered at the orphanage, or rather what she had not discovered.

"No, sir," Lily said quietly, all too aware that she could be wrong. A name embroidered on a strip of fine cloth and a bag of gemstones were her only link to her past. Perhaps her parents had been doctors and had caught the gray plague, like so many others—it might explain how they could afford gems, but not to keep their daughter.

"And the other girl?" the inspector continued, unaware of Lily's thoughts.

"I'm just an assistant," Benedicta called over cheerfully. "I lost my old job when my former mistress no longer needed me."

"Just the two of you?" the inspector asked incredulously.

"There's more coming," Benedicta continued, smoothing out a sheet. "My brother and sister are going to help us out with spreading the word. They're good at that."

"Benedicta has come to work for the Almshouse," Lily explained. "The doctor has given his consent."

"Consent to what?" Pauldron muttered, shuffling his notes. "You still have not admitted what exactly it is that this Almshouse does."

"That may be because we haven't asked her yet, Sergeant," the inspector said, deadpan. He turned to Lily and raised his eyebrows. He didn't need to ask the question.

"The Almshouse isn't a business, Inspector Greaves." Lily waved her hands as she tried to explain, although the truth was she sometimes barely understood it herself. "It's . . . an idea. A concept . . ."

"A flophouse for debtors and damaged goods," the sergeant remarked, distastefully picking at a heap of bedding as Benedicta folded it.

"Among other things," Lily replied, keeping her voice level. "We feed those who have nothing to trade for food, and give some of them a place to sleep and wash under a roof. The doctor has agreed to treat some of those who are ill—they're sleeping down in the cellar at the moment."

"Sounds as if you are encouraging people to become debtors, Miss Lilith," the inspector said jovially, but with a hint of steel.

"We're planning to ask those who can to make food," Lily hurried on, trying to put forward the simple parts of her plan first, "and find work for the healthy, to help them to return to their own lives."

"Maybe even train them in new skills,' Benedicta added. "You'd be amazed how many people can't read, not even contracts."

The inspector furrowed his brow.

"Unusual, and probably pointless, but it's not our business to stop people from enterprise," he murmured, stroking his chin. "There is just one thing. Why haven't we received any contracts from this? I hear there was a crowd last night and many more expected. There must be many for us to collect."

Lily took a deep breath. This was going to be the hardest part to explain.

"There aren't any contracts."

The sergeant's charcoal stopped moving. The silence was deafening.

The inspector leaned forward. "No contracts?" he asked. "Then how can you make sure that these debtors give you what they owe for your services?"

"We don't ask for anything in return, sir," Lily said in a still, firm voice. "We give our food, our skills, without reward."

This time even the inspector looked shaken. He breathed in as if to speak, but seemed to think better of it. Sergeant Pauldron, however, was not so quiet. He threw his notes to the floor.

"Didn't I tell you, sir?" he said, red with anger. "I said that was what they were doing! Undermining the very bedrock on which Agora is founded—"

"Thank you, Sergeant," the inspector said hurriedly, but this time Pauldron was not to be silenced.

"You think it will stop here, sir?" he continued, growing louder. "Once it gets around that you can be a debtor and still be fed for free, who will want to work or trade or . . ."

"That is enough!" The inspector barely increased the volume of his voice, but suddenly it seemed to resonate within the temple.

Sergeant Pauldron was instantly quiet. The inspector frowned.

"You are becoming overagitated again, Pauldron. Take some time off and I'll meet you back at the barracks this afternoon. I shall finish here."

The sergeant looked as if he was about to protest, but the inspector turned away. Scowling, Pauldron made a stiff bow and opened the door. As he left, he shook his feet, as though the very dust on the floor was polluted.

After the sergeant left, Inspector Greaves sat and closed his eyes for a moment. When he opened them, Lily saw that his composure had returned.

"Sergeant Pauldron is a young man, very passionate about his work and about our glorious city," he began, reaching down to one side to pick up the notes. "However, he makes a good point. Our system is based on trade. Without it we grind to a halt. It makes this place suspicious. Highly suspicious."

Lily caught Benedicta's eye and saw her own nervousness reflected there. If the receivers wanted to close them down, they could, and they wouldn't even have to compensate them, because technically nothing would be lost.

"Just answer me one thing, Miss Lilith," the inspector continued. "Is it your food that feeds these hundreds? Is it your possessions alone that will be split among thousands of debtors?"

Hurriedly, Lily pulled a sealed contract out of her apron pocket and handed it to the inspector.

"Signor and Signora Sozinho have agreed to supply us regularly with art objects to trade for food and blankets. They have asked for nothing more than to know that they are helping others, as we helped them. They are our first patrons, and our only ones, at the moment. We are trying to encourage others to do the same."

Lily watched as the inspector read the contract, his eyes lingering over the seal of the Sozinhos, which was covered in musical notes. He finished and rolled it up.

"May I speak bluntly, Miss Lilith?" he asked.

Lily looked at the inspector. There was a curious gleam in his eyes, as though he was taking apart every word she said, testing her to see if she was up to the job she had set herself. For a moment, she wondered what the right answer was. And then, as if they were sharing a secret joke, she understood. What she said did not matter. He wanted to see if she would be confident enough to give an answer of her own.

"You're going to anyway," she said, raising an eyebrow, "so why should I say no?"

The inspector gave a grunt of satisfaction.

"Very true. Then let me say this. If you think that this will do any good, then you have no idea of the number of debtors, of hopeless wretches, in this city." The inspector rose, his tone reasonable but firm. "You will run yourselves into the ground with this and pour your little wealth into it until you are debtors yourself. If you think you can make something out of nothing you are fools, all of you, arrogant fools." He paused, his gaze taking in the whole of the temple, his eyes sparkling in the colored light streaming through the stained-glass windows. "However, the last time I looked there was no law against foolishness." He smiled, but his eyes were serious. "Take records of everything and forward them to me; I shall follow this case personally. My advice to you is that you stop immediately. I know very well that you won't take it. Good morning, Miss Lilith."

The inspector bowed, took one final look around and left, closing the door softly behind him.

Lily and Benedicta looked at each other in silence. Then Lily collapsed backward onto a pew, suddenly exhausted, and Benedicta burst out laughing.

Lily frowned. "It didn't seem very funny to me," she said.

"Who cares what he said?" Benedicta grinned. "He wasn't ever going to be thrilled about it, was he? The point is, they're not going to stop you!"

"Us, Benedicta," Lily said, a tired smile growing on her own face.

Never mind that in the back of her mind an unpleasant thought was nagging that Inspector Greaves might be right; Benedicta's enthusiasm was infectious.

"Nice of you to say, Lily, but it was your idea," Benedicta said dreamily. "I've never seen the Signora so happy. And I know we're going to make a difference, you, me, my brother and sister, if they ever turn up . . . I just know it! They're experts at praising and advertising. You'll see. Give them a week and we'll have rich patrons desperate to be part of this!"

Lily shook her head, amazed.

"That's not going to happen, Ben," she said. "Think about it — this place . . . It's completely different from anything they've ever seen. We'll be lucky if we get any more patrons at all for a long time. We've put everything we've got into this. If it fails — "

"Then it fails," Benedicta said quietly, her face more serious, "and if that happens we'll manage." She bit her lip. "If you don't laugh, then all you can do is — "

There was another knock on the door. Benedicta's eyes instantly began to shine again and the smile returned as if it had never been away.

"That's them!" she said as she hurried across the room. "I just know you'll like them, Lily. They'll be just what we need . . ." She opened the door and jumped with excitement. "Gloria! Laud! Come in and meet Lily."

As Lily watched, a familiar young woman entered the temple. Her curly red hair reached almost to her waist, and she seemed more pale and thin than ever, but there was no mistaking the figure she had seen flitting around Miss Devine's shop, or the delight with which she embraced her sister.

The young man who followed a moment later was new to her, but he too had a distinctive mane of red hair. He frowned as he looked around the temple, walking straight past Lily as she offered her hand.

"Needs work, don't you think, Gloria?"

"Laud!" the pale sister scolded him. "Don't start, not in front of—"

"I'm not saying it's a hopeless case," Laud continued, wiping one of his gloved fingers along the pews. He stared at it critically, before brushing it off on the lapel of his elegantly cut fawn jacket. "But I do think we'll have to play up the desperation angle, make it clear that this is positively the last hope and that no one else would ever come here . . ."

"Laud," Benedicta said quickly, "let me introduce Lily. She's the organizer," she added, placing particular stress on the last words.

Laud turned to look at Lily and hesitated, just for an instant, before shaking her hand briskly. Although he seemed to be only a few years older than her, Lily felt far younger under his critical gaze than she had just a few minutes before with the inspector.

Laud turned away and sniffed sharply.

"The smell could be a problem. Potential patrons may want to visit, and short of insisting that every debtor who enters find a puddle to wash in first . . ." He noticed something in the corner and stalked over to inspect. "Are these incense burners? They might just do the job."

"Ben's told us all about you, Miss Lily," Gloria said, taking Lily's hand with considerably more enthusiasm. "An astounding notion and one from which we may all reap great rewards."

"I really hope that these are *animal* droppings in this corner," Laud muttered.

Gloria twisted a strand of hair around her finger and continued as if she had not heard her brother.

"We won't be able to work on it full-time, since we're not charging our usual rate."

Benedicta gave Gloria a hard look, and her older sister hastily added, "In fact, we're not charging anything."

"For the moment," Laud added, in a tone that would brook no argument. "Benedicta has assured us that it is only a temporary measure, until you have enough donations. Then we shall draw up our contracts." He looked around the temple, its scruffy grandeur picked out by the multicolored light of the stained-glass windows. He raised one eyebrow. "Still . . . definite possibilities. It certainly has atmosphere." He shrugged. "That sort of thing appeals to those with more possessions than sense. We'll need to start spreading word of this throughout the grander parts of the city, of course. You won't find many willing to part with anything around here . . . Any other floors?"

It seemed that Benedicta was not the only one in her family to ask sudden, unexpected questions. Lily gave a stiff nod.

"There's a cellar, where the doctor takes his worst patients," she said, "and an open roof."

Lily found that her arms were very tightly crossed. Laud looked around for a moment, then located the stairs.

"Better look the whole place over," he murmured. "Perhaps if we sold patronage as a shortcut to moral worth . . . That would certainly get some of the more disreputable dealers interested, and they usually have wealth to spare . . ."

And, still thinking aloud, Laud ascended the stairs and vanished from view.

Lily felt herself relax a little and saw Benedicta do the same. Gloria gave Lily an embarrassed smile.

"He's very good at what he does," she explained, "but he tends to get wrapped up in his work. He always has."

"So I noticed," Lily said, trying to sound unconcerned. Internally, however, she couldn't help feeling that her idea, her dream, had just been sullied in a way that the receivers could never have managed.

Something must have shown in her face because Gloria continued, "I know he seems . . . a bit sharp, but — "

Lily held up a hand to stop her, trying to keep a polite expression.

"I'm sorry . . . I appreciate your help, but if you're about to tell me that your brother isn't really like that when you get to know him . . ."

"Oh no," Gloria said, with a smile, "when you get to know him he's even worse." Her smile faded. "But that doesn't mean he doesn't do his best. It doesn't mean we don't believe."

Benedicta nodded, laying a hand on Lily's arm.

"It's just the way it is, Lily. You need patrons and Laud knows how to attract them."

Lily bridled and shook Benedicta off.

"I'm not sure I want his sort of patron," she said tightly. "This isn't about 'selling virtue,' it's about charity. Even the receivers understood that."

Gloria gave a strained look, somewhere between a smile and a wince.

"Yes, Miss Lily . . . but they probably don't want it to succeed."

There was an uncomfortable pause, then Lily walked away.

Behind her, she was aware that Gloria and Benedicta were fiddling with the old brass incense burners in the corner, but right now she wasn't interested. Her insides were clenched like a fist. After everything she had done to get this Almshouse started, she wasn't going to let it be ruined by some patronizing advertiser. Determined to speak with Laud out of the hearing of his sisters, she began to climb the stairs to the roof.

Lily found him leaning on the brick parapet that surrounded the terrace. In the daylight, it looked even less grand than it sounded, a few square yards of roof hemmed in with walls, every inch of floor space covered with drying herbs. She picked her way across the floor until she was standing nearby.

"Not a good view," Laud said, without turning around. "I had thought perhaps a woodcut of the premises . . . It might be best if the patrons never visit at all."

"Wouldn't they prefer to see who they're helping?" Lily said, her irritation rising.

"To see them, possibly. Not to smell them. The wealthy are squeamish like that. The Almshouse has to be built in their imagination."

"I thought you were supposed to be good at praising things?" she said sarcastically.

"Only when I'm working, Miss Lily," he replied, turning around. "Would you prefer me to treat you as a buyer rather than the proprietor? I hear from Benedicta that you appreciate honesty."

"Do you lie to all the buyers?" Lily asked, meeting his gaze firmly.

Laud's look was intense, but not hostile.

"It helps," he admitted. "When they lie to themselves so often, truth is not really welcomed."

"Truth is what this is about, Mr. Laud," Lily said frostily. "This whole place is about facing reality."

Laud seemed to consider this, his eyes never leaving her face. His next words, when they did come, surprised her.

"How old are you, Miss Lily?"

"I've lived through thirteen summers," Lily replied cautiously.

"A little old for believing in ideas like absolute truth, don't you think?" Laud said, his tone oddly strained. "People want nothing to do with anything that disturbing. Still, if I don't live up to your standards, if I'm not allowed to play with your toys . . ."

Lily choked back her response, refusing to let herself rise to the bait. It would be so easy to throw him out: She had the power, she was the one hiring him, fee or no fee. But that would turn her into the little girl he so obviously saw her as, and she would not be caught that easily. Instead, she raised an eyebrow.

"How old are *you*, Mr. Laud?" she said.

Laud shrugged. "Seventeen."

"A little young to be quite so bitter, don't you think?" Lily said.

There was a long pause. Something in Laud's eyes seemed to darken, as though she had caught a glimpse of pain within. And then, in a sudden, percussive bark, he laughed.

"Fine, Miss Lily, we'll try it your way," he said, a hint of amusement still on his face. "Perhaps truth is about to receive a boost in value."

He held out his hand. Lily looked at it for a moment and then, relaxing, she shook it. Laud seemed pleased.

"Anyway," he said, in a friendlier tone, "I don't think there was ever much chance of my leaving. Once Ben sets her mind on something . . ." He shook his head and smiled fondly. "She has a lot of faith in you."

"I won't let her down," Lily said firmly.

As they stood there, facing each other, Lily became aware of a new scent in the air—a heavy, rich odor, far stronger than the faded whiff that had greeted her when she first entered the temple. Laud nodded, his face businesslike once again.

"Seems as if my sisters have the incense burning," he said thoughtfully. "Perhaps hanging one of the burners outside the door might attract some attention . . . Yes, that should certainly tell people that you've arrived."

But Lily was barely listening. Instead she watched as a tiny curl of smoke from the incense rose up the stairwell and dissipated into the air, its rich scent flowing out over the city. And although to Laud she only replied with a similar nod, inside she felt her heart leap in her chest.

She had begun.

INTERLUDE TWO

THE PEN SCRATCHES as it moves along the paper. The hand holding it is dry and withered, but does not falter.

"And so, our suspicions are proven correct, Miss Rita. Their rise has begun."

"Yes, sir."

Her hands are dark. Her nails are painted, but chipped. They dig into the sheaf of papers she holds to her chest.

"Already they flock to them," he says. "The highest in society and those who are left behind."

The pen is dipped into the inkpot without a splash. The ancient hands draw forth another sheet of paper.

"I have been thinking, Miss Rita, on the subject of fate."

Miss Rita's hands tense on the papers she holds.

"Fate, sir?"

"Our futures are tied to the scales of life, Miss Rita. A single grain of sand can tip the balance in our favor or against." The Director pauses, pressing an iron signet ring down into a blob of dark crimson wax. "One grain of sand, one thought or deed, can raise us up or plunge us into the depths." He places the last document to one side and puts the tips of his fingers together. "But we are apt to forget sometimes that it then takes only two grains of sand on the other side to tip our world upside down."

Miss Rita picks up the last document and turns away from the desk.

"They will not come to harm, Miss Rita."

The secretary freezes.

"But they will be in danger?"

"If there is a world without danger, Miss Rita, then it lies beyond our knowledge. But yes, they are in more danger than most. Particularly from those who believe that they are the two predicted by the Midnight Charter."

Miss Rita's hands clench so tightly that the knuckles turn white.

"Are they, sir?"

"I am certain. We have been wrong in the past, but now the final date approaches and it seems . . . fitting that they should be children. For the sake of the great Libran project, they must fulfill their role, must be watched but not influenced by the Directory. Not until the moment is right. The Charter demands it."

"But is the Charter right?" the secretary whispers.

There is silence.

"The Charter, Miss Rita, is always right. By definition. That is all."

"Yes. Thank you, sir."

The tap of Miss Rita's shoes fades away into the distance. The door at the far end of the room closes.

It is some time before the Director takes up his pen again, and this time when he writes he splashes ink as he dips his pen. As if his fingers are suddenly tense.

CHAPTER THIRTEEN

The Dance

"**M**R. MARK,** you look spectacular!"

Mark was not quite so sure. His new dress coat, so covered in golden thread that it almost shone, certainly caught the eye. But it had been measured for him months before and it was already too short, not to mention hot on this heavy summer's evening, on top of the starched shirt and embroidered vest. He tugged in vain at the scarlet cravat around his neck that seemed determined to strangle him. The tricornered hat perched neatly enough on the top of his head, but he wasn't looking forward to adjusting it all evening as it slipped down. He was glad now that he had kept his hair short—the fashion for men was to wear it long and tie it back with dark ribbon, as Laud did on formal occasions—but he didn't want it lashing his eyes. The mask, at least, was a simple, white eye mask—he had been worried that he would need to balance a mass of sequins and feathers on his nose until midnight. Still, he thought, looking at himself in the proffered mirror, he certainly couldn't be mistaken for just anyone.

Gloria swam into view, smoothing down tiny creases and flicking invisible fluff from his sleeves. Ever since Mark had hired her and her brother as his publicists, soon after his rise, she seemed to have adopted him. Laud had mentioned that she had cared for him and their sister, Benedicta, when they were younger, and Mark had certainly never felt more like a child than when Gloria was flitting around him. She seemed more fidgety than ever tonight, although it would have been hard for most people to notice. It was only because he had been around her for months now that he could see the telltale signs: the anxious tugging at the sleeves of her second-hand dress, the nervous flicker of the eyes.

"Have the guests arrived, Gloria?" Mark asked, keeping all apprehension out of his voice. He had become better at that lately. He had needed to.

"Many of them, Mr. Mark," Gloria said, peering out through a gap in the canvas of the marquee. "But not the most important ones yet. Remember, Laud suggested . . ."

"Not to make an entrance until I can be seen by the best people, yes, Gloria, I remember." Mark twisted a starfish-shaped button on his sleeve. "Let me see."

"Of course, sir." Gloria shifted to one side, and Mark put his eye to the gap.

Through it, crouching in the private marquee, he looked out onto a part of Agora that still made him gasp whenever he saw it. Before him, the gardens of the Leo District stretched out: rows of ornamental trees and flowers, elaborate trellises, and elegant sculpture. Beyond, beneath the gray mass of the city walls, he could see the agricultural fields of the neighboring Cancer District, where small fields of wheat and corn, ripening in the late summer heat, rippled in the breeze. The Leo District was called the soul of Agora, and

Mark had rented its most beautiful garden, the very center of the district, to hold his ball.

It had not been cheap. Mark still remembered wincing as he sealed the contract with the garden's keeper, but this was too good an opportunity to ignore. The chance to hold a ball in the Leo gardens, and in the month of Leo too — the symbolism alone oozed with success. As Snutworth had said, it was an investment worth making. A better investment than this jacket, Mark thought, as he felt the sleeves begin to creep up his arms again. His tailors were some of the best in the city, but they were not used to making clothes for their customers to grow into.

In the distance, he heard the voice of Laud, his customary tone of cynicism masked in grand, respectful formality, announcing the guests. It had been particularly difficult to hire both Gloria and Laud for the evening. They spent most of their time nowadays working for the Almshouse. Mark's heart sank as this thought reminded him, yet again, that another month had passed without him being able to visit Lily. Despite dozens of plans to meet up, they had not seen each other since Mark had begun his rise, nearly a year ago. There was just so much to do, he barely had time to write their weekly letters. Although, to be fair to himself, she sounded even busier and probably wouldn't have had the time to see him. Mark was just wondering if she had received his last letter, along with the invitation folded inside it, when Laud's latest announcement caught his attention.

"Ladies and gentlemen, may I announce the great Signor and Signora Sozinho, the angels of golden song, to bless our revels this evening."

Gloria smothered a laugh.

"Laud's in good form tonight," she said, adding mischievously, "I made a bet with Ben that he would get through more than fifty *greats* and thirty *goldens* before the end of the evening . . ."

Through the gap, the singers came into view, and Mark watched them mingle with the other guests. Masked and bewigged, covered in finery of every hue, the cream of Agora drifted around the garden in packs, stopping every now and then to take something from a silver platter. The first time he had been to one of these gatherings, Mark had wondered whether the really successful ever ate anything more than these tiny pieces of food. As one group of ladies passed the marquee, he recoiled from the power of their perfumes, trying to prevent anyone from hearing him cough.

"Sir . . ." Gloria began nervously. "I think I should go and see to the flowers, and the band will need to be briefed as to when to start the music. So if you don't need me . . ."

"Of course, Gloria," Mark said, reaching into his pocket. "Here, have a good time."

He slipped a tiny glass bottle into her hands, Miss Devine's finest. Her eyes lit up.

"Thank you, Mr. Mark. Always so considerate."

Discreetly, she retired to the far corner of the marquee, where Mark saw her pulling out the stopper and breathing in. When she returned, her eyes were shining.

"I just know this will be the best ball that Agora has ever seen, Mr. Mark!" she enthused, grabbing his hands. "Not even the skies can limit you! Not even the skies . . ."

With that, she pirouetted through the canvas flap and disappeared into the evening. Mark frowned, pacing nervously. He had to time this just right. He'd put a lot of his property into making the evening a success. He'd hosted a couple of dances before, of course, but nothing on this scale. If this worked out, Snutworth assured him, his influence would rise like never before — not just with his "astrology" but with all of the newer businesses. It had been Snutworth's idea to expand his interests beyond the stars, and success had followed success. By now, Mark had barely any idea of how many things he dealt in one way or another. But so much still rested on reputation — he couldn't afford to make a fool of himself.

He heard the sound of Laud clearing his throat and hurried back to the gap in the canvas.

"Will you welcome, please, Matron Angelina of the Future Workforce Trust."

Mark grimaced. He could hear the edge in Laud's voice this time, although hopefully no one else would. Ever since he had sat by, openmouthed, while Laud enthusiastically advertised a group of landlords, the very same ones who had nearly evicted him from his own house in payment for his rent, Mark had come to recognize when Laud was being sincere. It was usually when he was being scathing, and always behind closed doors. Mark was quite sure that, since his rise, Laud had thought up a few things to call him behind his back. Gloria said that this was just his way, a reaction to the constant stream of praise he had to come up with all day for his clients. But Count Stelli and Mr. Prendergast had been right about one thing: Laud was the best to be found. So when Mark could tell that he didn't like the person he was announcing, it signaled trouble.

Mark resumed his nervous pacing back and forth, pulling down his sleeves. He should be out there, directing the party. At the last one, just a couple of weeks ago, he had really been in good form. It had helped that Snutworth kept the older businessmen talking while Gloria directed the right people his way, but it wasn't as if everyone else didn't do it.

"Snutworth . . . what are you *doing* out there?" Mark muttered. He was twisting his fingers almost as badly as Gloria now.

Then a murmur passed through the crowd outside and he heard Laud, his voice oozing respect, call for silence.

"Ladies and gentlemen, it is my great honor and privilege this evening to introduce Agora's most respected lawyer. A man of judgment, honor and unimpeachable integrity . . . please welcome our Lord Chief Justice, Lord Ruthven."

Mark breathed a sigh of relief. Now his prize guest had arrived, he could make his own entrance. There had been rumors all day that Lord Ruthven wouldn't be coming. After all, the only reason half of Mark's guests had come was to meet the man who had the ear of the Director. Ever since Mark had inadvertently helped him to defeat Count Stelli, it was rumored that his political power had increased, and few doubted that to have him as a guest was a major achievement.

Nervously, Mark straightened his mask, plastered on a smile, and, trying to look ten years older than he was, and twenty more than he felt, strode out of the marquee.

"Lord Ruthven," he said, "how good of you to come to my gathering." He bowed slightly, just enough to show deference without being humbled. He'd practiced that movement for hours back at the tower, trying to get the inclination just right.

Lord Ruthven, resplendent in his robes of state and a sparkling mask that depicted the sun emerging from behind the moon, acknowledged the bow. Then, to Mark's delight, he returned it, and in everyone's sight.

"Not at all, Mr. Mark," Lord Ruthven replied warmly, "the pleasure is mine."

Mark straightened up. Was it time to press for a little more? To be seen starting a conversation? He cast a glance over to Lord Ruthven's right. Sure enough, Snutworth was there, unmasked, as was appropriate to a servant. He smiled, but gave a fractional shake of the head. Mark understood: Now was not the time.

"I hope to speak to you later, My Lord," Mark said, rushing a little with relief. "But for now — " he turned to nod to Laud — "let the dancing begin."

Mark waited until Lord Ruthven's party had drifted away,

toward the sound of stringed instruments being tuned, before sidling over to Snutworth.

"Enough?" he said.

Snutworth beamed.

"Perfect, sir. Naturally our work is far from over, but as an opening gambit . . . exquisite."

Mark relaxed, his formal poise dropped for a few blissful moments. He'd been doing this for months now and knew how to act among the wealthy: deferential, with just a hint that there might be more to him than met the eye. He'd put up with those who talked at him as if he had been in business for years, and learned not to recoil when some of them, usually the older women, chose to adopt him for the evening as if he were a brat of seven summers. He had to be all things to all people, but Lord Ruthven was the most important, and he did not want to waste this opportunity to be seen in his company.

"Can I stay out of it for a moment?" Mark asked. "I don't feel like mingling just yet. Those old ladies over there look like cheek pinchers to me . . ."

Snutworth laughed.

"I think you may leave it to Mr. Laudate and Miss Gloria to direct the proceedings for a while now. That is their field of expertise."

Mark looked over to where Laud was instructing the conductor of the string quartet, while bowing graciously to the guests who passed. Lord Ruthven's group received an extravagant sweep of the hat and a bow so low that Laud's nose nearly touched the floor.

"Isn't he going over the top?" Mark muttered, but Snutworth shook his head sagely.

"Do not assume that Lord Ruthven believes him anymore than Mr. Laudate means it. It is a game we must all play."

One of the servants came past with a silver platter. Mark didn't feel hungry, but Snutworth plucked off a couple of canapés and popped them into his mouth, crunching discreetly. Mark was too preoccupied with the crowd that had gathered around Lord Ruthven to even notice.

"Who are those people?" he said warily. "Laud didn't announce them."

"I believe they may be members of the Libran Society, sir," Snutworth ventured. "They have a tendency to turn up unannounced, particularly when Lord Ruthven makes an appearance."

"Again?" Mark said. "That's the second time this month they've appeared. I don't like it."

"They appear to be harmless, sir. A little secretive perhaps . . ."

"Secretive!" Mark muttered. "No one seems to know anything about them! Even the new head of the Astrologers' Guild goes quiet when I ask. Don't you remember Count Stelli talking about them? Telling Prendergast they were responsible for dreadful crimes — "

"With respect, sir," Snutworth said, cutting him off with unusual sharpness, "I would not have thought that you, of all people, would trust the words of the vanished Count."

Mark shivered. Thinking about the Count still made him uneasy. It wasn't that he was a threat. Not having been found, he had been officially declared dead months ago. He would have no right to reclaim his property now. It was more that, despite everything, Mark could not escape a lingering sense of guilt. However justified he may have been, he had still indirectly sent an old man fleeing from his only home.

"I know that," he continued awkwardly, "but those Librans still make me uneasy."

"The best guess of my associates," Snutworth said, "is that they are dealers in secrets. That would certainly explain their expertise in concealing their own. Then again, a surprising number of known members are grain merchants, and there can hardly be too many wheat-based conspiracies . . ."

"Look, Snutworth," Mark said, lowering his voice. "Maybe you should put a mask on so you can get nearer to him, see if you can overhear anything."

"Mr. Mark," Snutworth said, raising an eyebrow, "far be it from me to correct you, but masks here are nothing to do with hiding one's identity. Trust me, I shall be far more invisible without one." He smiled. "Meanwhile, your guests await you. I think they expect you to lead the dance."

In the distance, the band began to play a gavotte.

Mark winced.

The dance began.

It was the same as always. Mark shuffled along to the steps, trying to look poised. There was nothing complicated about the dance itself. It seemed to him to be entirely made up of walking in time and trying not to bump into people, and by now he barely paid attention to his feet. His attention was drawn to faces. To the parade of leering, grinning masks that spiraled around him, amidst the sea of color, and the muffled words and thoughts that lurked behind. With practiced ease he nodded to one, laughed politely at a joke, invited an older lady to dance with a gracious bow. Even so, he often felt like their pet. He was now nearly as tall as the grander businessmen, but he couldn't shake the feeling that he was being cast in the role of the jester, the mascot, the little boy playing at business.

Still, let them think it, he mused, as he took the hands of a plump, elderly woman whose fortune lay in flowers and who liberally displayed her wares in her wig. He glanced across the garden. Over by the marquee he saw a coterie of old astrologers picking at his food. He still received twice the number of requests for personal readings than any of them did and, unlike Count Stelli, he was only too pleased to oblige. It was the source of all his success, all his power.

When he thought about it now, it seemed so obvious, so simple, but it had taken Snutworth to explain it to him at first. He had shown Mark how the wealthy businesses lived in constant fear of uncertainty, of shifts in the never-ending market. That was the danger of contracts: No matter how valuable you thought your wares, they were never worth any more or less than what you were willing, or able, to trade them for. One moment a merchant could be on top of the world, and then a single dissatisfied customer, or smear on his reputation, could make his precious wares fall from grace, changing hands for a pittance. In an attempt to protect their friends from misfortune, the wealthy formed guilds and business consortia, but everyone knew, no matter how powerful they were, that tomorrow could bring disaster.

That was where Mark came in. People wanted security, they wanted to be able to predict what the future would hold, and trade only with those on whom fortune would smile. And if the stars happened to point customers in their direction, lightly veiled in mystical language of course, they were usually very grateful. The kind of gratitude that had to be kept in a vault.

At first, Mark had relied on Snutworth's guidance to suggest whom to support, but he had soon learned to read the web of alliances that held the city together. It was no different from this dance — bowing to some, passing by others, and being careful not to tread on the toes of anyone who could cause him harm. When he had begun, Mark had felt guilty about making his living from elaborate, mystical lies. He found himself unable to sleep at night, fearful that the stars would turn against him for twisting their prophecies and making them say whatever he wanted. But, as the grand deception met only with success, Mark found himself less and less concerned about the way he lived. Either the stars approved of him, or they truly were nothing more than specks of light in the sky. As Snutworth often said, everyone in Agora made their way by seeming more powerful and important than they were. Anyone who did not would be trampled into the dust, and Mark was not about to let that happen to him. He had escaped from the gutter. He was never going back.

As Mark changed partners, he caught a glimpse of Snutworth, in quiet conversation with a representative from the Tanners' Guild. Mark smiled. By tomorrow, he knew that the arrangements would have been made, and some of his surplus wealth would have been traded for an advisory seat on the guild. Another position of influence, another group of merchants who would listen to him. He had been in business for less than a year, and already he would never have been able to keep track of all of his dealings on his own. Snutworth had proved himself invaluable a thousand times over — he had devoted his every waking moment to Mark's success.

Of course the older merchants all pretended that Mark was little more than an amusing mascot for their guilds, the latest bright spark who would soon fade. No one liked to admit how far this thirteen-year-old from the slums had come, or how much power he held. But Mark knew better. Shifting his gaze, he saw the furniture maker, one of the best, who had decked out the tower in its new finery, particularly pleased to help after Mark had joined his consortium. All around him, weaving through the dance, he recognized the insignia of merchants dealing in meat or fish or gold and jewels. Half of them were already woven into his own business interests, the other half only waited on tonight to sign him up. Who cared if the whole city thought him their monkey? How many monkeys could afford a party like this?

He slipped through the dance, lacing in and out of every kind of wealth, the hems of their coats touching and sparkling with gold.

He passed the band and nodded to Laud, who gestured to the conductor. Immediately the music changed, becoming grand and stately. Mark looked around for a new partner for the next dance.

"Mr. Mark, a charming party."

A severely corseted woman of middle years, her graying blond hair aggressively scraped back into an elegant pleat, took his hand. A simple eye mask was perched upon her nose, but it covered little of her expression of polite determination. It was customary for the gentleman to ask the lady to dance, but her tone made it clear that failing to offer would cause great offense and may not be an option.

"My pleasure," Mark said, bowing to cover the discomfort caused by her fierce grip. "Would you care to dance, Miss . . ."

"I see you are quite a flatterer," she said with a mechanical smile. "I am no miss. My name is Matron Angelina."

Mark's mind buzzed. This was one of his star guests. Composing himself, he stood in a line with the other men, facing his partner, and then slowly stepped forward to walk round her to the beat.

"You honor me," Mark said, trying, and failing, to sound casual. "I hear your orphanages —"

"Future Workforce Centers," the matron corrected.

" — are the most successful in the city," Mark continued.

For once, the flattery was very close to the truth.

"Fine words from the prodigy of the Astrologers' Guild," Angelina replied, stretching out her right hand to form a star of four dancers with the next couple. "You really should visit. I'm sure my daughter would be delighted to meet you —"

"I believe they are talking business, *carissimo*."

"On such a night as this? Impossible!"

The voices of the couple they had joined cut across them. Mark looked up at Signor Sozinho, who had an impish grin on his face. His wife laughed.

"Perhaps the matron has more than work on her mind tonight?" she suggested, with a sly wink.

Mark winced. He had spent hours at his last gathering being talked at by this couple. It wasn't that he begrudged them their happiness, but they did seem determined that everyone should be aware of it. He blanked his mind as they launched into their favorite topic — Lily's Almshouse. As Matron Angelina's face assumed an expression of glacial politeness, he looked around the dance. That reminded him: If Lily was going to come, wouldn't she have shown up by now?

The star broke apart in a whirl of skirts. With a swift bow, Mark changed partners and the matron was swept away, still at the mercy of Signor Sozinho's unrelenting enthusiasm. Mark turned to his new partner, and stopped dead.

The Reaper stood before him.

Mark stepped back, colliding with another line, the dancers scattering around him. Suddenly he was no longer the successful young businessman, the shining prodigy. Now he was just a thirteen-year-old boy faced with the same hollow, black eyes and blank face of his memories, memories he had tried to push away.

The figure stepped forward. Something was wrong. It seemed shorter than Mark remembered.

It pulled off its mask.

"It's been a while, hasn't it, Mark?" Lily said.

Chapter Fourteen

The Secret

LILY DECIDED that Mark hadn't changed at all.

He was taller, of course. His dirty blond hair was combed and clean, and his rich clothes were more suited to this opulent party than the ragged castoffs he had been wearing the last time she had seen him, before his rise. After Laud had pointed him out to her, she wasn't sure whether this confident, elegant figure would even recognize her, despite the letters they had exchanged.

But as soon as he caught her gaze, he was instantly the frightened boy she had taught to read, his mouth slack from surprise.

"Shall we go somewhere else?" she said, looking around her at the dancers, who had stopped in midspin. "I think your guests are staring."

For a minute, Mark seemed dazed. Then, as if nothing had happened, he straightened, bowed, and offered her his arm, just as she had seen the other gentlemen do.

"Come and see the gardens," he said, and then added with an ironic grin, "Would the lady care to take my arm?"

"Thanks, but I can walk myself, you know," Lily replied, playfully pushing his arm away.

She strode off toward the gardens, planning to walk fast, but her heavy black dress and fashionable dark hooded cloak, some of Signora Sozinho's hand-me-downs, prevented her from moving freely. She heard Mark hurrying to catch up with her and slowed down, trying to relax. This was supposed to be a break, a chance to see an old friend, but it was getting harder and harder to push her daily life from her mind. She found herself looking at objects and wondering how many debtors they would feed if traded.

"Come on!" Mark huffed as he caught up to her. "Just a joke. Remember jokes?"

Lily shook herself and made an effort to smile.

"Sorry, Mark. I don't hear a lot of laughter nowadays."

Mark fiddled awkwardly with the lace on his shirt cuffs.

"Yeah, I got that impression from your letters," he said, adding hastily, "I meant to write back more often, honestly, but with all the meetings . . . and the lunches . . . all the endless parties . . ."

"Sounds like a hard life," Lily murmured, with the lightest hint of sarcasm.

Looking a bit sheepish, Mark stopped talking, and Lily couldn't help but smile.

"Anyway," she continued, with a streak of mischief, "tell me, since you obviously have plenty of experience of these events, will I get thrown out if I try hiding some of those canapés for later?"

Mark's face assumed a look of mock outrage.

"That would be deeply insulting to the host," he said.

Lily raised an eyebrow. "Aren't you the host?"

"Exactly. It's insulting to think that you'd have to hide them. I'll get you some from the food tents."

Lily smiled openly this time. "Don't you have other guests to look after?" she asked.

Mark shrugged dismissively. "None of them are interested in me. Most of them only came to be seen. Snutworth will let me know if anyone important wants to talk."

"Snutworth . . ." Lily mused. She remembered Laud talking about Mark's manservant once. The word he had used then was *slippery*.

"But who cares about that?" Mark broke across her thoughts with a laugh. "It's so good to see you!" Impulsively, he grabbed her hand. "Forget about the gardens, you can see them later. How about going back to the dance?"

Lily shook her head decisively.

"I'll get it all wrong," she protested, but Mark did not let go, and his grin widened.

"That's the point. This is revenge for you being better than me at everything when we first met."

Lily pulled her hand back, but not sharply, and considered for a moment. Then she smiled. She could never resist a challenge.

The evening wore on, the summer sun sank below the horizon, and still the party continued. Despite knowing that she was needed back at the Almshouse, that she had left Benedicta without any help, Lily couldn't quite bring herself to make her excuses. Partly it was the pleasure of seeing Mark again — so successful and confident. It was good to have a friend completely separate from her new work. But also, she had to admit, being entirely free of responsibility for one evening had a charm all its own.

Eventually, Lily found herself sitting next to Mark at one of the long tables set up in the central marquee, with a plate of meats and salads that looked almost decadent before her. Mark was eating ravenously.

"You know," he said between mouthfuls, "it was a really irritating party until you came. I should have invited you before, but your letters were always so full of this 'great project' of yours, I didn't think it would be your thing."

"It isn't really," Lily said thoughtfully, "but I'm glad I came. I've missed you."

"Yes, well . . ." Mark floundered. He looked down at the table, where she had placed Theo's old mask and goggles, the ones she had been wearing when she arrived. He reached out and took them, gazing down at the blank face. "Was that supposed to be a joke?" he said quietly.

Lily shook her head.

"No . . . I'm sorry, Mark. I'd meant to take the mask off before I saw you, but the gatekeeper wouldn't let me in without one and that was all I had. Sorry if it brought back memories."

Lily saw a tiny shudder pass across Mark's face.

"No more memories than usual. It's stupid. I know the doctor never meant me any harm, but . . . it reminds me of my dad. What he did." Mark paused, then brightened, pushing his plate to one side. "Let's not talk about that. Look, you've got to tell me more about this place of yours." He grinned. "I thought I might get involved, you know, as a patron. Snutworth isn't on board, but it sounds like a brilliant idea to me . . ."

"You think so?" Lily thought back to the ragged lines that stretched around the Almshouse night and day and leaned forward intently. "You really think what we're doing is the right thing?"

"Fantastic!" Mark said, waving his hands excitedly. "I mean, it's a perfect gap in the market. It's like selling happiness, satisfaction, and smugness all in one package. Even the best emotional distillers can't produce anything like it." He put his elbows on the table. "Honestly, Signor and Signora Sozinho can't get enough of it."

"They are good people," Lily replied slowly, disappointed that

Mark did not seem to understand, but still determined to encourage his interest. "They know it's about more than the effect on them. I wish other patrons could see it the same way, would come down and look at the good work we do." Lily sighed in frustration. "Even those we helped barely understood what we were doing at first. We had to convince them that there was nothing shameful about taking alms. Some of them would rather have starved to death than admit their troubles."

Mark opened his mouth, about to speak, but the voice that Lily heard was not his. It was a deeper, more mature voice and it spoke with easy authority.

"Even debtors have their pride, Miss Lilith."

Lily turned sharply. Across the table from her, where previously there had been only a row of empty seats, sat a distinguished-looking older man. He had placed his mask, the sun going into eclipse, on the table and was looking at her with appraising eyes. Despite his casual posture, there was something in the lines around his mouth that suggested this was a man used to respect and Lily self-consciously shrank backward.

Mark hastily rose and gave a bow.

"Lord Ruthven, I didn't mean to ignore you . . ."

Lord Ruthven shook his head and smiled, although Lily received little warmth from that smile.

"Not at all, Mr. Mark. I did not wish to let formality intrude on your discussion with Miss Lilith. It was certainly most enlightening."

"I wouldn't have thought that you would be interested, My Lord," Lily said cautiously.

Lord Ruthven held his chin thoughtfully. "On the contrary, as head of the receivers, one of the more tiresome duties of the Lord Chief Justice, I have read several reports about your venture. One of my sergeants in particular is especially . . . forthright in his opinions."

Lord Ruthven gestured with his other hand to the corner of the marquee. As Lily looked over, she could see the familiar deep-blue coats of a group of receivers. She immediately spotted the disdainful face of Sergeant Pauldron and bit her lip.

"The sergeant has made no secret of his dislike for the Almshouse," Lily admitted, well aware that every time he visited to check up on them, his scowl seemed to grow deeper.

Lord Ruthven nodded thoughtfully. "Pauldron is a boy of pure thoughts, Miss Lilith," he explained, adding with a note of amusement, "Though I suppose hearing a man of twice your age described as a 'boy' is odd to you."

Lily shifted uncomfortably. The pleasure of seeing Mark again had made her let down her guard, and Lord Ruthven had taken advantage of this. For all his courtesy, she was certain that he was mocking her.

"Sometimes I think age has nothing to do with how many summers you have seen," she said defensively.

Lord Ruthven leaned back. "Do not misunderstand me, Miss Lilith," he said condescendingly. "I have the greatest respect for those who achieve while young." He gave a little nod to Mark, who seemed very pleased. "But," he continued, "you are correct. There are some who seem to keep the innocence of the very young—the absolute devotion to simple ideals. You will never find a man of purer loyalty to Agora, to his duty, than Sergeant Pauldron."

Lily looked back at the Lord Chief Justice. There was something odd in his tone. Not quite threatening, but this was definitely a warning of some kind.

"Do you agree with the sergeant's view, My Lord?" she asked. "Do you think that charity is a dangerous idea?"

Lord Ruthven considered the question. When he spoke, his voice was quiet and meaningful.

"I believe very strongly in stability, Miss Lilith. In maintaining the way of life that has led to Agora's golden age. I think it is . . . unwise, and even dangerous, to disrupt such a delicate balance."

Before Lily had a chance to reply, he turned to Mark, who suddenly seemed very interested in the remains on his plate.

"What do you think about it, Mr. Mark? Would you become a patron of Miss Lilith's Almshouse? Would you consider it a good investment?"

Mark looked up, his eyes flicking from Lord Ruthven to Lily and back again. She could tell that he was trying to avoid answering the question. She supposed that Mark could not risk upsetting this powerful man, although it stung her that he would not think for himself. He had seemed very enthusiastic about the Almshouse a short while ago.

"I thought I . . . that is . . . I think it's always a good idea to invest in many different businesses . . ." Mark mumbled, not meeting Lily's eyes.

Lily frowned, unable to hide her disappointment, while Lord Ruthven smiled indulgently.

"Indeed, Mr. Mark, indeed. I was particularly pleased to see that you chose to join us in the latest Pescator deal . . ."

"Pescator?" Lily was startled. She had heard that name before, and recently.

Mark nodded. "A group of fish merchants who wanted some backing to improve the efficiency of the fishing in the Piscean slums." Mark gave a half smile and inclined his head toward Lord Ruthven. "You remember, My Lord, that I used to live there? Snutworth called me sentimental, but I wanted to help the local merchants, for a steady supply, of course . . ."

"Help?" Lily said icily. Now she remembered where she had

heard that name. Among the hollow-eyed men who crowded into the Almshouse, it was as bad as a curse. "Mark, those merchants have put half of the poorest fishermen out of business with their practices. I don't think you should join them."

"I'm afraid it is rather late for such advice, Miss Lilith," Lord Ruthven said. "Mr. Mark joined their planning committee two months ago."

Mark nodded. "A good deal too. I helped them streamline their plans. They weren't sure how to get the best deal out of all the local fishermen, and I suggested some kind of quality control to make sure everyone only brought in their best catch." Mark smiled confidentially. "Sorry, I mean, that's what the stars told me would bring them great fortune." He leaned forward, whispering so that only Lily could hear. "To be honest, I didn't understand it completely, but Snutworth said that sort of thing usually worked very well, and he's never let me down so far . . ." Mark trailed off. "Are you all right, Lily?"

But Lily was not all right. She suddenly felt cold and clammy. One month ago. That was when they had all arrived. All those ex-fishermen, forced out of their homes by landlords, telling tales of their catches left rotting on the wharves. Fish that no merchant would buy, thanks to the Pescator consortium's "quality control." The most important quality being that they had to be willing to trade for a cripplingly low return.

The heat of the evening seemed to have increased. The marquee was too stuffy, the food on her plate too greasy. Her mind in a whirl, Lily got up from the table so suddenly that her chair fell over and, barging through the crowds of the great and nearly great, left.

She walked quickly, dimly aware that Mark was following close behind her, apologizing. She still could not quite believe what he had said, but her horror drove her to the far edge of the gardens, where she stopped by a large marble fountain.

A few moments later Mark reached her, obviously anxious. She would not look at his face, staring at her reflection in the rippling water instead. Out of the corner of her eye, she saw him put her mask and goggles, forgotten in the rush, down on the edge of the fountain, then reach into his vest pocket and pull out a familiar kind of glass vial.

"Sorry, I suppose the party must have been too much. I forgot — I'm used to it. Here," he said, pulling out the stopper and pushing the vial into her hands, "have a little bottled calm. Call it in exchange for missing half the party."

Lily pulled her hands away with a jolt. Surprised, Mark lost his grip on the tiny vial and dropped it into the fountain, its blue contents mingling with the water.

"Lily!" Mark said, annoyed. "That was top-quality calm! Last of the batch too. I had to trade a whole gilt chair for it . . ."

"A couple of years ago you'd never even seen a chair," Lily spat back, her words rising up hot and fiery. "A couple of years ago you sat on crates and thought only legendary kings had chairs. Now you trade them away to drink the emotions sucked out of other people? Is this your success, Mark?"

"People sell those emotions, Lily. It's their choice. What's wrong with you?" Mark said, staring at her in disbelief. "Look, I'm sorry I didn't tell Lord Ruthven I was thinking of becoming a patron for your Almshouse . . . Some of these old men, they're set in their ways. You just haven't had a chance to get used to the way they do things in these circles. Not like I have — "

"I'd never get used to this," Lily growled. "Mark, do you realize what you're doing? Don't you know that your consortium is ruining people's lives?"

"Don't be stupid," Mark replied. "I made it better. I make all the businesses I join better, and that helps everyone. Look, why not come back to the party, apologize to Lord Ruthven for running away like that — " Lily grabbed his hand, interrupting him.

"Mark, stop this now. A fisherman died at my Almshouse today. If anyone had bought his fish he would have been able to have his disease treated, but Theophilus couldn't do anything by the time he came to us." Lily drew her face closer. "Mark, he had the same gray plague you had when you came to the tower. It hasn't gone away. He could have been you."

"So now the diseases are my fault as well?" Mark replied, an edge creeping into his voice. "I'm sorry, Lily, but bad things happen to people who don't deserve it." He pushed her hand away. "You should know that," he continued bitterly. "I do. I was ill, just like your fisherman. I was sold off like a rag or a blanket. I watched my whole family turn as gray as stone." He folded his arms. "If you want me to give something back, if you think I 'owe' something to them, fine. I'll be a patron for you. But after what my father did, after what the Count tried to do, don't I deserve something good in my life?"

"You call this good?" Lily said quietly, trying to keep calm. "Mark, your businesses — they're built on other people's pain. I understand . . . I don't think you knew what was happening. But you can't keep doing this. You can't treat people as if they don't matter."

Mark looked back at her then, his eyes cold.

"You told me to survive, Lily. Don't you remember? You said that's what we have to do, and I believed you." He moved closer to her. "That's why I'm here, grabbing every chance I get, wearing stupid clothes, acting like I've been doing this for years, not months. This might look like the high life to you, but it's still a fight to survive. I've just got more to lose than I used to." Mark set his mouth firmly and turned away from her. "I've been at the bottom, Lily." His voice grew quieter, more pained. "I'm not going to be worthless again. I'm going to keep fighting."

Lily stared at him, speechless. She couldn't believe that he could fool himself this much. She wanted to drag him by his ridiculous golden coat to the Almshouse and force him to look at the people he had trampled on as he clambered up. But she kept her mouth closed because he clearly wouldn't listen. All he had known for months was a world of fashion and fortune, the world that had seemed so carefree to her just a few hours ago. That was all any of them knew. They couldn't begin to understand the value of things that couldn't be traded for.

Suddenly, Lily had to get out. She felt the disapproving glare of the statues around her. Even the air seemed heavy, swollen with the scent of riches. She didn't belong here, where no one would listen no matter how hard she shouted. She reached down and picked up her mask and goggles. Then she turned back to Mark.

"The problem with fighting, Mark, is that it never stops." She fixed him with her eyes then, trying to burn her words into his mind, which was fogged over with glamour and dreams. "Eventually, everyone comes across a fight that they lose. After that, what then?"

She turned. She didn't want to witness his reaction, didn't want to hear him repeating the opinions of those who didn't see. Didn't even want to look at him anymore.

Lily barely noticed the irritation of the guests as she pushed past them on her way out of the gardens. Internally, she was cursing herself. She should have forced Mark to see how wrong he was, but the last months had made her so tired. She had tried everything, they all had, but nothing seemed to be getting better. Theo still searched the city for his grandfather whenever he could take a few hours away from his patients, although his initial panic had long since faded; nowadays he searched because he couldn't quite bring himself to give up on him. Meanwhile, she and Benedicta worked tirelessly to feed the debtors on the meager food they could afford. Nothing was changing.

Actually, that wasn't true, Lily thought grimly, as she rested against a building just outside the ornate iron gates. The Almshouse was growing poorer. Their few patrons couldn't keep them going much longer. She had even had to give up her search for any sign of her past, or her parents, as a lost cause. It nearly broke her heart, but the Almshouse needed her every moment of the day. Lily bowed her head, trying to ignore the guilt that was creeping over her. So much for her resolution not to preach. As usual, it had only made things worse.

The streets were strangely quiet in the Leo District. The ball, she noticed, was ending, and the guests were slipping away into the warm night. Lily found herself wishing, praying even, to whatever being had once been worshipped in that old temple where she lived, that something, anything, would stop this slow, painful collapse.

Lily looked up and a strange sight met her eyes.

Just a short way from where she was standing, Lord Ruthven was talking quietly to a couple of figures in black. Something was wrong. A man of Lord Ruthven's standing did not have to skulk in the shadows. Surely no one would have dared to stop anything he chose to do. Concealed in the dark shadows of the building, she leaned closer.

". . . the meeting is tonight, My Lord, they already await you."

"I thought they knew I was not available tonight," Lord Ruthven hissed, removing his mask and glancing around. Inwardly, Lily started, but managed to keep herself completely still and he did not seem to notice her. As she watched, Lord Ruthven hastily slipped an old, nondescript cloak over his fine clothes. Then he spoke again.

"I shall join them at the Clockwork House, but they should be reminded that I am the head of the society. They may not summon me on a whim."

Unless . . .

Even the Lord Chief Justice was not above the law.

As he slipped away into the shadows, Lily found her feet following him. She pulled up the hood of her borrowed cloak, clutching her white mask inside her long, black sleeves, willing herself to blend into the night. Somewhere in her mind, she was already forming reasons. Maybe if Lord Ruthven could be proved to be corrupt, the city would change its ways. Maybe his secret was damaging people's lives. Already she was discounting the most honest reason — sudden, burning, and overwhelming curiosity. She had to know.

Lord Ruthven was not easy to follow, especially once he padded through the empty stalls of Central Plaza and into the Piscean slums, where he mingled with the thousands of others in dark, mud-stained clothes going about their night activities.

Lily could not suppress a shudder as she slipped under the crumbling archway into the Pisces District, the two fish carved on it seeming to glare at her. Her only comfort was that the gray plague seemed to have almost died out over the last year. All kinds of disease were still rife in the slums, of course, but at the height of the plague she would never have ventured in, no matter how curious she was. Even now, this part of the city disturbed her, especially at night. This city never slept, but it showed a different side in the darkness: harsher, seedier. Lily heard the echoed sounds of laughter from a bar, smelled stale odors wafting all around her. But in the moonlight she could see the fragments of glitter from his mask still caught on a cloak whose quality was just a little too good.

Deeper and deeper they went into the tangled mass of streets: Fisher's Way, Weaver's Road. Lily tried to memorize the route, glancing over her shoulder to check the street signs. She kept her target in sight, but as she looked back again, she realized with a sickening lurch that she too was being followed. Every time she turned her head, they were there—a man and woman, their faces concealed behind heavy hoods, getting closer with every step. As an experiment, and at the risk of losing Lord Ruthven, Lily darted down a side street. Sure enough, mere moments later, the light of the woman's lantern appeared around the corner. Lily forced herself not to speed up, not to show the fear that made her heartbeat race. What if these were Ruthven's servants? There was no receiver patrol in sight, but even they would be little help if the Lord Chief Justice caught her spying on him. Despite herself, she felt her pace increase, desperate to break into a run. Up ahead, a crowd burst out of another side street, singing raucous songs and bringing with them the scent of gin and sweat. Lily plunged into the midst of them, feeling them press in around her, treading on her skirts and toes. Checking behind her, she saw her pursuers draw nearer, following her into the mob. For a few terrible seconds, she couldn't move, pinned between two large drunken men, and then, with a sudden inspiration, she jabbed an elbow into the nearest chest. The man turned angrily, flailing his fists, but Lily dropped to the ground, crawling through the muck to avoid the escalating fight she had started. Shaking, she ducked into Lock Street, leaving her hooded followers trapped by the brawl. As she stopped to catch her breath, she caught sight of Lord Ruthven once again, ahead of her. All of her good sense was telling her to turn around, that it was too dangerous to go on.

As if mesmerized, she began to follow again.

The narrow street opened up into a square. Nearby, Lily could hear the Ora lapping against its banks, thick and sluggish at its downstream end. She guessed that she was somewhere near the far edge of the city, where the river disappeared, seeming to melt into the vastness of the great, gray city walls. It was said that only the riverboat captains knew the exact place where the Ora left the city, or where it entered, the only breaks in the walls that encircled Agora, marking and enforcing the limits of the mortal world. Some even whispered that the captains knew how to leave Agora, but that was as far as the stories went. "To leave the city," in Agora, was another way of talking about death.

Lily snapped out of this train of thought as, up ahead, she saw Lord Ruthven in conversation with three other figures. He made some kind of sign — she was too far away to see what it was — and then he stepped through a door, into a building of ancient stone.

Lily moved closer, her mind buzzing. What would the highest judge in the city find in the middle of the slums? Who were these people?

And then she saw them. The man and the woman, still hooded, coming into the square from another street. Lily shrank back, flinching as their heads turned toward her, her whole body trembling. She watched as they drew closer, choosing her moment. She tensed her legs, ready to run from the square and lose herself in the twisting alleyways.

They looked away. Lily turned. She ran.

She ran straight into a man in a midnight-blue coat.

"Hunting for debtors, Miss Lilith?"

Lily stepped back, shaken. Sergeant Pauldron stood before her. His tricornered hat shadowed his face, but even in the moonlight she could see his look was not friendly.

"There are many unfortunates in the Pisces District, Sergeant," she replied, keeping her voice as still and reasonable as she could, despite her thumping heart. "Some are too weak to make it to the Almshouse on their own."

"So I noticed, Miss Lilith. Receivers are not blind, whatever you might think." He moved closer, his eyes accusing. "I saw very well all of the debtors you passed by. Not feeling quite so charitable tonight?"

"I . . . I was looking for someone in particular," Lily said. Even she could hear the tremble in her voice.

"And who might that be?" the sergeant asked, sounding reasonable, a sure sign of danger.

"Me, sir . . . I'm sorry to have caused so much trouble."

The voice was rasping but firm. Lily and the sergeant turned together. The old man who had been following Lily was now beside them, and the woman with him also came forward, lifting the hood of her cloak to reveal a mass of red curls.

"I managed to find him first, Lily. I hope you don't mind," Gloria said with a thin, nervous smile, raising her lantern to her face.

"Of course not, Gloria," Lily answered rapidly, relief flooding through her. "It's good to see you . . . er . . ."

"Pete, miss," the man said.

In the light of Gloria's lantern, Lily did recognize him. He had been at the Almshouse several times, another old fisherman if the smell of the river that clung to him and his clothes could be trusted. They had offered him a bed, but he hadn't stayed, probably out of pride alone if this was where he was living.

Lily turned back to the sergeant, who was still looking them over with a wary eye.

"Well . . . we must get back. We'll be on our way," Lily muttered, retreating but making a mental note. She wasn't going to forget tonight.

"Do that, Miss Lilith," the sergeant replied, stepping back into the shadows. "These slums are not a safe place."

Lily shivered.

"Come on, Gloria. Let's get back."

As they walked, Gloria seemed unusually calm. The usual fidgeting and sudden exclamations did not pepper her conversation, and she even accepted Lily's thanks quietly, rather than with her normal burst of overenthusiasm.

"It was nothing, really. I was just on my way home from the ball and I saw Peter here returning to the slums. I thought I'd try again to get him to come back with us."

Pete grunted, but in a friendly way.

"When a young lady puts herself out for someone like me, the least I can do is walk her back to the Almshouse," he said.

Lily raised an eyebrow.

"Quite the gentleman, Pete."

The old fisherman snorted.

"Never been one of them. But I wasn't always like this. Seen a lot of change."

Lily nodded thoughtfully. Change was what they needed now. She knew this walk home too well. She knew the sight of people still clinging on to their pieces of clothes and dignity, standing in line before their tiny door. She knew the bright voice of Benedicta as she welcomed her back. Even that smile, always there, seemed thinner nowadays. She was a great friend, of course, but sometimes Lily wondered how deeply Ben felt that cheer she tried to give to others. Lily knew that it helped the debtors and she tried to do it herself. But she also knew, even without looking in the mirror, that her eyes could not hide her thoughts.

"Lily . . ." Gloria lowered her voice as they entered the twisting streets of Sagittarius. "Could you keep quiet about my trip tonight? Laud doesn't like to think of me going into the slums."

Lily nodded and Gloria visibly relaxed, exchanging a glance with Pete. Inwardly, Lily sighed. Did Gloria really think that no one knew what she went there for? It didn't take a genius to notice that she was no longer visiting Miss Devine. Perhaps she had found a less expensive supplier.

"I won't tell him," Lily said, taking Gloria's arm, "but you should. They worry about you—both of them."

Gloria smiled wistfully.

"What else are families for?" she mused. "We worry, all the time. Ever since we lost our parents, I don't think there's been a day when I haven't worried about Laud and Ben. I haven't been as much of a mother to them as I should have."

For a while, they walked in silence. Then, trying to put her thoughts into words, Lily spoke again.

"I don't think they need a mother, not anymore. But they do want their sister. Their real sister, without other people's emotions inside her."

Gloria nodded slowly.

"It's hard, Lily. Until I came to the Almshouse, I used to feel . . ." Gloria seemed about to tell her something, but then she changed her mind. "I'll tell you soon. You've been so important, but Laud and Ben should be the first to know." She smiled, a quiet smile so different from the distracted grin she often wore. "It won't be long. I'm not there yet, but . . . you'll see a real change soon. I promise."

Lily looked into Gloria's unclouded eyes and believed her.

They got closer. In the distance, Lily could see another light. The guiding light, they called it. They had put a lamp up to show people the way to their door. It had been Laud's idea, a kind of symbol. The Almshouse wasn't the end of a journey, a place to die, but the way back for those who were lost. It wasn't until the first night after they put it up that they saw it also illuminated Miss Devine's shop, the glass decorations sparkling in the lamplight. She too was still open, despite the hour. As Lily, Gloria, and Pete approached, she appeared in her doorway, framed in light from within the shop. She nodded, her expression as always unreadable. She had reduced the rent recently. Lily had so wanted to believe, like Benedicta had said, that she had taken their charity to her heart. But it would have meant ignoring the steady stream of those with nothing else to sell who left the Almshouse and drifted into her shop. Miss Devine was doing a brisk trade. One of the regulars at the Almshouse barely spoke anymore; she seemed indifferent to the entire world. Nothing left to sell.

Lily let Gloria and Pete go ahead, wanting to stay a little longer in the night air. She hoped Theo would be in tonight. On the nights that he stayed in, he was usually a calming presence. Maybe she could talk to him about what Lord Ruthven had been doing. Around Benedicta and Gloria, she had to have all the answers. Lily shook her head. Right now she would even appreciate some of Laud's barbed comments, anything to get her out of her own mind.

Anything to drive Mark's words out of her head. She had thought he was better than that.

"Lily!"

Benedicta had appeared out of nowhere and was now grasping at her hand, her eyes shining with excitement.

"He's found him! We'd nearly given up hope, but he's found him!"

Lily let herself be dragged into the Almshouse. At first, all she saw inside was what she usually saw: row upon row of people who had nowhere else to go, slumped in pews, talking together, living despite everything.

And then she recognized him. At the back. Being fed a bowl of soup by Theo, who was holding the spoon so very carefully. Ragged, crumpled, but alive.

"Count Stelli," Lily breathed.

Theo looked up and gave her a tired smile. He seemed brighter than he had for months.

As Lily watched, she became aware of another person beside her. Laud had also returned, and he looked on with a less sympathetic eye.

"He doesn't deserve it," he sniffed, "not after he disowned him. Not after spending his whole life treating others as if they were worthless."

"I know," Lily mused, looking back at him. "But isn't that the point?"

Laud considered for a moment. Then, perhaps, the edge of his mouth twisted upward.

"True enough."

After that they just watched as Dr. Theophilus lifted another spoonful of soup to his grandfather's lips.

CHAPTER FIFTEEN

The Daughter

MARK HAD NO IDEA how he had let himself be talked into this.

That was a lie, but it made him feel better. He knew exactly how it had happened. It had been Lily's fault. He hadn't felt comfortable for days after his ball, no matter how much Snutworth assured him it had been a great success. Those words of hers kept echoing in his head.

Eventually, everyone comes across a fight that they lose.

It had been running through his mind when he met with the jewelry consortium the day before and the results had not been good. It had been echoing in his ears when he read the reports that spoke of a sudden downturn in his profits. And it had kept on at him, until Snutworth, ever observant, suggested that he might not be entirely satisfied.

"It's just . . . I don't seem to belong," Mark grumbled to Snutworth and Laud as he dined with them a few days after the ball. "It doesn't matter how much I do for them, they still keep me out, treat me like some sort of pet, not a real businessman. I'm sure that silversmith yesterday was laughing at me, and if those figures you gave me were correct, it's starting to have an effect on the business."

"Mr. Mark, these things take time," Snutworth purred. "You are still very young. I'm sure that you frighten some of these more experienced people. And then there is the question of recognition . . ."

"Everyone recognizes me," Mark said, thumping his knife on the table. "I'm famous. I've been in the newspapers three times this month alone."

Snutworth and Laud exchanged glances.

"What I mean, sir," Snutworth began again, "is not so much recognition in that sense, but — "

"You can move into Count Stelli's tower, you can take his place, but sixty years' worth of work and reputation might just be a little harder to trade for," Laud interrupted bluntly.

"Stelli never worked for anyone but himself," Mark replied fiercely, "you know that. Anyway, they hire you and you're not much older than me."

"True," Laud said with a shrug. "But I'm serving them, not competing for their position. And whatever you may think, these merchants have been at the top of their game for years. They don't appreciate being told what to do by someone who hasn't started shaving."

Mark sat back in his chair and crossed his arms.

"So . . . we need to make me look older, more respectable — at least as far as the other merchants are concerned," Mark mused. "Any thoughts?"

"A false beard?" Laud suggested, completely deadpan.

"Nothing so comical, Mr. Laudate," Snutworth said, as a light came into his eyes. "I have a much more workable idea . . ."

Which was why he found himself, freshly ironed and smartened by Gloria, waiting to be let into the most unappealing building in the whole of the Aries District. He didn't have a bouquet of flowers. That had been sent ahead.

The door creaked open and a thin, pale boy looked up.

Mark took a deep breath. "Mr. Mark, to see Matron Angelina and Miss Cherubina."

As he walked along the dingy corridors, Mark kept repeating a mantra. He had to remind himself why he was doing this, that Matron Angelina was one of the best-established figures in the city, that her orphanages were highly profitable, that her good word would cement him in position for years. That with the ball not having been the success he had expected it to be, and Lord Ruthven not treating him so favorably since Lily's outburst there, he needed every ally he could get to prevent his businesses from collapsing.

But that came with conditions.

"You must understand, Mr. Mark," the matron said as she poured the tea, "that Cherubina is my only daughter and you are a very young man. I know that in some circles it is usual to arrange these matters immediately after both young people have passed their title days, but I should want to wait at least a year before the marriage."

Mark swallowed his tea so fast that it burned his throat. Snutworth had implied that he could put it off for a few years at least! He looked up weakly through eyes still watering from the pain. The matron stared back at him appraisingly. From her tightly buttoned work dress to her scraped-back hair, everything about her seemed to be restrained. It made Mark, conservatively dressed in his most respectable blue jacket and somber vest, feel uncomfortably gaudy, and he found himself surreptitiously tucking his lacy cuffs inside his sleeves.

The matron pored over the bound copies of Mark's business receipts that she had requested from the Directory. To appear willing, Mark glanced at the records of the orphanage that lay open before him. They looked good, but he really wasn't that interested. He was far too conscious of the person waiting in the next room.

He had still not met the girl he was in the process of becoming engaged to.

Matron Angelina closed the book with a snap and peered at Mark hawkishly.

"All seems to be in order, Mr. Mark. I am prepared to seal the relevant documents if you are. Naturally when it comes to the marriage, further contracts will have to be made."

"Uh . . . naturally," Mark floundered.

The matron rose.

"Now, I shall go and have the contracts drawn up. If you wish, Cherubina is in the next room. We shall be agreeing to two visits a week and I do not object if you wish to make the first one now."

Mark rose in a daze, wanting to ask something else, anything to delay the moment. But Matron Angelina had already gone, as thrifty with her time as she was with everything else.

Mark looked toward the door to the adjoining room. His throat went dry. He should have been thinking of all sorts of things. He remembered Gloria teaching him how to compose himself and Snutworth advising him to stick to small talk. But, at this moment, all he could really think of was Laud's advice, direct and to the point.

"Remember, she'll probably find this as awkward as you will."

With that ringing in his mind, he knocked.

"Come in!"

The voice that came from behind the door was young. Mark breathed his first sigh of relief. Looking at Matron Angelina, he wouldn't have been surprised if her daughter had passed thirty summers.

He turned the handle.

"Mr. Mark! Do come in and have some tea! We've room for one more, don't we?"

Mark had no objection to pink. Pink, in moderation, was a perfectly good color. Cherubina did not have her mother's sense of moderation.

He could have coped with the dollhouse and the frilly curtains. It didn't bother him that he had to move aside a perpetually surprised-looking stuffed animal from his chair before he could sit down. He even didn't mind having to kiss a hand so covered in girlish glass jewelry that his teeth clacked when he touched it. What did disturb him, though, was the fact that the girl sitting across from him was surely seventeen or eighteen and yet, in her behavior, she reminded him of his younger sister when she was six.

"There you go," Cherubina said, coyly looking down at the table. "This is the best tea we have, Mr. Mark."

"I'm . . . I'm sure you can just call me Mark, Miss Cherubina, since we're about to be . . . um . . ."

"Well, yes, I suppose so," Cherubina replied, fiddling with her bracelets.

Silence.

Mark became aware that Cherubina, despite her apparent ease, had not looked at him once since he had entered. She seemed as confused by all this as he was, as though he was nothing like what she had expected.

Be charming, that was what Snutworth had said. Charm her, just as he had won over the businessmen. How did he do that?

"Charming—" he cast around, looking for a clue—"charming . . . dolls, Cherubina."

It was the right thing to say. Cherubina looked up at him and beamed a genuine smile of delight. "Aren't they? Why don't you meet them all?"

Mark smiled weakly as she began to place them on the table in front of him. One of them caught his eye. Dark skin and hair, wrapped in white. Only a baby doll, but something about its little bead eyes made him uncomfortable. He turned it over to face the table. Then he felt something on his head. He looked up. Cherubina, triumphantly brandishing a small silver pair of scissors, held up a piece of his hair.

"You don't mind if I keep this, do you?" she said earnestly. "I want to make a doll of you as well."

"Um . . ." Mark couldn't decide whether this was scary or flattering.

Cherubina played with the little lock of blond hair, holding it up to her own brighter ringlets.

"Yes, you'll look just right next to the doll of me."

Happily, she opened the front of the immense, elaborate dollhouse and pulled a blue-coated male doll from the sitting room, which even had a miniature fire burning in the grate. She skillfully snipped off the doll's brown curls, and tucked the piece of Mark's blond hair into the doll's collar, whispering something about gluing it on later. Then, with utmost care, she placed it next to another doll in an upstairs room. A doll with golden ringlets that was sitting at a tea table with even smaller dolls. In the corner, there was even a little dollhouse.

Scary, Mark decided. Definitely scary.

"Can't you just see the future laid out before us," Cherubina said dreamily.

Mark tried to speak, but nothing came out. His throat seemed to be constricting with horror.

She looked over at him quizzically.

"You're younger than I expected, but I don't mind that. In fact, if you want the truth — " she came closer — "I'm really glad. Some of the others Mommy invited over . . . Ugh!" She wrinkled her nose. "Old enough to be my daddy." She twisted a strand of hair around her finger and an oddly sad note crept into her voice. "I can't help with the business, you see. I sold myself back to Mommy on my title day, but I'm no real use to her. So I knew she would have to sell me eventually."

For a moment, her face seemed older, more like her real age, and despite himself Mark reached across to her. He could certainly sympathize with that. Then she giggled, instantly returning to her childishness, as if a door had snapped shut.

"Let me see your seal," she said, peering at his outstretched hand. "Oooo, you wear your signet ring. Mommy told me only very ordinary businessmen don't have a servant to bring it when they need it."

Mark colored, pulling it off his finger and handing it to her. Cherubina examined it thoughtfully.

"Still, Mommy can't be right about everything. You must be awfully rich." She giggled. "What is that, anyway?"

"It's a starfish . . ." Mark mumbled. "My family . . . um . . . dealt in fish . . . and I started off an apprentice astrologer so . . ."

Mark trailed off. Cherubina was not even pretending to listen. She was too busy hunting for something.

"Then your doll needs a golden starfish on his coat," she exclaimed, triumphantly pulling a spool of golden thread out of a drawer. "He needs to be just right," she added, frowning as she threaded a needle. "Nothing but the best for my Mark . . ."

Mark found himself concentrating on Cherubina's fingers as they moved over the cloth. Anything to stop him from looking around the room and meeting the stares of the thousands of glass eyes that peered out from every corner. He could cope with the animals, but something about the dolls' smiles made him shiver. Looking at Cherubina only made her turn away or coyly walk her fingers over the table to meet his. That made him jump, but when he tried to speak, she seemed completely absorbed in her work again. Only occasionally did their eyes meet, but when they did Mark felt more confused than ever. Because beneath the girlish simpering, he saw something else there — a look of utter relief. Almost unconsciously, Mark found himself wondering what the other suitors had been like.

Matron Angelina left them alone for an hour. When she entered, Mark got up a little too hastily, but before he could make his excuses, the matron laid out the betrothal contract on the table in front of him. Mark felt his throat go dry — in Cherubina's dreamy company he had nearly forgotten how much of his future was being determined. Maybe he could defer things for a while, try to find another way out of his business problems. Nervously, he reached to twist his signet ring. It wasn't on his finger; Cherubina still had it.

"That's all right," she said eagerly. "I'll do it for you. I never get the chance. Don't even know where my signet is."

And she pushed his ring down, sealing beside her mother's rising sun surrounded by six hands. The contract was signed and sealed, and Mark hadn't even had to lift a finger.

He kissed Cherubina's hand again as he left and bowed to the matron in a daze.

Once he had left the room, he jammed the signet ring back onto his finger so hard that it hurt. So, that was that, then. He'd been dreaming about his future for years and now officially his future was *that*.

Matron Angelina's business had better keep on being the best.

* * *

He stalked down the corridors, a hot frustration growing inside him. When the door opened and his carriage was nowhere in sight, his blood began to boil.

He swept through the streets, dimly aware that his fine breeches were being splattered with mud from passersby. The late-afternoon sun baked down on him. His coat was hot and uncomfortable, and every other thought was of that dollhouse, looming up before him, shrinking his life to fit inside.

He tried to avoid the crowds in the Central Plaza by pushing through the Taurus District, but the streets here wound around each other, matching his meandering, twisting mind. By the time the welcoming towers of the Gemini District appeared before him, clean and grand as they rose into the heavens, the sun was dipping below the horizon. The evening seemed even hotter than the day.

The tower door slammed.

Hurriedly, a crowd of servants rushed forward to take his hat and coat. Mark had never understood how the Count could live with only one servant, but now he was not pleased to see them and shrugged off his coat without a word. He stormed up the stairs, throwing himself down on a seat in the Observatory, which was now more of an office. He jangled the bell.

The worst thing about it was that the day had gone as planned. By rights he should be pleased.

He stared down at his signet ring. A little piece of the fatal wax was still clinging to it. Warm and slightly sticky, like the touch of Cherubina's fingers.

He rang the bell again.

"Snutworth! Laud! Where are you?" he called out.

He heard an approaching step on the stairs, and then a nervous tap at the lower door.

"Come," he shouted.

The door rasped open and a hurried step ascended the iron stair. Mark hissed in irritation.

"Gloria, what are you doing here?"

Gloria twisted one finger in her curls. If anything, she seemed even more agitated than usual, as though something had disturbed her.

"Laud asked me to stay until you got back," she said, her eyes flicking around the room. "He needed to go and see some other clients."

"Really?" Mark felt another surge of irritation. "Important clients?"

"I think so . . ." Gloria ventured, her eyes coming to rest on a wooden box on the table beside Mark.

"Oh, good," Mark snapped. "I'd hate to think I was being abandoned for anyone unimportant."

"Mr. Mark, Laud isn't your servant," Gloria began gently, but Mark wouldn't let her speak.

"Of course not. Just as loyal as his payment. Everything on the wording of a contract, right?" Mark felt the heat rise up into his head. "My life, everyone's life, just bought and sold on the market, right?" He sat back, already tired of her. "Well, no need to hang around here when your services are not needed, Gloria. You know your way out."

Gloria nodded, but stood still, her attention still pointedly on the box. Mark stared back, waiting.

"Mr. Mark," she said at last, "I wonder, just before I go, if I could have . . ."

"I don't remember any mention of your little treats in the contract, Gloria," Mark said darkly.

He knew exactly what she wanted. That was where he kept his regular order from Miss Devine.

"Well, no, sir. We agreed it wouldn't be in the contract, as Laud might not have liked it if he'd seen it, but . . . we agreed . . ."

"Can you prove that, Miss Gloria?"

Mark knew what they had said. But as far as he was concerned, he gave those "treats" to Gloria out of friendship. He was not feeling friendly tonight.

Gloria bit her lip, her hands fidgeting.

"No, Mr. Mark. I . . . I wouldn't ask, but . . . it's been days and I just need a little . . ."

She looked up at him then, her eyes imploring. But he met her gaze with a stony glare. When Gloria looked at him, all he saw were those dolls.

"I . . . I . . ." She bowed her head, defeated. "I'll see myself out."

Mark listened to her steps descending the stairs. Slowly, nothing like her usual anxious run. He carried on listening as they faded into the distance.

Awkwardly, he shuffled in his chair. He had never seen a look of such despair before. She really did need that stuff.

He heard the door below open again, but this time he heard no footsteps. That could only be one person.

"Snutworth, about time," Mark grunted as his servant glided up the stairs.

"My apologies, sir," Snutworth said smoothly. "I was fetching you today's reports when I bumped into Miss Gloria . . ." He paused tactfully. "She seemed in some distress."

"She was being annoying," Mark muttered, but already the sting of his earlier frustration was draining away. "I'll apologize tomorrow."

"Very well, sir," Snutworth replied. "Now, if we could get to these reports."

Mark listened distractedly. He got up and wandered around the Observatory as Snutworth read the reports aloud, staring at his

distorted reflection in the brass telescope. He looked disappointed somehow. The gold on his buttons didn't seem to shine as
brightly as usual.

He moved to the window and gazed down at the streets below the
tower, in a way the Count never had, watching the scurrying people
below.

He thought he caught a glimpse of Gloria as she moved slowly
away, walking toward the growing shadows. But in the evening
light it could have been anyone, their hair catching the setting sun
and turning blood red.

CHAPTER SIXTEEN

The Theft

IT WAS NOON before they heard.

It had been an ordinary morning. Theo did his rounds among the weaker debtors, checking for signs of illness. For a moment, he lingered by his grandfather, sleeping on the makeshift bed in the corner as he had every morning for the last week since Theo brought him in. Lily knew that the doctor was hoping the old man would speak. The Count hadn't uttered a word since Theo had found him, huddled and filthy, in the corner of an abandoned warehouse in the Aquarian docks.

Benedicta boiled up a broth and brought it around. No one knew what she found to put in it. Laud had once said, out of her earshot, that he hoped the debtors understood that it was the thought that counted because there was often little more than thoughts added to her boiling water.

Lily was at the old altar, grinding up medicines. The Almshouse could run itself for now; she never forgot that she was Theo's apprentice still.

Everything was normal — as settled as it ever got in a building devoted to those who had nothing.

Until Laud arrived.

Lily knew immediately that something had happened. Laud was a good actor, so he walked in without drama. But his eyes were fixed and his manner too quiet.

"Lily, could you get Benedicta for me?" he said hollowly.

"Of course," Lily said, frowning. "Laud, what's wrong?"

"Please, just . . . just get Benedicta." Laud leaned on the altar. "I'm sorry, Lily. I think . . . she should know first . . . before they arrive . . . They'll be here soon . . ."

"Before—" Lily began, but closed her mouth. Laud didn't want to say, so she just beckoned Benedicta without a word.

The girl came over, smiling to see her brother. He took her by the hand and held it wordlessly. And for the first time ever, Lily saw Benedicta's smile die.

The two walked out of the Almshouse in silence. Lily caught Theo's eye. Even some of the debtors looked curious.

Lily left the brother and sister as long as she felt she could, then she wiped her hands on her apron and made for the front door.

Inspector Greaves was framed in the doorway. Behind him stood a squad of receivers, including Sergeant Pauldron. All of them wore grim expressions, except for the inspector. His was sadder, graver, but utterly determined.

"I'm afraid, Miss Lilith, Dr. Theophilus, we shall need to investigate your premises and conduct some interviews. I would ask you not to let anyone leave or there could be dire consequences."

Lily stepped back, confused. Something wasn't right: They didn't look angry and they weren't trying to close her down.

"Inspector, if this is about the receipts I—"

"I regret to inform you that it is a far more serious matter," the inspector said, walking forward. "A theft, Miss Lilith, of the most serious nature."

"Inspector," Lily said, nervously, "I'm sure that no one here would steal anything. There's nothing worth stealing. You can search them if you . . ."

She trailed off as she realized that something didn't make sense here. There was a question that needed to be asked, and suddenly she would have given anything in the world not to have to ask it. Luckily, the doctor spoke first.

"If I may ask, Inspector," he enquired gravely, "what kind of theft?"

"A life theft, sir."

The doctor frowned in pain. Lily stared dumbly.

"And the victim, Inspector?" the doctor asked quietly.

"A young woman by the name of Gloria, Doctor. We believe that she worked here on occasion."

In the distance, Lily heard the sound of Benedicta crying.

The process was long and slow. At least Sergeant Pauldron, who was watching the Almshouse being searched with an uncomfortable expression of triumph, did not want to interview her, but he seemed to be the only receiver who did not. Lily found herself repeating the same words over and over again. Yes, the last she had seen of Gloria was a few days previously, when she had visited her sister. No, she had not seemed more agitated than usual. Lily was very careful with those words. No, she could not think of anyone who would want to kill her. Lily insisted on using that word, even if every receiver corrected it to "steal her life." No, she couldn't think of a reason why Gloria would have gone to the Piscean slums, where she had been found. No, no one suspicious had been loitering around the Almshouse. That never failed to spark off a hollow laugh from the receivers, as they glanced around at the hordes of debtors lining the room, trembling as they mumbled their statements. Even the inspector, who of all of them seemed to listen most attentively, shook his head when she said this.

"Miss Lilith," he said firmly, "you must accept that this Almshouse was a dangerous place for Miss Gloria to visit."

"These are just normal people, Inspector. Normal people who were unlucky or foolish or ruined by the greed of others."

The inspector looked up from his notes, a sympathetic look on his face.

"In my experience, Miss Lilith, most life thieves are normal people. And you must accept that this institution attracts the most desperate, those ready to slip from the touch of civilization." Greaves looked around the room, to where one debtor, one of those that always came in stinking of alcohol, was being restrained by two receivers and launching a filthy torrent of abuse at another. He gave a thin, sad smile. "Is it beyond the bounds of possibility that one of these wretches might have looked at Miss Gloria — young, attractive by all accounts, rising in success — and been taken over by some horrible jealousy?"

Lily turned her face away. She wanted him to gloat, to take pleasure in proving her wrong. She had no defense against reasonableness.

Between interviews, she wandered around, giving those who were ill their medicine and trying to stay away from the accusing stares of the receivers. She kept hoping that Ben or Laud would return, but Theo told her that they had gone to identify the body. Lily sat down beside him, her shoulders hunched. Despite the hordes of receivers, the Almshouse suddenly felt very lonely.

Theo was probing the sores on an old woman's arm, his attention apparently entirely absorbed. As Lily got up to leave, however, he spoke.

"They will come back, Lily, but you must give them time. They have only each other at the moment."

Lily suddenly felt guilty as she realized she had never thought to ask about their family. It came from living at the orphanage: You never asked, in case someone still had parents who had sold them.

"Is there nothing we can do?" Lily said.

Theo looked up at her then, surprised.

"You haven't needed me to instruct you for a long time now, Lily." He wiped his hands and attempted a smile. "We carry on doing all we can. Our work doesn't stop for this."

Lily nodded, feeling very young. She should have been the one to say that. The Almshouse had all been her idea and Theo had put up with it, even when she filled his practice with those who had an illness that no medicine could cure.

"If only there was a clue," she said. "If I could just *do* something and feel that I was helping . . ."

"Sometimes the best thing to do is let the receivers continue with their work," Theo said, although Lily could tell that it left a bad taste in his mouth. "If it helps, Laud mentioned before he left that they didn't find any bottles of emotion on her. He found that to be comforting."

"None at all?" Lily asked, surprised.

Gloria had tried to hide it, but they all knew how serious her problem was. She used to clink as she moved.

"She must have run out." Theo frowned. "It probably made her more nervous, less able to notice things . . ." He sighed, his face pained. "I have seen death so many times, Lily, but rarely anyone I have known. They always vanish from sight."

Lily gave the doctor's hand a reassuring pat, but already her mind was starting to buzz. Something was wrong here, something she couldn't quite put into words.

A triumphant shout broke into her thoughts. Lily turned in alarm to see Sergeant Pauldron in the doorway, framed by two other receivers. And between them, struggling, was Pete, the old fisherman. Inspector Greaves swiftly joined them and, after a hurried exchange of whispers, the receivers withdrew to the cellar, which they had requisitioned as an interview room, taking their prisoner with them.

Lily darted a look in Theo's direction. He nodded.

"I'll look after things here," he said softly. "Go and see."

Lily rushed down the stairs, just in time to see Pete being pushed onto an old barrel that served as a chair. Pauldron had picked up a lantern and was shining it in his face, while the inspector sat sternly before him, his customary geniality no longer in evidence.

In the crazy shadows cast by the lantern, Lily was all but invisible halfway down the stairs. Silently, she listened as Greaves cleared his throat, gesturing to another receiver, a young woman, to take notes.

"Your name is Peter, is that correct?"

"Yes, sir." Pete's voice was rough, but quiet. His whole frame was tense.

"And your age?"

"I have seen thirty-nine summers."

Pauldron leaned in, pushing the light from the lantern into Pete's eyes, illuminating the lines on the fisherman's face and the gray streaks in his hair.

"Strange. You look older than that," he said with a satisfied smile, "or could it be that you are such a liar you can't even be truthful about your age?"

"My life has been a hard one, Sergeant," Pete replied, with a defiant stare, "and the years have struck me harder than many."

Now that Lily looked at him clearly, she could see what he meant. He was not as old as she had thought at all, but his bearing was of a man weighed down by twice his age.

"We have no need to accuse Mr. Peter of anything so trivial, Pauldron," the inspector remarked, adding, with greater emphasis, "The evidence we have is more than enough."

"Evidence?" Pete seemed uncomfortable now, shifting his weight as he sat. "What do you —"

"All in good time," the inspector crisply retorted, then returned to his notes. "Mr. Peter, we have several statements from your fellow — " he hunted for a word — "clients here that mention you having regular conversations with Miss Gloria on her visits. Do you deny this?"

"No need to," Pete grunted. "Sweet girl, always willing to talk. They're good here, but they're busy. Sometimes I just needed someone to lend an ear. Are you saying we need to seal a contract to talk now?"

"Of course not, but these conversations were not limited to this building, were they? Miss Gloria came to find you in the Pisces District on several occasions, did she not?"

Now Pete was beginning to sweat. Lily could see him running a finger around the back of his grubby collar. She felt a chill, remembering the night of Mark's ball, only a week ago, where she had bumped into them herself.

"I . . . I . . ." Pete grasped for words, but Pauldron leaned in close to him again, his distaste palpable.

"There is no use lying, Pete. Remember, I met you there myself, in Miss Gloria's company. Miss Lilith will swear to it as well."

Pete looked down at his hands, clenched before him. He mumbled something into the ground.

"What was that?" the inspector asked, icily patient.

"It . . . it wasn't what you think . . . She . . . Miss Gloria . . . she had a problem. I used to help her out sometimes. It was . . . Glitter . . . you know, bottled emotions . . ."

"We have already noted from her receipts that Miss Gloria purchased an unusually large supply of these substances," the inspector conceded.

Pete gave a humorless laugh.

"She couldn't get enough. 'Obsession' — that was her favorite. She said it made the world seem so much brighter, more interesting. Even her worst clients were easier to praise when she was Glittering." Pete lowered his voice, shame in every syllable. "I know some people, in the slums. I did a few jobs for a cheap Glitter merchant, and he used to trade it to me. I think he thought he could get me hooked. So it wasn't hard to get some for her. Not a lot, but when she needed a little more . . . It's not illegal!" He looked up fiercely. "I checked. There's nothing wrong with me selling it to her."

"If there was nothing wrong, Mr. Peter," the inspector said with quiet intensity, "why is she dead?"

Silence.

"We have witnesses. They say the last time you met, yesterday afternoon, around the fifth hour, you were seen arguing with her. Some say you were shouting. That is the last report we have of Miss Gloria alive."

Silence.

"Tell me, Mr. Peter, what did Miss Gloria give you in return?"

"Food . . . blankets . . . I liked to earn them, not have to ask at the Almshouse . . ."

"Then why could we find no receipts for these purchases at the Directory?"

"You . . . you didn't have the time . . ."

"On the contrary, Mr. Peter, Sergeant Pauldron mentioned your name as soon as the body was discovered, having seen you with the deceased only a week ago. We had all of your receipts brought up from the vaults. They made very interesting reading."

Pete had gone pale now, all of the blood draining from his cheeks. In the midst of her horror, Lily was fascinated. After all that had been revealed, what could make him react like that?

"We found some records dated nearly two years ago now. A contract with none other than the good doctor who owns this establishment." The inspector paused, watching Pete's reaction. "It was for the sale of a child, in exchange for medical treatment."

Peter groaned then, a sound of agony wrenched up from somewhere deep and dark.

"I told myself I was saving him," he whispered, "that if anyone could cure him, the doctor could. I never thought I would get through it too. I thought I'd go the way of my wife, my other little ones . . ." He stopped, sighing. "When he never came back, I thought he'd died as well, until I started to hear about him, hear about his rise." Pete gave a tiny smile then, one filled with sadness and pain. "My Mark . . ."

"Your son, Mr. Peter," the inspector said softly.

Lily felt her breath catch in her throat. After all this time thinking that Mark's father must be a monster, he had been under her roof. And now she felt sorry for him. In a way, selling his son had been the best thing he had ever done for Mark.

She heard Pete take a shuddering breath and saw him wipe at his eyes with the back of his hand. When he spoke again, it was as if something had broken within him — a door that he had kept locked for years had burst open. He almost sounded relieved.

"All right," Pete admitted. "It was nothing to do with food. I gave her what she wanted and she told me how he was, how he was doing . . ."

"You hired her to spy on him," Pauldron said, his voice calm and deadly.

"No," Pete said, leaning forward, "not to spy. I just . . . I wanted to know. He probably hates me. I couldn't show myself to him . . . She was working there anyway . . . It all seemed so perfect . . ."

"Until she told you about the Pescator deal," the inspector said quietly. "There is no use denying it, Mr. Peter. It is registered that you, along with the entire Piscean Fishing Guild, were taken over by the Pescator consortium. It is also a matter of fact that when they introduced their new 'quality control' two months ago, you began to run up debts."

"It . . . it wasn't just me," Pete protested weakly, "none of us could live on what they wanted to trade for . . . not with any self-respect . . ."

"You lost your boat, your home, and finally your work. You became a debtor, thanks to your son." The inspector shook his head. "The Directory provides all records, Mr. Peter."

Pete sat for a moment, his shoulders sagging.

"I couldn't believe it when she told me. Poor girl, she just mentioned it in passing. She didn't know I used to work for them. I shouted at her, but afterward, when I'd thought, I reckoned it must be the stars, paying me back for what I did to my boy." He clenched his fists. "But Miss Gloria . . . she just ran away when I shouted. I didn't do anything else . . . I swear . . ."

"And then you came straight back to the Almshouse?" Pauldron asked softly.

"I . . . walked around, to calm down. But I was back here long before sunset, anyone here will tell you."

"You didn't threaten her?"

"No . . ."

"You didn't tell her she was a filthy liar?"

"No!"

"You didn't grab your old fish knife and . . ."

"I told you, NO!"

Pete tried to rise from the barrel, but the two receivers behind pushed him down. The inspector watched gravely, then he nodded.

"Mr. Peter, you are now a possession of the Directory. We will take you to be stored in the prison until your trial . . ."

"Just don't tell him!" Pete said, suddenly desperate. "Don't tell my boy about me . . . He doesn't need me pulling him down . . ."

Lily couldn't listen to any more. Her head spinning, she ran back up the stairs to the temple. There was so much to take in, yet one thought kept pushing itself to the forefront. She was certain that Pete was telling the truth. He wasn't one of the violent ones. She had seen them, the ones who lashed out from hopelessness. He had too much purpose, even in his new life. He would never strike.

But this wasn't evidence. She was forced to watch as Pete was marched out of the Almshouse in chains, forced to smile and thank the inspector as a guard of four receivers was left on duty to keep away other "undesirables." But she never stopped thinking. Gloria had to have gone somewhere else after she met Pete at five o'clock. Somewhere in the slums perhaps. But where would she have gone? Where could she get what she needed?

And as she stood outside the Almshouse watching the dust from the receivers' boots settle back on the cobbled roads, something caught her eye. It was a tiny piece of glass, fallen from Miss Devine's wall, sparkling in the summer sunlight.

Inside her mind, something slotted into place.

Nothing had changed inside Miss Devine's shop. Lily had been living beside it for over a year now, but she had never been in again. Not since that first time. Now, looking at the walls of glass vials glowing faintly in the windowless gloom, she felt the same fear that had assailed her younger self. But this time, there was something else — determination.

She found Miss Devine adjusting the emotion distiller, her hands scurrying across the controls. Lily glanced at the leather chair in the center, where an old woman who had come to the Almshouse a few days ago lay sprawled, asleep, her chest rising and falling.

"A lot of rage there," Miss Devine commented, without looking up, her expression as bland and businesslike as ever. She dusted her hands on her work dress. "Good-quality anger too. It should fetch a reasonable price on the market. The only difficulty is filtering out the righteousness. No one likes the flavor. It makes it too bitter." She adjusted a couple of controls and a red, fizzing liquid began to drip into a beaker beside her. She watched it, its ruddy glow reflecting in her eyes. "Now," she continued, "what was it you wanted? A little serenity would do wonders for you."

"I think I'd like something else, Miss Devine," Lily said, a hard, implacable calm settling over her. "Knowledge, perhaps."

Miss Devine looked up, one eyebrow raised.

"I don't think I have it in stock," she said carefully, watching for Lily's reaction. "Would you settle for curiosity?"

"Gloria," Lily said, refusing to be distracted, "why hasn't she come to visit you recently?"

Miss Devine shook her head dismissively.

"You might as well ask why the whole city doesn't come calling. Supply and demand, Miss Lily. Customers come and go — "

"Customers maybe, but not addicts," Lily interrupted. "I've heard people say that obsession is the most addictive of all. How much did you sell her to make her come back for more, Miss Devine?"

The emotion seller drew herself up indignantly.

"I don't think you appreciate how small a part of my business the emotions are. I'm a glassmaker by trade. I have no need to rely on — "

"But you do, don't you?" Lily felt the ice within her start to crack. "You prey on people who've sunk as far as they can go. It doesn't matter if they're lying in the street or sitting in mansions, they all come back to you in the end."

"I've never tried to sell to someone who didn't want it," Miss Devine replied frostily. "I'm different from some in that respect. Go into the slums, Miss Lily. At least I'm honest. I don't try to cheat them . . ."

"True. You were the best supplier she knew, so why did she stop coming to you? Why did she need to recruit an old fisherman to find her the emotion she needed?" Something else that Miss Devine had said started to fit into place, and the burning within grew hotter. "Why did she have to go to the slums to find it?"

For a moment, Miss Devine stared at her. There was something new in her eyes behind the disdain. A glimpse of fear.

"I am busy, Miss Lily. I think you know your way out . . ."

Lily felt her hands clenching. There was something here, something that would tie everything up. If only she could bring the threads together.

Her next words seemed to come out of nowhere.

"I listened to some receivers once," she said softly. "They were talking about the law. Do you know the worst crime in Agora, Miss Devine?"

Miss Devine was trying to look uninterested, but she was listening.

Lily continued, "Years ago there was a group of bakers who wanted to make their bread more valuable. But they didn't just use finer flour, no. They decided to talk to the other bakers. They agreed not to sell to everyone, to divide up the city and make people from each district go to one baker and one alone. Then they could trade for whatever they liked. Everyone needed bread."

"A clever strategy," Miss Devine replied slowly.

"Brilliant," Lily said, drawing ever closer, "and illegal. The greatest law in Agora — no one shall prevent trade. The ringleaders were sent to prison."

"The best place for them."

There it was, the halt in the voice, the pause that was a little too long. Lily felt utterly calm, even as, somewhere within, part of her was screaming at Miss Devine. She put her hand on the emotion distiller and met Miss Devine's gaze.

"And those who had agreed not to sell . . . they were arrested too, sold back as servants to the ordinary people they had cheated. Some were even executed, I think. Except for those who confessed and were released." Lily smiled mirthlessly. "After all, the city needed bakers."

This was the moment. Lily knew she mustn't break her gaze. If she did, she would be letting her go. An image of Gloria swam up before her and she kept steady. It was Miss Devine who looked down first.

"There is no record . . ."

"Of course not, but they must have given you something in return. Something that wouldn't have a receipt. But the receivers will find it, Miss Devine." Lily looked the emotion seller up and down. She seemed shrunken, smaller than ever. "You're a businesswoman, Miss Devine. You know when you've gotten a raw deal."

Miss Devine laughed then. One note, harsh and cold.

"We all get a raw deal, every time. We just don't always know it. Even those who think they're on top. Even those who deal in the weakness." Miss Devine picked up the beaker of anger and shook it, its red bubbles jumping in her hand. "That's the wonder of addiction — it holds us all. Whether it's wealth or power or thoughts of an old friend . . . a friend and more . . ." An odd expression crossed her face, almost wistful. Then she looked up at Lily, her eyes narrowing. "Even crusading can become an obsession, Miss

215

Lilith—truth is never more addictive than when it comes to you in the tiniest grains." Miss Devine placed the beaker back down with a resolute clink. "They say he's a prodigy. I don't know about that, but I'll give him this: He knows how to play the game. Keep them unsafe, make sure you're the only one that holds the key to their happiness, and you have their loyalty forever." She turned back to Lily. "Just like any other astrologer, make the future dependent on you."

Lily stepped back, her composure draining away. Her thoughts began to whirl, denying what Miss Devine had just said, trying to think of something else that it might mean, but knowing there was no other option. Gloria had only worked for one astrologer and she had certainly been loyal. There hadn't been a day when she hadn't gone to visit.

"If I find out you're lying," Lily hissed . . . But Miss Devine straightened up, her old confidence back as if it had never gone.

"My dear, I never lie. Lies have no power."

And Lily knew. She knew what must have happened. She knew that Miss Devine was telling the truth.

And she knew where she had to go.

CHAPTER SEVENTEEN

The Box

MARK HEARD the knocking all the way up in the Observatory, but it didn't concern him. He still had people visiting every day to beg for a reading from the great astrologer.

He barely looked up from his star chart when he heard his porter ushering someone in. Maybe it was a messenger from one of the consortia he had joined.

It was only when he heard the clatter of someone on the iron stairs to the Observatory that he looked up, just in time to meet Lily's eyes.

She stood there at the top of the stairs, her apron askew, her hair wild. She was breathing hard, as if she had run all the way up the tower. But her eyes were the only thing Mark could look at — hard, fierce, and accusing.

"Lily," he said, getting up, "I didn't expect to see you."

Lily said nothing, just kept staring. Mark shuffled from foot to foot. She was the uninvited guest, he was in his own home, and yet suddenly he felt like a thief caught in a searchlight.

"Would you like some tea? I could get Snutworth to send some up . . ."

Still nothing. Mark's voice died. The evening light streamed through the windows of the Observatory, catching Lily's eyes so they seemed to glow with their own inner fire as she walked toward him, every step slow and deliberate. Involuntarily, Mark shrank back.

"Lily . . . by all the stars, tell me what's wrong!" Mark said, coming out from behind his desk.

For a second, the two stood face-to-face, Lily looking him up and down, as though seeing him for the first time. Then, at last, she spoke.

"Gloria."

Mark frowned, puzzled.

"I haven't seen her since last night," he explained. "I can fetch someone to look for her if you like . . ."

"She's been found."

Each of Lily's words hung heavy in the air.

Mark shuddered. He felt that somewhere there was a trap here.

"Well, tell her that she should have been at work this morning. Snutworth had to go through my next appearance with me instead — "

"When did you see her last night?" Lily asked with sudden urgency.

"About sunset, I think."

Briefly, she looked relieved, but then her eyes hardened again, as if she had just remembered something.

"How was she last night?"

Her voice was quieter now, but there was nothing quiet about her expression. It seemed frozen in a look not unlike disgust. Mark frowned.

"You know Gloria, Lily. She was . . . nervous, as usual."

"Not being cooperative?"

"Look," Mark said, turning away, "if she's been saying bad things about me, I'm sorry. I had a bad day, but it was her fault for being so irritating . . . I'll apologize when I next see her, because she's a good worker . . ."

"So irritated that you didn't give her the usual bonus?"

Mark froze. His eyes darted to the wooden box on his desk. He had checked it that morning, still half full of little bottles of obsession, faintly glowing in their wooden slots. No one knew about that. No one except him, Gloria, and Snutworth. And Miss Devine too, of course.

He noticed Lily's eyes flick to the box, following his own. He sighed in exasperation and turned back, folding his arms.

"Miss Devine told you, then. Look, I know you've got a problem with bottled emotions, but they're not against the law." Mark shrugged. "I didn't like the time she spent getting her supply, so I arranged to have it delivered here. Always Miss Devine. She's better than most."

Mark looked up to find Lily still staring. He hunched his shoulders. He didn't have to justify himself to her. Business was business. There was a silence as he inspected his cuffs, waiting for Lily to say something, but she did not. Eventually, Mark spoke again.

"Look, I know Laud doesn't like it, but Gloria needs the stuff. It's better this way than her going to look for herself."

"In the slums?"

"I wouldn't know."

"What else wouldn't you know?" Lily's voice was still quiet, but the edge was growing.

"What do you mean?" Mark snapped with irritation. He didn't have time for puzzles.

"Maybe you wouldn't know that Gloria's supply had dried up. That the only safe person she could get it from was you."

Mark shrugged.

"Of course," he said. "What? You wanted her to start taking it more often? This way, she was never late for meetings."

Mark tried to crack a smile, but it wavered and vanished under the onslaught of that stare. Lily began to draw closer to him, her voice growing quiet and hoarse.

"Until you refused to give it to her. Until you took advantage of her problem and out of spite kept it from her."

There was something else in Lily's eyes now. A kind of desperation.

"Tell me you just forgot, Mark. Or tell me I'm wrong. Tell me you handed it over as usual and she went there for some other reason." Lily's face was almost touching his own. "Tell me it wasn't your fault."

"My fault?" Mark drew away as if stung. "What's my fault? What has Gloria been telling you? Look, Lily, I don't know what this is about but I'm busy, so just—"

"Answer me, Mark," Lily said, her voice suddenly loud and fierce.

Mark was temporarily silenced, but then he gave a defiant shrug.

"It isn't a right, you know; it's a treat. She bugged me last night, so I didn't let her have it. So what?"

There was a long silence. Lily seemed incapable of speech. She raised one hand and for a moment Mark thought she was going to strike him. Then she drew it back, stepping away.

"You sent her into the slums. You weren't happy, so you decided to make someone else pay . . ."

"What is this?" Mark asked angrily. "Did she go looking for some cut-rate emotion in the rough area? So what? She doesn't normally ride around in golden carriages, you know. She'll be fine."

"No, Mark." Lily stared back at him, quivering with rage. "She won't be fine. Ever again. She's dead."

Mark felt his stomach lurch, but Lily went on, driving her words into his skull.

"She went into the slums, Mark. You lived there once, so you know how dangerous they are. She went there because she needed her emotions back, the ones that you and Miss Devine and all the others made her depend on if she wanted to feel anything at all. And someone found her. You sent her to her death, Mark."

"Just a minute . . ." Mark felt sick, but at the same time indignation rose within him. "It's not my fault that this happened. You think I'm responsible for every madman or thieving debtor who crawls through those alleys?"

"You didn't think, Mark. You didn't stop for a second to think what she might do. What it would drive her to."

"How could I have known that?" Mark slammed his fist onto the desk, trying to release his pent-up energy. He took a deep breath. "Look, Lily, I'm really sorry this has happened, of course I am, but it was just bad luck . . . really bad luck . . ."

"We make our own fortune, Mark, you know that," Lily said, but there was something gentler in her tone now, she was more like her normal self. "Mark, I know you didn't hold the knife. But you know why she went into the slums, and you can help put things right. The receivers have an old man in custody, a debtor. They think he murdered her, but you can prove them wrong. He has an alibi from an hour before sunset — he was at the Almshouse. If you tell them what you know, that she was here at sunset, they'll have to consider it . . ."

"I would not advise that, sir."

Both of them jumped as Snutworth appeared out of the shadowed stairwell, his tread nearly silent. Mark frowned. Had he been listening in, just like the two of them had done nearly a year ago?

"What's this got to do with you?" Lily bristled, turning to Snutworth.

"Practically everything, Miss Lilith. As Mr. Mark's personal assistant and adviser, I am charged with protecting my master's best interests." He leaned forward, the tip of his silver-handled cane hitting the ground with the quietest of taps. "There is no real evidence linking Mr. Mark with the endangering of Miss Gloria's life, nor with restricting her access to her obsession. To suggest that there is would cause highly unfavorable publicity, which would be . . . less than ideal at present."

Mark was used to Snutworth's way with words by now, particularly his understatement. "Less than ideal" didn't even begin to describe it. Despite his other business deals, his reputation still rested on his predictions. His entire life was based upon people trusting him. A scandal like this would be enough to label him damaged goods forever.

"You think things are bad for you?" Lily replied, looking at Mark sarcastically. "How do you think they are for P—" Lily stopped herself, a look of concern crossing her face — "for this old man?"

"With all due respect, it seems that this old man is guilty," Snutworth added calmly, pulling a parchment scroll out of the pockets of his coat. "I heard about this tragic affair from my associates in the receivers a few hours ago. I had planned to inform you, sir, when I had been fully apprised of the facts." Snutworth unrolled the parchment and laid it before Mark with a flourish. "As you can see, sir, the receivers searched the old debtor's squat and found a most suspicious knife. Further tests have proved conclusive — the receivers have their man. So really, this little upset is entirely unnecessary."

Mark glanced down at the scroll, a report that went into sickening detail. He pushed it away, feeling ill. He didn't even glance at the name of the suspect.

"That's all in order, Snutworth," he said, before turning to Lily, who still stood, fuming, before him. "Lily . . . I didn't want this to happen, but it's just a coincidence that I had an argument with her. The receivers have the murderer. He must have sneaked out later that night."

Lily stared back at him, unspeaking, her brow furrowed as if she were making a decision.

"Mark," she said at last, "would you let the receivers execute a man without knowing all the facts? Don't you feel anything for him? He's old enough to be your father . . ."

Mark bridled.

"My dad has nothing to do with this. Don't try to blackmail me that way . . ."

"But he might have children your age. Won't you think about them?"

"Why should I? He's probably sold them off already and even that didn't stop him from becoming a debtor," Mark spat. "All children are orphans in this city, Lily, you should know that."

"You must forgive her, sir," Snutworth added, with a sad shake of the head. "Do try to see it from her point of view." He smiled patronizingly in Lily's direction. "Thanks to her Almshouse, her friend Miss Gloria was placed in constant contact with the lowest of the low, forever in view of the disturbed and the desperate . . ." Snutworth left the thought hanging in the air, before bowing his head. "Denial is part of mourning."

"I can't believe I'm hearing this," Lily shouted, turning back to Mark. "By all the heavens, can't you see what's happening? They want to brush this into the corner, just like we always do with something we don't want to think about. But you have an opportunity to change this, Mark . . . to save an innocent man and make them look for the real killer . . . Why can't you see? You have to, you owe her — "

"I don't have to do anything."

Mark glared back at Lily, Snutworth's words ringing in his ears.

"Snutworth's right. It's just as much your fault as mine. I don't care how you dress it up, Lily. It's your fault that she met this old murderer. I'm not going to ruin my reputation to make you feel better."

Silence. The last rays of the sun hung in the tower, illuminating two faces. Mark saw his own — defiant, resolved — reflected in Lily's dark eyes. Then, in one sudden movement, she swept her hand across his desk. The wooden box crashed to the ground, the little vials of obsession bursting out and smashing on the floor.

Nobody moved. Mark wasn't going to give her the satisfaction. Eventually, it was Snutworth who spoke.

"Naturally, Mr. Mark will expect a contract within the week offering items to trade for that."

Lily's eyes never left Mark's face. The flash of anger had left them hard and cold.

"Congratulations, Mark," she said at last in a hollow voice. "You are a true son of Agora."

Lily bowed stiffly, as if she were a tradesman calling on business, and stepped away. She left without another word, the sound of her footsteps echoing all the way down the tower until the front door closed behind her.

For a while, they stood in silence, then Snutworth looked down at the shattered box and prodded it with the end of his cane.

"It will not stop here, sir," he said softly. "She is a crusader. She will find some way to get her story known."

Mark leaned forward on his desk, looking bleakly at the star charts spread out there. There was nothing in them to guide him. They seemed like meaningless patterns of dots.

"What do you advise?" he said finally.

"A truth will emerge, that is inevitable," Snutworth mused. "But it cannot be one that damages you, sir. There is too much at stake. In a few years, you could be the greatest force in the city. She is merely the custodian of the debtors, but they will never go away. The receivers must understand how her Almshouse does nothing but cause chaos, and will do so again and again. May I suggest a word with the Lord Chief Justice? A letter expressing the concerns of an important businessman should be all the excuse he needs to take action—an answer to the protests of her patrons, to ensure that the receivers do not look biased. It will not be difficult, I gather that the Almshouse is already highly distrusted by the receivers and as Lord Ruthven happens to be their commander . . ."

"If I do that," Mark said, thinking aloud, "they'll close her down."

"That is entirely possible, sir."

Mark ran his hands through his hair, looking up and out through the windows of the Observatory. A few stars had appeared now that the sun was sinking below the towers of the city.

"There must be another way."

"Give and take, sir; her reputation for yours. Someone will have to be blamed. Which of you is going against everything that our great city holds dear?"

More stars came out, emerging in the darkness.

"I can't. She's my friend."

"A friend who is perfectly prepared to put the interests of her murderous debtors above your future," Snutworth replied quietly, reasonably. "She must think that you are worth very little."

Mark stared as the last of the twilight gave way to the night sky.

"Snutworth . . ."

"Sir?"

"Find me Lord Ruthven's address."

"No need, sir. I shall deliver your letter personally."

Mark sat down, dipped his quill in the ink, and began to write. He felt empty, as if something had left him. He knew what he was doing as he formed the words, knew that he should be feeling something—remorse, anger, pain. But it was as if Gloria's death, and Lily's accusation, had left him hollow. All he could see was the scandal, his own fall, a return to that slum world where people were murdered — the world outside the tower. A world he never wanted to see again.

It was too late for Gloria, and as for Lily . . .

But he stopped himself from thinking about Lily. Her final stare was still burned into his mind.

After Snutworth had gone, bearing the letter laying out his concerns over the Almshouse and its part in causing violence, Mark sat for a long time at his desk. He didn't light the lamps.

"You or me, Lily," he said at last, to no one. "You or me."

Chapter Eighteen

The Night

WHEN THE ALMSHOUSE was a temple, the open roof had been used to hold midsummer services for its tiny congregation. The old priests would have been amazed to see how many it held most nights now, as people wrapped in fraying blankets slept in the late summer heat.

Tonight, though, there was only Lily, leaning on the parapet, staring out across the twisting streets of the Sagittarius District. The Almshouse's guiding light had been extinguished, so now it was just the waning moon that provided illumination. Occasionally, a rush of sparks would fly up from Miss Devine's chimney as she worked at her glassblowing furnace late into the night, tinting the shadows with crimson flame. Below, people moved back and forth as always, but tonight they seemed subdued. Sometimes, one of them glanced toward the Almshouse, before turning away with a shudder.

Clasped in her hands, Lily still held the document that Inspector

Greaves had handed her that evening. Officially, it claimed that the receivers were shutting her down only while they continued to investigate the life theft, but Lily could read between the lines. It had talked too much of the Almshouse's role in causing "unrest" and "dangerous tension." Lily had heard those same sentiments only two days before, in the mouth of Mark's assistant. But no mere servant would have been taken seriously by the Lord Chief Justice.

Lily had read it through twice, unspeaking, and then looked up at the inspector, his face solemn and grave, and asked if Mark had sent a letter. If he had used his influence to make this happen.

Greaves had not lied to her. He had not answered.

"Miss Lilith," he had said, "I am sorry that this had to happen."

"Did it?" Lily had said, feeling the bitterness well up inside her.

Greaves had put his hands on hers.

"This was the inevitable result of mixing with debtors. I should have warned you, but—" he had paused and given a sad smile— "sometimes I am too curious for my own good. It comes from being an inspector."

"You're wrong," Lily had said, withdrawing her hands. "The Almshouse had nothing to do with Gloria's death."

"Everything is connected, Miss Lilith. Everything." He had glanced at a pocket watch attached to his midnight-blue coat by a long silver chain. "If you will excuse me, duty calls."

She had not spoken after that. She had remained silent as the announcement was made by the receivers. She did not cry out as the debtors left, some having to be dragged, clinging and flailing. One had even attacked a receiver. The debtor had quickly been clubbed senseless, but the wounded receiver was still below, being tended to by Theo. He was the only patient left in their sanctuary that night. She forced her lips closed, knowing how many of the receivers were waiting for her to protest, to raise her voice against them so that she too could be marched off to prison. When, at last, the Almshouse stood empty, she met Theo's gaze.

"Lily . . ." he said, spreading his hands hopelessly.

But Lily couldn't reply. Not then. She held up one hand and, ever sensitive, he understood. He turned back to his work.

Now, up on the roof, Lily had nothing but her thoughts for company. Thoughts that she desperately didn't want to have. Thoughts that reminded her that she had invited Gloria to start working here. Thoughts that made her look at the crumbling stonework around her, at Theo's practice, which was itself on the verge of destruction. No ordinary patient had visited for months. She still heard herself shouting at Mark, giving in to the terrible anger that came over her when she was so sure that she saw injustice, and that, like any fire, burned her as badly as anyone else. A better person would have persuaded, not accused, not made an enemy of her oldest friend, however wrong he was; would have had the courage to tell him about his father, even if it was certain to make things worse.

And then, when she thought of her other friends, Lily let the Closing Order flutter to the ground, her hands slack. She had thought she had sacrificed everything to her vision, but this night all she had lost were a few dreams. But Theo had given his practice; Benedicta, her innocence; Gloria, her life. She had taken everything they had offered and barely noticed. And she was supposed to be the one who believed in helping others.

She heard a step behind her. Theo, she thought. More than anything, she needed to talk to him now. She turned.

Laud looked back at her.

Lily froze, unable to speak. In the moonlight, he looked ghostly, his pale skin stark and his eyes shadowed. Only his hair, grown longer than usual, glowed red in the silvery light. For one dreadful moment, his resemblance to Gloria struck her and Lily had to turn away, unable to bear looking at him. He came forward and stood beside her, also staring out over the streets. He didn't speak.

"How is Benedicta?" Lily said at last, feeling the silence weigh on her.

"Better," Laud said, his voice tired. "She's below, with the doctor. She wanted to return earlier, but there were . . . things to sort out."

"Of course." Lily said hurriedly. "You didn't need to come back, you know. It must be hard . . ."

"Ben will survive," Laud said, still looking out, not meeting her eye. "She's stronger than I imagined."

Lily nodded but did not reply. The two stood in silence for a little longer.

"Did Theo tell you about the closing of the Almshouse?" Lily asked. "Because I want you to know that I won't ask you or Ben to fight for me. It's my responsibility, mine alone," she rushed on, babbling out her thoughts. "I'll do what I can. If it doesn't work, so be it, but I'm not letting anyone else . . ."

"That's not your decision, Lily."

Lily stared at Laud then. He kept his eyes fixed ahead, out into the distance, but now his hands gripped the balcony edge with greater force.

"Decisions are a strange thing," he continued reflectively. "When our parents disappeared, it was just the three of us. We had to fight to keep Benedicta. She had just turned ten at the time. I was thirteen, a man in the eyes of the law, but I still looked up to Gloria. She was the big sister, she had seen sixteen summers, so she had to be mother. We all had to choose how to survive." Laud gave a low chuckle. "Benedicta could stay the child: She made herself laugh and smile until it became second nature. I built a shell of words: I used them as a weapon. But Gloria — " he bit his lip — "Gloria was the one that carried us, who would put up with anything. That's why she started to praise people for a living. That's why I followed her." His smile vanished. "I was expecting our customers to be not worth our words and I was right. I never used to mean what I said. But for Gloria, sincerity was everything. She had to believe, had to force herself to admire our clients. In the end, even her enthusiasm wasn't enough. But she couldn't stop. We needed her too much." Laud cast down his eyes. "They say obsession is just concentrated enthusiasm. I wanted her to give it up, and so did Ben; she couldn't keep it hidden from us. We both knew the signs: the nervousness, the unnaturally bright eyes. But neither of us knew how much she needed it. And all to keep praising those who never deserved it. Not as much as she did."

Lily looked away, her eyes hot and blurring, and felt Laud's hand on her arm.

"Then, over these last few months, I saw something I never thought I'd see again. There was a project that Gloria was working on so hard, almost running herself into the ground to promote. I thought she'd started taking a larger dose, but when I looked at her, it *was* her again. The Gloria I knew, before she had started to buy her emotions. I asked her what had changed and she told me."

Laud grasped Lily's shoulders and turned her around to face him. His eyes shone fiercely in the moonlight.

"She told me that she didn't need the obsession when she was working for the Almshouse. She said she was planning to stop all other projects because this was the one that was worth something." Laud's eyes darkened. "A few days later, it was over. But in those few days she was my sister again."

His grip on Lily's shoulders tightened, while his voice sank to a whisper.

"If you give up, Lily, you'll be killing her all over again. I won't let that happen."

For a moment, Lily stared back. And then she understood.

"Thank you, Laud," she said simply, and Laud nodded.

A tiny smile played on his face. Lily returned it. They didn't speak.

Then they heard a discreet cough. Both turned, Laud letting his hands drop to his sides. Theo had appeared at the top of the stairs, a quizzical expression on his thin face.

"I think I may have found something interesting," he said.

Lily and Laud followed him quickly back down the stairs into the main room of the temple. There, the wounded receiver slept on a wooden cot, his cuts freshly bandaged. Benedicta stood nearby, looking down at him.

Lily rushed over and Benedicta turned to greet her. For a few seconds, they shared a wordless hug. Then, as Ben pulled away, Lily looked into her face. It was still the same Ben, but there was something new there, something hard and determined. Now was not the time for comforting.

Benedicta held up a sheaf of papers.

"Dr. Theophilus found these in the receiver's pockets," Benedicta began. "They seem to be a progress report on the investigation. I've been reading them."

"Doctor, I thought I left her in your care," hissed Laud.

"I did not suggest it," Theo added, anxiously picking at his mustache, "but Miss Benedicta insisted. I thought it might be too distressing—"

"I've had my time to mourn," Benedicta snapped, cutting him off. Seeing their surprise, she softened her expression. "I know what you're doing, but you can't shelter me anymore. Maybe if Gloria had confided in me more often . . ." A look of pain crossed her face, only to be swiftly banished. "Come on, listen to this."

She began to read:

*As the recent arrest of Peter of the Pisces District has
provided conclusive evidence, the search of this area will be
halted. Reports will be provided on the following areas . . .*

"They think they've found the right person, so they've just
stopped! They haven't even looked carefully around the place
where they . . . found her . . ."

Lily put a comforting hand on Benedicta's shoulder, but her
mind was already whirring as she looked down the list. Despite the
tone of the report, everything seemed to have been done. There
had been an extensive investigation. Except . . .

"Ben," Lily said, "where exactly did they find her again?"

Benedicta looked over at her brother. He frowned and pointed
to a spot on the map at the end of the report.

"Lock Street, on the corner," he muttered. "But give them some
credit. They were competent enough to search the scene."

"Then why haven't they searched the square at the other end of
Lock Street?" Lily said.

Something about the pattern of alleyways, right up against the
city walls, stirred something in her memory.

"Lord Ruthven . . ." she said, grasping at the memory.

"He won't help," Theo mused. "He has no love of charity . . ."

"No, not help," Lily said, still thinking. And then it hit her. "Lock
Street! That was where I followed Lord Ruthven, after Mark's ball.
That was where . . ." She paused, suddenly realizing what she was
saying. "That was where I bumped into Gloria. Near an old building
by the city walls. And the receivers haven't searched it. Look . . .
there's a cross on the map. They've been told *not* to go there."

Laud shook his head.

"It's a chance in a million. What's to say that this one building is
more significant than any other?"

"Most slums don't get visited by the Lord Chief Justice," Lily

233

replied darkly, another memory stirring. "I think I heard him talking about it. He called it the Clockwork House."

Laud looked as if he was about to raise another objection, until he caught Benedicta's eye. Something passed between them, a kind of understanding that Lily couldn't catch. Then he nodded cautiously.

"All right, perhaps we should investigate . . ."

"We?" Theo queried, alarmed. "Surely this is a matter for the receivers."

"They won't do anything, Theo," Lily said. "They think they have their man." She stood back, joining Laud and Ben. "We won't ask you to come with us, but we have to find out the truth." Lily drew a little closer and whispered so that only Theo could hear. "If we can't find the truth, we'll never be able to let her go."

Theo looked back at them, then glanced over to where Count Stelli slept fitfully on a cot against the wall. He frowned.

"Just let me check on Grandfather, and then I'll get my lantern. We'll be safer in greater numbers."

In the end they kept the lantern shuttered. It was far better to slip along the moonlit streets without attracting attention. Even past midnight the alleyways of Agora were far from deserted. As they ventured further toward the Pisces District, Laud and Theo drew their tricornered hats down over their faces, while Lily and Benedicta, who had insisted on coming, pulled black cloaks around their shoulders. All four walked close together. It was not for warmth, as the late summer's night was almost sultry, but for protection — from the shadows around them, a thousand eyes watched their progress.

It was almost a relief to near their goal. When they came to the corner of Lock Street, though, Lily couldn't suppress a shudder. It looked just like the rest of the slums. They could tell where Gloria had been found only from the small patch of cobblestones that had been swept clean. A bright spot among the filth-blackened streets.

Benedicta swallowed, her face paler than usual.

"Please . . . let's get this over with," she said.

Soon after that, they arrived. It was as unremarkable a square as Lily remembered, although now, in the small hours, its only occupants were curled in corners and doorways, sleeping. In the silvery light, the ancient building seemed out of proportion, looming up before them larger than it should be, both falling into the square and leaning back to rest on the vast city walls behind.

Without conscious thought, they moved as one, Lily leading the way while the others kept watch.

Lily reached out her hand. She tried the door.

Without a creak, without any sound, it swung open.

Theo opened one shutter on his lantern. A beam of light extended into the darkness beyond, but illuminated nothing. Lily looked around at her companions. They didn't need to say anything.

They stepped inside.

The silence within hung heavy on the air. Lily could hear her own breathing, quick and high, more nervous than she would admit to feeling. Something was wrong. The door had been left unlocked. Any other house would have been crowded with squatters sheltering from the eyes of receiver patrols. Lily followed the beam of Theo's lantern. It swept over a dusty stone floor, over old oak beams, and stopped. In the darkness, the light gleamed off something metallic. And sharp.

Lily caught her breath as Laud fumbled with the shutter of his own lantern, inwardly cursing that she had not brought one herself. She felt Benedicta take her hand in the dark.

Laud's shutter opened. Another beam. For a moment, relief flooded into Lily's mind. It was not a weapon. Then she looked again.

"Well," Theo whispered in awe, "that's why he called it the Clockwork House."

Dominating the room, stretching back into the house, was a vast tangle of machinery. Cogs, crankshafts, and wheels rose up to the ceiling and plunged down to the flagstones beneath them. Aside from the shiny and sharp-toothed cog that had caught the light, the whole edifice bore the rusty marks of time. Fascinated, Lily touched the nearest part. Its surface was rough and cool. No one had used this machine for years. Standing there, she felt dwarfed by this vast, incomprehensible secret. Turning, she could see Benedicta and Laud examining the walls of the house, perplexed, while Theo stared up at the works with foreboding.

"Just a damp old house," Theo muttered, a tremble in his voice. "Nothing particularly strange about it," he added, as if trying to convince himself. "Probably some inventor down on his luck, years ago . . ."

"Which of the Lord Chief Justice's duties requires him to inspect ancient machinery?" Lily replied, raising an eyebrow.

"Who would bother making something that size for no reason?" Laud added, straightening up from his investigation. "I can't find any controls. If only there were another door, or perhaps . . ."

"A staircase?" Benedicta said softly.

The other three turned to see her moving aside a loose floor slab made of much thinner stone than the others. Beneath it, a set of wooden stairs descended into darkness. Hurriedly, Lily knelt down beside the hole in the floor and peered in. Something on the stairs below sparkled in the lantern light. The tiniest piece of gold leaf, fallen, Lily was sure, from an ornate mask of an eclipsed sun. The events of the night of Mark's ball flashed before her again.

"Lord Ruthven must have come this way," she murmured, looking up at the others.

Laud shone his lantern further down the stairwell, to the bottom. A solid oak door stood at the end of the steps, an elaborate design of a set of scales carved into its surface.

"Libra, the scales . . ." Theo said quietly. "Grandfather did manage to teach me something . . . Wait . . . Libra . . ." Then, suddenly, he seized Lily's arm. "You never told me this had anything to do with the Libran Society!"

"Libran Society?" Lily replied, confused, pulling her arm out of his grasp. "Who are they?"

Theo shook his head.

"I don't know. That's just it — no one does. No one outside the highest in the city. Grandfather hated them. He said they were dangerous, that they had too many secrets . . ."

"And this is one of them," Lily replied. "We won't find the truth by running away from secrets."

Theo thought for a moment, then bowed his head in submission.

"I'll stand guard. But please, be as quick as possible."

Leaving the doctor at the top, Lily, Laud, and Benedicta crept down the stairs. The handle of the oak door moved easily in Ben's hand, and Laud held his lantern out into the darkness. Lily half expected shouts of surprise, or running footsteps, but there was nothing. Nothing except Benedicta's gasp at the room beyond the door.

The house above may have been decrepit, but the secret chamber was furnished for comfort and grandeur. Elegant tapestries of stern men and women hung on the walls. A few embers glowed in the grate of an elaborate fireplace. On the low ceiling, a design of interlocking arcane symbols stretched from corner to corner. The room was dominated by an ebony table, with padded chairs spaced around it. Laud put down his lantern, all of its shutters open, in the center of the table, and its light cast flickering shadows on the walls.

Lily peered around the room, searching for some kind of record or logbook, anything to hint at what was discussed in this hidden meeting house. At the head of the table, a sheaf of papers lay next to an inkwell and pen, but as she riffled through them she found that they were all blank. As she put them back, however, her gaze fell on something that had been underneath them — a pile of flat disks, glittering gold in the lamplight, inscribed with strange designs.

"Do you think they deal in jewelry?" Laud asked, holding up something between his thumb and finger. "I found some of these at the other end of the table."

It resembled a piece of smoky crystal, intricately cut and faceted. As Lily looked at it, the lamplight seemed to be drawn in, a tiny flame forming in its heart. She blinked, telling herself not to be distracted. This was just a trick of the light.

Lily held out her hands and Laud dropped the gemstone into them. Staring at it, something stirred in her memory, something distant and dreamlike. Just as she reached for it, however, a more recent memory forced itself to the surface. An image of her record at the orphanage, and the payment for her care, left in strange gemstones that shone with an inner light . . .

"Laud! Lily!" Benedicta called over from the fireplace, interrupting Lily's thoughts.

Lily hurried over in time to see Benedicta pull something from the ashes beneath the grate with a set of fire tongs. She held it up for Lily to see. It was a piece of parchment, scorched and nearly illegible, but some words were still clear.

"The Midnight Charter . . ." Lily read aloud, squinting at the lettering. ". . . hereby agreed that . . . until the time when the

Antagonist . . . preserve the structure . . . the Protagonist must, with full support . . . lead to dissolution . . . as stated below . . ."

She pulled the charred paper toward her, trying to read it better, and the bottom part crumbled away, leaving her with only the title, unburned, grasped in her hands.

Benedicta brushed the fragments from her dress.

"It doesn't seem to make much sense," she mused. "What's a charter anyway?"

Lily frowned, trying to remember.

"I think I saw a couple at the bookbinder's, in the record books," she said. "It's a foundation contract, a kind of list of rights and aims when you start something new, like a guild or — " Lily paused, struck by a thought — "or maybe a society. But it didn't look like anything I've seen before."

Laud came over to join them, scowling.

"It must be important," he mused, before adding irritably, "They had to make it so complicated, didn't they? Would it kill them to write something simple?"

"Simplicity is so rare nowadays, isn't it, Mr. Laudate?"

The voice came from the doorway.

All three spun around. Framed in the entrance, one foot still on the stairs, stood a figure in an all too familiar midnight-blue coat.

"Sergeant!" Lily said nervously. "We were just — "

"I think the term is breaking and entering," Sergeant Pauldron continued smoothly, stepping into the room. His eyes caught the lamplight and gleamed as he surveyed them. "An unusual method of mourning, Miss Benedicta, Miss Lilith. Anyone would think that you knew more than you had admitted about the unfortunate incident."

"Not at all, sir," Lily said, hastily dropping the charred fragments into the pocket of her apron. "We thought, perhaps . . ."

Lily's brain raced wildly, trying to think of an explanation that did not involve reading an unconscious receiver's report. "A fresh pair of eyes . . . and some debtors told us that they thought this place was strange . . ."

Lily's voice died away under Pauldron's gaze. He was utterly still, but there was some kind of suppressed energy about him. He took another step forward.

"Miss Lilith, I thought you realized that the case is solved. There is no question of who took Miss Gloria's life . . ."

Benedicta bounded forward, seizing Pauldron's arm beseechingly.

"But that can't be true! Pete wouldn't do that, not in a thousand years . . ."

Pauldron put a hand gently on Benedicta's shoulder.

"Child, you must know that everyone has their secrets."

Lily frowned. Something nagged away at the back of her mind. Something important. Something wrong. If only she could . . .

"Sergeant," she said slowly and deliberately, "where is Dr. Theophilus? We left him standing guard."

Almost imperceptibly, she saw Pauldron's fingers tighten on Benedicta's shoulder. Lily looked for his other hand, but it was out of sight.

"Ben," Lily continued, "I think you should come over here."

"I . . . don't think I can," Benedicta said, her voice high and strained.

"It might not be a wise idea," Pauldron agreed, "but you can turn, a little."

Slowly, stiffly, Benedicta turned. But it was not her pale face or trembling hands that caught Lily's attention. It was the long, slim-bladed knife that the sergeant was pressing against her stomach, just hard enough to cut the fabric of her shawl. It glittered in the lamplight, as cold and hard as his eyes.

Laud started and Pauldron turned his attention to him with a flick of his head.

"Be still, boy. This doesn't concern you. If you are fortunate this sister will not go the same way as the last one."

There was a horrible silence. Laud's eyes seemed riveted to the knife, but Lily's were looking into Pauldron's oddly impassive face.

"The knife is clean," Lily said quietly, keeping her voice level.

Pauldron gave the tiniest of nods.

"A truncheon saw to the doctor. Quieter. I think he may only be unconscious, for the moment."

Lily swallowed. Her throat was suddenly dry and her heartbeat pounded in her ears so loud she could barely hear herself speak, but she continued, not daring to crack.

"Why Pete?"

"What makes you think I wish to answer your questions?" Pauldron asked, his mouth cracking into a sneer.

Lily held his gaze.

"Why else keep us alive?" she said.

She could see Pauldron weighing the question. His tone was light, the most casual he had ever sounded. If he had not had Benedicta at knifepoint it could almost have been a normal conversation.

"At first, I think, little more than an old-fashioned scapegoat. But now I know his family secret," he smiled, but his eyes did not. "I think that the execution of the father he thought was already dead will be a good distraction to put Mr. Mark off his guard. And after Peter is executed . . . the son will soon be reunited with the father."

"I see," Lily said.

Her tone was the height of calm but internally her mind was screaming, trying desperately to think of a way out. Then she heard Laud speak in a voice of barely suppressed rage.

"First Gloria, then Mark! What possible reason . . ."

Pauldron shook his head, slowly and deliberately.

"Sorry to disappoint you, Mr. Laudate, but Miss Gloria is not relevant. She never was. Not that it really matters to her now."

He moved the knife up Benedicta's dress, cutting the merest wisp of fabric as he went. Benedicta grew paler, but said nothing.

"You know," Pauldron continued, "I doubt she felt a thing. She was so very — " he gave a hollow smile — *"emotional* that night. Then again, those slum dealers are very reasonable. It only cost me a week's rations to get hold of enough. Even so, she took some persuading before she would follow me here. But it had to be here, you see. I had to lead you here. To the place of my epiphany."

Lily's heart sank, even as Pauldron went on.

"The Clockwork House is a very special building. The original purpose of the machinery is lost, but the society continues to meet here because it is such a wondrous symbol. A symbol of Agora and of the harmony that they — that we — wish to achieve. Every cog interlinking, every part working together for the glory of the whole, no one piece trying to set itself up as higher or worthier than the others." He fixed Lily with a stare and touched the tip of the knife to Benedicta's throat. "Do you believe in fate, Miss Lilith?"

Lily looked back at him, inwardly berating herself for not seeing that finding that report had been all too convenient. She sized Pauldron up, trying to decide what answer he wanted, but those cold, dead eyes were inscrutable. Eventually, she chose the truth.

"No," she said.

Pauldron nodded.

"Neither do I. I believe that we can choose our future. And I will not have the one that you will bring." He looked over at Laud, who was trying to sidle toward him. "Attempt that again, boy, and you alone will be responsible for the consequences."

He didn't raise his voice or show any sign of anger, yet as they watched, a spot of blood welled up on the tip of the knife. Laud stepped back, shaken.

Lily's mind began to whirr, slotting together things he had said.

"My future?" she said tentatively. "You mean the Almshouse?"

Pauldron's lip curled.

"A festering sore in Agora's heart. But no, not the Almshouse. That's nothing more than a symptom." His voice sank to a deadly whisper. "The Almshouse is not the source of the poison."

He looked straight at her then and the cold, impassive eyes gave way to an expression of utter hatred.

"We take an oath, Miss Lilith, when we join the receivers. To serve Agora and her virtues for all our life. We seal a contract with the city. A contract I saw my fellow receivers breaking every day, looking the other way, ignoring the law. Some of them said that I didn't live in the real world. I began to falter in my belief, to compromise."

Pauldron started to shake. Benedicta shrank back, but he kept a firm grip on her shoulder. "But higher wisdoms prevailed. They saw my devotion, my purity. They inducted me into their deepest secrets. They led me here to this house, to this room, to the center of this wonderful, glorious dream." He stared into the distance, an ecstatic smile on his face. "They led me to the Midnight Charter."

Pauldron moved suddenly. For one horrible moment, Lily saw Benedicta stagger, but the sergeant had only pushed her to the floor, unharmed. Benedicta tried to struggle away from him, but he placed his foot on her back.

"Not just yet, little one," he cooed. "Soon, but not yet."

"It's not her you want, is it?" Lily said, the last of her thoughts aligning. "It's me."

Pauldron gave the tiniest of nods.

"You and that impostor Mark. Strange, I often wondered why so many patrols were sent to observe you. No one would ever tell me why. My superiors always said it was too complex to understand.

But actually, you see, it is very simple. The Midnight Charter is not long. It nearly made me wake up from this beautiful dream."

At the edge of her vision, Lily noticed Benedicta slowly inching across the floor. She looked away, focusing on Pauldron. She had to keep him talking.

"Dream?" she said, almost casually.

"Agora itself, Miss Lilith. Nothing but a dream. None of us real, all locked away in our perfect, pure city. Until you two, Miss Lilith. Until both of you destroy us." His face twisted with anger. "You, whose fire will consume everything I swore to uphold. I found my own fire. I burned away its dreadful words, but still they remained. Still they were not destroyed." He leaned closer. "But it can be stopped. Two years to go, but I will save everything. I will take his place and defeat you. So you see, Miss Lilith, in the end it isn't complicated at all. It is simple. And Agora lasts forever and ever, thanks to the simplest thing of all." Pauldron raised his knife. "Come then, Antagonist. Come and die."

But as Pauldron lunged forward, Benedicta grabbed at his legs, pulling him over. He snarled, lashing out with a foot and kicking her to one side, then struggled to his feet.

Meanwhile Lily stooped down to the fireplace, wrapping the corner of her cloak around her hand.

The sergeant turned on Benedicta, but as he sprang Laud seized him under the arms, buying his sister time to stagger to her feet and run up the stairs. They struggled, but Pauldron was stronger. With a twist, he slashed at Laud's arm, opening a red, shining gash. The younger man let go, grimacing in pain, and fell back, knocking the lantern from the table. It burst on the floor, splashing burning oil across the room, catching on the tapestries and papers. Pauldron turned back to Lily, his eyes glittering in the firelight. He raised his knife.

Lily brought up her hand. In it, readable despite the smoke, she held the remains of the Midnight Charter. Pauldron stared, fascinated, his breath coming in gasps, his shoulders shaking with rage. For just a moment, he was gone, retreated into his own mind. It was long enough. Lily drew back her other hand, the one wrapped in her cloak, and threw a handful of hot embers into his eyes.

Pauldron howled in pain, bringing his knife down inches from Lily's head. In desperation, she tried to slip past him, but his flailing hands caught her by the hair. He peered at her through weeping, burning eyes.

"You will never destroy us," he hissed, "not even if the Director himself wills it."

He raised his knife to strike, but Lily refused to close her eyes. She waited for the blow.

Instead, she heard a dull thud and saw Pauldron slump to the ground.

Emerging from the greasy smoke wielding a truncheon, Inspector Greaves stood over the crumpled form of his sergeant. Lily felt a thousand words rise to her mouth, but the inspector raised a weary hand.

"There will be time later, Miss Lilith. Let's get you and your friends out of here."

For the first time ever, Lily agreed with everything the inspector said.

CHAPTER NINETEEN

The Trial

*. . . Our latest reports say that Mr. Laudate and his
sister are recovering well from their injuries. Inspector
Greaves, while still making no comment on how his own
sergeant could have become suddenly deranged,
remarked that he was glad that Miss Benedicta had had
the presence of mind to fetch the nearest patrol. When our
reporter questioned him on why he was patrolling the
slums himself, far from his usual duties, the inspector
declined to comment . . .*

Mark put down the newspaper, his head spinning. He had already
read it three times since Snutworth had brought it in that morning
and still he found the story hard to believe.

He looked over at his breakfast congealing on a tray and found
that he was not hungry. His eyes drifted back to the newspaper.

They hadn't mentioned why Gloria had been so easily tempted into the slums. He was safe.

Edgily, he glanced toward Snutworth, who was still standing to one side of the dining table. His face was utterly neutral. This unsettled Mark. Snutworth seemed to be waiting for his reaction. It felt like a test, and Mark wasn't sure what the correct response was. He certainly knew that the feeling that had robbed him of his appetite was not relief.

"A terrible thing," he said at last, cautiously.

Snutworth nodded.

More silence.

Mark looked down at the newspaper again, studiously avoiding his servant's gaze.

"I'm glad that Lily and her friends are recovering. It says here that Dr. Theophilus was even well enough to treat the others himself after a few hours."

"That is certainly good to hear."

"Yes," Mark muttered. "Only caught him a glancing blow in the dark apparently."

"How fortunate."

Mark rolled up the newspaper and bit hard into a piece of toast. Snutworth was still waiting, expecting something. Mark desperately wanted him to go but could not bring himself to send the man away. He really shouldn't allow himself to be intimidated by his own servant. Anyway, there was something he needed to do.

"Snutworth, I'm going out."

"Very well, sir."

"I won't be back for a few hours. Will you deal with any business?"

"Naturally, sir."

Still that expectation, that watchful eye, as Mark brushed the crumbs from his mouth and slipped on his coat. It was too warm for it, of course, but Mark couldn't look like just anyone.

And then he realized what Snutworth was waiting for. He paused, choosing his words very carefully.

"Snutworth," he said slowly, "if anyone comes asking about this . . . you will be very sorry that we don't know anything, won't you?"

Snutworth gave a satisfied smile.

"That, sir, goes without saying."

As Mark closed the front door of the tower behind him, however, he was not satisfied at all. If anything, the tightness in his stomach had grown worse. As his feet unconsciously propelled him forward, he found he was barely noticing the people thronging around him, most hazarding a respectful nod to the famous astrologer. He was still trying to work out whether the feeling was guilt or fear.

It wasn't that he had done anything wrong, not really, but it could be made to look like that, and after their last meeting he knew he couldn't count on Lily's goodwill.

Mark shivered. The newspaper report said that Pauldron had felt no remorse. He'd treated Gloria as if she was worthless.

Worthless.

Mark shook his head. He was at the Central Plaza now and had to keep his wits about him. He had never been this way before, but his visit was long overdue.

The streets of the Sagittarius District twisted before him. The smells of a late summer day rose up from the mud of the street and the press of bodies. Mark wrinkled his nose but pressed on. Living the good life had not made him forget these smells, or how easily they faded into the background in time.

Eventually, he saw a gleam of light in the distance. There was the shop of the "glassmaker." Snutworth had described it well after he had been to make purchases for him. The pinched face of the owner peered at him from the doorway, but he hurriedly glanced away. There was something in the woman's eyes that made him feel that he was being appraised for sale.

Around the side, he had said. Look for the lantern.

There it was, a plain wooden door, blackened with age. The handle was within his grasp.

It turned. He entered.

The smell of the streets faded, to be replaced with that of thick, sweet incense. In the colored, stained-glass shadows, piles of rags shifted and muttered in their sleep. A few debtors looked up from the communal cooking pot when he entered, but they quickly turned away. Even in here, they avoided those who lived in the other world.

Mark glanced around, trying to find someone he recognized. He didn't particularly want to see Laud, or even the doctor, but he hoped to see them before he saw Lily.

Instead, in the furthest corner, he recognized a face he had never thought to see again. The Count had always been thin, but now his sunken cheeks made him cadaverous. His worn-out clothes had lost their sparkle, and so had his eyes, as they flitted over the room. For an instant, they came to rest on Mark, who thought he saw something twitch within them, some distant memory. But just as quickly it was gone and, dull again, the ancient nobleman opened his mouth. Another man beside him pushed in a wooden spoon containing porridge. And Count Stelli, the greatest astrologer the city had ever known, closed his withered lips around it and sucked, without seeming to notice.

Mark came forward, stunned, and sat on a pew in front of him. The man holding the porridge glanced around, but Mark saw only a glimpse of grayish hair and a lined, smeared face, before he went back to stirring the porridge, facing away from him.

"If you're looking for the doctor, sir, or Miss Lily, they're out," the man mumbled.

"Out?" Mark asked distractedly.

"At the trial, sir. The trial of that receiver who stole Miss Gloria's life."

Mark's heart sank. The newspaper hadn't mentioned when the trial was scheduled. He felt that he should be jumping to his feet and running to the courts, but something stopped him. He caught a whiff of fish in the air and, for a second, felt a pang of something old, like a memory long lost.

"The Count," Mark said at last, "what's wrong with him?"

"Age, sir," the man said, keeping his back to him, sliding another spoon of porridge into the old astrologer's mouth. "It catches all of us in time. Of course, they say that he kept it from his mind for years with his work, but that was before his time on the streets. It adds years to a man, sir, and he had too many to start with."

Mark stared, watching the hand that fed the old man. Lined, but strong. It made him uncomfortable.

"Why does he let him stay here?" Mark said at last. "The doctor, I mean. Didn't the Count disinherit him?"

The man put the spoon back into the bowl and stirred it thoughtfully.

"Perhaps. But that's just words on a contract, isn't it? Blood now, that's important. We all learn that, sooner or later. He's still the doctor's grandfather. Nothing can change that. No one should put a price on it."

Mark frowned.

"Some have," he replied darkly.

"So I hear, sir."

Silence again.

Mark rose, feeling the air, scented with bodies and perfume, starting to close in on him.

"Where are they?"

"The Sun Court, on the border of Scorpio and Libra. The highest court. I should be there giving evidence."

Mark paused, staring at the man. It was hard to tell whether he was old or young. Something about him made Mark feel very small.

"Were you a witness?" he said.

The man gave a low chuckle.

"No, sir, I was the man that they arrested first. But they have enough evidence from the receiver patrol now. I'm not important anymore."

"I . . . I'm sorry," Mark mumbled, not prepared to meet the man who had said he didn't matter.

"Thank you, sir. You didn't need to say that."

Mark nodded. The man was right, he didn't. Not legally. And yet . . .

Mark shook his head. The trial would already be in session. He had to get there. If any of them revealed his part in the affair, it would be all over.

And that was important. Very important.

Yet still he had to force himself out of the Almshouse, away from the innocent man's voice and the Count's dreadful, empty eyes.

Mark walked through the streets, wrapped in his own thoughts. He emerged from the twisting alleyways and strode past the grim prison and receivers' barracks of the Scorpio District, until it gave way to the elegant government towers of Libra. And there, on the cusp, the vast and classical courtrooms, standing firm between them with an air of finality. Neither the gold statues of justice nor the graceful murals of the sun shining down on a world of order could hide its function: The court loomed like an implacable judge ready to pass the harshest sentence. Mark shivered as he walked between its twisted columns.

It was not difficult to squeeze himself into the public gallery, although the courtroom was packed. Obviously he was not the only one who had been able to locate the trial. As he pushed his way to the balcony and glanced down, he saw Pauldron at the defendant's table, staring straight ahead, his eyes fixed on something only he could see. Every now and then, his hands rose to his chest, to pick at the badge he no longer wore, or smooth down a midnight-blue cloak that had been stripped from him. On the other side of the courtroom, Mark glimpsed Laud's red mane, and beside him, a smaller figure. His other sister perhaps; Mark had never met her. Behind them, he caught a glimpse of Dr. Theophilus, in conversation with Signor and Signora Sozinho. It looked as if everyone with any connection to the Almshouse was here, except the one person he was most expecting to see. In vain, he searched for Lily, listening to the expectant whispers around him. A verdict was being reached.

And then there was a loud rap from the high bench.

Mark looked at the presiding judge and caught his breath. Lord Ruthven sat there, gazing down at the court, resplendent in wig and robes. In the back of his mind, a little voice protested. This was only a common life theft. Very sad, of course, but not worth the attention of the Lord Chief Justice himself. Mark was still trying to puzzle this out as Lord Ruthven cleared his throat and spoke.

"We have heard all the evidence and Pauldron has confessed to his crimes. Not even a receiver is above justice. In accordance with the laws of Agora, I have reached a verdict and will now pass sentence. Since he has stolen a life from the family of Mr. Laudate and Miss Benedicta, they have the right to his life. They shall determine whether he lives or dies."

A buzz filled the courtroom, but Lord Ruthven brought his gavel down with a sharp rap.

"However," he continued, placing the weight of a decree on each word, "the family has requested that another be allowed to speak for them, to put forward their position on this matter. Considering the seriousness and delicacy of the matter, this has been permitted. She will now speak."

Lord Ruthven gestured, reluctantly, Mark thought, and sat. Laud put his arm around his sister's shoulders. Pauldron stared forward, his features set in a mask of contempt. The crowd's rumble rose higher.

Mark saw all of this, but took none of it in. His attention was fixed on the witness stand, which was below Lord Ruthven. Now he saw her stand up and look over the courtroom. He saw her quiet gaze ripple out across the crowds, stilling the mutterings, focusing their attention.

And then, she looked up and noticed him.

For a second, he could see nothing else. A look of utter clarity, not condemning or welcoming, just a command to listen.

Mark sat down, spellbound.

Lily began.

CHAPTER TWENTY

The Speech

LILY PLACED HER hands on the rail in front of her. All around her, she felt the pressure of a thousand eyes and ears, the air thick with expectation. Slowly, deliberately, she took a breath.

"The family have asked me to give their response to the verdict," she began, her voice not loud, but spreading out through the whole courtroom. "They find it strange." Lily swallowed, trying to keep her thoughts straight. "They can't understand how one life can be worth another. Maybe they could if Pauldron's life could be traded for Gloria's, if his death could bring their sister back. But it can't. That is beyond even us."

Lily looked around the courtroom. Already she could see restlessness. They had only been expecting a short declaration, a token of grief before they hurried back to their lives. But it was now or never. This was her chance, and Laud and Benedicta had insisted that she take it. She raised her voice.

"So what use is another's life to them? They could demand blood, send him to the gallows, and no one would bat an eye. Or they could make him work for them, bound in chains. Both are what normal people would do." Lily swept her gaze over the courtroom. Glimmers of interest were appearing, so she plunged on. "But there was nothing normal about this. Pauldron wasn't trying to kill her, or me, or anyone in particular. He was trying to kill an idea."

Lily glanced up at Lord Ruthven as she spoke. The Lord Chief Justice looked back with shadowed eyes. He had made it very clear to Lily beforehand that nothing was to be said about the Clockwork House or Pauldron's connection to the Libran Society. The list of charges had made no secret of Pauldron's hatred for the Almshouse, however.

"But an idea cannot be destroyed," she continued. "Even if he had drowned Agora in the blood of those who believed in it. Because ideas come back. It doesn't matter who first speaks them; they have a life all their own. And Gloria believed in this one. Believed that the lives of people—living, feeling people—cannot be reduced to words on a contract."

Lily became aware of a buzz going around the courtroom. There was no way to tell if it was approving or not, but she felt the temperature of the room rise. She risked a glance over at Laud and Benedicta. They sat there, holding hands, both willing her on with intense expressions. Behind them, smiling cautiously, Theo too gave an encouraging nod. She turned back to the crowd.

"You may know that during their investigations the receivers closed down the Almshouse. It might surprise you to hear that in recompense for one of their own men being responsible for Gloria's death, they have agreed to let it reopen." Lily leaned forward, gripping the rail of the witness stand. "I don't pretend that Gloria knew she was giving her life for it or would have chosen to do so. We don't want her remembered as a martyr. What I do say is this: That in trying her best and giving her time and herself to work for others, Gloria showed true charity."

Murmurs arose from the courtroom at this, but Lily pressed on. "Charity is nothing to do with buying the feeling of virtue; compassion is not something you can measure. It's there when we don't check that we're always getting the best deal, when we stop seeing others as traders or merchandise, and see them as people, as those who deserve to live. Charity knows that humanity is worth more than the market price."

She turned her head then and stared directly at Pauldron, who met her with a cold and unblinking look. "We believe it is the same for everyone, even a murderer. We don't want his life. We ask only that he be allowed time and a place to heal his shattered mind."

There was a loud rumble from the crowd. People were rising to their feet confused and disgusted. Lily could see some beginning to storm out, while others sat in surprise or shock. But as she looked up, she could see one figure unmoving. Mark still sat, waiting. He could tell that she hadn't finished. Theo told her that sometimes she got a look in her eye that no one could turn away from, and she used this in the court now. People stopped, silenced, giving her their attention.

"I know that you're shocked by this. Perhaps it isn't the way of Agora. But remember — " she flung her hand toward the unrepentant Pauldron — "that was what *he* said. That was his justification for thinking a life was worth nothing. We believe life is worth more than anything. There can be no middle ground."

Lily paused, drawing the silence into her before letting her voice resonate out. "So, do you want to live in his Agora or ours?" she asked, looking around. "How much do you value yourselves?"

She sat down.

* * *

Lily leaned back, drained, as Lord Ruthven summed up the end of the case. She watched, almost detached, as Pauldron was led out, his expression of blank, implacable hatred still burned into her mind. It was only when a shadow fell across her and she looked up into the patrician face of the Lord Chief Justice that she roused herself. He extended his hand.

"A most spirited argument, Miss Lilith," he said. His voice seemed warm but faintly patronizing. "I imagine it has given us all plenty to think about."

Lily took his hand cautiously, but did not smile back.

"I will find out the truth, you know," she said simply.

Lord Ruthven's hand tightened on hers a fraction, but otherwise he kept the same determinedly bland expression.

"Miss Lilith, you know the arrangement. In return for over-looking your invasion of a private meetinghouse of the Libran Society, you and your friends are not to give any specific mention of what you found there, or any revelations made." He withdrew his hand, brushing it neatly on his robes. "I have invoked the seal of the Director on this matter. None but he himself can overturn it." His eyes narrowed and he leaned closer. "The Libran Society has several privileges, including the right to arrest without public trial. Prove yourself a sensible young lady, and do not interfere."

He moved away, clearly believing that he had had the last word, but Lily jumped up and blocked his way.

"This isn't public, Lord Ruthven," she persisted. "This is just the two of us." She looked up at him, folding her arms. "Tell me, what is the Midnight Charter?"

Lord Ruthven recoiled, then shook his head.

"Good day, Miss Lilith," he said, pushing past her.

She grabbed at the sleeve of his robe.

"What could be in it that is so terrible it drives men mad?" she hissed.

Lord Ruthven stopped and gave her a strange look, almost one of fear. Then, very deliberately, he unhooked her hand, flinching as if her touch caused him physical pain.

"Think about your own question, Miss Lilith. There are some things that are a curse to know, some secrets that must be guarded. Look at the effect that this knowledge had on the sergeant." Ruthven looked her in the eyes, and Lily felt it again, a strange mix of fear and steely resolution. "I shall not warn you again, Miss Lilith," he continued, "but if you believe nothing else, believe me when I tell you this—I am protecting you. One day, perhaps, when it no longer matters, you will find the answers you seek. And when you see what could have happened, when you understand what you might have become, you will look back on today and thank me for sparing you."

Without another word, he walked briskly away. Lily had the strange impression that if he could have run without damaging his dignity, he would have.

Lily glanced around. Most of the court was empty now. She saw Benedicta waving from the exit. Some of her old sparkle had already returned, and Lily couldn't help waving back. Time for everyone to put their everyday masks back on. Behind Ben, she saw the Sozinhos waiting and remembered how she had to thank them. Without their influence, the Almshouse would never have been able to open again so rapidly.

Then she saw someone else she had to talk to. She caught him just before he left, sidling out of the building.

"Mark!" she called.

He turned, his eyes haunted, and shuffled back toward her. He stuck his hands into his pockets.

"Thanks for not saying anything," he said after a moment. "About me, I mean."

"It didn't seem important anymore," Lily mused, also feeling strangely awkward. She still wasn't sure how she felt about Mark. In a way, he was right; he hadn't been responsible. And yet . . . he had still betrayed her. He was the reason they had closed the Almshouse.

"Even so, thanks," Mark insisted, trying to sound gruff. "You didn't need to help me."

"No, I didn't," Lily agreed and looked at him curiously. "But everyone deserves another chance."

Mark nodded, his eyes flicking away to the door. Lily wondered if he had listened to her speech. She had felt almost as if she had been speaking directly to him. She knew that if he apologized, she would forgive him at once. She cleared her head. Now was not the time for this; she had to tell him something.

"Mark," she said, low and urgent, "be careful. It wasn't only me that Pauldron was after. He wanted you too."

Mark jumped, alarmed.

"Me? But . . . I thought you said . . . I mean . . . I've nothing to do with the Almshouse . . ."

"It wasn't just that." Lily glanced over her shoulder, to see if any receivers were close by. "It's the Libran Society. They've got this document . . . Pauldron thought it had something to do with us."

Lily flailed her hands. The truth was that she had understood very little. Not for the first time she wished she had managed to keep those few charred fragments of the Charter. She grabbed Mark's arm and looked him in the eye.

"Just be careful, all right. This is bigger than us. Bigger than our differences." She leaned closer. "I'll let you know if I find anything out. Will you look as well?"

Lily saw fear and indecision flicker across Mark's face. But then he nodded.

"It's a lot to take in," he said quietly, "but I'll try."

Mark moved away, pausing in the entrance. Behind her, Lily heard Benedicta calling. There was much to do now that the Alms-house had reopened.

Lily didn't move. She stayed staring at Mark, wondering what he was thinking.

For a moment, a look passed between them. It wasn't quite the same as before — not the friendship that had endured even when they had seen so little of each other in the months before Mark's ball. But as they drew apart, Lily got the impression that if they had ever been enemies, they weren't any longer.

It was an oddly comforting thought.

INTERLUDE THREE

THE WINE IS DARK and oily. It sits in the three glasses but reflects no light.

"Come, Miss Rita, join us in the toast."

It is not a command. The Director never needs to command. Cautiously, she takes the glass from his desk and raises it to her lips. The taste is sharp, acidic, but she hides her wince. The Director holds his glass up to the light of the candle, but only a murky glow shines through. As for the third figure, he sips silently. Miss Rita shivers. She wishes he would make a sound.

"An ancient vintage, Miss Rita," the Director says, a faint smile on his thin, dry lips. "It was laid down in our cellars the day our city was founded. Can you imagine such a length of time?"

Miss Rita purses her lips and glances again at the third figure. He meets her gaze and smiles. He too knows that this is not a question that requires an answer.

The Director puts down his glass, the wine untouched.

"Undrinkable, of course. Wine does not mature at the same rate as cities. Nevertheless, I feel that our founders would expect a symbolic gesture as we approach the fruition of their finest project. All is prepared, Miss Rita?"

"Yes, sir. The arrangements have been made."

The Director brushes his lips with the tip of one finger.

"Then you know your role." He turns to the third figure. "You, too, are prepared to honor our agreement?"

The figure nods.

"With pleasure, sir."

"I don't doubt it. But do be swift. Mishaps would be — " the Director frowns, his face becoming a mass of shadows in the candlelight — "regrettable at this stage. Ruthven looks at this office with hungry eyes. It would not do to please his supporters. Already they are calling the destruction of one of our copies of the Charter a bad omen."

For a moment there is silence, broken only by the ticking of a clock lost somewhere in this vast, ancient space. Miss Rita raises a hand to her mouth and coughs. The Director looks over to her.

"Of course, Miss Rita, you have work to do. Please, leave us." The Director turns back to the other figure. "We have much to discuss."

"Of course, sir," Miss Rita says.

She is only too glad to retreat to her own office, back into the world she understands. She is a woman who keeps many secrets, but they still make her uncomfortable.

The door closes behind her. The Director leans forward.

"Now then, Mr. Snutworth, it is time for you to act."

Snutworth puts down his empty glass and smiles.

CHAPTER TWENTY-ONE

The Fall

MARK SIPPED TEA with as much daintiness as he could manage.

The businessman in him knew that Cherubina was bound to him now by the strongest of contracts. Short of leaping up and striking her with the teapot, there was very little he could do that would make her break things off, and even then her mother would probably talk her out of it. Nevertheless, he found himself making an effort to fit into her world. In his business life, he stood up straight, inflating himself in the eyes of the world, but here he hunched in the delicate chairs and tried to smile, like the doll of him that sat on his left.

He became aware that Cherubina was talking again.

". . . don't know how you manage up at that tower, with barely a servant to wait upon you. The orphans are very useful, of course, but I don't like to have them hanging around, and no servant can ever make tea properly. They're all far too fond of the stronger stuff, if you know what I mean . . ."

She laughed at a pitch that made Mark wince.

"It's not so bad," he said. "Snutworth's a reasonable cook, and it's only until the next deal comes in."

He stopped, realizing that Cherubina was simply not paying attention. She appeared to be dabbing the mouth of a stuffed bear. This time he wasn't particularly annoyed. He was rather hazy himself on why he had had to fire most of his servants. Snutworth had said there had been another downturn.

Not surprising really. As the nights got longer and summer had faded into autumn, however, he had expected his business to increase. But the stars didn't seem to come together as they used to. So often he looked up there and found himself gazing at blackness rather than spots of light. Even this year's prediction at the Grand Festival over a month ago had hardly set the crowds ablaze. There had been no prodigy this year.

"Only one year," Mark muttered to himself. "Feels like a lifetime."

"Mmm?" Cherubina asked, looking up, her blond ringlets falling in her eyes.

Mark smiled.

"Nothing, um . . . dear . . ."

The future had certainly looked bright then. Back when he was starting, when his new life was full of excitement. Of course, every businessman had their bad days, but there was no denying the fact that people no longer looked over when he entered a room. His new businesses were good, but not spectacular; his life was depressingly predictable. Even Snutworth's investigations into Lily's so-called Libran conspiracy had achieved nothing, except to lose him the good opinion of Lord Ruthven, who had broken off contact with him only a few days after the Almshouse was reopened. A few weeks short of his fourteenth birthday and he was rapidly becoming old news.

He felt a hand resting on his shoulder and looked up. Cherubina playfully flicked a strand of his own dullish blond hair out of his eyes.

"Now then," she said coyly, "my Mark can't be sad." She pushed a plate under his nose. "Not when there's cake with icing!"

Mark stared at her eager, shining eyes and laughed. It was ridiculous. It was childish. He was engaged to a girl who seemed never to have advanced beyond the age of seven and had barely seen the world outside her front door.

Still, the cake looked good. He picked it up and took a bite.

And, he had to admit, it was a relief, occasionally, to talk to someone who cared about things other than business. Sometimes he felt like the only real thing in Cherubina's world.

"You'll stay for dinner?" Cherubina added eagerly. "Mommy wants to celebrate. She's just sold a new batch of workers to the paper mills . . ."

Mark shook his head hurriedly.

"I've got to get back to the tower. Snutworth is going to bring me the latest figures."

He stopped. Cherubina had turned away. There was something new in her expression, a kind of distaste. It made her look more her proper age somehow.

"I wish you wouldn't let that servant of yours come around here," she said, fiddling with one of her many bracelets. "I don't like the way he looks at me."

Mark blinked. The image swam before his eyes for an instant, before it collapsed.

"Snutworth?" he said incredulously. "He's old enough to be

your father! Anyway, I've known him for ages. He's not interested in anything outside of trading."

"That's just it," Cherubina said, still twisting her bracelet, not raising her eyes. "You're not the first potential husband, Mark. I've been looked at a few times by older men than him. It's not so bad." Distractedly, she began to comb a doll's hair. "What do you see when you look at me, Mark?"

She looked up and Mark took a moment. He saw a young woman still pretending to be a girl, wrapped in frills and lace and ringlets. But this time, there was nothing playful in the set of her shoulders. Mark bit his lip. He didn't want to get the answer wrong and, to his surprise, he found that it was because he didn't want to hurt her feelings.

"You," he said, already wincing, prepared to be told that it was the wrong answer.

Instead, Cherubina smiled, but more sadly than he would have thought possible.

"Snutworth doesn't see me. He sees the room," she said.

There was a jangling of the bell and Mark got up.

"That'll probably be him," he said awkwardly. "I'll meet him at the door."

Cherubina nodded, rising also and proffering her hand. His mind elsewhere, Mark took it to kiss, a strange ceremony but one they had been told to observe.

Her hand was colder than usual and, as he pulled away, she held him back.

"You'll come again tomorrow?" she asked.

Mark almost began to put it off, as he always did, explaining about the pressure of constant trading. Instead, he found himself nodding, gently releasing her hand. Despite everything, despite the giggling and the dolls and the silliness, he had started to like this strange girl. She might have wealth that his family could only have dreamed of, but in the end she was being sold by her parent, just as he had been.

He stepped backward out of the room. For one moment, Cherubina was framed in the doorway, her look haunting. Then, the next moment, it was closed and he was walking along a dark, drab corridor, everything as it always was.

Mark didn't stop when he reached the open front door. He felt Snutworth falling into step beside him as they made their way through the streets.

"What's the report?" Mark said, drawing his coat around him against the chilly wind.

"Not as bad as we had predicted, sir," Snutworth said, his tone as respectful as ever.

Mark sneaked a glance at him. Although he was by now nearly the same height as his servant, he still had to fight the urge to look up. It didn't matter what the contract said, he relied on Snutworth to be more than an organized assistant. He searched for something different in that concentrated frown, looking down at the papers in one hand, or for even the slightest change of beat, as he tapped his silver-handled cane, his one vanity, on the ground with each step.

There was nothing, no difference. Snutworth was Snutworth, as he had always been, working invisibly and essentially.

"The jewelry trade is going well?" Mark asked.

"The Grand Festival is a good time of year for them. The news is positive from that front. And the fishing has seen an upturn . . ."

Mark saw a flicker of midnight blue out of the corner of his eye and let Snutworth's voice fade into the background. It wasn't unusual to see receivers moving the drifting crowds along, but he seemed to notice them more and more nowadays. Ever since he had been to that trial and met Lily again. Maybe it was the thought that one of these men had been out to murder him. Yes, he thought, that had to be the reason.

Nothing to do with the ragged figures they were carting away.

Mark shook himself, casting his eyes down on some papers that Snutworth had handed him. He had left that part of his life behind and not even Lily would make him remember it now. He smiled at the freshly stamped contracts before him. If anyone wanted to know what he was worth, they only had to look at these. That was power.

Despite that, he couldn't help shivering as another receiver patrol passed by. He wanted to share his thoughts with Snutworth, but he knew that the servant would quickly turn the talk back to business.

He thought of Lily. He would write to her. Even if she still didn't trust him, he really needed someone to talk to — to confide in. Cherubina had proved herself to be a much better person to talk to than he had expected at first, but she had never quite been the same. She never really thought about anything outside her own life. Lily had always been a wonderful listener.

Just then, a coach rattled past and Mark jumped aside to avoid a spattering of filth, his thoughts banished.

"Are we ready to take on the other servants again, Snutworth?" Mark grumbled. "I hate this walking everywhere. First thing to do is to get the coachman back."

"I shall make a note of it, sir," Snutworth promised. "However, for the moment, there are a few last pressing orders of business. If you would just place your seal here."

Mark felt himself jostled as they pushed their way toward the Central Plaza. He glanced over the stack of papers uncertainly.

"Can't this wait until we're back to the tower?"

"Naturally, sir, but I thought that I might make a detour and hire some new staff before returning today. You can have a new cook by this evening, sir."

Mark sighed, looking around.

"Light the sealing wax, then. I'll have to find a stall counter to lean on."

"Sir."

Mark soon found a stallholder who was finishing for the day, and willing to clear a space. He tried to get back into the usual rhythm, pressing down his signet ring into the soft wax, but he still could not stop his mind from wandering. He thought about this new cook. Would they be male or female? Old or young? Over the last year the cook had been nothing but a means to an end. He had had three at the tower and could not have picked one of them out in a crowd. When he thought of the kitchen, he still saw Lily there, stirring the pot with one hand and pointing to the lines of unfamiliar words with the other.

"I think," Mark said cautiously, as he handed back the documents and they set off again, "I'll go with you to choose the new servants. I should know them, after all."

"If that is your choice, sir." Snutworth sounded doubtful. "But I can hardly see the point."

"If I want your opinion, I'll ask for it," Mark snapped.

"Sir."

They continued for a little further in silence, Mark still brooding on his new thoughts. He began to reason that if he knew who his servants were, why not his other workers in the businesses? Why not those who bought his fish, and jewelry, and prophecies? Did he really know anyone he dealt with? He stared about him, at the sea of faces that swarmed past, avoiding each other's gaze, plunging through on errands of their own.

Did anyone ever stop and look?

"Nearly there, sir," Snutworth said, the tapping of his cane quickening.

Mark looked up. In front of him, through the broad streets of the

Gemini District, he saw the great tower rise up. The late autumnal sun glinted off the glass of the Observatory; its thin, ancient shadow fell forward, stretching toward him. And Mark smiled. He owned this wonder, the finest in the city outside the Directory itself. From its topmost windows, he would really begin to see.

A hand grasped his shoulder. A hand in a midnight-blue glove.

"Mr. Mark?"

Mark turned his head. It was not an old face, but it had weathered a few storms. It wasn't harsh, but there was something firm in the set of the mouth that would stand for no argument. He looked down at the badge of office being presented to him.

"Yes, Inspector—" he squinted to read the lettering—"Greaves." Mark felt a chill, remembering the name from the report into Gloria's death. "Can I help you?" he asked anxiously.

"You could say that, sir," the inspector said grimly.

Suddenly Mark became aware of the other receivers standing around him in the crowd. He noticed people turning to each other, whispering. And above all he noticed Snutworth take two deliberate steps away from him.

"What's going on?" Mark said, nervousness flaring up within him. "Snutworth, what—"

"Mr. Mark," Inspector Greaves continued, in a reasonable but firm tone, "by the authority of the Directory of Receipts, I am taking you into custody for illegal dealings and for possible involvement in the life theft of Miss Gloria."

Mark tried to step back. He felt more hands on his shoulders and arms, rougher ones. The crowd around him was filled with blue coats.

"You will be a property of the Directory and stored in prison until the investigation of your case is concluded."

"Snutworth!" Mark called out, struggling against the receivers. "A lawyer . . . Find me the best . . ."

"Everything will be fine, sir," Snutworth replied, his expression unreadable.

"This way, sir," Inspector Greaves said softly. "It's best if you don't struggle. We don't want to cause a scene."

As Mark looked up, the tower faded from view, blocked by a wall of receivers. A whole patrol, just for him.

Special treatment.

"Yes, Inspector," he said.

CHAPTER TWENTY-TWO

The Scroll

A SICKENING SNAP, a groan, and the work was over.
Gently, Lily poured one of the doctor's concoctions
down the patient's throat. After a few minutes, the moaning subsided. By the time she had finished binding the wrist she had
reset, he had lapsed into a fitful sleep.

As always at moments like this, her fingers went to her throat, to
the little bottle that had once held her disgust. As she touched it,
she felt her queasy feelings subside. Her disgust was within her,
but she could control it.

She stepped back to observe her handiwork. Not bad, although
she had seen neater splints. It had been a while since she had put
the training Theo had given her into regular practice, but now, as
she looked around the Almshouse, she could see three of their new
helpers dealing with the basic care, and it was time to put her own
skills to use.

She wandered over to the cooking pot by the altar, checking to see if any of the daily broth remained.

"There's nothing left," Theo remarked as he joined her. "We've had a lot of new arrivals today."

Lily nodded thoughtfully.

"It's getting colder, so more come every day."

"I'll make something to eat when Laud gets back with the supplies," he said.

"Isn't that Ben's job?" Lily asked.

"Usually, but I think she's gone to visit Pete at his new workplace." Theo chuckled. "Now, that was unexpected. But he says he's happy there."

Lily rolled her eyes.

"Trust Ben, shining her light into any dark corner," she said fondly. She idly ran her finger along the rim of the cooking pot. "We'll be needing something bigger soon."

"Or perhaps a larger almshouse," the doctor said. "I've heard that the spice merchant on Aurora Road is planning to sell and the new patrons may be persuaded to assist."

Despite her tiredness, Lily matched Theo's encouraging smile. It hadn't been an overnight change. The day after the trial the street had not been thronged with silk-robed merchants donating all their worldly goods to help their fellow men. But somehow, ever since that speech, a trickle of people, some far from wealthy, had knocked on their door to give, not to take. At the same time, the Sozinhos had seized the mood of the day and finally managed to persuade some of their wealthy friends that becoming almshouse patrons would be good for their public image. Lily remembered Laud summing up their position the day before with a wary observation: "Well, it seems that we have become fashionable."

There was no guarantee that it would last, but for now the donations were flowing in steadily.

"There's a long way to go," Lily said, half to herself.

Theo nodded.

"A disease may linger for years, or even many cycles, and for most of that time medicines will only soothe, not cure." Theo shrugged. "But that's no reason to give up hope. Stranger things have occurred."

Lily frowned. Too many strange things had happened recently. She had tried to forget about them, to immerse herself in her work, but she could not push the thoughts of them from her mind. In her dreams now she saw shadowy figures closing in around her and Mark, knives flashing in the dark, the golden scales of the Libran Society branded on their hands and foreheads.

"Theo," she said quietly, "how deep do you think the illness goes?" She faced him, trying to read an answer in his sympathetic eyes. "How sick is our city?"

Theo did not at first reply, running a finger thoughtfully over his mustache.

"We cannot solve everything on our own, Lily," he said at last.

"I just feel sometimes that we're only treating the symptoms, not the disease."

"We are already doing so much. And you knew that it wouldn't change overnight . . ." Theo stopped, a curious expression on his face. "This isn't about the Almshouse, is it?"

Lily tried to put her thoughts into words, but she couldn't. Instead, she reached into the pocket of her apron and withdrew something she had hidden there since the night at the Clockwork House. Holding up the gemstone, she watched as it seemed to draw in the colored light filtering through the stained-glass windows.

"There are so many secrets in Agora, Theo," she said, "so many lies." She set her jaw in determination. "I can't go on skirting around, almost knowing. I don't care what Lord Ruthven says. Even if I have to go over his head and force my way into the Directory itself. I need to know."

"Is knowledge worth so much, Lily?" Theo said, his tone quietly desperate. "You're still so young. Can't we search with you carefully?"

Lily shook her head, clasping the gemstone tightly. "You don't understand, Theo. This is my only clue. You see, I think it's one of the gemstones that were left with me at the orphanage."

"Don't you think you're jumping to conclusions?" Theo suggested. "How can you be sure?"

"Look at it, Theo," she said, holding it up to the light. Slowly, the smoky crystal seemed to begin to glow, a tiny sparkle like a flame springing to life in its heart. "It's just how Miss Cherubina described them. There are no others like them in the whole city. I've looked everywhere, from the Virgo District jewelers to the Gemini museums. The Librans must know about me . . . know who I am, who my parents were . . . know what this Charter says or doesn't say. I need to know what I'm involved in, Theo, and the Charter might have the answers. I can't just wait for another attempt to kill me."

"So instead you plan to seek out those who wish you dead?" Theo said. "Hardly the most sensible idea."

"At least then none of my friends will get in their way again," Lily said.

"Don't you think we need you here?" Theo replied, more heatedly. "Is the truth more important to you than the Almshouse and everyone who needs it? Is it more important than us?"

For a moment, Lily couldn't think how to reply. She had never seen Theo like this, half angry, half pleading. She tried to articulate her feelings.

"But what if this truth is something terrible, Theo?" she said at

275

last. "Pauldron said that Mark and I would destroy Agora. I don't know how, or why us, but as long as you, Laud, and Ben are here . . . I might be putting you in danger. At least if I know what is happening I can make a decision."

They stared at each other. Around them, the usual sounds of the Almshouse—the groans of the hungry and the desperate—seemed distant. Theo appeared to be making his mind up about something.

"Let me tell you a secret, then," he said at last. "There are those who say that the Director never sees anyone, that his vision extends across the whole of Agora, through everywhere a deal is made or a trade is sealed." He smiled wistfully. "Perhaps that is true, who knows? But the Director does see people. The heads of the guilds and of the most important societies are summoned occasionally, and all such elite men and women may demand an appointment, once in their lifetime."

Theo reached into the pocket of his stained, dark coat. He pulled out a tiny scroll, sealed with black wax. There was no mistaking the symbol upon it—an unfurled scroll, the Director's personal sign.

"My grandfather was elected to the head of his guild for life ten years ago," Theo continued, almost whispering. "I don't believe he held even the Director in high esteem. He never bothered to go." He tapped the scroll thoughtfully with one long finger. "It took some explanation. I couldn't pretend that you would be on the astrologers' business, or say why the Count wasn't requesting it in person." He glanced over to the old man, sitting blankly in a chair on the far side of the room. "But in the end, people have a tendency to see me as harmless."

He put the scroll on the altar before them. Lily stared at it. An appointment with the Director himself. She felt her throat go dry. It was like meeting a figure from legend. The man who ran the world, who pulled the strings of the whole city, the one who knew every secret.

She reached out her hand and stopped.

"Why?" she said.

Theo sniffed.

"Your gratitude is touching," he muttered, turning away.

Hastily Lily laid a hand on his shoulder.

"I don't mean . . . I . . . Thank you. It's more than I could have dreamed of, but . . . if you don't want me to go . . ."

"I don't," Theo said, still looking away into the distance, "none of us do."

"I *will* be back. I don't care what the legends say. They can't make me disappear."

Theo turned back, his eyes endlessly sad.

"Grandfather was not the type to tell bedtime stories. But once, when I was small, he told me something. He said that Agora held secrets that could destroy you, just by hearing them. Secrets that could drive you mad. Secrets that would make you vanish and never return." He gave a hollow chuckle. "Who knows? Perhaps that's why I turned out to be such a coward."

"You're not a coward, Theo," Lily replied. "You're a healer."

"I was a survivor. A survivor who wanted to help a few others survive too. But I never had the courage to change things, to challenge. Like I do now." He sighed. "It isn't just you that we'd lose, Lily. I don't know if that spirit will last without you. I'm a better man with you around."

Lily stared at the doctor. It was strange to see him like this, looking back at her like a lost child. Yet this was the same man who had never complained, who had gone on treating patients, paying and debtors alike, through the worst of their times, when they were only a day or two from becoming debtors themselves. The man who had been the stable point in her world since she was first pushed in through the doors of the tower. Dr. Theophilus, never tiring, the healer of everyone.

"I won't go if you tell me not to," she said at last. "You're still my master. It's down on the contract." She fixed him with a stare. "But you must command me. I need to know that I have no choice."

Theo shook his head.

"I haven't been your master for a long time, and we both know it."

For a lingering moment, they stared down at the scroll, its black seal glistening in the autumnal light streaming through the stained-glass windows. Then Lily looked up and around at the Almshouse that she had started, that was going on around her, an idea that had been set in motion a year ago and, she fervently believed, could not be stopped.

She put her hand on the scroll.

Theo turned away.

"The appointment is in three days' time," he said softly, "at the twelfth hour of day." He moved across the room, agitatedly picking up his outdoor coat. "I think . . . I'd better go and check on the slums; it looks like there might be another outbreak of the gray plague, and I think I've perfected the cure . . ."

"Theo—" Lily began, but the doctor interrupted.

"No time to talk, I'm afraid," he said, pulling on the coat with unusual speed. "I've got lives to save, you know . . ."

Now that he had seen her decision, he seemed desperate to get away, as if her choice had caused him pain. Lily hurried after him, her mind now focused on the time ahead.

"I promise you, Theo. I will be back."

Dr. Theophilus stopped in the doorway and turned around. The pain in his eyes had softened to something else.

"Please, Lily. Don't make promises that are not within your

power to keep." He picked up his mask and goggles. "Hope, wish . . . but don't promise."

He slipped on the mask, covering his face with blank white authority, and stepped through the door, vanishing into the crowds.

Lily watched him, losing him in the throng, and clasping the little scroll so tightly in her hand that the seal cut into her palm.

CHAPTER TWENTY-THREE

The Cell

MARK WAS AWAKENED by the sound of stone scratching on stone.

For a moment he considered opening his eyes, but then he chose to keep them closed. As long as he lingered between sleep and wakefulness, he could believe that the prisoner in the opposite cell had loosened a stone and was even now tunneling through the walls to freedom.

It couldn't last.

As he lay there, Mark became more and more aware of the cold stones beneath him. More conscious of the aches in his arms and legs, more conscious of the feeling of dirt coating everything in grime.

He opened his eyes. A trickle of light made its way through the high window, casting shadows on the rough stones of the walls and the rusty bars of his cell door. Rusty, but firm. Mark had tested that while he still had the strength. But a few weeks of prison food had soon left him weak.

Listlessly, he turned his head to peer into the cell opposite. The scratching was still going on, louder and more furious than ever. Mark watched the prisoner, who was pushing greasy hair out of his eyes as he scratched furiously on the walls with a stone. The walls of Ghast's cell were covered with script. They looked like calculations of some kind, or maybe a diary. The truth was, Ghast had scratched over them so many times that they had lost any meaning they once had. He could cover all the walls in a single day. No wonder the skin sagged from his frame, for he never stopped moving.

Mark closed his eyes, determined not to spend another day watching the madman's scrawling. The problem was, there was nothing else to do, except remember, and Ghast was always preferable to that.

"They killed him, you know . . ."

The voice drifted across the gap between their cells. Mark sat up blearily, but Ghast still had his back to him. The old prisoner rarely seemed to care if anyone was listening.

"They cut him up and sold him off, pound by pound," he muttered, scratching a thick line diagonally across his cell. "But they couldn't stop him thinking, couldn't pull apart his mind. Not if he hid it. As long as he knows where he put it . . ."

He spun around, grinning at Mark. Mark shuddered. There was something wrong with that grin. It seemed too large for the drawn, hollow face.

"He was always looking for the big ones, the ones who kept their knives sharp and clean. He knew where to look for them, among the lights, and the ladies, heads in the feast. But the little star and his shadow were too quick." He sank back toward the other wall. "Win some, lose some . . . Win some, lose some . . . The walls are only there if you let them be . . . The mind wanders free . . . free to buy with its eyes and sell its breaths . . ."

Mark stared down at his bare feet, numb from the cold and bitten with fleas. Could he sell his mind? Why not? You could sell everything else. What else could he trade? Even the stench that he had never minded back in the slums repulsed him now, hanging on his breath and hair like the stink of failure.

He shook his head, staring down at the band of pale skin on his ring finger, not touched by the previous summer's sun. He couldn't trade anything anymore. Prisoners were not people. They did not have signet rings. He looked up and forced himself to listen to Ghast's ramblings. He would not think about the past. Not today.

"When is an end a beginning?" Ghast continued to himself, scraping a circle on the far wall. "Always? Until the end of time? Never? Because every beginning is also an end. Or maybe sometimes. What do you think?" He paused and laughed. "Always yes, sir. Meaning no. Or sometimes yes. Hide every meaning in the simplest words, why don't you? You always did . . ."

Mark stuffed his face inside a piece of old sacking, trying to block out the light. It was easier when he slept, because the time passed faster.

He heard the rattle of the keys and the heavy footsteps of one of the jailers. Voices spoke just out of earshot, then there was another set of footsteps, quiet and purposeful.

And the brisk tapping of a cane.

Mark flung away the sacking, pulling himself to his feet. A figure in a long, black coat was studying Ghast.

"Snutworth?" Mark croaked. It had been a few days since he had last spoken.

The figure turned.

"Correct, Mr. Mark."

Snutworth stood still, the little light there was in the prison slanting down to his face, forming deep shadows over his eyes, and glistening off the silver handle of his cane. There was a silence. Mark kept expecting him to break it, but instead he stood, looking at him.

Finally, it was Mark who forced out more words. "Have they said when they'll hear my case?"

"More than that, sir. You have been tried in your absence," Snutworth said matter-of-factly, never changing the tone of his voice.

Mark gripped the bars.

"They can't do that! What about my lawyer . . . ?"

"A lawyer was chosen for you. She pleaded your case most eloquently."

"But I should have been there!" Mark shouted, as loud as he could in his weakened state. "Even Pauldron was allowed to be at his own trial . . ."

"The law does not require the presence of the accused," Snutworth replied, his voice expressionless. "Not unless they are requested to appear by the prosecutors or the victims. I suspect Miss Lily wished to use the sergeant to illustrate her appeal. Prisoners have no rights."

"But . . . but . . ." Mark's voice faded. It was useless to shout at Snutworth. He had spent every day in his cell working out what he would say at the trial, and it had all been for nothing. There was only one question he could ask now.

"And . . . the verdict?" he said.

"Guilty as charged."

Mark felt his hands slacken on the bars.

"But . . . guilty of what?" he cried, the words bursting out of him. "I didn't do anything, not really, nothing that everyone else doesn't do . . ."

"There was a small matter of business malpractice," Snutworth spoke slowly, his eyes never moving, his hands resting lightly on his cane, "bribery and corruption. The twisting of astrological readings to benefit your allies. And then there was Miss Devine's evidence on the issue of preventing the free sale of emotions. All of this would have been trivial were it not for a string of charges of attempting to alter contractual records — an offense against the Directory itself. The court declared itself surprised that you had the time for your crimes . . ."

"I didn't . . . I don't understand . . ."

Mark tried to gather his thoughts. Had he really done that? So many meetings, so many decisions to make and contracts to seal . . . contracts he had often barely read, but that Snutworth had assured him were in order . . .

"As your worst crimes were against the Directory, it was decided that no reparation could be paid." Snutworth stepped forward, his eyes cold. "You have been declared a property of the Directory. Perhaps when you are older they will make you work. Then again, there is so much paperwork. Sometimes prisoners are simply forgotten."

Mark sat down heavily.

"They . . . they can't do this . . . I swear, Snutworth, I never tried to cheat the Directory."

"They had the documents. All signed and sealed. The most damning were sealed on the day they arrested you, as I recall."

Mark gripped his head, trying to stem the rising wave of panic.

"The tower . . . I'll trade away the tower . . . I can buy myself back with it . . . You'll deal with that for me . . ."

"I certainly could," Snutworth mused.

"Then we'll find out who was fixing the documents, you'll see. We'll . . ."

"I believe you miss my meaning. I said that I could do that. I did not indicate that I was going to."

Mark looked up. Snutworth loomed over him, the bars between them casting thick, black shadows.

"Snutworth . . ."

"Consider, boy. You have no family and no other servants but me. The state does not claim your property for your guilt." Snutworth smiled. "I have no intention of selling my tower in exchange for you."

Mark stared, feeling all his emotion drain away. He was vaguely aware of staring at Snutworth, of trying to speak, but he couldn't. All he could see was Snutworth, handing him those documents to seal on the day they took him, and for weeks beforehand. Documents that were unlike any he had sealed before—so long and complex that he had barely glanced at them. Snutworth leaned closer.

"Then there is your share of the businesses, really quite satisfactorily successful. I would have preferred to have waited for a better upturn, perhaps another few years or so, but . . . well—" Snutworth gave the tiniest of shrugs—"the time was not of my choosing, only the method."

"Why?" Mark began to say at last. His voice felt like it was coming from very far away. "I trusted you . . ."

"Trust?" Snutworth looked thoughtful, considering the word. "I regret to say that the going rate for trust is very low, despite its rarity. No demand, I'm afraid. And if you looked to either of us for a source of this commodity, then honestly, the market was against you." Snutworth stepped to one side, casting an eye at Ghast shivering in his cell. "Or perhaps you assumed that our betrayals of our former masters were isolated events."

"That was different," Mark said, shakily pulling himself to his feet, his legs weak with dread. "They were going to use us . . ."

"And so we used them, to take advantage of your blunt vocabulary. Or did you simply assume that they would disappear, happy, contented, but out of your life?" Snutworth tutted. "Rarely the case, right, sir?"

Snutworth directed his question at the scrabbling prisoner, still scratching his symbols on the wall. Mark followed his gaze.

And then he recognized him. The fat had shrunk to hanging skin, the greasy perfumes to bodily stench. But the smile—the smile had been the same.

"Prendergast . . ." Mark murmured.

The madman barely looked up, but Snutworth nodded.

"The name reduced along with his stomach. Rather fitting, I feel." Snutworth turned back, a flash of triumph in his eyes. "So, if you are quite finished retreating from the moral high ground, I believe my business is concluded here, and I have a very busy day. Preparations must be made for the wedding."

It took a while for Mark's anguished mind to take in what Snutworth had said, but suddenly a chill ran through his whole body. He didn't want to ask, but he couldn't help it.

"Wedding?" he whispered.

Snutworth nodded.

"Everything goes to me, Mr. Mark. Your possessions, your position . . . and your betrothed. Those contacts will serve me well, and it is only right that a powerful man should have a wife. I think that Miss Cherubina will be far more satisfied with me than with a useless, filthy little boy."

Mark sprang forward, his mind clouded with a sudden rage. No reason, no horror, just a sudden urge to squeeze his hands around Snutworth's neck. He clawed through the bars, as if he could push them out of their sockets with anger alone.

There was an explosion of pain in his chest.

Mark found himself lying on his back at the edge of his cell, his body pinned to the ground on the end of Snutworth's cane, thrust through the bars with icy efficiency. Snutworth's eyes were hard and cold.

"You can't," Mark hissed painfully, finding it hard to breathe.

"Your property is mine, Mr. Mark, in its entirety," Snutworth replied with a twist of the cane.

"At least let Cherubina go . . . You don't need her."

"The daughter of the most successful orphanage matron in Agora?" Snutworth mused, increasing the pressure. "I beg to differ."

"But, you don't care about her . . . do you?"

Snutworth laughed.

"And you *do*, I suppose, boy? The arranged fiancée you could barely stomach visiting? No . . . it's not that, is it?" he said, leaning closer. "I wonder, do you want to save her from being sold off by her mother because you couldn't save yourself? Or is it perhaps that after everything you've done, she was the only friend you thought you had left?" Snutworth forced the tip of his cane a little harder into Mark's chest. "Look at the stargazer taken in by his own legend," he said. "Look at the child reaching for the skies, when all around him the real things, the solid things, everything that matters, are taken away. And no one will shed a tear because he didn't have the sense to stay in the mud, or the wisdom to look at the hands he chose to hold him high and guide his path." Snutworth's mouth twitched into a thin, humorless smile. "Worth so much to everyone else, worthless to himself."

The pressure released and the cane slid back through the bars. Mark coughed, clutching at his aching chest, pulling the dirt of the cell floor out of his hair. When he looked up again, Snutworth was already closing the door to the cells behind him. Ghast watched him go.

"The shadow and his imp, they cause mischief," he muttered, before going back to his scraping.

Mark lay there shivering. He barely noticed the pain in his chest or the new rasp in his breathing. All the memories of his life at the tower that he had been trying to keep away had crowded to the front of his mind, forcing him to see them again, making him watch as Snutworth, with a word or a gesture, effortlessly pushed him in the direction he wanted. All his great decisions, all his success, came down to the servant in black. In his mind, Snutworth rose up, not the icily calm man who had just left, but a demon, laughing, triumphing, and dancing upon him, each thud of his hooves another spasm of pain in his chest.

He slipped between waking and dreaming, never moving from the floor. He heard footsteps and voices. Dimly he saw that it was night, and then day, and then night again, and still the dreams attacked him. Snutworth cut off his legs and wanted to trade them away, but his father had rights to the left one and wasn't selling. Cherubina wanted his hand as a wedding present. A school of fish swam through the air, a starfish leading the way, laughing as it sank into the muddy ground. A crowd danced around him, then rose up like a flock of birds and tore at his clothes, his hair, his face. He tried to run, but the city walls loomed up before him, topped with jagged teeth closing in, crushing him as he tried to struggle free, to claw his way out. Then he was back before his tower. But it was swaying, tilting in the breeze, ready to topple. He turned to escape, but Count Stelli held him fast in a clawed grasp and he couldn't move. The Observatory plummeted. He could see the telescope turning end over end.

And a dark hand stopped it.

Lily stood before him, her eyes pits of fire. He cried in pain as her gaze burned him. He felt his finery turn to ashes. She extended her hand, but she seemed further and further away.

Mark reached out.

His hand closed around the hand of a pale, red-haired girl.

Mark blinked, his eyes blurry. He was lying on his back. He tried to move, but the girl pushed him back gently onto the straw pallet.

"Hush," she said, rubbing his chest with a rag that smelled of something medicinal. "The fever's broken, but your bruise is still a little tender."

Mark stared. The dreadful visions were gone. The walls of the cell still rose about him, but now he saw that the door to the cell stood ajar. In the shadows beyond he could make out the jailer, standing guard, and a sleeping Ghast. He felt an old blanket wrapped around him, against the chilling drafts. He turned his attention back to the girl. She laid a cool hand on his forehead.

"Back to normal," she remarked. "The doctor's remedies are getting more effective every day."

Mark looked at her. There was something familiar in the turn of the nose, the shape of the eye. And now he could see that she was not quite as young as he had first thought. About his age.

"How . . . how long . . ."

"Three days. The fever broke last night," the girl said, bathing the bruises on his chest where Snutworth's cane had dug deep. "It's the last day of the month of Scorpio." She smiled. "Two years since your title day. You should have a celebration."

"How do you know when . . ." Mark began. And then, in a flash, he recognized her. "You're Gloria's sister," he said, pulling back.

She nodded.

"That's right. I'm Benedicta," she said. Her balm tingled, spreading a soothing feeling. "You missed Lily. She was here earlier, when you were asleep, but she has an important appointment today. She's been here every day since we found out . . ."

"Benedicta, I—" Mark stopped, looking into her gentle, open expression. He felt quite a different pain this time, but memories of his fevered dreams came back and he had to continue. "I'm sorry about your sister," he said. "I never wanted —"

"Of course you didn't." Benedicta cut him off. "Only a madman would have wanted it."

"But still . . ." Mark struggled to speak. "I should have . . . I shouldn't have . . ."

He held out his hands and Benedicta nodded. So many things he could have done and hadn't. So many ways he could have helped her and didn't. It wasn't worth counting them all. She understood. He could see it in her face. A sad smile hung there as she looked into the distance.

"I told Lily that would be the first thing you said. She thought it would be about Mr. Snutworth." She shrugged. "She can be severe sometimes. But I think she was hoping I'd be right. She believes in you, you know. Which with Lily's standards is pretty impressive."

"I wish *I* did," Mark said, lying back down with his cheek on the cell floor. "It's not worth much now, but . . . I'm sorry."

"I know," Benedicta said. She paused, putting the herbal balm away in the pockets of her apron. "I forgive you," she said.

Mark twisted around, not noticing the fresh pain.

"Why?" he said.

Benedicta brushed her hands on her apron.

"Why not?" she replied. "I believe you, and we can't change what has already happened by blaming people." She leaned forward earnestly. "Don't grudges only cause pain?"

Mark stared at her. She sat in the filth and the despair of a prison cell beneath the receivers' barracks and talked about forgiveness. He opened his mouth, expecting disbelief. That was what he felt. Benedicta's expression stopped him. There was a hard look there, beneath the friendliness. And something else too, lost in the depths of her hazel eyes. It was almost desperation.

"Yes," he said. And to his surprise, he found that he meant it.

For one brief moment, he watched the smile that grew on her face and felt his own mouth twitching in response. Then he dropped his gaze to the ground.

"Look . . . I appreciate this, I do, but . . . you don't need to keep visiting. And thank Lily for coming too. She didn't have to."

"If you think that, then you don't know her at all," Benedicta said, getting up.

Mark nodded. It felt sometimes as if they were destined to keep crossing each other's path.

"I suppose she wondered where I'd gone," Mark mused, "but I don't know how she tracked me down here."

"She didn't," Benedicta said.

Mark looked up. Benedicta stood, leaning back on the bars. Behind her, the shadow of the jailer loomed. Mark sat up.

"We didn't even know you'd disappeared," Benedicta continued, "not until three days ago. By the time we found out, you were already ill." She walked past him, to stand in the shadows under the high, slitted window, through which a few beams of afternoon sun streamed across the cell. "Such a coincidence really. I was only coming to visit a friend who works here. I bumped into Mr. Snutworth on the stairs." She stopped, twisting her fingers. "He married Miss Cherubina yesterday morning. I'm sorry." She paused and then half smiled. "Laud refused to organize it. He won't work for just *anyone*, you know."

Mark heard a shuffle behind him as the jailer entered the cell. He felt a spark of anger and, without looking around, snapped, "Can't you just leave us alone a little longer?"

There was silence.

"Mark . . ." Benedicta said slowly. "This is the friend I was telling you about."

"The jailer?" Mark said disbelievingly. "When did you come across him?"

"I meet all sorts of people at the Almshouse, Mark." Benedicta said, keeping her eyes fixed on the jailer. "Some just need a bed for the night. Some need food or attention or medicine. Some we can help to find a new job, to stop being a debtor." She paused and then, weighing each word carefully, said, "He used to be a fisherman."

Mark froze. He could hear nothing but the sound of his own breathing. His mind was racing, trying to think what the jailer looked like, but he had never seen him out of the half-lit gloom.

He turned.

The jailer stood illuminated in the light falling from the window. The hardness of life had added more lines than two years should, but now Mark looked into his face, now he really looked with clear eyes, there was no mistaking him.

"Dad . . ."

"Son."

Mark stood, barely feeling the emotions struggling inside him. The last time he had seen his father, the man had seemed like a giant. Now they were the same height.

"You . . . you sold me." Mark's voice was empty and strained.

"I thought you'd be safer in the care of a doctor," he said, his voice trembling. "I thought I was going to die and leave you with no one. Then, when I saw how great you had become . . ." He dropped his hands to his side. "Who'd want an old debtor like me spoiling their dream?"

Mark stepped forward. A storm of emotions was waiting beneath the surface, straining for release. But for now he just stood and looked at his father's face.

He heard the rustle of a skirt. Benedicta was next to them. She grasped Mark's right hand in hers and, with her left, took his father's right hand. Gently, she brought them together and then stepped away.

Mark clasped his father's hand. It was solid and real. Then he squeezed it, tighter and tighter. His vision began to blur. And then he pulled him closer.

He felt the tears stream down his face as if they would never stop. He felt his breaths come in great shuddering gasps. He felt his insides twisting with sadness and regret.

He felt the warmth of his father's embrace.

And that was worth something.

CHAPTER TWENTY-FOUR

The Director

THE DOORS of the Directory were vast — two great slabs of ancient oak, carved with baroque representations of all twelve signs of the zodiac, with the scales at the top, picked out in gold leaf. Around them, sculpted angels held scrolls of pure white stone that poured down the supporting pillars and spread out to touch the gray solidity of the walls. And above, piercing the overcast morning sky, the towers stretched away until they vanished from view. It was breathtaking. Even the courts could not compare with it for grandeur. And it was as if it were invisible.

The square before it was almost deserted. Those that did walk past kept their faces huddled in their collars, their eyes fixed on the ground. Even the occasional receiver seemed to flinch away, as if those doors shone like the sun and would burn the eyes of those who sought their splendor. But Lily looked straight at it, the appointment scroll clutched tight in her hand, her borrowed cloak tight around her shoulders, and the great building stared back, its presence flooding the square and filling the sky.

Lily turned to her companion. Laud was not keeping his eyes averted. He stood, his shoulders squared, his jaw tightly set, looking at the Directory as if his gaze would make the marble crack. His eyes didn't move, not even when she came to stand next to him.

"Are you all right?" Lily asked haltingly. "You didn't have to come with me."

"Couldn't let you come alone," Laud said, his voice clipped and strained. "Not here. Benedicta wanted to come too, and if Mark hadn't looked as if he was going to come out of his fever today I couldn't have said no." A shadow of amusement crossed his face. "The first time I've been happy with something that Mark's done for a long while."

Lily stared up at the Directory of Receipts. She could see now why the passersby averted their gaze. The longer she looked at it, the larger it seemed to be, as if it was pushing itself forward to emphasize its importance. It impressed itself upon her eyes like the stamp of a signet ring.

She turned away, disturbed.

"It's only a building, Laud, no matter what the legends would have us think," Lily said, not sure who she was trying to convince. "I mean," she added with an attempt at a grin, "you don't really believe that they can just make people disappear? That's impossible . . ."

"It happens," he said coldly. "It happened to our parents."

Lily stepped back, her hand rising to her mouth. All her forced jollity froze in her throat and she couldn't speak. In the end, it was Laud who broke the silence.

"Ten years old," he said, "that's how old Benedicta was when they went through that door. Special debts, they said. We searched every prison in the city but we couldn't find them. We never cried. We had to look after Ben, register her as our property." Laud made a bitter sound that was nearly a laugh. "I was thirteen, and already a father to my sister." He walked away, not looking at Lily. "I can't let her see another person she cares about go through those doors." He dug his hands deep into his pockets. "It looks like everyone leaves us in the end."

Lily found she was biting her lip so hard that she tasted blood. She reached out her hand and pressed it against his sleeve. She touched the outline of the scar on his arm through the fabric, still raised and lumpy after Pauldron's attack. Her mouth was dry and guilt dripped coldly down her spine, but still Laud wouldn't look at her.

"If there was another way, anyone other than the Director himself to ask," she began, but Laud stopped her, turning around and putting his hand on hers.

"I know," he said, his voice quieter. "And there's no point in trying to talk you out of it." He met her gaze, his expression holding the same burning intensity that she had seen once before, when they had stood on the roof of the Almshouse that terrible night. "But I doubt if any secret is worth it."

And for a moment Lily felt the urge to reconsider. It would be so simple to turn back. She could continue her apprenticeship with Theo. She could be useful at the Almshouse. She could help people one at a time and see the good she did.

She could stay, and never know who she was, or what might happen.

She looked back at Laud.

"Tell Mark I'm sorry I missed him," she said.

Laud nodded. There was another expression on his face now — a look of pain, but far gentler than the scowl he usually wore.

"Anyway," he said, "I'd like to see them try to make *you* disappear." A ghost of a smile crept onto his lips. "You'll be back at the Almshouse dispensing the secret of eternal life by sunset."

Lily smiled too. It lasted no more than a couple of seconds, though it felt longer.

And then, without either of them noticing when he had arrived, there was a third person present: a receiver, and a familiar one.

"Miss Lilith," Inspector Greaves said with a small bow, "you are expected within." He turned to Laud. "The appointment is for one only, Mr. Laudate."

"I understand, Inspector," Laud said brusquely, stepping away, turning his back on the Directory.

Lily looked over to the inspector, who regarded her with curiosity.

"Are you ready, Miss Lilith?"

Lily glanced sideways at Laud and then turned to face Greaves, the Directory looming behind him.

She nodded and stepped forward.

For a second, as they passed each other, Laud's hand brushed hers and their fingers interlocked. Neither of them looked at each other. There was nothing more to say. She took another step and felt his hand fall away.

Greaves went ahead, across the square, as the two receivers on guard hauled open the vast doors. Lily followed, gazing into the shadows beyond.

As she crossed the threshold, a sudden pang gripped her from within. She turned back, hoping to catch Laud's eye, but it was too late. Quietly, without fuss, the doors had closed behind her.

The Directory smelled of parchment and ink, overlaid with the strange, all-pervasive scent of age. In that, it reminded her of the bookbinder's — a temple to the written word. As she followed Greaves down the wood-paneled corridors, the windows were fewer and farther between, until he was forced to take an oil lamp from the wall to light their way.

Just as they were passing a small side door, almost invisible among the paneling, Lily heard voices approaching them from further down the corridor. To her surprise, the inspector stopped dead, his expression troubled. Then, in one purposeful movement, he opened the door, which led into a dark storeroom, and motioned Lily inside. Instinctively, she obeyed, knowing that she had to be quiet. The inspector shut the door behind her.

For a few minutes, she waited in the dark, listening to the tap of footsteps outside on the stone floor. Every now and then she heard muffled greetings from Greaves. She could not be sure, but at one point she thought she heard him address someone as "My Lord."

Once the footsteps had died away, the inspector opened the door.

"My apologies," he said, as Lily emerged back into the corridor.

"What was that?" she asked pointedly.

The inspector looked as if he was not going to answer, but then he sighed.

"Your presence today could cause some . . . difficulty if it were widely known."

"But surely if the Director has authorized it," Lily began, but Greaves held up a hand to stop her.

"There are some who disagree with the Director about you, Miss Lilith. If they saw you here . . ." He looked straight at her. "I was instructed to ensure your safety. I have already almost failed once. I do not intend to again." He turned away. "We're nearly there. Shall we keep moving?"

Surprised and silenced by this new knowledge, Lily nodded, and they continued to walk.

Sometimes they passed a door ajar and Lily would snatch a glance inside to a vast hall filled with the sound of scratching quills, or perhaps a library stretching down into the earth. The stone floor was polished with age, but an endless coating of fine dust overlaid everything.

Lily looked up at the face of the inspector. The lamp cast strange shadows, deepening the worry lines on his craggy face. He turned his head.

"Are you all right, Miss Lilith?" he said, sounding genuinely concerned.

"Yes, of course," Lily said.

The truthful answer would have taken too long, but as the corridors grew grander, and paintings began to dot the walls, she could not tell whether the tension that was now spreading through her, from her deepest thoughts to the tips of her fingers, was caused by fear or excitement, curiosity or dread. Here, in the half-light, she almost expected to see the fabled book, where it took only the stroke of a pen to remove a person from existence. In a building with so many legends attached to it, anything seemed possible.

And then they were standing before an ordinary doorway in an anonymous corridor. Greaves knocked and the door opened.

Inside a woman was framed by lamplight from the room beyond. A woman whose skin was as dark as Lily's.

"Miss Verity, this is Miss Lilith," Greaves said, gesturing to the woman. "Miss Lilith, this is the Director's personal secretary."

Miss Verity extended her hand.

"Please, call me Rita," she said, in a voice that was making an effort to be welcoming. Had it not been for the awkwardness of the woman's hand as she shook it, Lily might have believed her.

"Lily," she said, returning the favor. She felt the hand in hers relax a little.

"The Director will see you at the twelfth hour. Please come in."

Cautiously, Lily entered Miss Verity's office. She noticed the coffee cups, chipped but clean, clustered on an antique desk. Saw the ebony door on the other side of the room, its brass handle shiny from use. Saw the piles of papers still to be sorted in an otherwise immaculately neat room. For some reason, Lily knew that it was today's work, and today's alone, that had been left undone.

Miss Verity and Greaves had a brief conversation in the doorway, their voices hushed. Lily could only make out some thanks for escorting her, before Greaves bowed and left, closing the door behind him. Miss Verity moved over to a coffee pot.

"Would you like some coffee?' she asked, her voice formal and tense. "Or perhaps some tea . . . I think we might have some here somewhere."

"That's kind of you, but no, thank you," Lily said.

Miss Verity fiddled with a strand of black hair that had fallen out of its tight braid. Her eyes flicked to a wooden chair in the corner.

"Please, sit down," she said hurriedly. "Unless you'd like another chair . . ."

"Everything's fine, really," Lily said soothingly. "I prefer to stand."

Miss Verity nodded distractedly and began to shuffle some papers on her desk. There was something unsettling about the secretary. Lily found herself watching the woman as she moved about the office, peering into the cubbyholes of a large bureau, glancing at the wall-mounted clock that ticked away the seconds to the meeting. At first she had thought it was nothing more than the lamplight playing tricks, but, as Lily continued to watch, the feeling grew stronger. It was in the way she moved, the way she spoke — looking at this woman was almost like gazing at herself after twenty more summers had passed. As she thought about this — a strange and wonderful thought forming in her brain — Lily caught Miss Verity staring back at her.

"Is something wrong?" Lily asked, feeling odd as she did so. It was she who was the intruder in this world, and yet she felt almost calm, the constant ticking of the clock pushing her ever closer to the appointed time.

Miss Verity looked back at her, clutching a new pile of papers to her chest. She breathed out.

"Forgive me. I didn't know what to expect from you." She put down the papers and stepped around her desk. "I've read about you in the files, but — " she reached out a hand to touch Lily's face, a faraway look in her eyes — "that's only facts. It couldn't prepare me . . ."

The clock struck twelve with a sonorous clang. Miss Verity withdrew her hand, the moment broken, and smoothed down her dress. In an instant, the nervousness was gone, suppressed with the tiniest shudder. Her tone, when she spoke, was one of simple efficiency.

"The Director of Receipts will see you now."

She reached out to the handle of the ebony door and turned it. The door opened inward. Lily looked toward Miss Verity, feeling a sudden sense of loss, but it was as if any trace of the woman who had reached out for her had vanished, leaving only the Director's secretary in her place.

Confused, fearful, but determined not to show it, Lily stepped through the open door.

It took a moment for her eyes to adjust to the darkness. A moment for the marble floor to gain its quiet gleam and for the starry ceiling to come into focus. A moment for the portraits of past directors in their gilt frames to swim out of the shadows and glare down at her with haughty eyes. A moment before she saw the pool of light halfway down the room where four burning candles stood on an ancient desk.

She heard the click of the ebony door closing behind her and the scratching of a quill stop. The figure at the desk looked up.

"How pleasant to meet you at last, Miss Lilith. Please, come forward."

His voice was quiet, but it carried through the vast office and seemed to resonate in the air. Lily walked forward.

The man behind the mahogany desk came into view. His dry, withered hands lightly brought together, his thin lips half smiling, his white hair swept back from a face that bore a look of quiet power. His eyes glimmered in the candlelight. Lily felt herself stepping more reverently. She found that she wanted to bow, but inwardly stopped herself. This was just an old man. He didn't shine in glory or touch the sky. His ceremonial robe was in black and gold, but faded and slightly fraying. Even his signet ring, dully gleaming on one finger, was not golden. It was made of iron.

The Director's gaze moved over her. Lily had the strange feeling of being cataloged. And then he spoke.

"Aren't you going to bow?" he said calmly, without a trace of annoyance or anger. "It is customary."

"Do you want me to?" Lily replied coldly.

The Director raised an eyebrow.

"Not particularly. The bowing accomplishes little. It is the choice that interests me."

"Then no."

The Director nodded, seeming satisfied, and picked up a long quill from his desk. With practiced ease, he dipped it into a brass inkwell and began to write on the parchment in front of him.

Lily stood. All she could hear were the sounds of her own breathing and the relentless scratching of the quill. The Director seemed barely to acknowledge her presence. Suddenly she felt a flash of anger and pulled the appointment scroll out of the pocket of her apron. She dropped it on the desk in front of him.

"I am quite aware of that, Miss Lilith," the Director said, without looking up. "I, after all, agreed to the time."

"Then why bother to see me if you are busy?" Lily said, trying to keep her voice level as her fists clenched.

The Director looked up placidly.

"I am not, Miss Lilith. I am merely passing the time until you see fit to tell me the nature of your business here."

Lily glared, thrown off guard. She tried to catch a spark of triumph or contempt in those aged, sunken eyes, but saw nothing. The Director was giving nothing away. Consciously, she slowed her breathing, regained her composure.

"I want the truth," she said.

The Director put down his quill.

"A vast request, Miss Lilith. There are so many things that are true."

"Not as many as the lies."

The Director considered for a moment and shook his head.

"I cannot agree with you. The truth consists of everything there is. Lies are limited by what the human mind can conceive."

"That doesn't sound very limited to me."

The Director paused then, his hands touching at the fingertips, looking at her as if appraising her worth. He seemed to come to a decision.

"Very well, what do you want to know?"

Lily looked back at him. There was something new in his stare, almost a kind of eagerness. It made her uncomfortable, but she knew what she had planned to say.

"Who am I?"

The Director sighed, and Lily thought that he seemed disappointed.

"You know the answer to that question. You are Miss Lilith, known as Lily. No more, no less than yourself." He met her gaze. "Perhaps, though, that is not what you meant . . ."

Involuntarily, Lily shrank from his gaze, trying to piece together what she knew.

"Pauldron . . . when he had me cornered, he called me something. He called me 'Antagonist.' "

"Yes, Pauldron." The Director frowned. "A highly regrettable occurrence. Greaves is normally so reliable. Had your friend not escaped and raised the alarm . . . but that is irrelevant now. He has brought you here safely today."

"Yes," Lily persisted. "If I'm nothing special, why was he sent to look after me? He's always been around, ever since I started the Almshouse."

"Initially, his only duty was to report on you to the Directory. But then Miss Rita suggested that you might be in danger and Greaves is a highly reliable man. He never asks to know more than he needs. I believe he prefers his world view simple." The Director gestured into the darkness behind Lily, back toward the ebony door. "So you have Verity to thank for his presence. She has quite an interest in you."

Lily froze. The idea that had been growing, just below the surface of her thoughts, since the first moment she saw the Director's secretary crystallized into a question. She wanted to ask, but at the same time she didn't want to know. She steeled herself. This was the only chance she was going to get.

"Director," she began, feeling the mythical name roll off her tongue so easily, "is Miss Verity . . . is there a reason for her interest?"

The Director's mouth twitched. There was a definite smile there, although whether it was friendly or not was impossible to tell.

"You have noticed the similarities in your appearance?"

Lily nodded, her heart beating faster.

"No, Lily," the Director said, shaking his head, "she is not your mother."

It was stupid. They had only met minutes ago. She had spent her whole life without parents. But it felt like a blow to the stomach. When Miss Verity had touched her face, it had felt comfortable somehow, like coming home. For a moment, she wondered if the Director was telling her the whole truth. There had to be some significance, she didn't believe in coincidences like that. She gritted her teeth, ready to ask another question about the secretary who had looked at her with such pained eyes.

"Not that you are truly an orphan," the Director added, almost casually.

Lily stared, her prepared words deserting her. So many shocks so close together were too much. Her emotions slipped away. She faced the Director, matching his icy calm.

"Where are my parents?"

"Not here. Outside."

"Outside the Directory?"

The Director shook his head.

"Outside anything and anywhere you have ever known. Outside of our world. Beyond the city walls. Beyond Agora."

"Can I find them?"

"That depends."

"On what?"

The Director looked her in the eyes.

"On your next, and final, question."

Lily opened her mouth, but the Director raised a hand.

"Do not be surprised," he said. "There are some who would deny you even this much knowledge. But I believe that this trade is just. One more piece of truth, Miss Lily, one more idea to be given to you in exchange for that which you do not know you have given. One question."

The Director put the tips of his fingers together, and waited.

Lily's composure faltered. She could feel the turmoil lurking beneath the surface of her mind waiting to engulf her once this light was snatched away. One more thing to be illuminated before this window was closed.

And then, out of it all, came the question. The question that should have been first.

"What is the Midnight Charter?"

The question hung in the air, resonating up to the ceiling, seeming to deepen the frowns on the portraits of the past directors. The Director thought for a moment and then, as if unburdening himself of a secret that he had kept for far too long, he spoke.

"The founders of Agora were idealists. They looked at a world torn between extremes and dreamed of another way." His voice filled with reverence. "They had a vision of a city where all were equal — where balance, barter, and give-and-take were woven into its very heart and soul. Where value was judged by every individual, and no one could force something out of nothing. Where their symbol, Libra, the scales, would be revered as the highest virtue." The Director bowed his head and rubbed his temples. "A fine dream, one worthy to be believed in. But they also saw how easily it could be corrupted." He smiled wearily at Lily. "There is no vision so strong that people cannot trample it into the dust. So, on the night the first of Agora's stones were laid, at the midnight hour, when one day is balanced against the next, they signed the Midnight Charter. The most ambitious plan ever devised by the Libran Society. An agreement that, when the time came, their own city, their own dreams, would be tested and proven worthy. Agora itself would be weighed in the balance and tempered with fire."

"How was it to be tested?" Lily asked breathlessly.

"There would emerge, the Charter says, two judges, one for each side of the scales. The first, the Protagonist, would thrive on the city, express fully everything that Agora and her system could be. The

306

second, the Antagonist, would take the opposite view. They would see every failing, every crack and fault in their wonderful project, and would try to change it. The two would be equal and opposite, linked in their lives and destinies. They would not judge in the traditional sense, they would be granted no power that they had not found for themselves. Only in their struggle, their judgments, their trials, would we see which is the stronger. Only through them could the city reach perfection or destruction." The Director looked straight at Lily. "Over the years, there have been many whom we have suspected of filling these roles. Many Protagonists who soared to great heights in the city, many Antagonists who spoke out. Yes, more than are common knowledge. But always they have disappointed us, or they have never emerged at the same time. But now, we think, you have."

Lily stepped backward, stunned. A thousand questions tried to form themselves in her head, but, oddly, she asked the one to which she was sure, somehow, that she already knew the answer.

"Who is the other?" she said.

In reply, the Director fished an object out of his pocket.

"At first, we were not sure about either of you. You were one of our many projects — merely a possible pair. But after that memorable Agora Day, after we saw his rise and then your Almshouse, and we noticed how your lives seemed to constantly interconnect . . ." He held out the object, a worn brass signet ring with a starfish carved into it. "We were surprised to see that even after everything that has happened, you came to him in his illness. But it seems oddly fitting that our great opposites should also be friends."

Lily stared at the ring.

"Mark," she said.

Even though she had been correct, the thought gave her little comfort. As the Director dropped Mark's signet into her hand, she struggled with this new knowledge. It all seemed to fit so perfectly.

And yet she knew, more certainly than anything else at this moment that she did not believe in destiny.

She raised her head to speak again, but just as she opened her mouth she heard a noise behind her, a sound like raised voices moving nearer.

The Director frowned, showing a trace of annoyance.

"It appears that we are about to be interrupted."

A moment later, with a crash that seemed deafening in the previously hushed office, the ebony door to Miss Verity's office was flung open. Striding through it, his normally composed features twisted with anger, came the Lord Chief Justice. In his wake, Miss Verity followed, casting apologetic looks at the Director.

"I'm so sorry, sir," she said hurriedly. "He insisted that — "

"I shall speak for myself, thank you," Lord Ruthven growled. "Leave us."

Miss Verity looked at Lily and then at the Director, who gave her a tiny nod. Bowing, she exited. The Director turned his attention to Lord Ruthven.

"Now, Ruthven, to what do we owe this interruption?"

"This meeting is unacceptable, Director," Lord Ruthven fumed. "The girl has no right to know our secrets. How can she presume to judge everything we have spent our whole lives building?"

"There are many kinds of judgment, Ruthven," the Director replied calmly. "You of all people must know that. And perhaps the young may see things more clearly than we ever could, with all of our experience."

Lily's head was still spinning, but she managed to speak up in her defense.

"My Lord," she said, "I've never tried to judge anything . . . only to do what is right."

"You see, Director?" Lord Ruthven spoke confidently now, his voice hard with scorn. "This impostor cannot understand. The true Antagonist would have no doubts, no confusion. She does not have the purity for this calling."

Something in Lord Ruthven's words struck her as familiar. Slowly, as the two powerful men continued to argue, all of the things she had been told began to click into place . . . thoughts about purity, truth . . .

"Have you ever come across any other with such passionate beliefs, Ruthven?" the Director continued, still the voice of reason.

Who else believed passionately in what he did? Lily asked herself.

"Have a care, Director," Ruthven said icily. "You rule this city, but I am head of the Libran Society and we have the power to suspend you if — "

"It was you!"

Silence. Both men turned to look at Lily. For an instant, she doubted herself, but as she spoke again, breaking the silence, it was as if she had found a new strength that she had never touched before. She stared at Lord Ruthven.

"Back in the Clockwork House, when Pauldron tried to kill me, he said something. Something that made no sense at the time." She lowered her voice, but never broke her stare. "He called me 'Antagonist' and said that 'higher wisdoms' had revealed the truth to him." She came closer, growing in confidence. "Back at Mark's ball, you praised Pauldron's purity, his devotion to Agora. You told him these secrets, didn't you, My Lord? You showed him the Midnight Charter because you wanted *him* to be the Protagonist. That was what made him call Mark an impostor and want to defeat me." Lily stopped, horrified by her own realization. "And that was what drove him mad."

There was a long pause. Lord Ruthven stood frozen. He seemed to age before her eyes.

Slowly, the Director rose from his chair. "Is this true?" he said.

His voice, though quiet, filled the room. It would be impossible to lie to that voice. Ruthven drew himself up stiffly.

"Pauldron was far more suitable than that boy," he said coldly. "He was a man who passionately loved his city." He faltered, looking away. "I . . . I did not foresee that it would disturb the balance of his mind."

"You showed him the whole charter?" The Director spoke with quiet anger. "Could you not see, Ruthven, what a terrible thing it is to read if you have confused the dream of an ideal city with the flawed, unfinished reality? A dreadful uncertainty—enough to drive one whose whole life was founded on love for that city onto a path of darkness, to protect his own vision of perfection by striking at those who would test it."

"I did it to preserve our city!" Ruthven shouted. "He was stronger than the girl! He would have won the struggle, proven the Glory of Agora is everlasting." His voice grew quieter, but no less intense. "The Charter says that, despite their powerlessness, these two will change Agora forever." He turned to Lily, a look of hatred in his eyes. "I have served Agora for over fifty years, given my whole life in service to our city. I will not have that ruined by a pair of ignorant children."

The silence that followed seemed endless. For a long time, the Director stared at Ruthven, his face unreadable. Eventually, and with great precision, the Ruler of Agora spoke.

"You are fortunate, Ruthven, that I do not wish there to be a scandal," he said. "I shall not ask you to step down as Lord Chief Justice immediately. You will take your time to find a suitable successor. Everything will be done as if you have simply chosen to retire. But before a year has passed you will be gone. Otherwise, scandal or no, I shall break my silence. I will tell the whole city that you so poisoned the mind of a receiver that he killed a young woman. And then—" he paused and, when he spoke again, he placed great stress on his words — "then the damage to your good name may be irrevocable." The Director sat again, his expression one of disgust. "Now, get out."

Lord Ruthven's face drained of color. He cleared his throat to speak, but the Director refused to look at him. He turned to Lily, but she too looked away, staring at the wall. He would get no help from her. A few moments later, she heard his slow footsteps, followed by the door opening and closing. Only then did she breathe again.

Lily took a minute to compose herself. Soon she would need to have a long think, to organize her thoughts and feelings into some kind of order. For now, however, it was time to bring this interview to an end.

"Director . . ." she began.

The Director met her gaze, his face as calm as ever.

"Yes?" he said.

"What happens now?"

In response, the Director reached under his desk and opened a drawer.

"Now you must make a choice." From the drawer he pulled a rusty iron key. It seemed heavy and unwieldy, out of place in his hands. "There are many legends told about the Directory, strange and terrible stories. One is that people who visit here disappear, never to be seen again." He turned the key over in his hands, gazing at it thoughtfully. "But legends are all about drama. It would be such a disappointment for them to know about the door in the city wall."

Lily felt her heart jump.

"But . . . I thought there was nothing outside the city," she said.

The Director shook his head.

"Surely you never believed that. Surely you, Miss Lily, know that the only way to truly understand something is to see it as a whole — from outside."

Lily stared at the key.

"Are you banishing me?" she said hesitantly.

Part of her was horrified, but she could not ignore the fact that another part, deep within, flared with excitement and curiosity. She remembered, back at the tower, peering out of the windows, trying to see as much as she possibly could. It had been the best feeling she had ever had.

And, of course, her parents were somewhere out there in that unknown world.

"No, this is not a banishment," the Director said, bringing her back to the present. "I shall not force you to go. At least one of the judges must choose their destiny."

"One?"

The Director gave a half smile.

"If you accept this path, Lily, then you must take the other judge with you. No one will notice his departure from prison." The Director's smile faded. "It was . . . distasteful to convince his man-servant to close his trap a little earlier than he had intended, but sadly necessary. It was only a matter of time before you came to me and the disappearance of such a famous young man as Mr. Mark would have attracted too much attention unless he first vanished in a more conventional way."

Lily bit her lip, feeling the temperature in the room drop. The Director had defended her against Lord Ruthven, but she could see that in some ways he was no less ruthless.

"And if I don't leave Agora?"

The Director frowned.

"Then I have been sorely mistaken in you, but you will receive no punishment. You will return to your Almshouse, which in time will

312

fade away. You will perhaps live an easier life, with your friends, but Mark will remain in prison. And nothing will ever change."

Lily swallowed nervously. She wished that she could discuss this with someone, or ask Mark what he thought. But she knew that the Director did not waste his words. He had said only one of them could make this decision, and it was her. She hoped, whatever decision she made, that Mark would forgive her.

"But how can we judge anything?" she asked. "Who will obey us?"

The Director smiled.

"It is written in the Midnight Charter that your judgment will not be a conscious one. You will judge with every word and deed through your own natures. You will barely see the full effect of what you are doing, until the end. And then you will look back with wonder at what you have done."

Lily wanted to protest, to say that this made her task no clearer, but her voice died under the Director's stare.

"No more words," he said. "Now you must choose."

The Director placed the key on the desk in front of him. It shone in the candlelight.

"Take this key and become the Antagonist. Be reborn into an alien land, free the Protagonist from his cell and seek your parents. See Agora for what she truly is." He frowned. "Alternatively, do not take the key and return to the life you knew. Unchanged, unknowing, and unimportant. But safe." He sat upright now, with power in his eyes. "Choose, Miss Lilith, but be wary. Walk out of the Directory and live the rest of your life as any other citizen. Walk out of Agora and you will never walk back in."

Lily looked at the key. Every speck of rust seemed sharp in her vision, as though all the light in the dark office were concentrated on it. She thought of Laud and Theo and Benedicta, waiting for her back at the Almshouse. She thought of her parents, somewhere out there in the unknown. She thought of Gloria and of how little she had wanted to have anything to do with the conspiracy that had robbed her of her life. She thought of Mark, lying fevered in his cell unless she set him free. She thought of the good she was doing, the hundreds of debtors she had helped and the hundreds more that appeared every day. She thought of the city in all its awful, soulless splendor, and its crowds seemed to pour through her head, all unknowing, all part of an idea, the dream of long-dead founders.

All asleep and not wanting to be awakened.

The city waited.

She made her decision.

CHAPTER TWENTY-FIVE

The Promise

MARK AWOKE to the click of approaching footsteps.
He pushed himself up on one arm, squinting at the
window, which let in a little chilly predawn light, and rubbed his
shoulder, which ached from another night on a straw pallet.

He listened. The footsteps were too light to be his father's. He
had said he would be back in the morning with some blankets.
He couldn't let him go free, but for the moment he didn't need to
go anywhere.

He listened again as a door in the corridor creaked open. They
were too sharp to be Benedicta. She walked as gently as she spoke.

Mark started as a thought struck him. Could it be Lily?

Blearily, he reached forward, grabbing the bars and hauling
himself to his feet. The figure was close now. The last door between
them opened.

It was not her. For a few seconds he thought that it was, but this woman was older, more smartly dressed. She entered briskly, a lantern in one hand, a ring of keys in the other. She stopped before Mark's cell. As he stared, she selected a key from the bunch and slipped it into the lock of his cell door.

It turned with a clink.

Mark stepped back, confused. Perhaps he was still asleep.

The woman stared at him.

"Most prisoners wouldn't step back from an open door," she said.

"Uh . . ." Mark's head was still fuzzy from sleep, but he found himself pulling on his ragged shirt, stepping through the door, watching as she locked it behind him.

"This way," she said, turning on her heel.

Mark followed.

They walked deeper and deeper into the prison. Soon the cells gave way to stone corridors, damp and empty. He felt the floor slope down, then up, until he could no longer tell where they were, and still the woman marched ahead, never speaking, her lamp leading the way.

Finally, Mark found his voice.

"Look, it's not that I'm not grateful to you for getting me out of that cell, but—" he stopped walking—"who are you?"

The woman came to a halt. She turned, holding the lantern to her face. There was a look of sadness in her eyes.

"My name is Verity, and I'm here to show you the way out."

Mark stared at her. He would have thought it some kind of cruel joke if her expression had not stopped him.

"Thank you," he said, feeling that it was not enough. Verity turned away.

"You have Miss Lily to thank for this."

After that, Mark barely noticed where he was walking. His head was filled with visions of the future. Of starting again with a new trade. Of building up another tower better than the one Snutworth had stolen from him. Of bringing his father to stay with him. Maybe he'd even become a patron of the Almshouse. If Lily had given him a second chance, then he would pay her back, even if she didn't want it. That was how Agora worked. Finally, Mark thought as they approached an ancient wooden door, he could see a future that was right for him.

Verity stopped before the door. She pulled another key from her pocket, a large old one, flecked with rust. She pushed it into the lock and stopped. She turned to Mark, her voice low and urgent.

"Are you grateful, Mark?" she said.

Taken aback, he nodded fiercely. "Of course . . . Sorry, it's all been so sudden. I'd have said . . ."

"To me?" she said, in the same tone of voice. "And to Lily?"

"Yes," Mark said, watching the woman's hand tighten on the key.

The old lock made a grinding squeal as it turned.

"Then promise me something," she said, grasping him by the once fine shirt he wore, pulling his face close to hers. "Promise me that you'll look after her."

Despite himself, Mark laughed.

"Lily's never needed protection from anything," he said.

Miss Verity tightened her grip.

"That's what makes it so dangerous," she whispered. "Now, promise me."

Mark looked into eyes that were sorrowful but steely, glimmering in the lamplight.

"I promise," said Mark.

Verity drew back, seeming satisfied.

"Good," she said, and opened the door.

For a moment, Mark's eyes were dazzled. The low light of a winter sunrise flooded through the door. He put up his hands to shield them from the glare and took a few steps.

He felt Verity push him forward. He stumbled through the door.

There was a creak of hinges. Then a click.

Then the sound of the key turning once again.

Mark spun around. Here the door was small and inconspicuous, set into a wall.

A vast wall, stretching higher and farther than he had ever seen. Except for the city walls, of course.

The city walls . . .

Mark hammered on the door, clawing at the rough wood. He heard himself shouting that everything he had was inside the city, that he finally knew how it worked, that his future was imprisoned in those walls.

There was no response from within. He sank to his knees, huddling against the door, his fingers raw and bleeding. Behind him, he could feel a vast emptiness. A gust of wind made him shiver. There was nothing beyond the city walls, nothing.

Agora was the world and he had left it, as surely as if he had dropped dead.

A shadow appeared on the wall beside him. He pressed his head against the door, closing his eyes, not wanting to see. And then he heard a familiar voice.

"It was the only way, Mark," Lily said, soft and gentle, "the only way out of both of our prisons. There's so much you need to know, Mark . . . so much to say . . ."

Mark didn't respond, dully running his fingers over the wood of the Agoran door.

"Look, Mark," she said. He felt her hand rest on his shoulder.

"Look out there. A new world, Mark, a new life!" He heard her kneel down beside him. "It's beautiful."

Confused, bewildered, and more frightened than he had ever been since that day he had come back to life in the astrologer's tower, Mark turned his head.

And he opened his eyes.

GOFISH

DAVID WHITLEY

What did you want to be when you grew up?
A writer! I've been very lucky, really.

When did you realize you wanted to be a writer?
I must have been about six years old, and I was watching a cartoon. It came to an end, and somewhere in the back of my mind, I thought *That wasn't the right ending. If you'd done* this, *it would have been much better!* I've never looked back.

What's your favorite childhood memory?
This really should be something uplifting and unusual, shouldn't it? Pity, because nothing beats the first time I tasted ice cream in Florence, Italy, where it was invented. Pure heaven.

As a young person, who did you look up to most?
My cousin, Emma. She is ten years older than me, and when I was about twelve, she was just beginning her career as a playwright. I went to watch a production of hers—an excellent adaptation of *Little Women*. I remember being struck by the amazing fact that someone I knew well could be a writer—that it really was possible, and not just something that "other people" did. A couple years later, my first piece of writing for a public audience was a stage adaptation of an Agatha Christie short story. That was my only foray into writing for the stage so far, but a pivotal moment for me!

What was your worst subject in school?
Sports. I'm much better about exercise now (you have to be if your profession involves sitting at a desk all day), but I must admit, at the time, I failed to see the attraction of standing in a muddy field and occasionally being knocked down by a horde of other boys.

What was your best subject in school?
The one I enjoyed most was English, but funnily enough, the one I got the best marks in was physics. I haven't yet found a satisfactory way to combine the two . . . time to go into science fiction, I think. . . .

What was your first job?
I was very fortunate indeed—I've never been anything other than a writer.

How did you celebrate publishing your first book?
Back home in Chester, we organized a launch event in my local book-shop. All of my friends came, and cheered! It was such a special evening.

Where do you write your books?
At my desk, with many mugs of tea on standby and a note pointedly telling me to keep working and not get distracted by the Internet.

Where do you find inspiration for your writing?
Absolutely everywhere! It could be as grand as reading a great work of literature and being struck by A Profound Thought . . . or as simple as wandering past a shop window or into a museum, seeing a strange or unusual object and thinking *I'm having that*. And once I have an idea that works, expanding it into a full story, working out all of its implications and results, is my favorite part of the whole process!

Which of your characters is most like you?
All of my characters have a little of me in them—a different aspect of my personality. To my alarm, that does include the more morally dubious characters. Though I'd never really act like them, it's startling how easy it is to slip into their personality, once you start looking at life from their point of view. . . .

Having said that, there are some characters who I hope are particularly like me. I love to write about Dr. Theophilus. There is something very inspiring about his story—a good man who has suffered much, and nearly given up, but who finds new purpose in the actions and ideals of his friends. I try to live up to him.

When you finish a book, who reads it first?
My agent and his editor. I don't like to show it to friends and family until I have a professional opinion on whether it is any good!

What's your idea of the best meal ever?
Paprika would be involved, as would chicken, tomato, roast potatoes, chocolate, and maybe some raisins. No, not all in the same course, don't be silly. . . .

What do you value most in your friends?
Patience! I can be dreadful about keeping contact with my friends—sometimes, more than a year goes by in between visits. But that doesn't mean I'm not delighted to spend time with them, just that the writing has taken over for a while.

Where do you go for peace and quiet?
There's a wonderful zoo only a mile from my house. When the wind's in the right direction, you can hear the lions roaring! It's a brilliant place to wander, and it's doing a fantastic job of protecting so many endangered species. I've been going there since I was tiny, and I've always loved it, although it has made me surprisingly blasé about exotic animals. My parents often remind me of the time when, aged five, I ran straight past the elephants, excitedly shouting, "Oh look, a squirrel!"

What makes you laugh out loud?
Wordplay humor, usually silly and frequently surreal: "A man answers a ringing phone and asks 'Who's speaking, please?', and the voice on the other end says, 'You are!'" Classic.

What's your favorite song?

"Giants in the Sky" from Sondheim's *Into the Woods*. There were so many songs that I could have chosen by this composer, but this one wins for its sheer brilliance in telling a whole story in two breathless verses, and really capturing the excitement of experiencing something wondrous that completely changes your world.

Who is your favorite fictional character?

Arthur Clennam from Dickens's *Little Dorrit*. Not the most extraordinary man, nor the most powerful or world-changing. But he is honestly the most humanly decent person I have ever come across in fiction, trying to make the lives of everyone around him better. Even when he fails, his modest goodness is wonderfully appealing to me—a real example of being good and self-sacrificing, without heroics.

What are you most afraid of?

Heights. I know, it's ridiculously common, but any kind of precipice will result in a lot of walking with my weight on the back foot, constantly looking out for stray gusts of wind.

What time of year do you like best?

Early autumn. There's something wonderfully fresh and crisp about the air, and it's not too far away from my birthday!

What's your favorite TV show?

Doctor Who—wonderful concept, often brilliantly and wittily written. Above all, it's the variety that makes it so good—almost any story could be waiting when the doctor steps out of his time machine. . . .

If you could travel in time, where would you go?

Eighteenth-century London—to the Halls of the Royal Society, the greatest scientific body in the whole of the Age of Enlightenment. I would love to meet the people who changed forever the way we looked at the world, discovering new planets, new species, new understanding. They revealed the wonders of the earth and the universe with unrivalled passion, and I think it would be awe-inspiring to watch them at work!

What's the best advice you have ever received about writing?

It's actually a quote from Clive James, but it sums up the writer's life perfectly: "The art of a writer is to turn a phrase until it catches the light." Beautifully expressed—and perfect in showing how so much of writing is crafting your words until they achieve exactly what you want.

What would you do if you ever stopped writing?

I would probably become an academic of some kind, I certainly enjoyed my time at university. Then again, I suppose that would involve quite a lot of writing as well. . . .

What do you like best about yourself?

Enthusiasm. I can generally get excited about and interested in anything!

What do you consider to be your greatest accomplishment?

The youth drama productions that I have directed, with the most fantastic young casts imaginable. From the start of the rehearsals to the final performances, they were brilliant!

What do you wish you could do better?

Find my way. I have absolutely no sense of direction. Really, it's a good job that I do most of my travelling by train.

SQUARE FISH

THE AGORA TRILOGY

Children
of the Lost

DAVID WHITLEY

CHAPTER ONE

Foraging

GRADUALLY, Lily became aware that she was being watched.

Shielding her eyes against the low, winter sun, she swept her gaze over the gnarled, bare trees that stood gray and silent around her.

Nothing.

But still, she couldn't shake the feeling that somewhere, a huge pair of eyes had turned upon her.

When Lily had first glimpsed the forest, a couple of days before, it had looked forbidding—a silent, dark mass at the base of the mountains; the leafless, twisting branches clustered so thickly together that the light barely penetrated.

But as she took her first steps on the soft leaf mold beneath the trees, she had begun to hear it—the rustling in the undergrowth, the flap of wings overhead, the occasional birdcall, so harsh in the still air that she would jump and turn, and catch only a glimpse of black feathers. The earth shifted beneath her feet and yielded up things that moved and writhed and scuttled. Even the trees themselves, within their thick, cold bark, were alive. She had always known that; she had seen a few trees in the orchards of the city, but these were nothing like those ordered rows. Those trees were tamed; these looked as if they could reach for you.

Something moved in a nearby tree, and Lily jumped, letting the mushrooms she had been gathering fall to the ground. She looked closer.

Two dark, round, shining eyes peered back at her from the ancient bark. She caught her breath.

Then, there was a faint ruffle of feathers. Lily breathed out. The eyes belonged to a large, gray owl, which sat, brooding, on a branch, just next to the trunk, its mottled plumage making it almost invisible against the mossy bark.

The owl regarded her with a penetrating stare, and Lily returned it, unblinking. She tried to imagine what it would make of her. Would it see this dark-skinned human girl, wrapped in a mud-streaked apron, as a curiosity or a threat? Was she a guest here, or an intruder? The rational part of her nature laughed at the notion that the tree itself had been watching her. But at the same time, the owl was no less fascinating.

After all, she had seen streams of pure, liquid anger, and watched a captured voice float through the air. She had known things that seemed supernatural. But in all her fourteen years of life, she had never been so close to a wild animal.

A moment later the bird ruffled its wings and swooped down and away, breaking the stillness. As it did so, the breeze began to stir, and Lily shivered, wishing she had not left her cloak at the camp. Now was not the time for nature watching. Wearily, Lily gathered up the small pile of mushrooms again, and, feeling the ache of the cold in her steps, she made her way back through the forest.

As she walked, Lily began to smell the smoke from the campfire. Now she could make out a dark shape against the brightness—the silhouette of a boy, the firelight darkening his blond hair. He sat hunched against the cold, his legs drawn up to his chin, Lily's cloak tight around his shoulders. Unlike Lily, who was wrapped up in many layers of dress, petticoats, and apron, the boy wore only a shirt and breeches, which looked as if they had once been of fine quality, back when they were clean and new. Every now and then, he poked the fire with a long stick. He did not look up as Lily approached, or when she sat beside him. His gray eyes stared into the flames, his expression grim.

Lily spread out her apron on the ground, showing the pile of mushrooms. She hoped she had brought enough. They were not appetizing, but they had been eating them for three days and they had not been poisoned yet.

"I brought some food," she said cautiously. The boy didn't reply. Instead, he pulled his stick out of the fire and, without looking at her, he speared a mushroom and held it over the flames.

Sighing Lily did the same. She was not especially talkative herself, but the forest magnified their endless silence. Every tiny rustle or distant call of an unknown animal seemed huge and terrible.

And still, Mark would not meet her eyes.

It had not been so bad, at first, back in the mountains. But then, the first couple of days were a blur in her mind. She remembered being ushered through the tunnels beneath the city, saw the door being opened for her, and the light streaming through, and then . . .

It wasn't seeing Agora from the outside that had shocked her, even though it was an amazing sight. Without the city buildings to

3

hide them, the stark gray mass of the city walls had loomed over her. She had spent her whole life believing that Agora's walls were the limit of the world, and for the first few minutes, she found herself touching the stone, unable to accept where she was. But even so, she had prepared herself for that. She had made the decision to leave the city.

No, it was when she turned away from the walls to look outwards, that her senses deserted her. The mind-numbing grandeur of the mountains rose up on all sides, shielding Agora in a deep, wide valley without blocking the rays of the low winter sun. Lily had seen the most incredible sights of Agora, from the Directory of Receipts to the Astrologer's Tower, but beside the rugged peaks, silhouetted against the dawn, they were nothing at all. By the time she heard Mark shouting, screaming to be let back into the city— she could barely speak. She thought that she had mumbled something about it being "beautiful."

At first, they had tried to find the river Ora, walking around the city until they reached the place where it flowed out through a vast, rusty grille set into the base of the city walls. Mark had insisted that they stop, to see if there was any way of lifting it, of getting back into the city that had been their world. But although huge, ancient chains plunged into holes in the walls, they couldn't move the grate. Even so, they camped there the first night, huddling together for warmth, just in case anyone appeared to tell them that it was all a mistake and to welcome them home. No one did.

The next morning, they had turned their backs on Agora, and Lily, steeling herself, had told Mark everything.

After that, Mark had stopped talking. But at least in the mountains, it had been a passive quietness—almost as though he was elsewhere. It had been as though the shock of this new world had left him without anything to say.

But over the last couple of days, as they had entered the forest, that had all changed. He was still tight-lipped, but now one look at his face told her that he had plenty to say. And once he started, she knew that she wouldn't like what she heard.

The last of the evening light faded away. As they ate, the world around them shrank until it extended only as far as the circle of light cast by the campfire. Lily glanced up again at her companion and, tentatively, she reached out a hand to him.

"Mark . . ." she began.

He snatched his hand away and turned, hunching his shoulders. He had grown early, and could sometimes be taken for older than his fourteen years, but sitting like this, he seemed so like a child.

On previous evenings, this had been how it had ended. Lily had scanned the clearing for lurking creatures, and then settled down by the fire and tried to sleep. Neither of them had slept well. Not that Mark told her, but she could tell from the dark circles forming under his eyes. It was as though the tension of the days, the oppressive atmosphere between them, was seeping into their nights. The next day they would take turns searching. Lily said that they were looking for food, but both of them knew the real reason. They were looking for any signs of another human being.

But tonight, perhaps because her nerves were frayed from lack of sleep, Lily jumped up and stalked around the fire, until she was facing Mark again. She knelt down in front of him, forcing him to look at her.

"Mark, we have to talk . . ."

"Go on, then," Mark replied, staring back at her, his eyes cold in the firelight. Lily, taken aback, lost her resolve and sat back on the ground to gather her thoughts. She knew what she wanted to talk about, and also knew that if one thing were guaranteed to make Mark worse, it would be that.

"We need to keep moving," she ventured after a moment's thought. "We should try to find the river again. If anyone lives out here, they must live by the river, there's no other freshwater—"

"Seen anyone yet?" Mark cut across her fiercely, "or is this another guess?"

"There must be someone else," Lily said soothingly. "The Director said that others had left the city before . . ."

Lily stopped herself too late. She had not meant to mention the Director again.

"Pity he didn't tell us what happened to them," Mark said, and then added, in a strained voice. "Sorry, pity he didn't tell *you*."

For the hundredth time, Lily wished that she had not told Mark about the agreement she had made with the Director of Receipts, the ruler of Agora. It had seemed so simple—the chance to leave the city, to escape those dreadful streets, where everything and everyone was for sale. The chance, moreover, to find out the truth behind the dark secrets that had plagued their lives, plots that had already led to the death of a friend. The possibility, somewhere in this strange world, of finding her own vanished parents. It had been a once in a lifetime offer, and the price had seemed so tiny— that Mark would accompany her. At the time, Lily had been sure that he would leap at the chance. How could he complain, when he had lost everything? When Lily had last seen him, he had been rotting in a prison cell, dying from fever, and being watched over by a man he hated for selling him when he was younger—his father.

If his fever had only lasted one more day, Lily would have been his savior. If he hadn't had a chance to meet his father, to talk, and to forgive him.

"I've told you," Lily said, as gently as she could, "I didn't know he was going to offer a way out, Mark. I never thought he'd give you the chance to escape from jail . . ."

"Don't pretend you did it for me," Mark growled. "You talk to

6

the ruler of Agora, and he drones on about some ancient secrets, and suddenly nothing else matters—"

"This is something bigger than us, Mark," Lily said intensely. "Didn't you always want to be important? The Director said they've been waiting for us ever since the city was founded. Hundreds of years, Mark, long before the Golden Age began . . ."

"He said it *might* be us," Mark replied. "It's *possible* that we're these legendary judges that they've been waiting for. You said that they'd been wrong before."

"But what if they're right, Mark?" Lily interrupted, with sudden passion. "Think about it. The Director said that we would make a real difference. That we'd change Agora forever! Wouldn't that be worth it?" She sat forward, letting the firelight shine full on her face. "We could change it for the better, Mark. We could make it a place where children don't get sold by their parents, where secret societies don't kill our friends without a second thought, where people don't have to sell their own emotions to survive!" Lily was getting heated now. "You were thrown into prison without even being allowed to speak at your own trial, Mark, thanks to Mr. Snutworth. My friends spend all their time running an almshouse, a charity, that's always on the verge of collapsing, and why? Because people don't care. Agora is our home, Mark, and it's sick. It's broken. And the Director told me that we, the two of us, can make it better! All we had to do was leave the city."

Mark stared at her. Then, suddenly, he gave a hollow laugh.

"And you believed him?" he said with scorn. "He spins some story about ancient prophecies and documents from the foundation of Agora, and you do whatever he says?" Mark leaned forward. "I was an astrologer for over a year, Lily. I built my life on making up stories like that. And let me tell you something—prophecies are worthless. They're all just big words and guesses. I thought you didn't fall for that sort of thing."

7

It was Lily's turn to be silent, then. She so wanted to tell Mark that she believed every word the Director said. It had certainly felt real when she had been standing in his presence, with the weight of history pressing down upon her. At that moment, it had been so easy to accept that she and Mark were the legendary judges that the great Midnight Charter had predicted—the "Protagonist" and "Antagonist" who would, without realizing it, shape the future of Agora. But now, they had spent days in this bleak and empty landscape, and they had found nothing. No sign to tell them where to go, no guide to explain what they should do to fulfill their destiny. And when she thought back to what the Director had said—really thought, away from the awesome grandeur of the Directory—she realized that he had told her nothing. Given her no guidance, no idea of what they needed to do.

And yet . . .

"Why would the Director bother to trick us?" Lily said reflectively. "Why would the most powerful man in the city need to banish us?"

"Us!" Mark said, his anger flaring. "There isn't any *us* about it. He wanted to get rid of *you*, Lily. You were popular. The whole city was talking about your Almshouse, about how it was a new way of life. You were already making a difference, don't you see? Do you think the Director wanted that?" Mark shook his head in exasperation. "Did he even show you the bit in his precious Midnight Charter which mentions us?" Mark stared into the fire. "Think like him for a moment, Lily. He couldn't stop you openly. Not after one of his receivers tried to kill us."

"He didn't organize that," Lily said, defending the Director, but Mark's look silenced her.

"Doesn't matter," Mark continued. "You threatened his power, Lily. So when you go to see him, he dangles this 'great quest' in front of you, and off you go. Problem solved." Mark's eyes filled with bitterness. "Only the stars know why he wanted you to take me too. Then again, if he and Snutworth really were working together, maybe I had to be silenced too."

"No," Lily said hastily, trying to ignore the awful feeling in the pit of her stomach that what Mark was saying made sense. "No, you're wrong. There has to be more to it than that." She looked at Mark, her calm evaporating under his relentless stare. "You'll see, we just need to keep going for another day or two."

"Where?" Mark leaped up. "Where are we going, Lily? Are you still expecting there to be a welcoming party for us, the Great Judges?" He flung his half-eaten mushroom to the ground. "I certainly hope they bring food." Before Lily could respond, he threw his head back and shouted into the night sky. "Hey! We're over here! The Protagonist and the Antagonist! Did we miss the party? Anyone out there? Hello? HELLO!"

Lily struggled to her feet, her head whirling.

"Mark, don't do that!" she shouted. "There might be wild animals—"

"Why are we here, Lily?" Mark ignored her, shouting louder than ever. "Who do you think is out here in this forest?"

"We'll find someone."

"Who? Who are you expecting to find?"

"Someone . . . anyone . . . The Director said . . ."

"What did the Director say? What are we looking for?"

"He said my parents are here!"

It was out of her mouth before she could stop it.

There was dead silence. Mark stared back at her across the campfire. The anger that had been there a moment ago was gone; now his eyes showed only pained shock. Lily tried to say something, to tell him with all her heart that this was not the only reason, that she really meant what she had said about making Agora a better place. But it was Mark who spoke first.

9

"So," he said dully, "That's it."

"Mark . . ." Lily began, but he would not let her continue.

"You don't really care about any of this," he interrupted, his voice growing in power. "You're pretending it's all about these high ideals of yours, but really you just want to find your parents. You tore me away from my father because that was the price of finding your own."

"I rescued you, Mark, remember?" Lily said, the words coming out harsher than she had intended. "Yes, I want to find my parents. I didn't tell you because I thought you'd react like this, but I also wanted to get you out of that prison cell . . ."

"But you didn't ask me!" Mark shouted with rage. Lily felt herself take a step back. For the first time, she noticed that Mark was taller than her. "You didn't even try to get a message to me! Did you think I wouldn't have understood? I spent two years thinking my father was dead, thinking the last thing he did was to sell me. I had twelve hours back with him in that cell. I was just getting to know him again—"

"You wanted to stay in prison?" Lily snapped, the last of her patience ebbing away. "Locked up for crimes you didn't commit, dying from fever and nearly going mad? What would it have been like after a week, a month, a year? In the end, you'd have had to face the fact that your father was your jailer, keeping you locked up in a stinking cell. I set you free."

"Free?" Mark replied. He turned his head away, his voice quiet again. "I'm not free, Lily. I used to be locked up. Now I'm locked out. Cut off from the only home I've ever known."

And in one, painful moment, Lily understood why he was so angry. Despite everything that had happened to him there, despite its flaws and corruption, Mark loved Agora in a way that Lily never had. In hopeless sympathy, she reached out a hand to him.

Mark turned his head back, and Lily pulled her hand away,

shaken. She had never seen a look like that, not even on the faces of the worst debtors that had come to the Almshouse. His eyes seemed hollow, as though he had lost something that could never be regained.

He moved to the edge of the circle of light cast by the campfire, his face half in darkness.

"Where are you going?" Lily asked. There was no response. "We have to stick together, Mark," she said hopelessly. "We're all we've got."

Still silence.

"Mark, where are you going?"

"Home," he said, his voice steady, almost detached. "I'm sorry, Lily. I'm going home."

And he walked out of the light.

A few seconds later, Lily heard him break into a run, his feet crunching on the dead leaves.

It was only a minute before Lily overcame her surprise and shock. Only one short minute before she began to call after him, her voice rising thin and desperate in the night air.

But by then, Mark's own sounds were gone, swallowed by the silence of the forest.

CHAPTER TWO

Running

MARK LEANED heavily against a tree, his head spinning. Already his legs had begun to ache, and his chest to heave. He braced himself, trying to clear his thoughts.

The night closed in around him, utterly black. Against the clouded sky, one shade lighter than the forest itself, the branches bore down on him, crooked and accusing, like claws.

He shut his eyes and concentrated, listening. For a moment, the only noise was his own breathing, and the thud of his heart echoing inside his head. But as that grew quieter, he heard what he was listening for. The far-off sound of running water.

The river was not too far away. The same river that wound its way through Agora, miles upstream. Maybe if he set off now, he could be back in the mountains before next nightfall. Maybe this time, if he waited long enough, the door in the walls would open again. He was prepared to sit there until it did.

Mark walked on, his feet sinking into unseen moss and mud, already picturing his trek up the mountain passes that he and Lily had half skidded down. It was hard to remember exactly where Agora was, but the river would be his guide, his ally. There were lots of warehouses near the river, back in Agora. He could hide there, once he got back in. Find himself a new name, forge a signet ring, contact his dad through his old fishermen friends. There had to be people who did that for escaped prisoners.

There had to be a way.

Mark held out his hands ahead of him, and his fingertips brushed cracked, ancient bark. The sense caused a sudden stab of memory, so sudden and painful that he found himself pulling back as though burned. He felt, again, his own raw fingers, scrabbling at the door in the city walls, begging to be let back in, and hearing only Lily's voice, telling him to turn his back on Agora, on his home. She had done everything except drag him away.

Mark buried the memory and strode on, barely noticing the scratching of thorny undergrowth on his bare shins. Breeches were not designed for forests, and without stockings his legs were already numb from cold. But still, he kept on, toward the hiss of rushing water.

It hadn't been so bad in the mountains. But ever since they had arrived in this dark, endless forest, it was as though he couldn't avoid his worst thoughts. Every night he dreamed about striking Lily down, about screaming at her for stealing away his home. And every day he had bitten back his words and accusations, leaving them to fester and grow strong. By the time he ran away from their camp, it had felt as though his mind was on fire.

Mark stopped, feeling the rough fabric of Lily's cloak around his shoulders. As he stood there, the cold prickling his arms, he listened.

Silence.

He turned his head again. Still nothing. Had he been going the wrong way? The river had to be in this direction. Perhaps if he kept on moving . . .

Something shrieked.

Mark flung up his hands in front of his face, darting his eyes around into the utter blackness that hung, thickly, about him. There it was again, that noise, piercing the night. An agonized, inhuman wail.

Mark stood, every sense strained, the cold banished by his rushing blood.

Silence again. It was gone.

Mark sank to his knees, barely noticing the mud. It had just been an animal, some strange creature that he would never see. Not a person.

He realized that this was not a comforting thought. Even in the midst of his fear, there had been a tiny hope. An idea that it might be a human voice calling out. But out here there was no one. No one but ghosts. Hadn't they always said that to leave the city was the same as death?

Mark sat back on his haunches. He knew that he should keep moving, but his legs were already numb from the cold, the pain of his feet had dulled into a throbbing ache that spread through his entire body. Even his thoughts, which up until now had been racing, slowed to a trickle. He was tired, so very tired.

Gently, he lay down on the frost-covered earth. Maybe he would rest for a few moments. Or perhaps sleep. It would be easier to find his way back in daylight.

"Mark . . . Mark!"

Lily's voice. Mark stirred, sluggish.

"Mark!"

Blearily, he opened his eyes.

And saw the red glow of a burning branch.

Lily was coming. With a torch from the fire. She'd find him; she'd take him back. Suddenly, he didn't care about being alone in the darkness.

Before he was even conscious of it, Mark was up onto shaking legs—legs that grew stronger with every step. First he was walking, then running, faster and faster, pounding across the ground, dodging between trees that loomed out of the murk. No time to think, no time to wonder, only time to run away from Lily.

Roots rose up to grasp his ankles, branches lashed across his eyes. Blinded, he plunged into a mass of thorns like a thousand tiny knives, but still he had to keep moving.

He couldn't go back now. Not back to Lily and her dead, silent, new world.

And then, without warning, the forest was no longer silent.

A hideous howl filled the air around him. Mark heard a panting, the sound of something bursting from the bushes he had disturbed and felt a rush of hot, stinking breath. He fell to the ground, his momentum carried him forward, and he tumbled over and over, jamming his foot against a tree in a bright flash of pain. Grimacing, he turned back, but even here, where the branches were thinner, he saw little more than a wild shadow, slipping through the trees.

Mark grabbed a stone from the ground. His hand trembled, but he was determined not to go without a fight.

Then it dawned on him.

The creature was not coming toward him. It was headed toward the light.

The light of Lily's torch.

He was running again, but this time it was back toward the light. He squeezed the rock in his hand, but had little idea of what he was going to do with it. All he knew was that it was his fault. He had disturbed it, he was the reason Lily was out in the forest, away from the campfire. The thought of it made him shudder with fright.

As he raced toward the torch, the shadows of trees seemed to dance before him. Every bound felt as long as three, yet at the same time he never seemed to move forward. A flock of birds flew down and next to him, their caws ringing in his ears. Except, somehow, the next moment they were gone, and the trees closed around him, poking and scratching with long, knobbly fingers. The howl returned, blasting out from all around him. He was shouting now, shouting Lily's name. And she was answering, but she seemed so very far away—too far.

And then, the trees parted. And Mark was staring across a clearing at Lily. She was holding the torch high in the air, staring back at him with an air of annoyance and relief.

The creature was right behind her.

Hidden in the shadows of a tree, its breath misting, curling out of its long muzzle, as though there was a fire lit within it. Very slowly, Mark raised the stone, motioning Lily to move sideways, away from the creature.

Confused, Lily brought down the torch.

"Mark? What do you—"

The creature lunged.

The stone dropped from Mark's hands.

Lily fell as the beast struck her.

The torch, thrown from her hands, spiraled through the air.

And Mark saw him. A man, standing by the edge of the clearing.

It was only a glimpse, just long enough for Mark to see his face, scarred and rough, and with a glint of wildness in his eyes. Just long enough to see him raise his arm. There was something in his hand. Something like a short metal truncheon.

There was a deafening explosion.

The creature was thrown back across the clearing.

Mark stood for a moment, paralyzed with fear, watching the beast lying there. Then, tentatively, he came forward, picking up the torch that lay, guttering on the damp earth.

The creature didn't move, even as Mark approached and reached out a hand to touch the matted fur.

His fingers came away sticky with blood. Mark looked—the creature's eyes were already beginning to glaze over.

"Lily," Mark said, his voice hoarse but excited, "Lily! It's dead . . . the man, he . . ."

Mark looked up, trying to find their strange savior who could kill beasts from many yards away.

He saw nothing but the shifting shadows. Whoever the man had been, he was gone.

Mark turned back to Lily's prone form and tugged at her sleeve, babbling in relief.

"We're safe! Don't you see? You were right; they've come for us! We're not alone Lily, we're . . ."

Mark stopped. Something felt wrong. Lily hadn't answered back. She hadn't even moved.

Cautiously, Mark shone the torch a little closer to her face.

And he saw the claw marks.